This land is ours

Jonathan Rush

Published in 2017 by FeedARead.com Publishing

Cover design by Paul Houlton, The Grand Design.

The young girl on the front cover is taken from a portrait of Mary Annie MacKay (1865-1949) and appears by kind permission of Rees and Robyn Mackay.

For Jenny

Acknowledgements

This book is dedicated to my mother, Leonora Matilda Rush (née MacKay) who was born in Rockhampton, Queensland, Australia in 1912 and died in Weston Turville, Buckinghamshire, England in 2013. I should also apologise to my mother whose stories about her family history I had at first dismissed as fanciful but, for the most part, turned out to be true.

I am indebted to my mother's aunt, Mary Annie MacKay, whose tales of her family's history, faithfully recorded and amplified in transcripts by my mother's cousin, Robert MacKay Brown, in *The MacKays of Dulcalmah*, provided the story upon which much of this book is based.

I must express my thanks and gratitude to: my cousins, Rees MacKay and William Ash, who kindly placed *The MacKays of Dulcalmah* at my disposal; Rees also generously supplied correspondence from the 1970s between his father and various people living in Prince Edward Island, Canada; another cousin, David Ash, for his opinion on historical legal matters; Melanie O'Flynn for her book, *Before the Line,* and her sound advice, which proved invaluable as I approached the end of *This land is ours*; Maureen Kingston, Secretary, Dungog Historical Society; Richard Walmsley, author of superb Italian crime fiction; Stephen Foster, author of *A Private Empire*; and my three children and their spouses for their encouragement and advice, particularly Jackie and Adam Collins.

Foreword

I had long been intrigued by the story of my mother's branch of the clan MacKay: how a family of tenant farmers and agents of the clan chief emigrated in 1806 from Tongue, in the most northerly part of the Scottish Highlands, to Prince Edward Island, Canada where they prospered. Mysteriously they left Canada by 1840 and ended up in 1877 living in Australia's Hunter Valley, New South Wales where they built one of the country's grandest mansions.

Why did they leave Scotland and then Prince Edward Island? How did they become so rich in Australia? My mother had only vague, unsatisfactory answers to my questions.

After my mother died, aged 101 in 2013, I decided, rather ambitiously, to write a book – part biography, part novel – based on the MacKays' story described in *The Mackays of Dulcalmah* and the major events which moulded the societies and attitudes in which they lived.

A great deal in this book actually took place and most of the characters really did exist. However, this is partly a novel so I hope the reader will allow the Cheshire Cat of fantasy to smile down, now and then, upon the stage and its players.

Even so, much of the fiction is plausible. To substantiate this claim I have listed some of my sources of information at the back of this book. With few exceptions, all of these and many more, too numerous to list, are available by searching the Internet.

A major theme in this story is the distress and hatred caused by land ownership disputes in the Scottish Highlands, Prince Edward Island and Australia: clansman against clan chief; tenants versus absentee landlords; and the fierce resistance of indigenous Australians to the British settlers' invasion.

Some of this story makes disturbing reading, not only to the descendants of British settlers in Australia, like me, but also to those of Aboriginal and Chinese descent. As is often the case, the truth turned out to be uncomfortable.

Jonathan Rush
Chalfont St Peter, England, November 2017

The MacKays

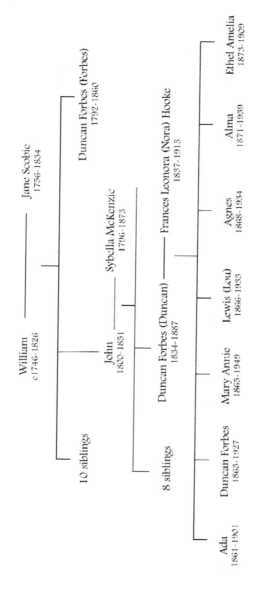

William
c1746-1826 — Jane Scobie
1756-1834

Duncan Forbes (Forbes)
1792-1860

10 siblings

John
1800-1851 — Sybella McKenzie
1796-1873

Duncan Forbes (Duncan)
1834-1887 — Frances Leonora (Nora) Hooke
1837-1915

8 siblings

Ada
1861-1901

Duncan Forbes
1863-1927

Mary Annie
1865-1949

Lewis (Lou)
1866-1933

Agnes
1868-1934

Alma
1871-1939

Ethel Amelia
1873-1909

Part 1: The Scottish highlanders

'Scotland is indefinable; it has no unity except upon the map. Two languages, many dialects, innumerable forms of piety, and countless local patriotisms and prejudices, part us among ourselves more widely than the extreme east west of that great continent of America.'

'The happiest lot on earth is to be born a Scotchman. You must pay for it in many ways, as for all other advantages on earth.'

The Silverado Squatters, Robert Louis Stevenson, 1883

The map overleaf shows the location of Strathnaver, the ancient country of the MacKays in the far north of the Scottish Highlands, taken from *The Book of MacKay* by Angus MacKay, 1906

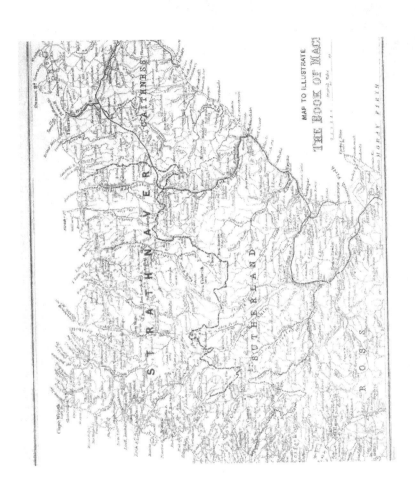

MAP TO ILLUSTRATE
THE BOOK OF MACK

Chapter 1: The drovers

In the summer of 1801 William MacKay shot a reiver – a rustler. This was the first time William had killed a cattle thief. Yes, he had fired shots in the direction of where unseen reivers were suspected to be creeping up, usually in the dead of night, on one of his herds. But his shots had never hit home on human flesh.

But this time, not long after daybreak, William had glimpsed a furtive, misty–grey figure creeping up on the herd and had let loose a shot. Now a corpse lay face down at his feet, sinking slowly into the edge of a muddy bog. The back of his head was a bloody soup of splintered skull and tendrils of brain where the flintlock pistol ball had penetrated.

William reached a hand down slowly, grabbed a shoulder and tried to twist the body round so that it would be face upwards. He grimaced as sucking mud forced him to use both hands and pull the corpse's shoulders with more force. An uplifted knee, caught in running, mid–motion, now rose from the ground and then slid softly down into the wet peat.

By now, squatting on his heels, William stared closely at the man's face. He winced as he looked at the protruding eyeballs glaring at him: half terrified, half surprised. The face was gaunt and its slack jaw revealed missing teeth. The man was short, emaciated and barefoot. His clothes were patchwork rags knotted together by fraying, coarse twine. William looked at the face again – although smeared with mud, he fancied he half–recognised the man.

Averting his eyes, William turned to his three–man crew of drovers who had joined him grouped around the body.

'Do you know him?' William asked, his strained voice permeating slowly through his crew's shock.

Two of his team shook their heads but the other nodded in recognition: 'Aye, I think I do.'

He paused for a second or two as he peered down at the muddy face again. 'The poor man's Dougie Chisholm. He used to go a–droving like us some years ago.'

The drover thought for a few seconds and then continued bitterly: 'He was a good man. I'd heard that his family was starving. They hadn't been able to make a living from harvesting kelp on the coast after they were cleared from their farm last year.'

William sighed inwardly: like all his crew, he had been horrified to hear about a year previously that the chief of the Catholic clan Chisholm had suddenly and brutally burnt the homes and expelled half of its members from their small farms to make way for more profitable sheep – one of the early, brutal examples of what became known as the Clearances. And now, here they were a year later driving through the Chisholm country, Strathglass, south of Inverness. They had passed several farms razed to the ground; their blackened stone chimney stacks pointing skywards like gigantic headstones.

William knew the Chisholm clan had never recovered from its support of Charles Stuart, the Young Pretender, and his defeat at the infamous Battle of Culloden in 1746 by the British Army and loyalist clans. William recalled with guilt how some MacKays, along with the other victorious clans, were said to have settled old scores by joining in the pillaging, looting and butchering by the British soldiers of the Stuart supporters after the battle.

The four men stared at the dead reiver, each absorbed silently in his own thoughts as they contemplated that they were accomplices in the killing of a man who had been driven to stealing.

The men twisted around, startled by the sound of the sudden, shocked gasps of two teenage boys.

'What are you doing here?' William demanded as he stood and roughly pushed his sons away from the scene. 'I told you to stay and look after the camp.'

'I know Father but after we heard the shot we were...worried about you,' 13 year–old George stuttered, wide–eyed fear writ large across his face. And then, staring horrified at the corpse, he added: 'You've killed him, haven't you?'

His younger brother by one year, Duncan Forbes, known by all as Forbes, said nothing as he stared at the dead man.

William did not reply but led his sons slowly by the hand back to the uneasy, lowing herd. They were followed by the rest of the crew who separated swiftly to different parts of the herd to calm any cattle startled by the shot.

Once he was sure there was no chance of a stampede, William sat on a dry rock and pulled his trembling sons towards him. Over their heads, William frowned. Had it been too soon to start taking the boys on his annual drive south to the cattle yards in Crieff? No, he swiftly dismissed his doubts. He had been the same age on his first drive. Besides the boys had also learnt how to butcher and cook beef – an essential skill for drovers who travelled light.

William crouched down and looked down into the boys' eyes: 'I'm sorry you had to see this.

'Please remember that to steal cattle or sheep is a terrible crime. Even if you thieve to feed your own family, it is no excuse. What will the family whose food you have stolen have to eat?'

William fell silent, gauging his sons' reaction.

George was quivering, still in shock. But his younger brother, Forbes, had quickly recovered and said calmly: 'I understand, Father. He was a bad man.'

'Yes, Forbes, he was a bad man.'

William now pulled the trembling George closer and tousled the boy's thick, black wavy hair and said softly: 'You are right to be upset. This is a serious matter.'

Unspoken were William and his sons' realisation of how desperate Dougie Chisholm must have been to try and steal from this herd. William was known as one of the best drovers in Strathnaver – the country of the clan MacKay – partly, it was whispered, because his crew were ex–reivers who knew every inch of the trails and the best places to try and rustle cattle.

William's reputation meant that his herds were usually large – the biggest he'd had was 2,000 head. But since the Clearances had begun numbers had started to dwindle, year on year. This one was a modest 750. His crew had started early in April to buy the cattle before the June roundup. William had been disappointed in the low head count

15

but had hoped to buy more cattle on the trail. Clearly, he now realised, there were no cattle for sale in Strathglass.

The crew had been divided on whether they should bury the dead reiver. 'He got what he deserved,' was the consensus and should be left to rot, hidden in the heather for foxes and lynx. But William had insisted. It would be bad enough to have Chisholm's death on his conscience, doubly so if he did not give him a Christian burial.

Although the boggy ground was soft, the crew did not possess any digging tools. Even a shallow grave for Chisholm took them over an hour, using knives, sticks and stones. William's nails were broken, black with dirt and his knuckles bleeding by the time they wedged Chisholm into his final watery, resting place. They hastily covered the corpse, avoiding the man's bulging eyes. A large stone was manhandled over the disturbed mud and the little group stood around. William swiftly repeated a prayer taught to him by his father. At last it was done.

The crew shrugged their shoulders and got on with their work. The killing of a reiver was not uncommon and there would be no complaints. Yes, there would be gossip over whisky and beer in pubs once they had arrived a few weeks later at the sales yards in Crieff. But there would be no legal consequences.

'What will we tell Mother?' George had asked in an unsteady voice after the burial.

William had said sternly: 'Let us not concern ourselves until we arrive back home. I will tell your mother when the time is right.'

But the time was never right. And the incident was never forgotten by the boys.

Chapter 2: The Call of St John's

About five years before William Mackay shot Dougie Chisholm, he was sitting with his two elder brothers sipping whisky and warming himself in front of a big log fire in the Belfast officers' mess of the clan MacKay volunteer regiment, the Reay Fencibles. The eldest of the three was John, a sergeant and a guest of his two officer brothers in their mess. The other brother was Donald, a few years older than William.

The two officers' single–breasted scarlet jackets were buttoned done up tight and their gold epaulettes flickered in the reflected light from the fire. John's uniform was different: over his coat, he wore a belted plaid which formed a small kilt below his waist. On a side table near a wall his two younger brothers' carelessly discarded, fur–crested helmets cast menacing, swaying silhouettes on the wall like crouched cats preparing to pounce.

Although it was early Spring, the damp Northern Ireland weather still retained a late winter's chill. The building's thick stone walls and massive slate roof required several minutes of burning a big pile of logs to heat up the large room.

A big spark from the fire suddenly flew out and landed in William's lap. Swearing softly to himself, the officer put his glass down irritably and rubbed the ember out before it could burn his breeches.
'You're lucky you weren't just wearing a kilt like John's,' chuckled Donald, 'otherwise you might have been singed in an awkward place.'

Their Gaelic conversation was interrupted by the bar steward who enquired whether the brothers would like another dram.

Why yes, thank you, they certainly did fancy another tot. It was Saturday night and it was their roster turn to stay in the Belfast barracks. They had the mess to themselves. The room was now, at last, heating up, the chairs comfortable and the excellent Islay whisky was warming the blood.

Talking about kilted soldiers caused William to muse idly, while sipping his drink, how the Fencible's command structure mirrored the social make–up of the clan MacKay. Their commanding officer, Hugh MacKay Baillie, was a member of the aristocracy and landed gentry,

17

related to the clan chief, Lord Reay, who was suffering from a tragic accident and unable to take his place at the head of the regiment. Next came Major Scobie, a prominent tacksman – a rent collector and major tenant of Lord Reay's land – which he or she sublet to common clansmen. The major was related to William's wife, Jane, who was born a Scobie. Then came Donald who had several years' service as a professional soldier, some of which were as a prisoner of the French. In recognition of his experience he had been appointed a captain. There were a couple of others who had also been given the same rank because of their age and social position. The junior officers were young sprigs of MacKay gentry, land owners or tacksmen, like William. Then followed the sergeants who, like John, had some learning and were generally prosperous tradesmen. The soldiers under their command were, by and large, ordinary clansmen who were small–farm tenants of the tacksmen or cattle herdsmen, kelp harvesters and agricultural labourers. Everyone knew their place. And all felt secure within a strong clan which looked after its people.

William eased himself back and stretched out his shiny booted legs. After a few further moments of gazing at the bright flames, the young officer raised his glass; this time he took a moody mouthful, looked across at Donald and said bitterly: 'I came here to fight damn Catholic rebels and the French. Not sit around on my arse doing endless drilling and marches around the town.'

Donald sighed: 'I know brother, I know. I feel the same way. It's been, what, two years now?' William nodded, gloomily.

In 1794 George III, the Hanoverian king of all Britain, ordered the loyal northern Highland clans to raise regiments and cross the Irish Sea to help quash the Irish rebels and the expected invasion of their French allies. The MacKay clan had always answered the call to fight for Protestant kings and country. This time the clan chief's heir, Eric MacKay, had written to the clan's leaders, exhorting them to raise as many soldiers as possible. The clan had responded well: within a few weeks 800 men had answered the call from every part of the MacKay country.

The brothers had expected to see action quickly. But the inexperienced Fencibles had been held in reserve in Belfast's Infantry Barrack, while the regular regiments of the British Army were patrolling the rebellious areas.

As one of the few experienced officers in the regiment, Donald was even more frustrated than William and John. He totted up the time to himself: yes, fifteen years in the British Army. Donald had seen action in the West Indies in 1783 fighting the French and their American rebel allies in St Lucia. Although the British were victorious, the fighting had been hard. This had been followed by a short posting in Nova Scotia, guarding against the threat of an attack by militia of the new American republic and its marauding privateers.

Donald gave his drink a swift swirl. Looking down at the gleaming brown and gold whirlpool in his glass he casually asked his brothers: 'Have I told you about my time in Nova Scotia?'

William nodded lazily.

Donald paused and then asked: 'Did I tell you that I also visited St John's Island?'

William sank further into his chair's warm cushions. He wasn't really that interested in old soldiers' tales of the New World.

'Listen to me you two,' Donald said sharply.

William reluctantly cocked an eyebrow: 'Aye?'

John grunted to confirm he was lending half an ear.

Now he had his brothers' attention, Donald continued: 'I took my time off duty to catch one of the ferry boats across to Charlottetown. That's the island's capital. In fact I went twice. The second time I went across in a carriole, horse–pulled across the frozen sea. It was about seven miles. People are making money there. There is plenty of lumber which is fetching a good price for ship building. The sea is full of fish. Yankee boats regularly fish them. And once the land is cleared of trees, the soil is fertile.'

Donald gave his brothers a few minutes to digest what he'd said before he continued softly and slowly: 'And what's more, the ground is much better for crops than for sheep.'

William frowned and sniffed his drink uneasily. He knew only too well the reasons why his brother had emphasised the last point.

The year of 1792, not long before, had become known to the Gaelic–speaking Highlanders as the *Bliadhna nan Caorach* – Year of the Sheep. Farmers in Strathrusdale, not far from Inverness, the main city of the Highlands, had protested after their cattle had been impounded. The livestock had strayed on to land cleared of small farms and was now reserved for the newly–introduced sheep.

In retaliation, the Highlanders from all around started to drive more than 6,000 valuable sheep off the land. A riot ensued between the respective owners of sheep and cattle. Vastly outnumbered, the Cameron brothers, who owned the sheep, appealed to the army to save their livestock.

Their alarm reached the highest levels of government in London. Scotland's most famous British army regiment, the Black Watch, was hastily dispatched. The ring leaders were arrested and sent to trial. They were found guilty but escaped and mysteriously disappeared into the glens.

The incident in Strathrusdale sent a tremor through the Highlands whose traditional way of life seemed threatened. Suddenly animals seemed to be more important than people. This was the start of the Clearances, when the clans were run off their land and replaced by more profitable sheep.

In Strathnaver too, the process of decanting small farmers had already started. The increased yield from the sheep meant more rent money for Jane and William and for Lord Reay. But William was uneasy. In the long run, more sheep meant bigger farms. And wouldn't that mean fewer tacksmen? Once their tenancies had expired, wouldn't Lord Reay get rid of his superfluous agents too? But William had always dismissed such thoughts as pessimistic. The rights of tacksmen were as ancient as the clan chief's, although not legally binding.

'I know what you are implying, Donald,' William said. 'But our chief would never replace all of his people with sheep. And he would never ignore the rights of his tacksmen.'

Donald looked steadily at his younger brother: 'Are you certain, William? Really certain? Don't the Reays always need money? And, as a tacksman, you must know his estate is barely profitable.'

It was certainly true that the Lords Reay were well known as warriors but had a poor reputation in financial management. But now the current crop of Reays did not even seem to be fighters. Eric, the heir to the title, was conspicuous by his absence from the Fencibles, named in honour of his family.

What's more, in William's pocket was the latest news from his wife. Jane's letter was a litany of hard times, with their men absent in Belfast, being felt by the women of the parish. Jane was worried that she might have difficulty in meeting her next tacksmen rent payment to Lord Reay.

She also observed tartly: 'I saw Eric MacKay a few days ago coming out of the Ben Loyal hostelry. He looked the worse for wear.'

Jane had finished her letter plaintively: 'I wish you were here. I do not trust Eric. He seems greedy.'

William frowned. He had previously heard discomforting rumours of Eric's dissolute habits and now his own wife appeared to be confirming them.

He turned back to his brother: 'Are you really contemplating returning to Nova Scotia, Donald?'

'That I am, William. But I think I might end up in St John's Island and see if I can succeed in trade.'

'What? You a storekeeper?' John snorted.

'Better a prosperous trader than a poor farmer,' smiled Donald calmly, to show he was not upset. 'I know my wife, Jessie, and my son will support me.'

Donald sipped his whisky and smacked his lips before he said purposefully: 'Yes, I shall use my small army pension to start a business.'

There was silence for a few moments while both his brothers mulled over the consequences of what had just been said.

Donald stood up, downed his glass and placed it firmly on a side table. He grinned at his brothers: 'Enough of this tomfoolery. I shall

21

resign my commission tomorrow. This is a volunteer regiment and the colonel can't prevent me.'

William too now rose to his feet, drained his glass and shook his brother's hand, seemingly to seal a pact: 'My patience has run out as well. I shall go with you to see Scobie.'

John stood slowly to his feet, shook his head and frowned: 'Not for me. My men need me. I shall remain.'

His two brothers glanced at John with familiar, filial affection because their sibling had never been known to do anything remotely disloyal.

'So be it, John,' William said. 'I admire your loyalty but mine is exhausted.'

John sighed and finished his whisky, adjusted his beaver–skin sporran and followed his two brothers.

Major Scobie was prepared to allow William to resign. He knew from his own family that there were difficulties at home caused by the increase in tacksman rents by Lord Reay. However, he insisted that Donald should remain for another six months while a suitable replacement for his rank of Captain was found.

After both officers had returned to Tongue, they were relieved to hear the news, just before Christmas, that bad weather had prevented the 15,000–strong French invasion army from landing in Bantry Bay in the far south of Ireland. The French did not return.

But had the two brothers had the patience to wait two more years in Ireland, they would have taken part with John in the Battle of Tara Hill in 1798 near Dublin, where the Fencibles covered themselves with glory and routed a far superior force, killing 500 Irish rebels for the loss of 32 men.

The glad news of the victory was tempered by a worrying message from Major Scobie to Donald that John, although alive, had been badly wounded.

Chapter 3: The call from Prince Edward Island

In 1806, five years after the killing of Dougie Chisholm, several events occurred over a period of a few months which, taken individually, may not have been compelling, but collectively convinced William, now aged 58, that he, at last, had to take his family and follow his brother, Donald, to Prince Edward Island – the renamed St John's Island.

Donald had not stayed long in Tongue after their return from Belfast. True to his word he had told William that his prospects in the New World outweighed those in Tongue.

'There is nothing to keep me here, William. I am not a drover. Nor am I a farmer. And I have had enough of soldiering.'

Donald was an infrequent but regular letter writer. The MacKays in Tongue heard from him about twice a year. William had read about the steady progress of his brother's import and export business with interest and some pride. The colonist had repeatedly tried to persuade his brother that he would do better in Prince Edward Island.

The first event was an explicit warning from Donald: unless William came soon, all the best timber–clad land along the coast, fundamental to an ambitious emigrant's prosperity on the island, would have gone. The number of immigrants from Britain was steadily increasing. Donald concluded: 'Dear brother you are almost 60. George is 15 and Forbes 14, young men who will be able to do the heavy work. And I will help finance you. Even so, if you don't come now, it will be too late.'

The second event was an announcement by the government on the 16th May that much of the continental European coast was to be blockaded by the Royal Navy. The war with France had dragged on since 1792. This latest measure would result inevitably in reciprocal action by the French causing the United Kingdom having to import more produce from its colonies. The timber trade with North America, already buoyant, was now sure to boom.

The third event was an advertisement in the *Aberdeen Journal*, the weekly newspaper of the Highlands, which had caught William's eye. Placed by an agent called David McNiven, it announced the departure in November from the port of Thurso, west from Strathnaver, of the

Elizabeth & Ann. Bookings from would–be emigrants to Prince Edward Island and Nova Scotia were invited. The ship was sizeable – a sturdy brig of some 400 tons. The number of steerage berths was only about one hundred and fifty. Conditions were clean. The late autumn voyage meant the price was low.

The fourth event happened in the tap room of Tongue's Ben Loyal public house in late August. Once a week, on Saturday mornings, William allowed himself the luxury of visiting the pub to enjoy a tankard of beer and read a newspaper. This Saturday William eased into his regular seat on a well–worn, darkly–smooth wooden bench and, with the contented sigh of a father relieved of domestic duties, spread out on the table in front of him a week–old copy of the country's leading newspaper: *The Scotsman.*

William knew how the recent blockade was already fuelling a boom in a two–way trade for ship owners, their vessels laden with timber sailing from Nova Scotia to English and Scottish ports and returning full of Scottish emigrants. The ships were the finest afloat, he read, and, provided their passengers could afford the fare, they were virtually guaranteed a safe passage to the New World.

Furthermore, the government in 1803 had passed The Passenger Act to improve conditions on emigrant ships and ensure a record of passengers was kept. William reflected ruefully that the owners of the large Highland estates, including Lord Reay, had lobbied the government hard to pass the Act, particularly its more onerous and expensive bureaucratic conditions. The land owners had been concerned at the rising rate of emigration by poor crofters which threatened the profitability of their kelping and fishing companies. Fares were now three times the amount they were before the Act – £9 for an adult whereas it had been £3 a few years ago. Many of the poorest crofters were now trapped.

The article went on to repeat an entry some years before made in Prince Edward Island's newspaper and register, *The Royal Gazette*, announcing the arrival of a ship with Scottish passengers: 'There is not a doubt but they will receive a kind reception and experience that hospitality which so characteristically and eminently distinguishes the

Highland race.'

But today, savouring his beer, reading on to about a third of the way through the newspaper, William's eyes were suddenly snared by the headline to an article: *The Improvements*.

Although he had long agreed, albeit reluctantly, improvements to the Highland economy were needed, it was with mounting anger he read the piece which advocated expulsion of the clans and concluded: 'Collective emigration is, therefore, the removal of a diseased and damaged part of our population. It is a relief to the rest of the population to be rid of this part.'

William shook his head and wondered how educated, Christian Sassenachs (lowland Scots and English) living in the capital, Edinburgh, could revile their Celtic compatriots as if they were a grotesque growth which should be cut out by a surgeon.

'Good morning William,' a cheerily familiar voice in Sassenach–accented Gaelic, accompanied by a friendly squeeze on his shoulder, interrupted his gloomy thoughts. Looking up from his newspaper William lifted his head and forced a smile at his friend, Peter Dunlop. He slid across the bench to make room for the village schoolmaster.

'Why such a long face, William?' asked Peter.

William flicked a disgusted hand at the article: 'Am I diseased and damaged, Peter?'

'Let me see.' The teacher frowned, sat down on the bench, squeezed up next to William and pored over the newspaper through his lunettes. William watched keenly the expression on Peter's face.

The village schoolmaster was a Glaswegian. As a boy he had done well at school but his shopkeeper father did not have enough money for his son to continue his education. Like many in a similar situation, Peter had decided that he would rather tutor a rich man's children than tend the till in his father's shop. On a whim he had taken on a six month contract to teach the son of a merchant in the busy port of Thurso in the county of Caithness, east of Strathnaver. His contract fulfilled, Peter took the opportunity to explore Scotland's northern edge. Heading west from Thurso, he travelled along the coast. He didn't get far. After a couple of days he reached Tongue where he stopped one Sunday to attend church.

As the congregation exited Peter was approached by William (non–Highlander strangers were rare in Tongue): 'Welcome to our parish, sir. Did you manage to follow our service in Gaelic?'

Peter nodded: 'Enough of it, thank you. In any case Sir, the language of God is international.'

William nodded in approval and introduced himself as a kirk Elder. The conversation developed along polite lines: the two men agreed it was a fine day; the view across the water of the Kyle of Tongue was handsome; and the congregation had sung lustily. After a few minutes Peter let slip that he was a teacher on a touring holiday.

There was something about Peter's demeanour that both attracted and reassured William. He decided not to waste the God–given opportunity. He informed Peter that Tongue had recently need of a new master for its village school. The previous much–respected incumbent had departed this world unexpectedly, leaving his flock in dire need of a replacement.

'I would be very happy to show you our school and introduce you to our kirk minister.' Not wishing to offend this friendly, albeit somewhat presumptuous man, Peter nodded, even though he thought that the minister had, to judge from his gesticulations, overdone the fire and brimstone in his sermon.

The meeting later that day with the stern minister went well. William skilfully kept the conversation on educational rather than liturgical matters.

'I have little Gaelic, gentlemen. Would that not be a problem for the children?' Peter asked. No, it appeared not: the minister and Elders, including William, would continue religious education in Gaelic. The children who attended the school came from the better off homes and most spoke reasonable English. Those who couldn't would soon catch up. Children from the poorer families had to work and school was an expensive luxury which they could not afford.

Subject to references, would Mr Dunlop consider a trial period of six months?

Peter nodded again. Why not, he thought? Despite the post's meagre stipend, funded by the Society for the Propagation of Christian Knowledge, Tongue seemed a pleasant place and he had nothing arranged in the foreseeable future. The master's post came with free lodgings which made up somewhat for the low pay.

'And you'll get all the losers from the cock fights, Mr Dunlop,' said William chuckling. Peter wasn't sure if the Highlander was jesting. The minister allowed himself a thin smile: 'It's true Mr Dunlop. A local tradition, you see. Every year the pupils bring cocks to school for a fight. Those which lose become your property. To eat, sell or do what you will.'

The trial six–months quickly lengthened into a couple of years and then Peter realised he had found his vocation. He settled into the quiet rhythm of life in Tongue and its surrounding parish and was gradually accepted by its farmers, fishermen, drovers and kelp harvesters. And, most importantly, by their children. His Gaelic rapidly improved. After a couple of years he was as good as fluent.

Lifting his head up from *The Scotsman*, the teacher looked William straight in the eye and said slowly: 'Regretfully I agree with the author's proposition that the Highlands cannot continue to support its population.'

Peter tapped the article and continued gently: 'I agree too that improvements are needed.'

The schoolmaster now looked at his friend quizzically: 'I thought you acknowledged this?' William nodded glumly in assent.

Peter continued: 'But to compare the Highlanders to a disease is disgusting and not worthy of one of our country's leading newspapers.'

'William,' Peter pressed on, 'we all know most tenants are too heavily dependent on subsistence farming. The price of kelp goes up and down. There are not enough fishing boats to provide employment. And the price of beef is far less than that for sheep.'

'So you think that one day sheep will replace nearly everyone in Strathnaver, tacksmen too?' William asked his friend disconsolately knowing that confirmation of his own fears was imminent.

'I do. More's the pity. And I also think this Lord Reay will sell his estate. We all know he wants more money.'

27

Eric, the seventh Lord Reay, had finally inherited the title and lands from his disabled uncle in 1798, the year William had returned from Belfast.

Remembering Donald's words, William took a swig of beer and tested his friend: 'But he's our clan chief!'

Peter sighed: ' It may not be this year or the next or twenty years from now. Maybe not this Lord Reay, perhaps his successor. But sell they will.'

William slammed his pot down, ale splashing onto the table. Irritably mopping the puddle off the table with his handkerchief, his eyes noticed a few red stains on his friend's outstretched shirt cuffs.

'My shirt still has blood from last week's cock fights, William,' Peter explained, as a wan smile flitted across his face.

Ah yes, William remembered the dead cocks with their twisted necks being ceremoniously presented by the pupils to their schoolmaster. William shivered: Would his family suffer a similar fate if they stayed in Tongue?

He drained his pot suddenly and made angrily for the door without looking back. Peter watched him go without calling his friend back. He realised sadly that William was contemplating leaving Tongue. Peter wetted a finger with his beer and tried unsuccessfully to rub a blood spot off his cuff. 'Damn,' he cursed unhappily in English under his breath.

William irritably slammed the door of the Ben Loyal behind him and strode off with the heavy tread of an unhappy man. On the way home, on the outskirts of Tongue, William sat down by the side of the road on a way stone. He wanted to collect the thoughts, which were swarming around inside his head.

It would take a lot for William to leave Tongue. He had a respected position in society. The son of a surgeon, William was educated, widely–read and bilingual. In addition, to his native Gaelic, he spoke fluent English. His mother was the granddaughter of the Honourable Charles MacKay of Sandwood, a son of the first Lord Reay. But that meant little in Strathnaver. Large families, ten or more children, were common, and frequent marriage among cousins meant many of the clan were related. Although Jane was, in fact, the real tacksman – she had inherited the position from her Scobie mother – the family prosperity was also based on William's droving. He was often joined by larger landowners and their sons who valued his knowledge of the Highland trails. Although not wealthy, William's family never had to go short. Yet he had to agree with Peter, and Donald before him, that the Clearances were gathering speed elsewhere in Scotland and like a distant thunder storm threatening to inundate all Strathnaver. After all, he had already participated in their early introduction to Strathnaver but progress had been deliberately slow and conducted in as humane a manner as possible.

A letter from Donald had arrived a few months later in which he expressed fear that the fate of the Chisholm clan would be shared by the MacKays. 'Leave Strathnaver and join me in Prince Edward Island', Donald had urged. William had voiced Donald's fears to Jane.

She had waved them aside: 'Bah, what does Donald know? He's been in the army most of his life. Reay will never turn all of Strathnaver to sheep, William. In the end he will prove as loyal to the clan as we are to him,' she said.

Jane wiped her hands on her apron as she reminded her husband: 'Tacksmen have clan rights too, William. This land is ours as well.'

But William had again remembered Donald's words in the officers' mess ten years ago and shook his head gloomily: 'Like all Lord Reays he needs money. He lives a grand life in Edinburgh and London. And we have all heard the scandal of his godless life.'

He had whispered so none of the children could hear: 'He has fathered a daughter out of wedlock, Jane. He admits the bastard is his natural daughter. He will need to dower her generously to arrange a good marriage.

'And you told me last week he's increasing our rent. And he is starting to clear out the smaller farms at a faster pace. If this continues he won't need tacksmen.'

William had added softly: 'I'm sorry Jane, but in the eyes of the law your tacksman rights mean nothing.'

Jane had to admit that Lord Reay was taking ever more money from his tacksman. All the same she disagreed with her husband: 'We can cope. He's our clan chief, William. He will never force his tacksmen out. He needs us.'

William now looked out across the Kyle of Tongue and watched, with the detachment of someone whose heavy thoughts were elsewhere, how the clouds suddenly parted and the sun lit up the summit of Ben Loyal mountain. Subconsciously, his spirits rose at the sight but then he frowned as he caught out of the corner of his eye, further along the shore, Tongue House, Lord Reay's seat.

William sighed. His waning resolve to stay in Strathnaver snapped. He had made up his mind. He would have to tackle Jane again and convince her that the family really must join Donald in Prince Edward Island.

He stood up slowly from the stone road sign and looked back at Tongue. The brief break in the clouds suddenly closed and a sharp shower headed towards him. William turned the collar of his coat up and ran for home where he knew he would face a hostile reception. As he feared, William, once again, could not persuade Jane for the enterprise: 'Why, William, why?' she'd cried. 'We are happy here. There will always be a healthy living for the likes of us.

'And we wouldn't own the land in Prince Edward Island. We would have to rent. No different from here.'

'Yes, but Donald says...'

'Donald says, Donald says,' mimicked Jane scornfully.

William took a deep breath: 'He says the rents are so low that proprietors' agents hardly bother to collect them.'

Jane glared at William: 'I have grave doubts about that brother of yours. He is more a gambling soldier than a solid merchant. Why do you accept his opinion as if it were gospel?'

In sudden frustration, William slammed his fist down onto the thick dining table and shouted: 'I've told you why, Jane. Our future here is bleak. Donald offers us a new life. A new start.' The children stared in astonishment. Their father was normally mild–mannered and disapproved of excessive displays of emotion.

William retreated into silence regretting his intemperate outburst which had upset his children. He looked at his wife across the kitchen table as she angrily spooned the simple Saturday lunch into the family's bowls. He saw a grey–haired woman in her late–forties but, for all that, still handsome. Her pale face was creased with the deep lines of bearing eleven children. And the sorrow of losing six at young ages since their marriage in 1774.

Sensing his mother's distress, their youngest child, and his namesake, William, raised his hand and pointed a chubby, three year–old finger accusingly at his father and gurgled: 'Why, William, why?'

Caught unawares his father stared at his little son and then burst out laughing, glad that the small boy had broken the tension. The other four children around the table smiled, relieved that further argument between their parents had been avoided.

That afternoon William and Jane avoided the subject of the family's proposed emigration. William helped the boys with some Latin texts while Jane and Joanne had sat sewing shawls. A long spell of sunshine through the windows beckoned the family outside for a promenade up towards *Caisteal Bharraich* – Varrich Castle – overlooking the Kyle of Tongue. After ten minutes or so they stopped. None of them tired of this view. They stood watching how the swell from the open sea vigorously surged inland but was gradually tamed by the narrowing inlet and its muddy foreshores. Strong gusts of wind sketched dark, swiftly–shifting patterns on the stiller inland water before mounting the banks and tossing the tall Scots pines to and fro.

Jane and William looked at each other. This wild landscape was home. How could they leave, Jane's eyes pleaded. William's answered sadly: how can we stay?

After supper and the children had been put to bed, Jane and William retired to their living room. Black–dog silence cloaked them. William sat by the peat fire reading his Bible, seeking solace and a text to guide him and persuade Jane that they should leave their home. Jane had recently started reading the popular book, *Castle Rackrent*. The similarities of the satirical tale of aristocratic estate mismanagement to Strathnaver's situation were obvious and planted a seed of doubt in

Jane's mind. Had she been too hard on William? Too hasty to reject his arguments?

The candle next to Jane flickered. She sighed and put the book down on her lap.

'William?' Jane said softly.

'Yes?'

'I don't wish you to think that I have dismissed your proposal without due consideration. You must realise that what you are asking me to give up would be difficult. I inherited my tacksman income and rights from my mother.'

Jane drew a disconsolate breath: 'She would be extremely distressed if she knew that I had relinquished them.'

William looked up, relieved by Jane's conciliatory tone: 'I know, dear Wife. I understand how difficult it is for you.

'Please be assured I have every confidence in your ability to reach a sound judgement.

'I am content to abide by your decision.'

Jane's face softened and managed a small smile: 'Thank you, Husband. Please give me some time to deliberate.'

'Of course, my dear.'

The next day after the Sunday morning service, William left Jane and the children talking to some neighbours outside the kirk and sought out his brother, John, who had been honourably discharged after he had been badly injured at Tara Hill. Although he suffered from constant pain in his right leg and walked with a bad limp, he had recovered enough to resume his work as a blacksmith.

John had never taken to books as his brothers had. Their father had wisely apprenticed the muscular boy as a blacksmith – a trade which would always be in demand. John's lack of enthusiasm for book–learning was more than compensated for by his common sense. This was much valued by his family, and his ability to see the kernel of a problem and give sound advice.

William described his belief that prospects for his family had become so poor that he believed a new life in Prince Edward Island would be better. To his surprise, John did not hesitate: 'Yes, William, I agree you should go. I have been pondering this matter for some time.'

Noticing the look on his brother's face, John explained: 'I have seen a slow but steady decline in my income.'

The blacksmith shrugged his shoulders: 'There are fewer horses. This is a result of fewer farms.' The blacksmith paused: 'And more sheep.'

John placed a large hand on William's shoulder: 'Yes, even the demand for blacksmiths is dwindling. Who knows? We could all be thrown off the land. Thank God we are not penniless crofters.'

John was quiet for a second or two. He nodded his head in affirmation of what he then stated: 'I think for the good of the family you should follow Donald to Prince Edward Island.'

Looking closely at William's slim figure and thick, wavy grey hair, the craftsman added: 'Even though you are nearly sixty, you still have good health. And your boys will soon be men and can help as you get older. If the expedition is not a success you can return home and we would assist you get back on your feet again.'

There was a short silence before John put into words the conclusion which was arching over their discussion: 'But if you prosper like Donald, it might be that we join you. Yes, even I, who has just turned sixty, would consider a new life. And I am sure my good wife, Ann, and our children would support me.'

William nodded and looked at his brother: 'In the end it is Jane's decision. She is the tacksman and has most to lose. Jane may decide we should stay.'

But William turned out to be wrong. As she had promised, Jane had indeed pondered William's arguments over in her mind and was forced to agree her husband had made a strong case. But she was still not in favour.

Then, a few days later, a letter had arrived from Lord Reay announcing yet another hefty increase in rents, more clearances and hinted at the need for fewer tacksmen. Jane had to admit there was a clear trend: Lord Reay was determined to squeeze his tacksmen hard. To her horror she could see that there was no clan loyalty being shown by its chief, neither to his tacksmen nor to the ordinary clansmen.

Jane donned a shawl and bonnet and wandered along Tongue's main lane, arms folded and deeply depressed. She realised that even her Scobie family, prominent tacksmen though they were, would not be able to help her and her family for long. They too would be threatened. With an involuntary intake of breath she suddenly realised that the tacksman class was doomed.

A fine carriage trotted past; it could only be Lord Reay's. Jane caught a glimpse of the clan chief's plump, florid face. His predecessors would have acknowledged her, perhaps even stopped to greet her. But this Lord Reay looked straight ahead. It was as if she didn't exist.

Jane suddenly realised that everything William had said was right. If they stayed they would soon be solely dependent on his cattle droving earnings which were now not enough. Worse, they might even be cleared off the land and forced to become crofters. Reay would show no mercy. She shuddered. They should leave Strathnaver. As quickly as possible.

Chapter 4: Goodbye to Thurso

William had hardly looked back as the *Elizabeth & Ann* had slipped her moorings in November 1806 from the port of Thurso. The boat was a sturdy 400 ton brig with two main masts and fore and aft sails, registered in the northern English port of Newcastle. The family was travelling steerage – the cargo hold converted for passengers. Cargo ships had few cabins and they were occupied by single people or the occasional couple. Why pay a lot more for most of the ship's cabins for the whole family? The voyage should only last a couple of months. The reasonable sum of money they'd received for their cattle and the for the remainder of Jane's tacksman tenancy, sold to her Scobie relatives, would be better spent on setting up their new home in Prince Edward Island. Even though November weather could be inclement, the seasonal reduction in price was an added attraction.

Peter Dunlop had felt compelled to accompany his friend and his family to the port of Thurso to say goodbye. He was convinced that he was responsible for finally persuading William that he could do better in the New World. The teacher had taken turns with William's brother, John, to lead the horse as it pulled the dray over the coastal track and then helping it brake on the decline towards the port quayside through the grid of Thurso's Newtown streets.

Located at the mouth of the Thurso River, the port was doing good business. The children were fascinated by the unloading, loading and carting of goods in a busy port. They gawped at the dress of strangers from countries they had not heard of, speaking in unknown tongues. Timber cranes creaked, pullies squealed and ropes became as taut as iron as dray horses hoisted heavy flagstones from Caithness quarries destined, ignoring the embargo, for the pavements in Europe's major northern cities, from Napoleon's Paris to Sweden's Stockholm, onto vessels settling low in the water. The salty spray of surf from the wide beach over the other side of the breakwater wafted across the river and mixed with the lingering smell of the early morning herring catch. Lumber from Prince Edward Island and Nova Scotia was arriving and being loaded onto carts, southward bound for Inverness and onwards to Edinburgh. And nearby, in disconsolate groups, queuing to board the *Elizabeth & Ann* were other emigrant Highlanders – MacKays, McLeods, Chisholms, Sutherlands and Gunns – saying tearful goodbye to relatives. Jane noticed a few dark looks sent their way and thought she caught the hissed word: 'Tacksman.'

At the foot of the gangplank, the ship's master, Thomas Wynn, started to check their names on his manifest and suddenly frowned. Sucking his stubby pencil he looked inquisitively at William's wife and inquired, not unkindly, in a Newcastle Geordie accent: 'I have a Jane Scobie but no Jane MacKay?'

Jane nodded: 'Yes, that would be right, sir. My full name is Jane Scobie MacKay. No doubt your agent assumed my family name was merely Scobie.'

Wynn ran an experienced eye over William and Jane. They were clearly not impoverished crofters fleeing from a brutal landlord. Nor did they look out of wedlock. There were rings on their hands. He saw instead a tough–looking father in his fifties and his wife, a comely woman in her forties, who radiated determination to withstand whatever adversity life would throw at her. The family was simply, but well–dressed. The children were not undernourished. In short they were a respectable family. He ticked off their names and ages on the passenger list: George (15); Duncan Forbes (14); Joanne (13); Hugh (8); John (6); and William (3).

'Welcome to the *Elizabeth & Ann,*' Wynn said, nodding his head in approval. 'We aim to cast off quickly. The tide will turn soon and we have a fair wind.'

William smiled to himself at Wynn's accent which he had not heard since his army days in Belfast. Well, he thought to himself, I am going to hear many different accents over the next few years.

'God speed, William,' Peter had said when Wynn was finished, tightly grasping his friend's hand on the quayside.

Thank you, Peter,' the Highlander had replied stiffly, embarrassed that he might be showing unmanly emotion on his face.

'I will write. Who knows, perhaps you might join us some day,' William added, with a wistful, fleeting smile. Peter had nodded sadly, unsuccessfully concealing that he thought it was likely that the friends would never meet again.

It had not taken long to load the family's belongings onto the boat. Most of them were carried by the passengers themselves.

In contrast to William, Jane had not been able to fight back her tears. She wept openly as she stood with one arm around the children, the other waving at her Scobie and MacKay relatives on the quayside. She knew that she would not see Strathnaver again.

The oarsmen in the half a dozen or so tugging boats strained to pull the ship's bow into the middle of the river. Gradually the outgoing tide in midstream wrapped its arms around the ship and gently rocked her towards the harbour mouth. Now the wind filled the ship's foresails: with a startling crack of unfurled, stiff canvass and a sunlit, darting shimmer of dried salt she gathered speed and responded to the helm. Wynn smiled with a master mariner's pride that the exit from the port was going well. He waved his cap at the spectators gathered to wish Godspeed at the harbour mouth and, faintly on the breeze, caught sad shouts of farewell in return.

'Cast off,' he ordered the release of the now superfluous tugging–boats, their oars raised in the air as they slipped back along the sides of the *Elizabeth & Ann*, followed shortly by: 'Unfurl the first mainsail!' The ship's bow smacked into the first ocean wave and the cold November spray flew over the ship and showered onto the emigrants crowded on the deck looking back towards Thurso. With a cry of alarm most scuttled below.

Looking along the coast towards Strathnaver, William could just make out the gloomily–named Cape Wrath. He turned away and went below to join Jane and his children with his heart full of fear of the unknown. Under full sail, the *Elizabeth & Ann* scudded along, settling into the rhythm of the waves. Soon the disappointed seagulls wheeled away back towards Thurso, squawking to each other there would be no scraps of food from this mean ship.

Standing on the poop deck, his hands tightly clasped behind his back with his feet feeling each bow–thudding wave, Captain Wynn had eyes only for the west, already imagining the first port of call: Charlottetown, the capital of Prince Edward Island.

Chapter 5: Steerage

'Well, gentlemen this is where you shit or puke,' the seaman had said, emphasising with a sarcastic smirk, through his few front and tobacco–stained teeth, the word gentlemen. He gestured towards half a dozen flat boards with well–worn and stained circular holes, cantilevered out over the water from the top deck.

'Hang tight on to the ropes otherwise you'll follow your turds down into Davy Jones' locker,' he'd grinned.

'We have the same boards on both sides and another two at the bow – the heads. You can piss over the side wherever you wish. But, whatever your need, never piss or shit into windward!'

A couple of seasick Highlanders were already bending over the side, vomiting through the holes. Showing surprising kindness, the seaman handed a bucket of sea water to one of the men who was now wobbling on his feet, trying to stand upright: 'Here, take this. Wash your face when you're done. It'll take you a few hours yet to get your sea legs.'

The same seaman had been more polite down below in steerage where he had shown the women the two privies, one on either side of the ship.

Opening one of the privy's doors, he had gestured awkwardly towards a wooden seat on top of a bend in a large pipe, fastened to the bulkhead: 'This, ladies, is where you and your little children do your business,' he'd said.

Turning to their men folk he'd shown them a nearby large tank and a bucket: 'You use this to flush their waste away.'

Bending down he pointed to where the pipe ran from out of the privy, along the deck, through the ship's wooden and copper–bottomed hull and out onto the sea: 'This takes it into the ocean. Do not let your women put waste cloths into the pipe. It will become blocked,' he warned in a stern voice.

'If they do, you will have to dismantle the pipe and clear the blockage. This is a very unpleasant task. Your hands and clothes will stink for days afterwards.

'And ladies, remember also please, you can only use the privy which is on the leeward side'

The women looked blank. Most of them could only speak Gaelic and those, like Jane, who spoke English, had to translate. But even Jane had not heard the word leeward before.

The seaman saw the puzzled looks and held a horizontal hand up. Slowly tilting it he said: 'When the wind blows the ship leans over. The side which is not on the windward side, the leeward side, is lower and the pipe tilts down towards the sea.

'This means the waste water from the privy will run down the pipe.'

The sailor didn't need to explain what would happen if somebody unfortunately used the windward side toilet and tried to flush the waste away. The stench of excrement would make the close confines of the steerage deck unbearable. The noise of a women retching in one of the privies had already set the stomach churning among several of the others. Some of the women had to run for the deck, hands over mouths.

Jane sat down on the bottom bunk and surveyed the part of the ship which would be her family's home for the next six weeks. Running down the centre of the steerage was a long run of tables and benches where meals would be taken. At the end of the run there was a small 12 by 6 foot galley with a wood burning cast–iron stove. Next to it were a bucket of water and one of sand to extinguish accidental fires. Nobody needed to be told the danger posed by flames on a wooden ship. The ceiling was about 6 foot above the deck. If he were wearing his cap, William would be one of the few men who had to stoop.

The double–deck bunks, made of rough boards, were set up along both sides of the ship. The wide bunks slept five people each. Jane, William, Joanne and young William would sleep in the lower bunk and the other four bigger boys would sleep in the upper one. There was enough headroom between the bunks that an adult could sit up in bed. The bunks had straw mattresses. All the emigrants had been told to bring their own pillows, blankets, animal hides and other necessary bedclothes.

Jane counted the first weekly ration she had received from the ship's purser for each person in her family: 5 lbs. of oatmeal; 2 1/2 lbs. biscuit; 1 lb. flour; 2 lbs. rice; 1/2 lb. sugar; 1/2 lb. molasses; and 2 ounces of tea. There was a limited amount of salt beef too but that was to be shared out weekly on an ad hoc basis. Rum could be bought but was expensive. Although expressly banned, whisky had been smuggled on board by many.

There were only about 100 people in steerage so it was not full. Cargo was used to divide the passengers into quarters for single men, families and single women.

Jane wandered up to the end of the family section, nodding and smiling to other women and their families. As she approached the wall of wooden crates, she saw that one was addressed to D. MacKay & Co. Could this be William's brother, she wondered. She took a closer look at the paint and saw that on an attached ticket the crate's contents had been described for customs purposes as: Tools for ship building and lumber.

At supper time, while Joanne served everyone their porridge, salt beef and biscuit, Jane mentioned the crate to William.

'It could be for Donald,' William agreed. 'But I doubt it. There are bound to be other D. MacKays on Prince Edward Island.'

The family settled quickly into the daily routine of life for the steerage passengers. Provided that it was not too cold, rainy or windy Jane, William and the children escaped the fetid air and inevitable steerage smells by spending a lot of time outside on the top deck. William enforced a strict timetable of scripture, English, Gaelic, Latin and geography lessons.

William and the two elder boys, George and Duncan Forbes, were watching a sailor one late afternoon letting out a knotted rope from the stern of the ship. George, who, since coming on board, had become fascinated by all things nautical, turned to his father and asked: 'Is that man fishing, Father?'

'No, young man, he is casting out the log line so that we can determine how fast we are sailing,' said Captain Wynn, who had overheard George, as he passed the boy on his way to join the busy sailor.

Wynn looked down at George: 'The more knots we count when we pull the line in, the faster we are moving. We do this every hour so that I can estimate how far we have travelled.

'From observing the compass and my knowledge of tides and currents, I know roughly our direction and where we are on the ocean.'

William and the boys fell silent. Was this the only means of navigation?

The captain noticed their worried expressions. 'But for a more accurate estimate I use my sextant. At twilight I measure the angle between the North Star and the horizon. 'This gives me our latitude. I can then determine with reasonable accuracy our position.

'And when we get closer to land, we start to measure the depths using a lead line. I compare these with our charts for further confirmation of our location.'

Wynn smiled at George: 'Do not worry Master MacKay. I have crossed the Atlantic a dozen times. God willing, I am confident we will make Charlottetown safely.'

William looked at Wynn: 'Thank you kindly, Captain. We found that most interesting. And reassuring.'

Wynn stroked his beard for a few moments as he considered his next words: 'Mr MacKay, I have observed you giving your children religious instruction. A very commendable exercise, if I may say.'

William nodded his appreciation of the captain's words: 'I am a Christian, Captain Wynn. I was an Elder in our parish kirk. I shall ensure my children are educated accordingly.'

Wynn responded: 'I thought that might be the case. Would you think it amiss if I asked you to assist me in conducting our Sunday service, Mr MacKay? Particularly since most of our congregation only speak Gaelic,' he added.

'I would be honoured to be your servant, Captain,' William replied.

While William taught the elder children, Jane concentrated on teaching young William to read. In addition to her lessons, Joanne helped her mother sew and knit coats, caps and scarves. The winters in Prince Edward Island were expected to be colder than back home. In their spare time the children played games. On weekdays there was often dancing and concerts on deck.

Captain Wynn had ordered that the steerage must be brushed and its tables and benches washed down every day to prevent the spread of disease. Beds were stripped, their sheets and blankets shaken to combat fleas and lice. Any dirty patches on sheets and blankets were cleaned with a damp brush. It was too cold to hang a whole washed sheet on the top deck and expect it to dry. Once a week the steerage deck, tables and benches were thoroughly scraped, scrubbed with brushes and soap and dried with cloths.

Jane and Joanne prepared the meals, negotiating with the other women times when they could use the small kitchen. Late one afternoon, Jane and Joanne were in the kitchen washing rice before boiling it in a large communal pot for their evening meal. The weather outside was rough, the hatches were closed and the steerage was crowded with passengers There was a queue of women waiting to use the kitchen.

'Does the Lady Tacksman believe she owns the kitchen?' a voice suddenly screeched, the words slightly slurred. Jane glanced up and recognised the woman from the quayside who had sent angry looks in her direction.

'You've been in there too long. Hurry up. It's my turn now,' the voice continued to interrupt, this time the words louder and more slurred.

Puzzled by the hostile stranger, Joanne glanced at her mother. Tacksman? Wasn't that an honourable position in the MacKay clan?

Jane answered the woman politely but firmly: 'I agreed this time with the other women. We will be as quick as we can.'

'You can't be high and mighty with me now, Jane Scobie. There's no Lord Reay here to protect you.'

Jane looked at the woman: 'I do not know you Madam. But I am sorry if I have offended you.'

'All you Scobie tacksmen have offended me, Madam. My name is Mary Gunn. My sister was forced onto a miserable croft by your cousin.' This time the smell of cheap whisky seeped right through the angry woman's words.

Jane didn't bother to ask which one of her several cousins stood accused or how the woman recognised her as a tacksman. Wiping her hands on her apron she stared her accuser down: 'Whatever wrong you imagine I have perpetrated let me assure you that we are now equal. My family is going to start a new life in a strange country. In this endeavour, we are no different to you.'

Another woman who was also waiting clucked in annoyance: 'That's right. We are all emigrants now. Tacksman or not makes no difference where we are going. Let her finish Mary. There are many waiting to cook.'

Mary Gunn stood unsteadily aside. The unpleasant episode was over as suddenly as it began.

After Jane and Joanne had spooned their rice into a large pot they started to make their way gingerly along the narrow gap between people sitting at one side of the long table and the adjacent bunks. William and the hungry boys were waiting impatiently, sitting either side of the table, about halfway along, in their section of steerage. Jane gripped the family's pot of rice firmly with two hands. Her face showed a mix of anger and, yes, remorse after her encounter with Mary Gunn. Following close behind her mother, Joanne was frowning, still puzzled by the unknown woman's outburst.

With the ease of a mother accustomed to small children Jane swayed left and right to dodge young boys chasing each other. Kicking legs and knees protruding from bunks and pistoning elbows from benches added to the hazards. Black, wispy smoke from swinging lamps made the air hazy and difficult to see from one end of the steerage to the other. Everyone's nostrils had become accustomed to the pervasive smell of sweat, babies, toilets and cooking. The hubbub of noise from a cooped–up crowd gathering to eat had drowned out the noise of the altercation.

After Jane and Joanne had served the rice and William had said grace, Joanne took the opportunity of the family's hungry, chewing silence to ask: 'Mother, why was that woman so hateful about tacksmen?'

Jane put her spoon down and wiped her lips with her apron, gaining time for herself as she debated how to answer the question. Apart from baby William, all the children were aware of the economic upheaval taking place throughout the Highlands.

'Many tacksmen, some of them Scobies, are being over–zealous in moving people into crofts, Joanne. That's why she hates me.'

Jane paused and then surprised William and the children: 'And I think the poor woman has some justification. The Improvements will destroy the MacKay clan, no different from all the others. I was stupid not to recognise this sooner.'

Jane reached across and held William's arm. 'Forgive me Husband. You were right all along.'

William smiled, not in triumph, but in relief that Jane at last had expressed her complete support for their emigration so forcibly in front of the children. He felt full of a new confidence: come what may they would succeed in Prince Edward Island.

Chapter 6: A Christmas sea dance

It was Christmas Day. A cold, cloudless winter's day in the mid–Atlantic. Everything had turned a faint, pastel blue. The wind was so light that the *Elizabeth & Ann* felt almost becalmed. Only the faintest of ripples indicated that her bow was moving. Jane, William and the children had joined the circle of people on deck to watch some festive dancing. The family clapped their mittened hands to the foot–tapping music provided by a couple of quick fiddlers whose repertoire included fashionable waltzes and traditional reels. One of the few remaining Highland harpists gave some respite to the fiddlers between dances.

Bows zipped back and forth and sweat dripped off the musicians' noses onto their wooden instruments and became frozen tears. Faint steam wafted up from the fiddlers' caps into the air.

Captain Wynn was a keen dancer. He was walking around chatting to passengers, nodding to men and tipping his hat to women, while keeping a look out for a suitable partner. Through the throng the sailor spotted William's tall head above the crowd and then, next to him, Jane, her face only partially hidden by a thick shawl and heavy bonnet. Jane had not danced with a stranger for nearly 20 years. As the wife of a kirk Elder and daughter of a minister, her first reaction to Wynn's invitation was to hesitate. But she knew men far outnumbered women on board so even a delicate refusal might be misconstrued as rudeness. William also gave the faintest, stiff bow of assent. Jane handed her shawl and bonnet to Joanne and linked arms with Wynn.

'Thank you Captain, it would be an honour.'

Wynn was a good dancer. Jane realised the sailor must have had plenty of practice at sea with emigrant women like herself. The captain guided Jane around, covering her rustiness with a quick–tempo waltz and steering her clear of other couples. Despite his reservations, William watched with pride as the years fell away from his wife, twirling away on the wooden deck, her face floating in and out of focus through the frosty, glinting mist of the dancers' exhaled breath. Joanne and the boys saw once more the side to their mother which they had almost forgotten as she had become careworn from the loss of young children over the last few years. Jane's pale cheeks became rosy and laughter filled the lines in her face.

William couldn't remember the last time his wife had appeared so gay. Although they did not know it then, their surviving children, when asked by their own offspring what their grandmother had been like, would recount with love how her bright smile once lit up a ship on a dark, icy ocean.

The music stopped and after the flourish of one final twist, Wynn bowed to Jane.

'Thank you Madam.'

Jane curtsied in return: 'No, thank *you*, Captain. I fear I was somewhat out of practice.'

'I didn't notice, Mrs MacKay,' Wynn dissented gallantly.

Recalling something Donald had written, William gently interrupted: 'I hear from my brother that the settlers on Prince Edward Island have regular entertainment with music. I suspect my wife will be grateful for her dance with you, Captain Wynn.'

'What is your brother's occupation?' asked Wynn politely, half–expecting a reply that William's brother was just another Highland farmer.

'He owns a trading company buying and selling goods. He tells me he has a warehouse in Charlottetown.

'Perhaps you might know of him? His name is Donald MacKay.'

Wynn nodded in surprise: 'Yes, I believe I do. By coincidence I may have met your brother about six months ago. He sought me out to tell me about his plans to charter ships also across the Atlantic for his lumber. He asked me whether I might consider being the Master on his first ship.'

The short, northern winter's day was closing and the pale sun was fading fast. Wynn turned, looked up and, with a navigator's eye, caught the North Star gently pin–pricking its way into the enveloping twilight. He tugged his beard thoughtfully: 'In fact I think we are carrying cargo for him below.'

They all turned as a piper suddenly struck up a lament. Those emigrants who knew the Gaelic words began to sing. Others gradually joined in the chorus and the sound swelled. Some wept for homes they would never see again. Their sad voices floated above the deck's softly swaying lamplight and then drifted down onto the limpid sea to be hushed into gentle silence by the murmuring wake.

Wynn saw that Jane was on the point of tears and, from William's strained face, that her husband was also finding it difficult to control his emotions.

The embarrassed captain cleared his throat and asked William: 'Will you join your brother in his business, Mr MacKay?'

Grateful for the interruption, William nodded but glanced at Jane before replying: 'Only indirectly. We have spoken about supplying him with lumber.

'We hope to lease land on the northern shore of the island. My brother mentioned French River in one of his letters.'

Wynn nodded: 'Ah yes, I believe I spotted it on my new large map of the island. A very fine, detailed production, indeed. Would you like to view it?'

'I know, why don't you and Mrs MacKay join me for a cup of tea in my cabin?'

Jane replied: 'Thank you kindly Captain. Could we first take the children below and join you in about fifteen minutes?'

'Yes, that would be more convenient, Mrs MacKay. My cabin is not large.'

Despite their protests at being banished to their quarters, the children were taken down below and ordered to behave themselves while their parents were away.

Chapter 7: Mapping the future

'This is Prince Edward Island.' Pleased at the chance to show off his valuable, new map, Wynn gave a dramatic flourish with an outstretched arm as he and his cabin boy unrolled a wide parchment across the large chart table. Once the corners were clamped, Jane and William drew closer, fascinated by the clear detail. Both had seen maps of the island before, but they had always been small enough for Donald to fold and post to them.

Wynn spoke as if he were a school master giving a geography lesson: 'Prince Edward Island is about 150 miles long. Its breadth varies between three to fifty miles. The land is mainly flat, pleasantly undulating in the middle. Once cleared of timber, the soil is fertile and good for crops. All in all it is about 1.4 million acres. The first census of ten years ago gave its population as less than 5,000 people.

'Now, Mr MacKay, tell me again where does your brother think you might settle?' Wynn enquired, his fingers inquisitively drumming the edge of the table.

William's eyes scanned across the north shore of the island shown on the map but could not find the place he was seeking. He saw the island was divided up into rectangular areas. He knew that these were the sixty–seven large Lots of land which, following a British government lottery, had been awarded to proprietors, nearly all of whom lived in the UK, as a reward for loyal services during the ultimately victorious war to wrest Canada from the French and their native allies in 1763. Most of the original French colonists were forcibly driven off the island and transported to France.

Donald had written to tell William that the proprietors had agreed to pay the London government rent – called a quitrent – and allow their Lots to be leased by settlers. However most of the proprietors failed to pay their quitrent, calculating correctly that the London government would overlook the little colony, while engaged in other more weighty matters. In turn, few settlers felt obliged to pay rent to proprietors who showed little interest in helping them turn virgin land into viable agriculture property.

William remembered Donald had said that in fact the settlers hoped the London government would confiscate the proprietors' land for quitrent arrears – a process called escheat – and sell or grant it to the settlers. Settlers had been intermittently lobbying the London and island governments to adopt a policy of escheat, against the fierce protests of the proprietors. The latest squabble had reached an uneasy truce earlier in the year.

'French River in Lot 21,' replied William finally, giving up his search.

'Let me see. Ah yes, here we are,' Wynn's rough finger stubbed a spot where French River was written in small print at the entrance to an inlet from a larger river, flowing into the Gulf of St Lawrence.

Glancing shrewdly at William, Wynn continued: 'A good choice. The river banks and coast are still thickly–wooded. Chopping down trees and preparing lumber next to water is always more profitable.'

Wynn continued thoughtfully: 'And French River has a good anchorage. Along with several Yankee fishing boats, I sought shelter there once from a sudden storm when sailing back from the West Indies to Charlottetown.'

The tapping sound of a boiling metal kettle on the cast–iron hob of a small corner stove interrupted the group's thoughts. Jane and William's nostrils twitched with delight at the aroma of good quality tea from a china pot. They sipped appreciatively. Their palates had become accustomed to the rough leaves of the ship's rations served in half–washed clay mugs.

'This part of the island has an interesting history,' continued Wynn. 'Did you know that it was the site of a previous failed colony?' Jane and William frowned. Donald had kept this dispiriting event to himself.

Wynn raised his eyebrows in mock surprise: 'A Quaker merchant, Robert Clarke, bought the Lot and set up the Elizabethtown settlement in 1774 for about one hundred people of the same religious persuasion as himself. Today we call the area New London.

'Some say he was inspired by William Penn. Unfortunately the venture failed.'

Wynn lowered his voice: 'It is said one winter was so harsh that the people starved and' – Wynn hesitated – 'that they were forced to eat the bodies of dead friends. Whatever the truth, by about 1800 there was little left and Clarke died a bankrupt. A sad tale.'

'Oh no, that can't be true,' exclaimed Jane.

Wynn sighed: 'Yes, your brother's wife too was clearly upset by the story.'

'So you've met my sister–in–law. How was she?' William asked, surprised.

'Mrs Jessie MacKay was in good health when I saw her in the Pictou, a short distance across the Northumberland Strait in Nova Scotia. She is of great assistance to your brother in his business. Like me, she divides her time between Pictou and Charlottetown.'

'You seem to know a lot about my brother's affairs, Captain Wynn?' William enquired, faintly puzzled.

'Yes, I do indeed, Mr MacKay,' Wynn agreed with a wry smile.

'You see, the number of people who have positions of responsibility in the shipping trade is small. Ship builders, merchants and captains, we all know each other.'

'Do you live mainly in Pictou, Captain Wynn? Is that where you last saw my brother and his wife?' William asked.

'I still have access to lodgings there,' Wynn replied crisply. 'But I prefer to spend more time in Charlottetown these days when I am in between commissions.'

'Why is that?' Jane asked inquisitively.

'Unfortunately Pictou has succumbed to the evil of cheap rum from the West Indies, Mrs MacKay. The lumberers drink to excess and indulge in godless ways.

'The high price of timber means even the most humble farmer is tempted to neglect his fields and fell trees to join the alcoholic festivities.

'There is also a seductive system of loans, which encourages excess, provided by a very powerful man who has the town in his grip. Some call him the King of Pictou.'

'What is his name?' William enquired.

'Mortimer, Edward Mortimer.'

Wynn paused and said guardedly: 'Your brother and his wife would certainly know him through commerce.'

Jane and William looked at each other and digested Wynn's words for a moment. Both were concerned by the implication that Donald was doing business with an unprincipled person.

'Will you be hoping to buy land in French River, Mr MacKay? Wynn asked suddenly.

William was caught off guard: 'Why no, Captain. I had assumed that renting from a proprietor would be the only option.'

'That would almost certainly have been the case until recently,' Wynn agreed. 'But the situation has changed somewhat. The island's own government has begun demanding arrears in rent from some proprietors to finance the pay of their officials.'

Wynn smiled: 'Obtaining the rent arrears is proving difficult. Nonetheless I have heard some resident proprietors are selling parcels of land to raise money to pay at least some of what they owe.'

A weak flickering light caught Jane's eye as she looked out over William's shoulder through the cabin's large stern windows. She could vaguely see an enormous moonlit, shiny shape not far away, gradually fading away into the darkness. Alarmed, she pointed and exclaimed: 'What on earth is that?'

Captain Wynn swivelled around: 'Damnation!' he swore. With a face suddenly red with fury and in a strained voice, he said: 'Excuse me, I must go on deck.' Wynn grabbed his overcoat and cap and moved swiftly to the door. Over his shoulder he gabbled: 'Iceberg, Mrs MacKay...lucky escape...lookout failed in his duty...cabin boy will see you out.' And then, barely audibly under his breath and halfway out of the door: 'By God, I will have him whipped.'

The door slammed shut after Wynn. The stunned silence he left behind was punctured by the young cabin boy's polite enquiry: 'Would you like more tea, Madam?'

Jane recovered first from her shock. She raised her eyebrows: 'We may not have such nice tea again until Charlottetown, William.' She smiled at the boy and held out her cup and saucer.

'I would like another cup too, if I may,' added William.

Jane's mind returned to Wynn's question before the interruption. She reached out and clasped her husband's hand: 'William, dare we hope that we might actually own some land ourselves?'

William too had been dwelling on what Wynn had said. Was the captain correct? Had the situation really changed?

'I don't know, my dear. Donald will surely know the answer.'

Taking a fresh cup of tea from the cabin boy, William said: 'Let us not raise our hopes, only to find them cruelly dashed.'

William calmly looked at the map again. Putting his cup down on the side of the table, he beckoned his wife: 'Look Jane, it seems to be about 20 miles between Charlottetown and French River. And I can only see one road to the north coast, miles away from French River. I suppose Donald will take us by boat?

Suddenly there was a commotion outside, the door flew open and a sailor was shoved into the cabin. The man tripped and sprawled onto the floor and began to groan. He stank of rum. The prostrate fellow was followed rapidly into the room by Wynn and his first mate. Surprised to see William and Jane still in his cabin, Wynn said curtly: 'I would be grateful if you left, Mr and Mrs MacKay. As you can see I must attend to a disciplinary matter.'

Part 2: Prince Edward Island, Canada

Let's away to New Scotland where plenty sits Queen
O'er as happy a country as ever was seen
She blesses her subjects both little and great
With each a good home and pretty estate
Scots ballad, Anon, 1750

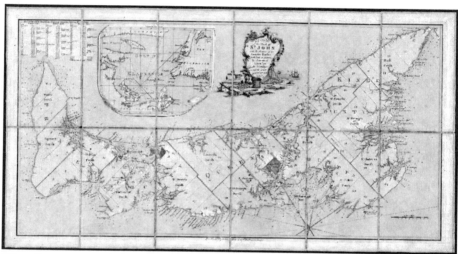

The first map of St John's Island (later Prince Edward Island) by
surveyor, Samuel Holland, 1765, courtesy of the Norman B. Leventhal
Map Center at the Boston Public Library/Richard H. Brown Collection

Chapter 8: A capital start

The *Elizabeth & Ann* docked in Charlottetown shortly after daybreak on the 5th January 1807. The previous evening, Captain Wynn had been forced to drop anchor a few miles out as a misty nightfall made further progress too dangerous. Not long after a murky dawn, all the immigrants crowded on deck to catch a glimpse of their new homeland as the *Elizabeth & Ann* crept past the brooding canons of the recently built Fort Edward and into Charlottetown harbour, towed by the tugging boats.

A fishing boat under full sail, low in the water and smelling of a large herring catch lumbered slowly past, escorted by a flock of swooping gulls. The fishermen waved up at the new arrivals and a couple of unfamiliar, large black and white dogs on the boat's deck spun round and round, barking excitedly.

'St John's Water Dogs,' a crewman explained to the immigrants around him while he fastened a towline. 'They help pull in floating net lines. They have webbed feet and thick tails and can swim as well as otters. Fishermen use them all along the coast as far as Labrador,' he added admiringly.

Donald was waiting in the milling, humming throng on the quayside, trying to discern his brother among the many faces along the side of the ship as she was towed in, splintering patches of thin ice out of the way. At last he spotted William, taller than most of the other Highlanders, and started to wave his large seal fur hat and shout. After a few seconds his brother recognised Donald's face.

'Look, there's Donald!' William yelled, delighted that his brother was there to greet him and his family.

The emotions of the *Elizabeth & Ann's* passengers were now the opposite of those they had felt in Thurso. Many wept with joy and relief at their safe arrival. Some knelt to thank God. On the quay stood relatives and friends, like Donald, waving impatiently, eager to embrace the immigrants.

Jane gave thanks to God silently. She had always feared the sea since she was a young girl when she had suddenly been struck by a large, rogue wave while walking on a beach with her father. On the

Elizabeth & Ann she had felt a slow, creeping sense of impending doom whenever she had looked up from the deck and watched the foaming, hostile waves.

Ropes were thrown and twisted around bollards. The crew heaved and the gap between the *Elizabeth & Ann* and the quayside narrowed. The rough hessian bag fenders squirted fizzy water as they were squeezed between ship and quay.

Only when Captain Wynn was certain that all ropes had been made securely fast did he order the main gangplank lowered. Wynn marched purposefully halfway down and grasped the side ropes.

Holding a megaphone to his mouth, he addressed the excited, pressing throng: 'Ladies and gentlemen.' But few could hear him above the hubbub and those who could took no notice. Wynn cleared his throat and started again. This time he yelled: 'Unless you make way and allow our passengers through, it will take two days to disembark.'

Annoyed, Wynn waved for a couple of his crew to stand at the foot of the gangway and elbow a space. The handful of cabin passengers went first into the narrow gap and pushed their way through. They were followed by the steerage families, single men and, lastly, the few single women.

William and the two teenage boys forced their way into the crowd, towing Jane and the rest of the family behind until they had wrestled their way into the more open space at the rear of the quay where Donald was waiting, arms outstretched.

The two brothers embraced. Donald found it difficult to stop his nose from wrinkling at the smell of two months in steerage which permeated William's clothes. He noticed that William seemed gaunt and a lot greyer.

For his part, William could see that Donald was expensively dressed. A thick brown seal leather, fur–trimmed coat, heavy woollen scarf, and his fur hat kept him warm. His brother had become plump and oozed prosperity, tinged with a whiff of Cuban cigars.

Donald greeted Jane and the rest of the family with boyish exuberance, hugging each of them in turn and wishing everyone A Happy New Year.

'My, my, how they have all grown!' Donald said admiringly.

'George and Duncan Forbes are already men.'

Tousling the latter's curly hair he said: 'Sorry my boy, I'd forgotten the family calls you Forbes for short.'

He smiled at Joanne: 'And you are already quite the lady.'

He turned and bussed Jane on each cheek: 'Your mother is still as pretty as I remember.'

Jane smiled: 'And *you*, Donald, are as I remember.'

'Where is Jessie?' Jane asked politely but not particularly surprised at the absence of Donald's wife, with whom she had never been close.

'My dear wife awaits to greet you in The Crossed Keys, the hostelry in which she is organising your rooms,' Donald replied gently. He turned on his heels and with a click of his fingers, authoritatively summoned the two men he had hired to carry the luggage.

'Come, follow me,' he said and led the family through the gradually thinning crowd, thumping his silver–topped malacca cane on the rough timber wharf with the self–confidence of a man used to getting his way.

Jessie had greeted Jane at The Crossed Keys with restrained enthusiasm and a peck on a cheek. But she seemed genuinely pleased to see her nephews and niece. William was rewarded with a close hug and a kiss. Unlike Donald though, she couldn't completely disguise her distaste at the smell of steerage. With her cologne–soaked handkerchief pressed gently to her nose and a swish of her heavy dress she quickly led Jane and the children upstairs to their rooms where hot tubs of water awaited them. Even the boys enjoyed their first wash in two months using water which was not salty.

While the rest of the family were washing and changing their clothes, Donald had linked arms with his brother and led him the short distance back to the quayside.

'Look William. Look at those ships.' Donald was pointing at two vessels being loaded, moored to the Charlottetown quay. Donald led William closer. The two brothers watched the crew on each ship, hoisting bundles of square–sawn lumber up from rafts floating next to the ships.

One of the ships was of similar size to the *Elizabeth & Ann*. The other was shorter, slimmer, more elegant and had less rigging. William thought she looked like a racehorse compared to the dray horse of the larger ship.

Donald put one heavy sleeved arm around his brother's shoulders: 'What do you see, William?'

Donald looked at the puzzled expression on William's face and cheerfully blew cigar smoke out of the side of his mouth: 'Look closer brother,' he urged.

William shook his head: 'I can see one ship is bigger. I recognise her as a brig. The other is an unknown type to me. I do not know what else you wish me to see, Donald.'

William crossed his arms and stamped his feet. He was tired, cold and hungry.

'As you correctly say, the bigger one is a brig. The smaller is a schooner. Faster and with a much smaller crew,' said Donald, ignoring his brother's discomfort.

'But most importantly, she can be loaded and unloaded twice as fast as a brig. See how the lumber can be hoisted straight up and onto the deck. There are no spars – poles – square to the masts with their rigging in the way. The schooner is not square–rigged. She has horizontal booms parallel to the ship's sides.'

Donald paused to let William absorb his words: 'Even though the brig carries more cargo, the fact that the schooner can be loaded quicker, has a smaller crew, and sails faster means it is cheaper to operate.'

William was quick to see the schooner's disadvantage: 'But it can't carry nearly as many passengers?'

'Yes, you are correct, William. The brig has the advantage of being able to ferry lots of emigrants back across the Atlantic. This is why schooners are used more for the coastal trade. Even so, they can still be profitable on the return leg if they carry smaller, expensive items. Like my shoes, for example,' he added with a self–satisfied grin.

Donald turned around and faced his brother: 'This schooner has been chartered by me. She will be delivering lumber along the coast to the Yankees in New York and Boston and then collecting molasses, rum and sugar from my agent in Jamaica for the return leg to Nova Scotia and here.'

Donald stopped and pointed his cane grandly around the harbour as if all the ships were his: 'And I am making a good living. Yes, a very good living.'

Donald patted his pale brother on the shoulder: 'I can see you would welcome a retreat to the warmth of The Crossed Keys. Let us return. I want to tell all of our family my plans during luncheon. I have ordered a feast for you.'

Washed and dressed in clean clothes the family sat down to eat at The Crossed Key's largest table. A fog of pipe tobacco smoke blanketed the crowded, noisy room full of happy residents and new arrivals speaking in a babel of tongues: English, French, German and, above all, Gaelic, with some of its Irish sister tongue, here and there.

At their table, William had insisted on saying grace before allowing his impatient, fidgeting children to eat a meal of fresh goose, potatoes, apples and cheese. Donald and Jessie chewed and drank slowly, watching the others hurriedly eating, remembering how famished they themselves had been after their own long Atlantic voyage.

'Don't gobble, John,' Jane admonished the six–year old boy who was stuffing his mouth with as much food as he could. Even Joanne was scoffing her food in an unladylike manner. Food and drink had never tasted so delicious. William savoured his beer, gently sloshing it round the tankard and sipping it slowly.

After Jane and William had eaten their fill and were leaning back contentedly, Donald tapped the side of his pewter tankard to gain attention: 'Welcome to Prince Edward Island, my dear family. William, with your permission, and yours too Jane,' he added hastily, remembering that Jane did not like people to forget she was the tacksman, not William, 'I would like to describe to you, if I may, the vision I have for us all to prosper.'

Seeing that William and Jane had no objection, Donald cleared his throat and continued, a trifle self–importantly: 'You know that I am already well established as a merchant. As I showed your father earlier this morning, I buy principally timber and charter ships...' Donald broke off as little William, seated on Jane's lap, beat a small wooden cup on the table and gurgled happily: 'Sheeps, sheeps.'

'No William, ships not sheeps,' corrected his brother, John, giggling.

'Quite so, young man. Our family's fortune will be in ships, definitely not sheep,' said Donald.

He looked around the table and gathered his thoughts before continuing: 'Now I would like you all to think how we could benefit if we not only harvested our own trees, but,' and here he paused to emphasise what he next said, 'also built and sailed our own ships.'

There was a silence around the table. The children were puzzled, failing to grasp the full significance of Donald's words, while Jane and William had expected Donald to expand only on how to maximise profits in the lumber trade.

'Donald, we know nothing about building and only a little of sailing ships,' said Jane, perplexed.

Her brother–in–law leant forward and, as if to emphasise the importance of what he was about to say, broke into Gaelic: 'Yes Jane, but look around you. On that table over there are probably a couple of shipwrights from Bristol. They have been left behind to build a ship over the winter.

'By the fire, your Captain Wynn is spinning yarns with other sea dogs. And at that loud table in the corner drinking rum is a team of French lumberers.'

Donald reassured his startled brother: 'Fear not William. The war with France is of little significance around here.'

'And your point about ships Donald?' said William, intrigued.

'Simply this, brother: All the necessary crafts and trades are available here. Lumberers, shipwrights, carpenters, sail makers, ship masters and sailors. One does not need to be an expert craftsman, only to know sufficient about their craft to supervise their work and pay a fair price.'

Donald looked around the table, his eyes focusing on George and Forbes.

'You two young men need only to work for a while with the people you employ to fell trees and prepare lumber. And shipwrights and carpenters are always looking for mates to assist with lifting, cutting, drilling and sanding. The same goes for sailing the ships. Captains are always eager for able–bodied seamen of good potential.'

George and Forbes followed every word that Donald said with increasing excitement. Building their own ships? Sailing them?

'And what of your own son? How is my nephew?' asked Jane, puzzled that Donald's son had not been mentioned.

'He sends his regards, Jane. He would love to be here.'

Donald frowned before continuing: 'The plain fact of the matter is my William dislikes the sea. He suffers from seasickness. Even the short journey from French River to Charlottetown makes him feel wretched for days. Besides which, William was born to be a farmer and is utterly content managing our property in French River.'

Trying brightly to conceal his disappointment that his son had not inherited his father's entrepreneurial zeal for seafaring and trading, he continued: ' He is looking forward to meeting you all.'

'Do Jane and I figure in your plan, Donald?' asked his brother, the edges of his mouth crinkling.

'Yes, of course. I did not mean to omit you, William. You and Jane will manage our French River affairs. We will all be partners. And as your land gradually becomes cleared of timber, like mine did, you will find the fertile soil is ideal for crops and pasture for cattle.

'My son, William, will be at your service to help in whatever way you need.'

'I do not wish to pour cold water on your plans Donald, but, to play our part, we will perhaps need more money than we have at present,' said Jane doubtfully.

Jessie, who had sat quietly during the conversation, now interjected: 'Dear sister, I am confident that profits from your timber will exceed your expectations. But, in any case, letters of credit are easy to obtain. D. MacKay & Co's reputation is sound. We regularly source funds from Pictou, where money is plentiful and interest rates low.'

Donald responded to Jane and William's surprised faces: 'Jessie looks after D. MacKay & Co's financial affairs and keeps our books. She is well respected in Charlottetown and Pictou.'

Jessie nodded her head in satisfaction at her husband's endorsement.

The table became quiet as Jane and William digested Donald's words.

After a few minutes Donald added: 'You see, my vision is to recreate here our MacKay clan from Tongue and Erribol so successfully that we can accommodate not just us, but also our cousins as their futures become ever more gloomy in Strathnaver.'

The table fell silent again.

It dawned on Jane she might have misjudged Donald. The free–booting qualities of a travelling soldier, which had made her doubt her brother–in–law's reliability, had clearly helped him become a successful merchant in a strange land. And to hear him declare so forcibly his loyalty to their extended family and the clan MacKay was a pleasant surprise.

Sensing that a change in subject might lighten the serious mood which had cloaked the table, Donald banged his tankard down: 'This is where the island's first Council – our parliament – sat. A queer place for a queer gathering, eh, William?' Donald chuckled, looking around the large open front room of The Crossed Keys.

'Do you mean exactly here?' said William.

'Yes. Around this very table on July 4th 1773, our House of Assembly first met to pass laws – provided the King's governor agreed.' Donald drew deep from his beer: 'Are you not drinking, brother?'

'I drink far less these days, Donald.'

Faintly disappointed, Donald smiled to himself, remembering their days with the Fencibles: 'Ah well, we drank enough in Belfast to last us a lifetime.'

'Yes, we did Donald. But since then the Good Book has taught me the error of my ways.'

Donald was not surprised. He had noticed from his brother's letters that once William had become a Kirk Elder their tone had gradually become censorious of excess of any kind.

Two men were making their way through the crowded, smoky room, when one suddenly turned to Donald and said in genteel English with a pleasant West Country burr: 'A Happy New Year Mr and Mrs MacKay. I trust you have enjoyed your meal?'

'Why, my dear Mr Cambridge,' Donald pushed his chair back and shook the soberly dressed man's hand, 'Thank you, we have indeed. Allow me to introduce my newly–arrived brother and his wife, Mr William MacKay and Mrs Jane Scobie MacKay.'

Donald looked inquisitively in the direction of Cambridge's companion, a tall, handsome man dressed in bright clothes at least as expensive as Donald's.

'Ah yes' – Cambridge moved to one side – 'Mr MacKay, permit me to introduce Thomas Douglas, the Earl of Selkirk.'

There was no need to ask why Cambridge's aristocratic companion was in Charlottetown. His purchase of several Lots on Prince Edward Island and the offer of free passage and land to poverty–stricken victims of the Clearances had made Selkirk famous in the Highlands and admired by many.

Donald said: 'It is an honour to meet you my Lord. We have all heard about your generous schemes. And we merchants are delighted they appear to be thriving.'

Selkirk smiled and extended his hand and, to Donald's surprise, replied in passable Gaelic: 'I am always delighted to meet fellow Highlanders in the Americas.'

Swiftly summing up the assembled MacKays he said: 'Forgive me if I seem presumptuous but, from your educated manner, I take it you are of the tacksman class?'

'I am, I was' – Jane corrected herself – 'a tacksman to Lord Reay. My maiden name is Scobie; several of our family are prominent tacksmen in our clan.'

Only faintly surprised at being addressed by Jane, Selkirk nodded: 'I have had the pleasure of meeting your Lord Reay a few years ago in

London.' Selkirk paused for a few seconds, rubbed his chin and awkwardly, and stared at Jane: 'How was he when you last saw him?'

'He was in fine spirits my Lord.'

'Ah yes, I often found him in good spirits, Mrs MacKay,' Selkirk said, allowing a suspicion of ironic amusement to dance around his eyes.

He looked at all the MacKays around the table: 'I find it encouraging that people of your class have come to this island. The more Highlanders of quality we have, the less easy it will be' – Selkirk's voice rose – 'for that set of lawless Yankee vagabonds to threaten the frontiers of our provinces.'

Selkirk reined himself in. He realised his fists were clenching involuntarily and felt his face was becoming red. Embarrassed by Selkirk's outburst, the older MacKays lowered their eyes. But Selkirk's hatred of the new republic was well known and stemmed from the time when the American privateer, John Paul Jones, had terrified the young aristocrat. Selkirk had been a small boy when the turncoat Scot had raided his family home in Scotland's Western Isles.

Cambridge took the opportunity of the silence to resume the conversation in English: 'It is a pleasure to meet another Mr and Mrs MacKay.'

Looking at William he said: 'I understand from your brother that you are interested in some land in French River?'

He raised his palm to indicate that there was no need for William to answer. Cambridge instead looked at Donald: 'Forgive me. We cannot tarry. Noon, tomorrow in my office?'

'No, Mr Cambridge. I would prefer my office, if you please. We are many and making arrangements for the children is not always easy at short notice.'

I am looking forward to it, Sir,' said Cambridge, as he and Selkirk nodded goodbye.

Looking at the back of the departing Cambridge and Selkirk, Donald said thoughtfully: 'Cambridge owns 16,000 acres. But the land I recommend you should lease, William belongs to Mrs Clarke. Cambridge serves as her agent. Thickly–wooded, fine, fertile land with fresh water at the entrance to French River. We call it Yankee Hill because their fishing boats load stores from a small jetty there.

'I thought Cambridge brusque, almost rude,' Jane observed. 'Unlike Lord Selkirk,' she added.

'That is his manner these days, Jane. He has business difficulties which are affecting his style. Do not worry though. Like most Quakers, I have found John Cambridge to be honest in business.

'Unfortunately he is in some disagreement with Mrs Clark who is trying to recoup some money from her dead husband's previous disastrous colony. Before the meeting tomorrow we should discuss Mr Cambridge in my office. Things have changed, possibly to our advantage.'

Donald leant to one side to allow a waiter to start clearing the empty plates.

'Provided we have reached an agreement with Cambridge, I suggest we leave as soon as possible for French River, say, two days from now. We do not have much time to waste. The sea could start to freeze any day.'

Chapter 9: Striking a hard bargain

'This is my office,' Donald said proudly, sweeping open the landing door at the top of a wooden outside stairway, surmounted by a large sign: D. MacKay &Co.

'Our office if you please, Husband,' Jessie sniffed as she strode past.

Turning to the rest of the assembled family she said: 'It's true I am not always at my desk,' she motioned with her hand to a heavily inlaid escritoire. Stepping forward she opened its ornate lid to reveal three neatly stacked, leather bound ledgers: 'However, I can assure you I am assiduous in my duties to our firm's finances.'

'I did not wish to imply otherwise, Jessie,' Donald said emolliently as he sat down at a large mahogany desk, puffing contentedly on a cigar, and waved his brother and Jane into well–padded chairs.

A wood–burning stove in the corner radiated warmth, its reflected flames flashing off the swinging pendulum of a nearby, large grandfather clock. Obtaining a nod of approval from his uncle, Forbes picked up a long, shiny telescope lying on a table and squinted through it in the direction of the harbour.

'What do you see Forbes?' asked Donald, lounging back, his fingers tapping on the fob chain across his paunch.

Twisting the metal ring into focus, his nephew replied: 'Men working, Uncle Donald. Many men. Loading ships and lifting wood off rafts.'

Donald nodded: 'Yes, everybody here wants to share in the bounty we get from timber before it runs out, which it surely will some day.'

His uncle chuckled: 'You see young Forbes, in Prince Edward Island money really does grow on trees.'

Between bookshelves and cupboards, the office walls were decorated with framed pictures and drawings. George was mesmerised by one painting which showed a speeding ship under full sail in a strong wind, the waves seeming to carry rather than impede her. He could make out the name on the bow: *The Grenville*.

'Is this one of your ships, Uncle Donald?' he asked eagerly.

'No, my boy. Grenville is a common name. I bought the painting because it caught the excitement of sailing.'

Impulsively, George spun round to face William: 'I want to be a sailor, Father. I want to become a captain.'

'That would be excellent, George. And Forbes can provide you with timber to make your ships profitable,' Donald said in satisfaction, pre–empting anything William might say.

Stubbing his cigar out, Donald looked at Jane: 'Perhaps you should take the children back to the Crossed Keys...'

'No,' Jane said flatly. 'I wish them to hear everything. Apart from little William, they are old enough to understand. It is, after all, their future we are securing.'

'Very well,' Donald assented.

'Let us turn to the subject of Mr Cambridge. He is one of the largest proprietors who actually lives on the island. Although wealthy in terms of his acres, I understand,' – Jessie coughed irritably – 'we,' Donald corrected himself, 'have reason to believe that Cambridge has an urgent need for some money in hand.'

'Indeed,' said Jessie, breaking in: 'Mrs Clarke informs me that she has reached a satisfactory agreement with Mr Cambridge. He will pay her an agreeable sum to settle their differences.'

'Furthermore,' Donald continued, 'the island government has demanded he pay some proprietor quitrent arrears or they will foreclose on part of his land.'

'How much rent do you think he will ask from me?' asked William, coming to the point.

Donald patted his hands on his tight waistcoat and thought for a moment or two: 'I expect him to ask a rent of £80 to £90 per annum and a substantial deposit of about £500. This is too high but will start the negotiation. You should offer £70 per annum with a deposit of £350.'

Jane interrupted: 'This is more than we were expecting to pay, Donald.'

Donald shrugged his shoulders: 'The war with Napoleon continues. The Royal Navy expands. More ships mean more wood to build them.

The price of land with good timber rises accordingly. Even during your two months at sea it has increased.'

William bent forward and stared down at his feet. The leather on his shoes was nearly worn through and cracked by the salt and wind of two months at sea. He glanced up at Donald's polished, outstretched leather boots, one leg crossed confidently over the other.

Suddenly William doubted himself. Was he up to the task of negotiating with a wealthy, experienced merchant like John Cambridge, risking all the money his family possessed? He looked at his elder brother who was watching him anxiously. William sensed that Donald was on the point of offering to negotiate on his behalf. Perhaps he should accept?

William felt Jane put her hand softly on his: 'Husband, you have negotiated as a tacksman between Highland cattle drovers and Sassenach beef buyers. And still made a profit. There are no cannier people on this earth. I trust you in this matter.'

William drew quick strength from Jane's words. He looked at Donald and Jessie and breathed: 'I...I am ready to deal with Mr Cambridge.'

'I believe you are, Brother,' said Donald – but a quick glance at Jessie betrayed he still had doubts.

Donald stood up and beckoned his brother to take his seat: 'Sit here, William, in a place of authority. We will sit Cambridge here,' he said, lifting a chair and putting it in front of his desk.

Jane forced herself to look at the clock and saw it was nearly noon. Only her moving lips showed she was praying: 'Dear Lord, I beseech you to permit a favourable outcome to this meeting. We have risked everything to come to this little island in the New World.'

William sat hunched forward, steeling himself to be ready to seize any opportunity.

Donald and Jessie exchanged glances. Their expressions softened as they felt empathy towards William and Jane. In the last ten years or so they too had shared similar moments of tension as they built their business.

Even though all had braced themselves, the noise of the first chime still felt like an explosion. Before the clock had finished striking twelve times there was a sharp tap of a cane on the door.

Even Jessie's hands were shaking as she greeted Cambridge and took his heavy coat, fur hat and cane. After the thin, angular Englishman had shaken hands, she ushered him into the chair facing William. Cambridge refused an offer of coffee and asked for a glass of water, which he sipped slowly as he took in the large comfortable room: 'I had forgotten what an elegant office you had Mr MacKay.'

'Thank you Mr Cambridge. We have indeed been fortunate,' said Donald.

As a precursor to the meeting, Donald indulged in some small talk: 'May I ask how Lord Selkirk fares today?'

'He is in a capital mood, Mr MacKay. Quite capital.'

Cambridge placed his glass down: 'I have facilitated his purchase of Lot 10.'

'But that is at the other end of the island from his settlement,' said Donald, puzzled.

'Yes, but such has been its success, he is contemplating another one on our island.'

Hearing a child sneeze, Cambridge twisted around to see the young MacKays standing with Jane in one corner: 'Your children will attend this meeting?'

'Yes Mr Cambridge, unless you have strong objection,' Jane replied firmly.

'No, no, not all, dear lady. It is unusual, but why not?' Cambridge said airily.

He stood up and took some papers from a small leather bag.

'May I,' he said, as he rolled out a drawing of an area of land on the desk in front of William.

'Mr MacKay, you will already know the tract of land in question, Yankee Hill, is at the headland of French River in New London with one side bordering the Gulf of St Lawrence. It is good soil, 615 and a half acres to be precise, well stocked with timber and its own French River frontage, close to deep water. Indeed, there is already a wharf which Yankee fishing boats use to load supplies. It also has a fresh water pond on the property's southern edge.'

Cambridge paused, and then added: 'Your brother, who rents land from Mrs Clark further up the river on the opposite bank, would confirm this, I'm sure.'

Donald gave the slightest nod of agreement.

Running a finger down a dotted line Cambridge continued: 'There is also a right of way from the edge of the property down this lane, Cape Road, to the jetty.'

Cambridge looked up: 'Otherwise some of your neighbours would be cut off from the wharf.'

William frowned.

The Quaker reassured him: 'It is not used frequently Mr MacKay. Perhaps two or three times a week. It should not unduly interfere with your commerce.'

Cambridge hesitated for a few seconds, slightly unnerved that William had not said a word: 'I propose a rent of £80 per annum with a deposit of £500, Mr MacKay.'

William did not immediately respond. Cambridge could see that the thickly bearded Scot was mulling over the proposal.

'Well, Mr MacKay, what say you?' Cambridge asked, cocking his head in enquiry.

'Thank you for your proposal, Mr Cambridge,' replied William eventually, his face expressionless: 'I would rather offer £65 per annum with a deposit of £250.'

Cambridge clucked his tongue: 'Come, come a fair rent for the land would be about £75 per annum, Mr MacKay. And £250 is too low.' However, Cambridge's guarded tone hinted there might be room for compromise.

'I am willing to increase my offer to £70 per annum with,' William paused and said slowly, 'a deposit of £500, Mr Cambridge.'

William ignored Jane's involuntarily gasp and placed both his hands, palms down on the table, lent forward and looked Cambridge straight in the face: 'Provided I have the option to buy the leasehold after five years with a further £200.'

Donald drew an inward breath in quiet surprise at his brother's demand. This had not been discussed. He looked quickly at Cambridge, fascinated to see what the man would say.

The Englishman thought quickly: the Scot's timing was impeccable. He must surely know I have an urgent need to find ready money for Mrs Clarke. And for myself. He glanced at Jessie: Of course, Mrs Clarke had probably gossiped about their agreement.

Cambridge paused. He disliked relinquishing ownership on any land but this was a generous offer. And after all, the land was not even his.

'I have no room for manoeuvre on this figure,' William prodded.

Cambridge smiled inwardly, believing he now held the whip hand: would the Scot agree to a condition? 'Three years, Mr MacKay. An option of five years would be too much for Mrs Clarke.'

William looked at Donald: was three years too soon? Would their enterprise generate enough profit in that period? Should he counter with four years? No need; Donald smiled confidently and inclined his head.

William stood up and outstretched his hand: 'Very well, Mr Cambridge. £70 per annum, a deposit of £500 and then a further £200 in three years. We have an agreement.'

'One thing more Mr MacKay,' Cambridge said, as he got to his feet: 'You are now the leaseholder. This means you have to pay the government its quitrent. At six shillings per 100 acres, a modest amount of 36 shillings per annum, nonetheless your responsibility.'

Now Cambridge held his hand out: 'Congratulations Mr MacKay. You are here on our island barely two days, but already a proprietor.'

Cambridge turned to take his coat from Jessie: 'I will have my notary draft the contract for your signature this afternoon.'

'I trust the agreement will accurately reflect our discussion, Mr Cambridge?' William could not resist teasing the Quaker, a man even more straight–laced than himself.

'Of course.' An Englishman's word is his bond, Mr MacKay,' Cambridge replied testily, his Bristol accent growling William's surname off his tongue like an old English sheepdog.

'I would rather trust in the good Lord, Mr Cambridge,' William said drily.

Furling the brim on his hat, Cambridge looked down at the two brothers. Donald he knew as a swashbuckling trader prepared to take risks and cheerily enjoy the fruits of his labours. This new brother was clearly made of different, God–fearing, dour material. He smiled inwardly: like a Quaker, in fact.

Cambridge said thinly: 'I'm sure God will guide my notary's hand, Mr MacKay. Your brother is familiar with my bank and can provide you with the necessary details for payment.'

The Englishman gave a small stiff bow to the brothers: 'Our meeting is concluded, I believe. Good day, gentlemen.'

William gazed down at the drawing after Cambridge had left. He whispered to himself: 'Our land.' He tilted his head sideways and stared at Jane: 'Look Wife, this is our land. MacKay land. But not Lord Reay's.' And then more loudly: 'Our land.'

Donald jumped up and slapped William on the back: 'Well done little Brother. I am proud of you.'

Puffing furiously on a new cigar, he placed a silver salver with four glasses on the table and unlocked a double bottle tantalus: 'I insist we all have a cognac to celebrate.'

He stopped his hand reaching for a French bottle: 'No, how stupid of me. I have an excellent Islay.'

He waved Jane down: 'No, I will not brook a refusal.'

Jessie added her congratulations as she took a glass from her husband: 'Yes, William, you handled that well. Very well.' There was a tone in her voice that neither Jane nor William had heard directed at them before: Respect.

Donald held his sparkling tumbler high: 'Let us drink to the MacKays of French River.'

'Red, red,' little William gurgled, pointing up at Jane's quickly–flushing face as she took a swallow of her whisky.

'Ah, Jane, can you not taste the peat, barley and the soft lochs of the Old Country in this?' asked Donald, smacking his lips.

Jane did not reply. She sat gripping her tumbler tightly in her lap with both hands, little William bouncing up and down on her shoes. The Old Country? Yes, how strange to call it thus. But that is what Strathnaver was now, she thought. How appropriate to toast the future with the drink of the past.

She looked up and said unsteadily: 'No, Donald, I fancy from now on I shall be content only to taste the fruits of our new home.'

'And your new home should not take too long,' said Donald cheerfully.

'We will have a Frolic. The dozen or so families around French River know you are coming.'

'A Frolic?' Jane asked.

'Yes that's what we name a cooperative gathering of people who will help build your new home. Our cabin is too small for your family for more than a little while. The Hardings, Sims and Orrs; all will welcome and help you.'

Donald sipped contentedly: 'When complete we will celebrate its opening with food and drink. I am confident that we will get about 15 men and boys to help us. Most have large families.

'Yes,' Donald beamed. 'My dear William and Jane, your new home in French River will be ready in less than two weeks.'

Chapter 10: *Manu forti*

Jane never tired of the view. She sat contentedly on the comfortable, smoothed tree stump at the end of the French River cape just where it started to slope down towards the bay. This was her favourite spot to relax, gather her thoughts and plan her housekeeping.

When Forbes had carved a seat out of the stump he had laughed: 'Look Mother, here's your chair. You can sit here and pretend you are back at Varrich Castle looking down at the Kyle of Tongue.'

Forbes had turned to join her looking down at the blue, calm of Grenville Bay's natural harbour, sheltered by its long, golden sandbank. Shielding their eyes from the bright summer sun, they could just see a lazy plume of smoke zigzagging up from the settlement of Cavendish, behind the thin, long smudge of the red–brown shoreline on the other side of the water. On their right behind the trees was the entrance to French River and on the left the wide expanse of the Gulf of St Lawrence.

Jane had to admit to herself Forbes had been correct. At first, when she had sat there, she had indeed spent many a time thinking about Tongue and whether the family should have stayed in Strathnaver. Even with Donald and Jessie's support, the family had struggled to adjust to their new, tough life during the first year. Their first home, built quickly during the Frolic in the middle of winter, was but a rough single–roomed hut, the gaps in the log walls and roof had been covered with birch bark and there had been a simple earth floor.

A hearth had been built at one end with an external timber chimney. The entrance door faced south to catch the sun and help tell them what time of day it was. She remembered how their only fire had once gone out. William had to walk more than mile in the cold to their nearest neighbours who had given him a live piece of coal. The same neighbours gave them hops, which they used to activate flour to make bread, and animal fat to make candles. Fortunately the storekeeper at the head of French River had been supportive, extending them credit for flour, oats, potatoes, sugar and salt beef. A diet that young William called *'Elizabeth & Ann* food.'

They eked out a living during their first winter. It was a relief when the ice melted and their diets widened in the Spring of 1807 to include mussels and eels, which were easy to catch in the river. The boys had laughed at how ridiculously simple it was to wade into the water with a basket and fill it with lobsters.

George had not stayed much longer than a year in French River. As soon as his parents would allow – they sensed he would run away if they didn't – the seventeen–year old had gone to sea. William had brought back from Charlottetown an excited, scrawled note from her son: 'Do not fret Mother. Father will tell you we are bound for the West Indies with timber and will return with sugar and rum!' Jane used the letter as a book mark and every evening she wondered where her eldest child was and prayed for his safety.

Jane smiled at the memory of her overwhelming relief – it had seemed almost overnight – when they prospered in 1808 at the end of their second summer. Yes, Donald and Jessie's optimism had proved to be well founded. The timber on their land had fetched a high price. French lumberers paid by Donald had come ashore and felled some of the best trees nearest the river.

But Jane's face now clouded with sadness: the relief at their sudden new prosperity had been marred by tragedy. Joanna had been bitten by a snake and died aged 15, on the cusp of womanhood.

In the following Spring they had employed a team of poor Scots itinerant field hands – there were many around – to help clear more land and plant their first crop. Donald's William had arranged for seed potatoes from South America and wheat seed from New England. The men and women – former crofters – worked together in the field and lived in a crude cabin which they built themselves next to the trees in the uncleared land leading down to the pond, which marked the southern border of their property.

Using a pair of horses, bought with money from the sale of timber, William and the boys had worked with the field hands to clear the stumps from the field behind where Jane was sitting, up to the western boundary with the Sims family's property.

Early one morning Jane remembered how she had gone to collect eggs from their chicken run. She had passed the field hands who were breakfasting on upturned chopped logs by a fire upon which their women were boiling oats.

One of the women had suddenly stood up and challenged Jane, hands on hips, in Gaelic: 'Nothing's really changed has it, Mistress Scobie?'

Startled, Jane turned and saw an emaciated woman dressed in clothes filthy from tilling the field and spreading mussel and sea weed fertiliser. The woman held her hands up to show Jane the rough calluses, freshly red from an early–morning shift.

'You don't recognise me do you?' the woman had said.

Annoyed by the sarcastic tone, Jane took a step forward. The woman's face was vaguely familiar.

'On the *Elizabeth & Ann*?' the woman prompted, glaring at Jane from sunken eyes.

Now Jane recognised her: the drunken woman who had complained that Jane was taking too long in the galley.

'You are still the Lady Tacksman and we,' here the woman stumbled, her hands hanging down and her voice now crumbling, full of defeated misery, 'we poor wretches have even less than in the Old Country. We should never have come.'

The woman began to weep, not the lachrymose tears of unhappiness, rather the arid, dirt–stained tears of despair: 'We were wickedly misled by the shipping agent's exaggerated accounts of this cursed island into quitting our homes.'

Jane looked at the woman's companions, who had fallen quiet as they shifted uncomfortably, staring at their bare feet, listening to the exchange: 'I am sorry for your distress. We too have endured hardship' – she suddenly recalled the woman's name – 'Mistress Gunn.'

'Aye, but you started with sufficient money in your pocket. And now you have land and a house. You are already building a new splendid home, I see.'

The woman paused to take a rasping breath: 'And we ... we have nothing.'

A man stood up from the rest of the sitting group and put a hand on the woman's arm. 'Come Mary, finish your breakfast,' he said gently as he led her back.

'We pay you well and provide you with enough food, don't we?' Jane barked at the retreating couple, irritated with herself that she sounded guilty.

'That you do, Mistress Scobie. We have no complaints,' the man replied calmly, over his shoulder. But Jane could tell he was lying.

Ill at ease, Jane continued with her eggs back home. She didn't mention the exchange to William because she thought it would only unsettle him. The next morning, a puzzled William told Jane that a man and woman had suddenly left their team of field workers without explanation. Jane thought it pointless to explain that she knew why.

They found the planting and growing season short from April to September. But the fertile soil and warm sun ensured a good harvest. Wheat had to be harvested quickly and threshed.

At the end of the summer their first crop of grain was taken by cart to the Tuplin mill at Indian River, only a few hours away. Oh, how Jane had wished Joanna was still with her to make bread from their own fresh flour. She smiled at the memory of how her daughter had cultivated a cane fruit and vegetable garden and had clapped her hands in excitement as her wild raspberries quickly bore fruit.

Jane clenched her fingers in her lap and looked across the short distance to where they had buried Joanna in the cemetery in a clump of spruce trees near the headland.

Jane did not sob. Her face merely registered resigned grief – death had become wearily familiar to her. She had now lost seven offspring: 'Please Lord, spare my remaining children,' she whispered, her dry lips barely moving.

William had reminded the family as they lowered Joanna's body into her grave that it was God's will: 'Some are taken earlier than others. We do not know why.' The boys had looked sideways at each other: they found little solace in their father's words.

In 1809 William had paid John Cambridge the final instalment of their agreement. That part of New London now became MacKay land.

Jane sighed. What should have been a cause for celebration slowly descended into an acrimonious dispute when some of their westerly neighbours began to drive cattle down the public right of way through their land to the jetty. Unfortunately the herds were poorly controlled and, on about half a dozen occasions, wandered off into the MacKay's fields.

William's patience became exhausted: 'These Sassenachs know nothing of droving, Jane,' he spluttered.

'Have you spoken to them?'

'Yes, I have warned them, at least twice. I am now determined to ask Donald to petition the Charlottetown Assembly to remove the right of way. I will suggest a detour, off our property down next to the pond.'

'But that is too steep for a horse and cart, Father,' exclaimed John.

Irritated, William looked at his precocious son, now aged nine: 'I do not agree young man. A road can be constructed'

Jane had vehemently disagreed to the legal action: 'Why are you doing this William? These are our neighbours. They helped us build our first home. Do you not remember our Frolic?'

William had retorted: 'Can you not see, woman, if I allow them to continue the right of way will become enshrined forever. And it goes right through our land.'

But their neighbours had successfully petitioned the Charlottetown court and William had been forced to concede defeat. During the dispute William had even forbidden access to the small graveyard on the headland where Joanna was buried along with other early settlers. Further escalating the quarrel, the building of a small chapel, which had been mooted next to the graveyard, was now also rejected by William.

And then, much to William's embarrassment, John Cambridge, who owned some land, south of the pond and next to the river, had been only too happy to donate an acre for a chapel and new graveyard.

In June 1810, Jane, William and the children, except for the sailor, George, travelled to the nearby large settlement of Princetown in the family cart and horse to attend the first ordination of a Presbyterian minister on the island.

The event drew nearly every family from miles around. Cape Road became a dusty, straggling line of carts, carriages and coughing pedestrians. Jane was discomforted to observe that the MacKays were shunned by many in the gathering congregation and during the post–service socialising. Even those who had come from afar had heard of the dispute and were reticent to engage in conversation, apart from the exchange of polite greetings.

After the part Gaelic, part English service William and the family were standing disconsolately, isolated near their cart, preparing to return home, when they were approached by Dr McGregor, the itinerant minister who had served the area for many years, and his newly ordained colleague, John Keir.

'Good day, Mistress MacKay,' McGregor said politely, doffing his hat to Jane.

'Please excuse us. May we have a word in private with your husband?'

Jane smiled in assent, fully aware of the reason for the minister's request and began to help the children into the cart.

William nodded warily as McGregor introduced the newly ordained minister: 'Welcome to our island Reverend Keir.'

'Thank you, Mr MacKay.'

'William, if I may address you by your Christian name, I met your brother, Donald, in Charlottetown less than two weeks ago,' McGregor said.

William was startled – he had not expected his brother to feature in the conversation.

Allowing himself a faint smile, McGregor continued: 'I was interested to hear from Donald about your time together in the Reay Fencibles. And what a fine, well trained body of Highlanders they were!'

McGregor looked at Keir to take up the reins: 'Mr MacKay, I have been until recently in Halifax. Relations between Washington and London continue to deteriorate. Most gentlemen of the first rank in

Nova Scotia's capital expect a second American War. The threat of raids by Yankee privateers increases day by day.'

'William, our New London flock will need to be ready to defend itself,' McGregor broke in, 'and you are the most suitable, no, the only candidate to raise and captain our own Fencibles.'

William still said nothing. He knew that the current argument with his neighbours would render the commission proposed by the two ministers impossible.

'William, I believe it is God's will that you should fulfil this military role. But, of course, we must first restore the previous harmonious relations you had with the other good folk around here.'

McGregor paused: 'I have already sounded all of them out and they are happy to shake hands for the common good. We hope also that you will agree to become an Elder again, this time in the new kirk, which will be built on the land donated by Mr Cambridge near your home.'

William remained silent. A face–saving opportunity to settle a quarrel had arisen. He would welcome a resumption of his position as an Elder. He felt keenly the diminution of the spiritual side in his life. Perhaps it really was God's will?'

He caught Jane's knowing eye from the cart. He realised, with a pang, that his wife must somehow have been already spoken to by McGregor and was ready to lend her support.

William forced a smile: 'Of course, gentlemen. How could I refuse? We must unite to defend ourselves.'

'Thank you William,' McGregor had said, holding out his hand.

As they shook hands, William had become aware of a faint collective sigh of relief from the many eyes watching them.

'I will need a lieutenant,' said William after a few seconds' reflection.

'Somebody with enough gravitas to deputise for me when I am absent.'

'Do you have someone in mind William?' asked Keir.

'You are in charge, after all.'

William swiftly ran through in his mind the list of candidates.

'Yes, I do. I would like to nominate my new neighbour John McKenzie. He has the necessary attributes. And his good wife is a first cousin of mine.'

'A good choice, William,' agreed McGregor, pleased that another Elder from the Highlands had been chosen. The minister spotted McKenzie in the crowd, his arm resting on the shoulder of his young daughter, Sybella, and waved William's neighbour over to join in the conversation.

As McKenzie stood talking, happy to accept his commission, Sybella peeped around her father's best Sunday coat and looked up at the MacKay's cart. She caught the eye of a young boy, not much older than herself. Sybella smiled cheekily and John looked away, blushing that he had been caught staring at a girl.

The Princetown Fencibles, as some called them, trained hard under William's command to repel any attempt by Yankee privateers to land and steal goods and livestock. Fortunately they were never needed.

Jane's reminiscing was suddenly interrupted by the bang of a hammer on a nail. William had hired Peter, a Bristol shipwright, to direct the building of their new, bigger home. The boys had learnt expert carpentry from the Englishman: how to hew beams, cut mortised joints and secure them with wooden pegs and nails. Forbes had proved particularly adept at learning the building trades of carpentry, masonry and roofing.

Their new home was substantial, with overlapping timber board walls, a shingle roof made from small wooden tiles cut from one–foot–foot square lumber, and a stone chimney. There was a wooden floor, glass windows and cast iron stoves in the kitchen and living room. Well away and down the hill was an outside wooden privy with a deep pit for the waste. Next to its door there was always a bucket of water for ablutions.

They now had a dairy in the cellar with shelves for pans to let cream rise to the top of the milk from their two cows. There was space for a barrel of brine with meat and another with fish. Come winter they would cut ice blocks from the river and store them in sawdust for summer refrigeration.

As their livestock increased in number they would join their neighbours in rotating the slaughter of cows and hogs so there would be a winter supply of fresh pork and beef for everyone in New London.

Jane looked around to look at their new home which was now largely complete, bar a few embellishments.

She heard William calling: 'Jane, Jane come here. Come here.'

Jane stood and glanced around the panoramic view and smiled. She felt content. This was home. At last.

As she drew near to the front porch, William put his hands over her eyes and steered her up the steps until she stood before the front door.

'What do you see, Jane?' William asked, releasing his hands.

Jane looked at a new door. It was well cut and fitted snugly into its frame.

'No, look up Jane,' William urged gently, his voice full of pride.

Above the door was an expertly carved coat of arms under which a Latin motto stood out in sharp relief: *'Manu forti'* – with a strong hand.

It was the insignia not just of the Lords Reay, but of the entire clan MacKay.

Jane grasped immediately the carving's symbolism. This was not just their new, grander home. It was a statement that the house and its land belonged to people who had a proud history. And were confident in their future.

Chapter 11: The Quoddy rascals

A stocky young man and a not–much–younger youth were standing in shirtsleeves, chatting at the prow of a schooner. Their weather–beaten faces were hidden in the shade cast by their salt–shiny straw hats, protecting them from the fierce tropical sun. One glance from even an inexperienced eye would notice all woodwork behind them was scrubbed clean, varnish glistened and ropes were stowed tidily. A cargo of timber was securely fastened to the deck. White mainsails gently billowed in the faintest, Jamaican summer breeze. The schooner's name, *Margaret,* stood out in fresh, bright gold against a black background on its name plate. The two young men gazed down idly at the ship's bow which was melting through the warm, syrupy water and occasional school of slapping, rubbery jellyfish.

'Some call it smuggling, but I call it free trade. And President Jefferson can go hang himself.'

Sam Cunard smiled at the listening younger man: 'And that's what his own people in the state of Maine also say, Master George MacKay.'

Cunard tapped George's chest: 'Now listen: once we have docked in Kingston, and loaded our rum, sugar and molasses from my father's agent we will sail to the border in Quoddy Bay, south of New Brunswick, and smuggle our cargo into Maine. In turn we will load flour and salt beef and ship it into Halifax.'

'But how Sam? How will we accomplish it? Isn't dangerous?' a wide–eyed George whispered.

'No: most of the Maine customs officers are in cahoots with the smugglers. The biggest danger is Yankee privateers who might surprise us on the way back. But the *Margaret* is fast, even when fully–laden.'

Cunard gave the younger man a mock–punch on the shoulder and laughed: 'You will see, George. You will see. And your share of our profit will make you very satisfied.'

George could not help but be swayed by his pugnacious captain. Although only 20 years old, Cunard had a mature way with words and his quiet air of determination inspired confidence in his crews. He had explained how the patience of the United States' President, Thomas Jefferson, had run out with the British embargo on trading with continental Europe, now controlled by Napoleon. The impounding of neutral American ships on the High Seas and the pressing of their sailors into the Royal Navy had become insufferable. But the president had overplayed his hand: in 1807 he imposed a draconian embargo on all United States export trade.

'Jefferson had not reckoned on the close links between the people in Maine and their Loyalist Canadian neighbours. Why, some of them were even the same families who were on different sides in the rebellion. My own father left because he preferred a King to a President. But we still have many friends who stayed behind and who resent being made destitute by Washington. There is even talk of secession from the republic.'

The young men fell quiet: the soporific sound of the gentle splashing water and hot sun was conducive to day–dreaming.

George stretched his arms and sighed in contentment: 'This is what I want. To be at sea. Always.'

'And I'm sure you will, George. You've learnt quickly. You will make an excellent ship's master some day.'

Cunard looked down at his rippling reflection: 'To me sailing is being at one with nature. But I want more than going up and down the coast to the West Indies.'

'And what is that, Sam?' George was allowed to address his captain by his Christian name, out of earshot of the crew.

Cunard glanced skywards at a solitary, shimmering cloud passing over the top of the foresails: 'Why George, I dream of starting a shipping line.'

Smiling whimsically, the youthful captain looked sideways at his younger companion: 'One that goes across the Atlantic, trading people and goods. I have already saved a goodly amount of money and my father is prepared to support me.'

George could see from Cunard's expression that the *Margaret's* captain was serious.

William and George had met Cunard by chance in Donald Mackay's office two weeks previously. The two French River MacKays had arrived, as usual, unannounced on one of their regular visits around the coast by cutter to Charlottetown to collect goods and money from Donald.

'Ah, William, well–timed indeed,' Donald had greeted them, looking up from his papers.

He introduced the person who had been sitting in front of him: 'This is Master Samuel Cunard, the son of a merchant in Halifax with whom I trade. We have just agreed the sale of some of our timber. Master Cunard will shortly be loading it onto his father's ship.'

'Master Cunard, it is always a pleasure to meet one of our customers,' William said, stepping forward with an outstretched hand which was met with a firm grip by the young man.

'What is the name of your ship?'

'The *Margaret,* sir.'

'And who is its Master?' William enquired politely, eyebrows raised, man to boy.

'I captain the *Margaret*, sir,' Cunard replied, allowing himself a faint smile.

'William, I advise you not to be misled by Mr Cunard's youth,' Donald warned.

'He already has a reputation as an expert seaman and skilful captain.'

'Why, thank you Mr MacKay,' Cunard said. 'I have been at sea since I was thirteen,' he added, looking at William.

Noticing George's rapt attention, Donald added: 'My apologies Master Cunard. I have failed to introduce my nephew, George MacKay. You may recollect I spoke about him on one of your previous visits?'

'Ah yes. I do recall,' Cunard said, turning to shake George's hand. 'Your uncle tells me you wish to become a sailor?'

'That is right, Mr Cunard.'

'Please call me Captain Cunard, George,' the young man replied, raising his voice slightly to ensure the two older men heard his preferred appellation.

There was a momentary, awkward pause following the mild reproof, which Cunard then quickly filled: 'Why, George your luck must be in. It so happens I have need of an educated person to be my mate,' Cunard said lightly.

'Someone to assist me in navigation and ensure the crew carry out my instructions. You have learnt trigonometry? You have Gaelic too?'

George nodded silently, dumbfounded, his head spinning in delight.

'That could be useful. Some of my deckhands are Highlanders,' Cunard said.

'Well, what say you George? Would you care to join my ship? As a trainee you would receive low wages. But you will have a fair share of the profit we make after delivery of our load.' Cunard ignored the faintest wink of amusement in Donald's eye.

'I would make sure you learnt quickly. There is no time for passengers on my ships,' the young captain added.

George gulped: the opportunity to join a ship's company as a trainee mate exceeded his most optimistic expectations. He looked at his father, hardly daring to hope.

But there was no resistance from William. Going to sea in a ship and a captain recommended by Donald allayed his misgivings. To be sure, seafaring was dangerous. But not so much more than life on land with its constant threat of illness, bears, snakes and freezing winters.

Two weeks later and the *Margaret* entered Quoddy Bay, as Passamaquoddy Bay was known, and inched slowly towards the border midway between the coasts. At dusk, Cunard ordered a sea anchor to be dropped.

'We are still in British waters, George. But by nightfall, the current will take us into Yankee territory. Our arrival will have been noticed by my colleagues in Eastport. You see how easy Free Trade is?' Cunard chuckled.

About three hours later a darkened ship loomed out of the gloom. Ropes were thrown and the two ships were fastened together. On top of groaning and squeaking gang planks, sweaty, heavily laden men carried bags and rolled barrels across as quickly as they dared. Flour and salted meat were carried in one direction, rum and sugar the other. Dawn came dimly through a morning fog while a land breeze started to whisper that it was time for the ships to part company.

With the sea anchor on board, the changed tidal current took the *Margaret* back northwards towards the British colonies, away from the republic. Cunard ordered the foresails to be hoisted. Just before the mainsail could be lifted, something caught George's eye. He grasped his captain's arm and pointed. Gleaming in the low rays of the bright morning sun, floating above the swirling mist was a flag fluttering in the strengthening land breeze: it was the Stars and Stripes. A ghostly–grey U.S. sloop–of–war under full canvas gradually took shape and loomed down on the *Margaret*.

'Ship ahoy. Heave to!'

'Hellfire and damnation seize it,' swore Cunard, lifting his telescope.

'It's the *Wasp*. I'd heard Jefferson had sent it to try and stop the smuggling.'

George bit his tongue to prevent himself reminding Cunard that he had said contraband was easy.

As if to forestall his mate's complaint, Cunard said: 'There were probably about 100 ships smuggling along this coast last night, George. It's just bad luck we encountered this one.'

The flash of a canon mounted in the *Wasp's* bow was followed swiftly by a loud bang and then, after a few seconds, a well–aimed splash of water on the windward side of the Margaret. 'Laconically wiping the spray from his telescope Cunard said: 'I am sorry George. We are within easy range of their canon. To try and run away would be foolhardy.'

For the second time within 24 hours the *Margaret* was fastened alongside another ship. This time though the traffic was human and one way. An armed skeleton Yankee crew, some of them English, climbed over the rails onto the *Margaret* whose crew was shepherded below and imprisoned under locked hatches. The *Wasp* went on its way along the border seeking other prizes. The Margaret now flying the Stars and Stripes of the Republic set sail out of Quoddy Bay and headed south.

Cunard addressed his crew: 'Well, we will have to make the best of our bad luck. I reckon we will be in Boston in a couple of days. After that I expect us to be released. We are not Yankee citizens and have not committed a crime. But we may be asked to 'volunteer' for their navy. However I expect to be able to raise enough credit to purchase passage for all of us on a ship prepared to bring us north again.'

But in a fortuitous, swift reversal of fortunes, not uncommon in the uneasy waters between the U.S. and British America, the *Margaret* herself was intercepted the following day by a Royal Navy frigate, HMS *Guerriere*, its crew released and the previous captors placed below among the flour and beef.

'You are fortunate, Mr Cunard, that I recognised your schooner, even from a distance. I had admired its tidy lines in Halifax a few months ago. I guessed what had happened when I saw the rebel flag,' Captain Skene, the frigate's commander added.

'Yes, we are indebted to you Captain,' Cunard agreed half-heartedly, knowing full well that money would be needed to release what was now a Royal Navy prize ship.

Skene grinned. Some of that money would be going into his pocket.

Followed by a watchful *Guerriere*, the *Margaret* headed off towards Halifax. But not before a stowaway deserter from the *Guerriere* was found trying to hide among the American crew below.

The deserter was hauled on deck by marines, his filthy shirt stripped off his thin back, tied to the *Margaret's* rigging and given 50 lashes. The man screamed as salt water was thrown on his back, the ropes loosened and allowed to slump onto the deck into a pool of blood–reddened water.

Skene shrugged to Cunard: 'If I don't wield the lash, half my crew would desert to work on American ships. Unpleasant I grant you. But necessary, Captain Cunard.'

Upon the payment by Cunard's father, Alfred, of one eighth of the estimated value of its cargo to the Court of the Vice–Admiralty in Halifax, the Margaret was released.

There was ample money still remaining from the sale of the flour and meat for Cunard to pay his crew off handsomely and plan his next expedition.

'Do you wish to accompany me again, George?' Cunard asked.

'I sail to the West Indies again in less than three weeks. My father has agreed a contract to take lumber from Pictou and return with rum. Not smuggling this time but liquor to slake the thirst of lumberers. The money is almost as good as 'Free Trade' with the Yankees. As far as I am concerned, you are now qualified to be a First Mate. I have signed your papers to that effect. You will be paid accordingly.'

George needed no persuasion. The incident with the *Wasp* had not dampened his desire to remain at sea.

The *Margaret* sailed up and down the American coast during 1808, sometimes smuggling to Maine, sometimes to and from the British colonies. The Cunards paid George well.

On the couple of occasions the *Margaret* docked in Charlottetown he deposited his savings with his uncle Donald. It was at this point that George realised Donald was involved in smuggling as well.

'The lumber you took on your first voyage to Jamaica – I provided that free of charge in lieu of a share of the eventual profits from the return leg,' Donald explained over a dram in his office, Jessie smiling along.

'Did my father know?'

'He didn't then but I have since discussed the situation with him. As you would expect he took a moral position. No, let me allay your fears, George,' Donald added hastily, hand raised, reacting to George's alarm.

'Your father eventually agreed that no government had the right to prevent Free Trade among its citizens and thus render them into poverty.'

George deposited his earnings with his Uncle who beamed with satisfaction, not just at the impressive amount of money, but also at the separate confirmation from Samuel Cunard that George would soon be capable of captaining a schooner in the coastal waters up and down the American seaboard.

In early 1809 the *Margaret* arrived in Halifax where it was greeted, as usual, by Samuel Cunard's father, Alfred, who escorted his son to the nearby family office as soon as the schooner had docked.

The *Margaret's* captain returned to his ship within fifteen minutes and took his mate out of earshot of the crew who were busy unloading the flour and meat.

'My father has just told me that President Jefferson has caved into the pressure and lifted his embargo. Apparently ports along the Maine coast were wildly celebrating yesterday and the news only reached here this morning.'

Cunard coughed awkwardly: 'My father says there will be a period of readjustment as everybody returns to normal trade. I shall dismiss the crew once they have finished unloading.'

He paused: 'For the time being we do not need your services George. But in six months or so?'

George smiled: 'Thank you Sam. But I think it is time I rejoined my family to see if I can assist with our own commerce.'

The young MacKay held out his hand: 'Sam, I shall always remain grateful for your fine tutoring.'

Cunard smiled and placed an affectionate hand on George's shoulder: 'I fear I may have reared some competition. But no matter. There is plenty of rum and timber and the demand for both keeps rising. America is growing quickly. Immigrants are pouring in from all over Europe.'

Cunard now pressed his fine telescope into George's hands.

'Take this as a memento of your time on the *Margaret*,' Cunard ordered.

'No, I will brook no argument. After all, I forced you to endure some distress during our encounter with the *Wasp*. Now God speed George MacKay. I fancy we will meet again one day.'

The newly qualified mate strode cheerily along the quay stopping only to ask other seafarers if they knew of a ship bound for

Charlottetown which might be hiring. After five minutes or so George found luck. He turned to wave goodbye with his new telescope to Cunard who could tell from George's delighted face that he had been successful.

As George stepped backwards, his face became partially obscured by the lattice–shaped shadow cast by the rigging of a nearby moored ship. From a distance George's face appeared uncannily as if it were behind prison bars. Samuel Cunard shivered with a sudden premonition that he would never see George MacKay again.

George worked his passage back to Charlottetown as a mate. He noticed with satisfaction that the skills he had learnt on the *Margaret* meant he was a better seaman than his new captain, whose orders he had to correct diplomatically on a couple of occasions.

Chapter 12: *The Jane*

'It is time to build our first vessel,' Jessie announced to the assembled MacKay family.

Donald and Jessie had sailed with George on one of the regular coastal cutters back to French River. Before leaving Charlottetown, Donald had sounded out his seafaring nephew about the proposal for the MacKays to build a ship.

'George, we have enough money put aside to pay for at least most of a new schooner. Certainly we will have to borrow the rest but that will be no problem.'

'But Jefferson has just lifted the embargo. There won't be any more 'Free Trade' with Maine. Will we make a profit?' asked George.

Jane and William voiced the same doubt as they sat with their other four boys Forbes, Hugh, John and young William in the family living room.

'Yes, as long as the Royal Navy needs more ships to fight Napoleon and the British embargo on European trade remains, North American timber prices will continue to rise,' Jessie replied confidently.

'Jamaica needs timber for repairs to His Majesty's ships stationed there and demand for rum and sugar seems inexhaustible in the U.S. and Nova Scotia,' added Donald.

'Yes Mother, Uncle Donald is right. When we brought good Jamaican rum to Halifax, it quickly sold at a high price,' George nodded, interrupting.

'And I now have a good knowledge of all the sea from here to the West Indies. I am ready to captain our ship,' he continued proudly.

His mother looked at her grown–up, sailor son for a few moments, her thoughts turning over the advantages and risks of the MacKays extending their commercial activities. She remembered clearly Donald outlining his plans for the family enterprise to include ships.

Jane's gaze turned to Jessie: 'But we have to borrow money to build this ship?' she asked doubtfully.

'Is it not too soon? Why not wait another, what, five years so we do not incur debt?'

'Because Jane we can build our ship over this coming winter and make more than enough money next summer to pay back the loan and reward ourselves handsomely,' said Jessie.

'And the following year our profits will be even more. Look Jane, you can see the evidence before you that your timber will run out in a few years.' Jessie pointed out of the window to the family's increasing acreage of cleared fields.

'The time is right – carpe diem, Jane.'

Jessica leant forward towards her sister–in–law to emphasise the point: 'And it is far more lucrative to own one's own ship than charter it from someone else.'

Before the family conference, Jessica and Donald had correctly deduced that Jane would be the person who would need to be most convinced. As the book–keeper, Jessie would advance the business case and ensure that her remarks were directed at William's wife.

In a role reversal from the negotiation with John Cambridge, Jane spoke and William listened. He now placed a reassuring hand on his wife's shoulder: 'Jane, it seems a small risk compared to those we have taken already in the last five years.'

Jane placed her hand on William's and turned to him: 'I know. But it's the sea. On the *Elizabeth & Ann* I came to hate it. I sense no good will ever come from the ocean for the MacKays.'

'Oh Mother, don't be silly,' George exclaimed – like a small boy embarrassed by his rudeness he placed a hand over his mouth, as if to undo what he'd said.

But Jane merely laughed: 'You are quite right George. I am silly.'

She nodded at Jessie: 'Yes, you have convinced me. Let us build our ship.'

Donald cleared his throat: 'There is still one matter of importance which we must decide, ladies and gentlemen.'

In good humour, the family turned to look at a smiling Donald: 'Her name, of course. I propose we call our ship,' he fell silent for a second, looking melodramatically around the room, *'The Jane.'*

'Hooray' shouted George, putting his arm around his mother.

Donald looked expectantly at his brother: 'So William, let us toast to the next chapter in our fortunes.'

William's boys shuffled awkwardly as their father retorted: 'I do not keep the demon drink in my house, brother.'

'Ah, I feared as much,' observed a downcast Donald to no one in particular.

'I..., I have some Jamaican rum with me,' George stammered.

'I keep it on board for purely medicinal reasons, Father,' he added nervously, looking at William's angry face.

'We use it to clean cuts or deaden the pain if someone is injured,' the young seaman continued hastily, this time with more confidence, looking at his father straight in the face.

'Come now, husband, let us make an exception,' Jane clucked setting some glasses on the dining table.

'After all, it is not every day that a ship is named after your wife.'

Jessie smiled to herself. She would need to travel to Pictou to arrange the finance – the cut and thrust of the meetings with Edward Mortimer were always memorable.

Chapter 13: The King of Pictou

'So Mistress MacKay, you propose to build a ship. Why?' demanded the man known, behind his back, as the King of Pictou, in his Banffshire–accented Gaelic.

Jessie had anticipated the question but did not reply immediately. Instead she took a moment to take stock of the handsome man dominating his desk in front of her. If ever a person merited the description larger than life, it was Edward Mortimer. He was tall, well over six feet, and broad–shouldered with a booming voice. He also had a forceful, bullying personality, complementing his daunting physical attributes. But Jessica noticed with some disappointment that Mortimer's face was becoming puffy and his stomach had grown substantially since last year. One of the buttons on his silk embroided waistcoat was straining and looked ready to pop off.

'Yes, Mr Mortimer. We wish to construct a schooner this winter and have her ready for next spring to sail to the West Indies,' replied Jessie, her hands demurely folded on her lap.

'As to why: although our family enterprise has grown pleasingly, we foresee more profit if we own our own ship,' Jessie continued, looking up at Mortimer with just the right amount of non–threatening femininity.

'But you do not have enough money for the whole project?'

Jessie sighed quietly and bowed her head.

Now Mortimer regarded the woman sitting in front of him. She and her husband had first come to him, what, ten years ago? He had lent them money because it suited him to have a timber merchant client in Prince Edward Island where he was just starting to expand his enterprise. He had also appreciated the chance to speak educated Gaelic with a pretty Highland woman. Which is why, he knew full well, that Donald always allowed Jessie to meet him unaccompanied by her husband. Something which would never happen back in the Old Country.

'And you thought I would be amenable to your request to borrow one thousand pounds?'

Jessie remained silent. She knew Mortimer was toying with her. If one borrowed money from the big man, one did not go elsewhere for more. There were no former clients of Mortimer. They were crushed and had an unfortunate habit of meeting accidents. The same was said of his competitors who dared to tempt away any of Mortimer's customers.

Mortimer turned his head towards his English secretary and barked: 'Fletcher, how fares our business this year?'

'Very well indeed, Mr Mortimer,' replied the bespectacled scribe promptly, scarcely looking up from his ledger. He was used to being asked by his employer to impress guests.

Mortimer raised his eyebrows, prompting Fletcher to continue: 'We are shipping timber to the value of about £5000 per week. I estimate we will fully load about 80 ships this year, all bound for England.'

Mortimer turned back to Jessie and shrugged his shoulders, as if to demand from his visitor why he should bother with small fry.

Undeterred, Jessie took up the challenge: 'If it pleases you, Mr Mortimer, although our venture pales by comparison, it entails two attractive aspects. The first is a generous percentage of our first year's profit.'

Jessie paused waiting to observe Mortimer's reaction. But the big man's face was a blank canvas.

Jessie continued, this time betraying a slight nervousness. If Mortimer turned her down there would be nowhere to go for finance.

'We would also supply you with high–quality Jamaican rum at a discount to the market price,' she said.

Now Mortimer registered some emotion: a small greedy smile creased his lips.

Inwardly Jessie felt vindicated. Donald had been doubtful that Mortimer would value rum so highly. But Jessie was adamant. She had heard the gossip that rum drinking in Pictou was fast approaching an epidemic. Jessie had also gleaned that rum was the currency Mortimer was increasingly using to his advantage as barter with lumberers and farmers, all desperate for the alcoholic beverage.

'I believe we can reach an agreement Mistress MacKay,' Mortimer said, inclining his head graciously after a few seconds.

Mortimer looked out through a window at the forest of masts crowded along the Pictou wharf. Skilled crews were in short supply and there was always the regular threat of the Royal Navy coming ashore and pressing unwilling sailors into service.

'Now, reassure me Mistress MacKay that your ship will be sailed competently. Who will be its captain?'

'We have in mind, Master Wynn.'

'Ah yes, a sound old sea dog. But getting a bit long in the tooth?'

'Yes, he is Mr Mortimer,' agreed Jessie.

'But he will have a mate who is familiar with the West Indies run and can take over after a year or so.'

'And who, pray, is that?'

'If you will allow, I have some young men waiting in your ante–room to meet you.'

Mortimer fluttered a patronising wave to Fletcher to fetch in Jessie's companions.

As their aunt had previously instructed, the MacKays lined up in front of Mortimer, as if sailors awaiting inspection by an admiral.

Jessie changed back to Gaelic: 'Mr Mortimer, allow me to present three of my nephews: George, Forbes and John MacKay.

'George is 18 and will be Wynn's mate. Forbes is 17, new to the sea so will be learning the sailor's trade. The youngest, John, is nine and will be our cabin boy.'

Mortimer looked keenly at the eldest of the three: 'Tell me Master MacKay: why should I invest in an enterprise with so young a person as you as its mate and soon–to–be captain?'

George knew this was a test so stared Mortimer, straight in the eye: 'Because I know every inch of water from here to Jamaica. I was shown by an expert.'

'And who was this magnificent tutor?' demanded Mortimer.

'Captain Samuel Cunard,' George retorted peevishly to the older man's sarcasm.

Mortimer chuckled: 'Who is not much older than you.

'No matter,' the merchant raised a languid hand to forestall George's incipient riposte, 'I grant you that young Cunard has a high reputation.'

Mortimer eyed the next brother: 'And you, Master Forbes, do you fancy a life at sea?'

'I am willing to learn, sir.'

'And I take it this same applies to you young man?' Mortimer asked John.

'Yes, sir,' the youngest MacKay replied eagerly.

Mortimer smiled at Jessie, keeping her in suspense: 'I congratulate you Mistress MacKay. You have not yet hammered a nail and you have already enlisted a crew.'

He turned to inspect the line of three brothers: 'They are fine lusty lads, Mistress MacKay and will surely make fine husbands not many years hence.'

George smiled at the compliment, a red–faced John giggled but Mortimer detected a faint blush on Forbes' face as the middle MacKay looked down at his shoes. The older man suddenly felt some empathy and, yes, a sexual frisson as he stared at Forbes. Mortimer was an experienced judge of character and guessed the middle MacKay was not the marrying kind. That is unless he felt the need to disguise his inclinations, as he, the King of Pictou had decided to do.

Forbes looked up and inadvertently his gaze crossed Mortimer's. For the merest fraction of a second they looked at each other in recognition. The older man's face flickered sadness; the younger one's panic.

The meeting was interrupted by the office clock chiming noon. Mortimer suddenly stood: 'Ah yes, forgive me. Time flies. I must away to our capital Halifax. I have pressing business with our Governor.'

He quickly picked his hat off a hook and grasped his cane: 'Yes, you may have your money, Mistress MacKay,' he said generously.

The big man stomped out of the door: 'A satisfactory conclusion to our business, I trust you will agree, Mistress MacKay?' he boomed dismissively.

Without waiting for Jessie's confirmation he continued: 'Fletcher will attend to the details. For this modest amount he has my power of attorney so can sign our contract.'

Nodding at Jessie, George and John but carefully avoiding Forbes' eyes, Nova Scotia's wealthiest merchant and most powerful politician strode out of his office. Forbes meanwhile unclenched his fists, struggling to conceal his inner turmoil: how had Mortimer guessed?

Chapter 14: The second American war

It was John, the youngest MacKay on board the Jane, about 400 miles south east of Halifax, who, on the afternoon of the 19th August 1812, about thirty–four years after the American War of Independence, first spotted the topsails of two naval frigates about 400 miles south east of Halifax. George recognised HMS *Guerriere* from about five miles away, using the powerful telescope Sam Cunard had given him. The Jane's course brought them closer to the two warships and he could just read the name USS *Constitution* on a longer and taller American ship. He was admiring the obvious faster speed of the Constitution when it suddenly slowed as it reduced to topsails and jibs. The British ship followed suit and the gap between the two ships gradually narrowed.

'By God, they mean to fight!' he shouted.

'Forbes: change course and head away from here!' George ordered his brother and ship's mate who was manning the helm.

Even though heavily–laden, the Jane tacked smartly away and, once the sails were set and helm lashed, the three MacKay brothers and the rest of the six–man crew stared back over the Jane's stern towards the impending battle.

The *Guerriere* opened fire first.

Forbes had snatched George's telescope away and was now watching agog: 'I swear that I can see splashes of cannon balls bouncing off the Yankee!'

George grabbed his telescope back and mocked his brother: 'Don't be stupid.'

The Jane's captain fell quiet for a moment as he stared again, focusing on the *Constitution*, before he exclaimed: 'Oh dear Christ, Forbes, I fear you are correct. That Yankee must be built of iron!'

The *Constitution*, with its seven–inch, American live oak hull waited until the distance between the ships was only 25 yards before unleashing its first broadside with its bigger and more numerous guns. Old, partly rotting French oak from the Limousin – the *Guerriere* had been captured by the British from the French Navy – splintered under 32 and 24 pounder cannon fire.

The *Jane's* crew gasped in shock as they saw something none of them believed they would ever see: a Royal Naval warship losing a battle.

George felt a pang of bitter irony because he knew that many of the *Constitution's* crew must be British who had declared allegiance to the US. He had read in a copy of the London *Times* newspaper that there were more than 10,000 former British sailors on American merchant and naval ships. Remembering the typical Royal Navy harsh conditions of poor pay, miserable food and reliance on the lash for discipline that he had seen for himself on the *Guerriere*, George muttered to himself: 'And who can blame them?' Apart from stopping trade with Napoleonic continental Europe, this was the reason why the Royal Navy, desperate for more manpower, stopped and seized British subjects on American ships in international waters. The republic's furious protests that the sailors were now American citizens were ignored by London, fighting an existential war against the French.

The *Jane's* crew could just see the *Guerriere's* main mast now toppling over. They shivered as they realised the British ship was doomed and its captain would be forced to surrender. If ever back in British hands he would face a court martial with the possible sanction of a death penalty. Royal Navy captains only surrendered under exceptional circumstances.

The *Jane's* crew had only heard after their arrival in Kingston in July with a cargo of flour from Boston Massachusetts, that the U.S. had declared war on Britain about a month before. The crew had shrugged off the news: they had believed that a war not wished for by many on the North American Atlantic seaboard would quickly fizzle out. But the evidence of this naval action suggested the contrary – that a war really was going to take place. Gazing at the smoke rising from the burning *Guerriere* as it slipped hazily below the horizon, George thought back quickly over the fortunes of his family since the launch of the *Jane* in the Spring of 1810. The speedy schooner had traded profitably up and down the east coast of America to the British colonies of Jamaica and Bermuda. George had assumed command after Captain Wynn had handed over soon after Mortimer's loan was paid off in early 1811. Donald and Jessie were joyful as the figures on the family's ledger grew more favourable with every month that passed.

With the naval engagement now out of view and *The Jane* free from danger, George stood behind Forbes, his mind thinking ahead. After a few seconds any initial fears were dispelled as he grew sanguine about the consequences of war with the U.S. He knew from the experience of the previous, recent embargo that the republic's citizens in New England would almost certainly refuse to stop commercial intercourse with the British colonies to the north.

He suddenly placed his arms around his two brothers: 'Well boys, I suspect I will soon be introducing you to the secrets of Free Trade in Passamaquoddy Bay.'

John punched the air in excitement. The twelve year old had been thrilled by George's smuggling tales during the last embargo.

Forbes kept his emotions to himself. He did not share his brothers' great enthusiasm for life at sea. He was a competent sailor but sometimes felt uncomfortable in the close confines of life aboard with others of the same gender. He had gladly agreed with George that the advent of war meant, once they had unloaded their cargo in Halifax, they should return home to discuss the family's future plans.

Not long after the *Jane* had been securely tied up to the refurbished Yankee Hill jetty, William beckoned George and Forbes into his study.

'Do you think you are ready to command a larger ship, George?' William asked his eldest son after they had all sat down in comfortable leather chairs.

George almost snorted his reply: 'I am indeed, sir.'

'But why do you ask, Father?' George continued, slightly shame–faced at his previous aggressive tone.

William drummed his fingers on the arms of his chair: 'There have been developments since you were last here.

'Our neighbours, the Cousins, McKenzies, and the Sims are keen to share in our success. They proposed that we jointly build a bigger ship – a brig.'

'We had intended to take timber to England and return with immigrants for which we would probably have had to hire Captain Wynn again,' William continued.

'But this unwanted war has changed matters.'

William paused and regarded his two sons: 'However, it has also provided an opportunity.'

Their father could see his sons' attention was wandering. He stood up and spoke as if addressing his kirk's congregation: 'Conscious of the economic threat posed by this stupid war to the colony of Nova Scotia, its canny governor, Sir John Sherbrooke, has persuaded London to allow him to issue licences to trade with northern Yankee ports. For their part they are eager to continue trading. As with the last embargo, they have scant regard for their political masters in Washington.'

William paused, uncertain how much his sons would understand of the nuanced politics of war and commerce.

'Those merchants of good repute and social standing in Nova Scotia's capital, Halifax, have been favoured first by Sherbrooke. Merchants such as the Cunard family,' William said, noticing that George's face grinned at the mention of the family name of his former captain.

'Yes, George, your high reputation with young Samuel Cunard has stood us in good stead. Uncle Donald has managed to persuade the Cunards to negotiate a licence from the governor for us.'

'In return for a generous commission, of course,' William added a few seconds later, almost under his breath.

'We now intend to use the brig to trade under licence between Nova Scotia's capital, Halifax and the northern Yankee ports. George, our fellow investors would like you to be its master,' William added.

Their father tapped his fingers again: 'I said that I would discuss the matter with you.'

The boys' father was now sixty–three. William still felt healthy but had noticed that he was increasingly mulling over matters rather than making quick decisions.

Perhaps the melancholic news from Tongue a year ago of his brother John's eventual death from his Irish war wound had affected him more than he cared to admit. Should he have simply told his neighbours immediately that George was ready to captain a brig?

Either way, the die was cast. Even with the contributions from their neighbours, another and bigger loan would be necessary to build a 400 ton brig compared to the 70 ton *Jane*.

Edward Mortimer had graciously acceded to Jessie's request for £5000. He had declared himself happy that George was up to the task of captaining the ship.

Once again Jane's instincts warned her that the enterprise was risky. But she kept her doubts to herself.

'What about me, Father?' asked Forbes, mildly irritated that George had attracted his father's sole attention.

William smiled at his second eldest son: 'Why Forbes, once George assumes his next command, you will become the master of *The Jane*. In the meantime, George I wish you to introduce Forbes and your brothers to Passamaquoddy Bay where we have already heard that Free Trade has resumed.

'Even when the brig is complete, Donald and I consider that the revenue we can get from Free Trade' – William could never admit that he was condoning contraband – remains attractive.'

Halifax was starting to boom once more from maritime contraband and licensed trade with the U.S. And further inland, the British army in North America could not survive without American farmers smuggling cattle and flour across the border to feed its hungry troops.

While William was discussing the project for a new ship with his sons, Donald was busy in his Charlottetown office buying plans and interviewing a team to build the brig at Donald's land on French River, which led into Grenville Bay. George remembered the name of the ship in the painting hanging in Donald's Charlottetown office. All agreed the name *Grenville* was suitable.

The project was proving more difficult and expensive than Donald had expected. The high demand for skilled craftsmen meant wages kept rising. He needed about 50 sawyers, carpenters, caulkers, blacksmiths, riggers, sail–makers, pulley–makers, and lumberers. And a large brig took twice as long as a schooner to build. Assuming a start in Spring next year, the ship would not be launched, ready for fitting out, until the late autumn of 1813.

Forbes and his brothers learnt as quickly as they could from George how to navigate around Quoddy Bay at dusk and dawn. But the small islands, channels, coves and tidal range took months to learn. George was a good teacher, passing on what he in turn had learnt from Sam Cunard. Sometimes it seemed that the biggest danger was colliding with one of the hundreds of other British and American small boats and ships engaged in the same work.

By September, George finally pronounced himself satisfied with Forbes' and his crew's knowledge of Quoddy Bay.

The Grenville put to sea early one morning in mid–December 1813, a good month before the first sea ice was expected to start forming around Prince Edward Island. Her cargo was timber from the woods around French River, including those belonging to the ship's investors, and potatoes left over from October's crop grown on land from which all the trees had been harvested.

An anxious Jane had asked why *The Grenville's* first voyage could not be delayed until the more clement Spring weather. George had patiently explained to his mother that Halifax never iced over so if *The Grenville* did not leave soon, she risked losing four months' trading, ice–bound in Grenville Bay.

Forbes was down at the Yankee Hill jetty standing at the stern of the moored Jane. As *The Grenville* slipped past, he gave George a mock military salute.

'See you in Halifax, brother,' George bellowed back into a brass loud hailer.

Further up the hill behind the jetty, the rest of the MacKay family and their neighbours had gathered to wish the new ship God–speed. George had waved his seal skin hat but Jane could only dimly see her son's face obscured by the cloud of his frosty breath. She shivered as her son gradually slipped away.

That evening as early winter's dusk began to seep in all around, *The Grenville* was hit by a sudden storm as she rounded Cape Breton. George had deliberately kept as close as he thought safe to the coast for fear of hitting St Paul Island, a few miles further offshore, which he knew was the site of many a ship wreck.

But the storm brought a quick change in wind direction and George was reminded, too late, that a brig was neither as nimble nor could tack into the wind as well as a schooner.

The Grenville was driven onto rocks, badly holed and sank within a few minutes. There was no time to launch a boat. George drowned along with all of his crew.

The pale face of his washed up body was found the next morning under a pile of criss–crossed, splintered wood. He looked like someone peering through the grill on a prison door, remarked the person who found George's body. He neglected to add that he'd also prised open George's fingers clenched firmly in rigor mortis around an expensive–looking telescope.

The storm unabated blew swiftly eastwards and reached French River within the hour. The fierce, swirling wind sent an eddy of ash scuttling down the chimney of the MacKay home and blackened rain drops spat out of the logs. In front of the fire, Jane jumped, shifted her shawl over her shoulder, and prayed that her son would be safe. But her pleading went unheeded: a week later a letter arrived with the grim news of *The Grenville's* loss with all hands.

Helped by William, Jane shuffled along the Cape Road and sat down on Forbes' bench, as she called it, and sobbed with the inconsolable grief of a mother who had lost her eldest son. And her belief that the sea would only bring disaster for the MacKays was cemented.

Chapter 15: The year of the burnings

Without a word Donald handed William a letter with a 30th June, 1814 Thurso postmark from Ann Calder MacKay, the widow of their brother, John. The letter was addressed to the two brothers at Donald's Charlottetown office.

William frowned as he forced himself to concentrate on Ann's writing – he read less and less handwritten Gaelic these days. He grimaced as he digested the first line and his hand clutched the arm of one of Donald's office chairs. He slumped down unsteadily to read the rest of Ann's letter:

My dear brothers,

I write with news of a heinous act committed against our noble clan MacKay. On Monday the 13th June, the Countess of Sutherland's factor, one Patrick Sellar, and his gang of Cheviot shepherds commenced a Clearance in Strathnaver which has shocked everyone in the Highlands. Over 250 homes were burnt to the ground by this cunning devil. Most of our men were in the hills participating in the annual cattle round–up. Our women, children, elderly and infirm were given only a few minutes to evacuate their homes before they were set alight. At least two people, including a 92–year old bed–ridden woman, Margaret MacKay, died as a result of this inhumane operation. Sellar was heard to shout: 'Damn her, the old witch. She's lived too long. Let her burn.'

One of the buildings destroyed was the smithy of my dear departed husband and your blacksmith brother, John. This has rendered impossible any chance that my son had of following his father's trade.

Although she did not dirty her hands herself, I accuse the Countess of Sutherland of being an accomplice in murder most foul. The high status of the countess and her rich English husband, the Marquis of Stafford, means they, of course, will never be charged with a criminal offence. But such is the public outcry, I cannot believe that Patrick Sellar will escape trial.

The land which was cleared had been previously sold to the countess by our clan chief. I have now lost any faith that Lord Reay

107

will have any regard for his duties to protect his clan and its traditions. It is as you correctly foresaw eight years ago. We have no future here.

I am now betrothed to William McIntosh. His wife departed this world a few years ago. The good Lord has enabled us to find solace in each other's company. With my five and his three children we now make a goodly–sized family.

We have resolved to leave Strathnaver and Scotland and now earnestly request your compassion for our family and beseech your advice on to where we should emigrate.

Yours, in hope

Ann Calder MacKay

William closed his eyes in despair. He tried to imagine the panic and hysteria among the women, elderly and children as they ran screaming out of their smoking homes. William realised that he must have known many of the victims. He could imagine the fury that the men must have felt returning from the hills with their cattle to be greeted by smoking pyres where once stood their homes. Some of them would have proudly served the clan under him in the Fencibles.

With a voice cracking with sadness, William whispered: 'May God curse the Countess of Sutherland and Eric Reay.'

Donald was shocked: he hadn't heard his brother swear since their soldiering days in Belfast.

The office fell silent as the brothers thought back to their happy boyhoods in Strathnaver. They remembered life in Tongue with their own parents, friends and relatives. The small shared incidents which form part of every family's collective memory, which become embellished with time and all the more precious for it.

William's eyes gradually filled with tears: 'This is the end of the clan MacKay, Donald.'

'Ann must come here, William,' Donald said gently, placing a comforting hand on his brother's shoulder. 'Your Kirk will extend a Christian hand, I'm sure. After they have been here a few months we can assess what options lie before them.'

Although still shaking, William stood up and shocked Donald once again: 'A wee dram, if you please brother.'

It was left to Jane back in French River, when she heard William's news, to react in a more practical manner: 'Husband, we must build a home here, next to ours, for Ann. We have land enough to accommodate her and her new husband's family.'

Heading off any resistance from William, Jane said: 'Yes, I know we are hard pressed to pay off our share of *The Grenville* loan but our state is nothing compared to the poor situation when we first arrived.'

Jane was pleased. She looked forward to some female companionship of her own age. She smiled as she started her book of Lord Byron's latest poems.

Ann Calder MacKay married William McIntosh about a month after Waterloo in July 1815. The family arrived in French River in October 1815. The timing was not auspicious.

Chapter 16: Of mice and dark summers

One day in the summer of 1815, fifteen–year old John MacKay tugged his mother's skirts as she was cooking the evening meal: 'Mother, come quickly, there's an army of small creatures destroying our potato field!'

Jane turned in alarm. They had all heard of the mouse plague on the eastern side of the island at the village of Souris – mice in French – in 1813. There had been outbreaks further west but nothing, until now, near French River.

Wiping her hands on her apron, she ran with John outside, the door swinging to and fro behind them, and ran into the Cape Road towards a strange humming, squeaking noise. What she saw made her scream. There was a wave of mice surfing through the family's potato field towards the MacKay home. On the other side of the grey, writhing torrent she could just make out other larger animals feasting themselves and encouraging the stampede. She stood mesmerised like a bird before a swaying snake.

'Mother we must return. The mice will get inside,' urged her son, grabbing her hand and pulling her back.

The mice were now within a few feet. John grabbed his mother's hand and they ran back towards the house.

Jane tried to slam the door behind her but desperately twisting incoming mice kept it wedged open.

About 50 or so mice had already run through and were attacking her pantry. Jane screamed again as mice ran over her boots, biting her laces right through to her skin. She quickly realised that trying to kill the rodents was futile. The food must be saved. She lifted bags of flour off the floor and placed them on tables, scraping those mice off with a sharp knife who were clinging through their clamped teeth to the hessian cloth. It was too late to save the potatoes. The bags on the floor were already split and the mice were gorging themselves.

The family's two black dogs barked hysterically in confused excitement, chasing the mice around the kitchen. The well–trained retrievers presented Jane and John with one dead mouse at a time, dropped at their masters' feet. They wagged their tails, waiting for further instructions, irritably growling and snapping at the mice running over their paws.

Then suddenly and inexplicably the mice scuttled away as quickly as they came out of the door and rejoined the thousands of their companions surging down the hill and then suicidally into the French River where their tortured rolling and splashing turned the shoreline into a muddy, foamy sludge. And then silence.

The crabs feasted upon the drowned bodies of mice for weeks to come.

Jane slumped into a rocking chair on the front porch as she surveyed the utter devastation in the MacKay fields. Where once the green leaves of potato plants had covered the ground, there was now nothing but bare, loamy red soil. A gust of wind whipped up some fine dry dust into her eyes. She wiped it clear with her apron and sobbed.

John felt for his mother's hand: 'Don't cry mother. I will look after you.'

Jane smiled and tousled the boy's hair: 'I know you will, my dear, dear son.'

Jane now stood up and put an arm around John and squeezed his shoulder. Mother and son stepped forward to the edge of the porch and stared out across the desolate field. They had no need to speak. Whatever adversity Fate threw at them, they were determined their family would survive.

'When I shut up the heavens so that there is no rain or command locusts to devour the land or send a plague among my people; if my people, who are called by my name, will humble themselves and pray and seek my face and turn from their wicked ways, then I will hear from heaven and forgive their sin and will heal their land,' the stern–faced Kirk Elder commanded his congregation.

William looked down from the pulpit and breathed retribution, laced with a modicum of forgiveness as he relayed to the congregation the Lord's reply to Solomon's prayer.

The Elder's passion was sincere. He wondered truthfully if his family's participation in smuggling during the recent American war had caused the Almighty to punish them. Not only the MacKays but many others in New London had seen their crops destroyed by the plague of mice.

The future looked grim for the MacKays. Money was in short supply. And Ann McIntosh with her extra hungry children were expected to arrive before the year's end.

William, now 67, was, at last, beginning to slow up physically and mentally. Jane, ten years his junior and still in her prime, was beginning to take the lead in all matters affecting the family.

'William, we will not starve. There is still enough fish to catch in the river. We will catch extra and salt them to eat over the winter.'

Her husband frowned: 'We will have to eat crab again, I suppose?'

Jane knew what William meant. So plentiful was the crustacean it had attracted the social stigma of being the food of the island's poor.

'Come now husband. Do not be so gloomy. It will only be for a year.

'We will enjoy next year's harvest. There will be corn, wheat and potatoes aplenty.'

Jane's optimism proved misplaced.

Following the end of the second American War, the years 1815 and 1816 should have been ones of celebration and renewal in Prince Edward Island, despite the fall in timber prices caused by the collapse in demand from the Royal Navy.

During the 1812 war the British defeated the attempted annexe of Canada by the United States, laying the foundation of pride in the nascent confederation. The republic's navy was eventually bottled up in its ports by the Royal Navy, leaving the U.S. economy in tatters. And the British Army successfully invaded the state of Maine, headed south and torched Washington. There was open talk of secession. In New England the governor of Massachusetts secretly discussed a separate peace treaty with the British. On the other hand, the British attempt to create an independent Indian buffer state between the US and Canada was thwarted. And the British invasion of the southern US was soundly defeated at the Battle of New Orleans. This major victory helped restore confidence and pride among the citizens of the battered republic.

Following the defeat of Napoleon at the Battle of Waterloo, the British could now supposedly turn their attention to its war with the American republic, hitherto accorded secondary status. Worried that the British might reinforce its army and navy, the U.S. government agreed to negotiate an end to hostilities. The U.S. needn't have worried.

Exhausted by years of Napoleonic wars and with a consequent national debt of more than 200 per cent of the country's annual economy, the British had no desire or money to continue the war, which, the Duke of Wellington advised his government, had been poorly led.

The 1815 the Treaty of Ghent settled terms between the two relieved nations and restored the status quo. Neither country won or lost. The British withdrew from New England. The defeat of Napoleon meant the enormous Royal Navy could be cut down and sailors dismissed. So there was no further necessity to interfere with U.S. shipping to press seamen into service. And the U.S. gave up any claims to Canada.

William's sermon commanding prayers to the Lord for his forgiveness from his New London congregation proved to be futile. Just as the mice destroyed their 1815 crop, their 1816 one was wiped out as well, this time by something, ironically, heaven–sent.

Unknown to everyone in Europe and North America, on the 10th April, 1815, the world's greatest ever recorded volcanic explosion took place on the island of Sumbawa in the Dutch East Indies. Day turned into night in the East Indies when Mount Tambora erupted in an explosion many times greater in magnitude than Pompeii. About 90,000 of its inhabitants were killed. Thousands of tons of volcanic ash were shot into the stratosphere and gradually went around the globe, blocking the sun and adversely affecting the weather in many places, including Western Europe and North East America. Harvests failed across Europe in 1816. The price of bread and rice soared. The rural, starving poor joined by thousands of unemployed army veterans of the Napoleonic wars crowded into the continent's towns and cities, begging for food and help. Obtaining little of either, rioting broke out

113

in many places. Governments feared that revolution was imminent. Severe epidemics of typhus followed famine. Perhaps as many as 200,000 people died in Europe. Emigration to North America rose and in New England people began to move west to colonise the less affected parts of the US.

In Prince Edward Island winter lingered on under a dark sky. Some days the sun could be dimly seen, on other days it was completely obscured and it was as black as night. In May the sea lanes finally became free and the MacKays decided to try planting their potato seeds. At last, one day in June, bright sun appeared and it became blisteringly hot. The family rejoiced. The cold period was over, wasn't it? But the following day the sun could hardly be seen. The temperature sank, dirty brown snow fell and the frozen ground crackled under William and Jane's boots as they surveyed their fields. There was not a single sign of green shoots.

Jane racked her brains. The price of grain and potatoes was already too high for the MacKay clan in French River. She frowned. More Yankee fishing boats were appearing off the coast daily and the supply of fish in the river was diminishing. Even the number of crabs was falling. Fish prices had soared as more and more people turned to the sea for nourishment.

Jane called a family conference. Donald and Jessie arrived from Charlottetown. Donald's son William, already in his mid–twenties, joined his parents from the family farm further up French River. He gave his mother a kiss on the cheek. A polite shake of his father's hand merely confirmed what they all knew: Donald and his son did not see eye–to–eye on much.

Ann MacIntosh and her husband sat in one corner, guilt etched on their faces. They knew the extra mouths of their eight children were placing a huge demand on the family's resources. All of the younger members of the family were scattered around the room, sitting on the floor or leaning against the walls.

Donald's William caught Barbara's eye and smiled at his pretty cousin. They both knew that there had already been discussions about a possible betrothal. Ann had pressed the matter with William's mother, Jessie: 'Barbara is already twenty–two. Almost an old maid! Surely William needs a female companion and children for your farm?' Jessie did not need much convincing. Only Donald had reservations which he kept to himself: he had hoped his son would secure somebody with a dowry.

Looking around the family gathering, Jane noticed wryly that there were now four William MacKays in the room, including her husband. She counted Donald's son; one of Ann's sons by her previous marriage to her husband's brother, John; and her own son. Jane chuckled quietly to herself, wondering how a future chronicler of the family could avoid becoming confused.

Jane stood next to the kitchen table, very much the *materfamilias.*

'Fish,' announced Jane.

She cleared her throat and repeated to the puzzled audience: 'Fish. Yes, fish will be our salvation. I have been giving the matter much thought,' continued Jane looking around at the dubious faces.

'Forbes and I visited Cavendish in the *Jane* last week to buy fish. As you know we need to make sure we have enough food to get us through this dreadful summer and the coming winter. We watched the fishermen unloading their catches to be salted and dried. We bought salted cod. And very expensive it was too!'

'Come, come Jane,' protested Donald. 'We are not fisher folk. We do not know how to use long lines. And we do not possess the small boats that we would need to work along with the Jane. Nor can we fillet, salt and flake a catch of fish.'

Forbes stood and joined his mother at the kitchen table: 'You are correct, Uncle Donald. But we don't need to be fisher folk. What mother is proposing is that we trade in salted fish.

'We hear the prices all the way down to New York are astronomic.'

Forbes looked keenly at his uncle: 'You are used to trading in timber and rum. Surely you can apply your merchant skills to dried fish?'

Donald nodded his head in slow agreement and turned to look at his wife.

Jessie, who knew the price and cost of everything, was running the figures through her mind: 'I would have to check, but if we took salted cod down to New York and continued to Jamaica and returned with rum and sugar, I believe we may be able to make a profit.'

Jessie looked at her sister–in–law: 'Jane, God bless you. I think you may have found a way for us to survive.'

Jane nodded in appreciation of Jessie's words: 'Of course the price of fish may drop once summer returns. But in the meantime, *carpe diem*.'

'Thank God we still have the *Jane*,' Donald said.

'Both of them,' added Forbes looking at his mother.

Ann and her William left the family meeting in a happier mood. Jane had shown a way forward.

There was a hazy sun. Although it was chilly, Ann knew the children were safe inside with their cousins. She suggested a walk down to the jetty where the *Jane* was moored. A short way along the planks William McIntosh suddenly grimaced in pain, grabbed his chest, stumbled and toppled into the shallow water.

Ann screamed and jumped in to try to rescue her husband. But, as she found her footing in the soft, muddy river bed, she realised William was already dead. His motionless body floating on his back, his face contorted in pain, was starting to drift away. Her boots stuck in the mud, Ann tripped and fell to her knees as she tried to reach out and grab William, her sodden skirts and cloak heavy with water. She gasped as the cold water pierced through to her skin. Thwarted, she sat sobbing in the shallows, unable to do anything as the gentle tide slowly carried William McIntosh away and out of her life.

Lightning suddenly pierced the sky out to sea, turning the darkening sky into vivid hues of red and yellow. A storm was coming. Ann slumped back onto her heels, utterly desolate. Rain arrived, the temperature fell and it started snowing. Ann sat shivering in the icy shallows with her eyes closed, snowflakes stinging her face. She suddenly felt something bumping heavily against her legs. Ann shielded her eyes against the driving snow and looked down. Forked lightning suddenly illuminated the bulging, shocked eyes of her husband staring up at her. The wind and waves had returned William to his wife.

Ann was overcome by shocked, hysterical terror. The body was no longer her husband but some strange life–threatening sea monster. She tried to push it away with her hands but the storm proved too strong. Still screaming she leant back and placed her hands on the river bed and, in a frenzy, managed to get a foot out of the mud and kick him away into the darkness. Exhausted by the effort and fading from hypothermia, Ann fainted.

It was Forbes and John who found her next to the jetty a couple of hours later after the rain had stopped. They carried their comatose, frozen aunt back to the house. This was when Barbara showed the first evidence of her skill in medical matters. But she and Jane were only partially successful. They managed to revive Ann for a day or so before she began to slip slowly into pneumonia. Her son William wept along with his brother and three sisters as their mother was lowered into the ground not far from Joanna.

William's body was never found.

About the same time as Ann and William died, in England a painter called Turner copied those bright orange and yellow sunsets to good effect in his paintings. Trapped in a hotel by Lake Geneva, a group of wealthy young English writers used a long, violent storm of never–ending rain, floods and lightening as inspiration. One of them was Mary Shelley who wrote her macabre novel, *Frankenstein*. Another one, the poet Byron, captured the extreme weather in his poem, *Darkness:*

'I had a dream, which was not all a dream.
The bright sun was extinguish'd, and the stars
Did wander darkling in the eternal space,
Rayless, and pathless, and the icy earth
Swung blind and blackening in the moonless air;
Morn came, and went—and came, and brought no day,
And men forgot their passions in the dread
Of this their desolation; and all hearts
Were chill'd into a selfish prayer for light.

Chapter 17: The *Jessie*

Sybella McKenzie married John MacKay in 1820 in the larger Princetown kirk instead of their Yankee Hill chapel, such was the high number of people expected to attend the union of the two prominent local families. When Sybella's mother had first spoken of the marriage she had said to her daughter: 'John is a fine looking young man, Sybella. I've spoken to his mother, Jane, who tells me he is likely to inherit the family's farm. His elder brother, Forbes, is more interested in working with his uncle, Donald, in their timber and shipping business. And don't forget his father, my cousin William, owns the leasehold. The MacKays are proprietors, unlike us tenants.'

Sybella knew all this. She also knew it was her duty to marry a suitable man, have children, produce food and milk from livestock, crops and fish, and manage a household. She had been well trained.

And John was only a few years older than me, Sybella thought to herself. If I do not accept a proposal from him, I may be forced to marry a much older man or become an old maid. She thanked the Lord for her good fortune that she actually liked John. Love, she reasoned, would surely follow.

Four years after their marriage, Sybella and John and their first child, a small three–year old boy called George, stopped momentarily at the entrance of a sunlit shipyard, startled by the high number of people who had come to watch the launch of a new ship. In front of them was an excited, gossiping throng walking around, poking and stroking the smooth copper–bottomed hull of a large vessel which towered over them.

Sybella felt silk slide along silk as a thinner, older arm gently linked with hers. The young woman turned to look into the smiling face of her mother–in–law.

'A penny for your thoughts, Sybella. What do you think of this grand MacKay occasion?' asked Jane.

Sybella paused a short while before she answered: 'I was dwelling on the great accomplishment of building this ship. Why, you arrived on the island less than 20 years ago and here you, we, are' – Sybella hastily corrected herself – 'launching our very own ship.'

'Yes, our very own ship,' Jane repeated doubtfully. She left the words hanging in the air that the last ship launch the MacKays had been involved in had ended in financial trauma and the loss of her eldest son. She looked down at the grandchild who had been named after him: George. But the last ship, *The Grenville*, had been owned by a consortium of New London families. This latest one was wholly MacKay.

'I haven't seen so many people together since you married my John. Was it really four years ago?' Jane mused.

Sybella nodded in agreement as she reflected that there had been a lot of marriages around French River as normal summers gradually returned from 1817 onwards. As expected, Donald and Jessie's son, William, had married his cousin, Barbara, the daughter of Ann McIntosh, and they settled down on his father's farm. Jessie had persuaded Donald to hand over the tenancy to the young couple. There were no trees left anyway and Donald was no farmer and Jessie no farmer's wife. She shuddered at the thought of having to give up her ledgers for a milking stool.

The remaining daughters of the ill–fated union of Ann and John McIntosh were married off, mainly to young men of fellow Presbyterian families. Finding eligible men had not proved difficult for Jane and William: young, educated women of good Scottish stock were in short supply on the island. For the most part the girls gladly accepted their chance to be mistress of their own house. Those that didn't were obliged to accept their lot in life – working as their siblings' servants.

Sybella's reverie was interrupted by a bounding, cigar–puffing Donald, resplendent in a magnificent, new sealskin overcoat, made for him personally by Jessie, who slapped John on his back: 'Welcome my dear nephew. Thank you for coming all this way.'

'Marvellous is it not, Sybella?' he added, beaming at the young woman and joining her, looking at the ship.

Donald nodded a curt good morning to Jane. There had been angry words when his brother's wife had refused to allow her side of the family to invest more than a modest amount in the new ship. Instead of the expected half share split of responsibility for the loan with his brother, William, the Yankee Hill MacKays had invested a modest £500 sourced from their savings.

Donald recalled Jane's words to William: 'Husband, did we learn nothing from *The Grenville* disaster? And now Donald wants us to risk even more this time.'

Jane lost her temper as she saw her husband was torn by filial loyalty: 'In God's name, William, Donald has already turned 80 and you are not far behind!'

It was a fact that Donald was a spritely 80 year–old with a full head of wavy, silver–grey MacKay hair. People often remarked that he appeared and behaved as if he were ten or even fifteen years younger.

Jane continued fiercely: 'Let our children save a few more years and build another schooner with their own money rather than saddle them with a large loan for years to come.'

Donald had winced at the furious tone of his brother's wife. They had all felt the loss keenly when they had had to sell the *Jane* to their neighbours, the Cousins, to keep up with *The Grenville* loan repayments to Mortimer.

'But Jane, that was ten years ago,' Jessie had responded patiently.

Jessie had then gestured towards her son's farm on the opposite bank of the French River: 'The trees on William's farm were exhausted a couple of years ago.'

Jessie had then pointed out of the same window that she had when trying to convince Jane to agree to borrow the money to build her namesake schooner.

'Look, now your own timber has also nearly run out. But there is still plenty of good timber on the eastern, Three Rivers side of the island which is why we have opened an office there in Georgetown.'

Jessie had stopped, sighed and looked around at each family member in turn: 'Without our own ship and timber the D. MacKay & Co business has become marginal. If we depend on the profits from the crops of our French River farms to build a new ship, without borrowing money, our children may have to wait a lifetime!' she exclaimed.

Looking at the older members of the meeting, Jessie took a few moments to gather herself and make a final appeal: 'A few years ago we were successful timber merchants and shippers. We were joining the first rank of society on this island.'

She sat silently for a few seconds to emphasise what she now said: 'Donald and I calculate there will only be another twenty years or so before all the best timber on the island has gone. If we don't take the opportunity now, our children will remain mere farmers, nearly all of them in thrall to their proprietors.'

There was an uncomfortable silence broken by Donald a few seconds later with forced good cheer: 'On a more optimistic note, I have been fortunate enough to have just negotiated on very favourable terms with Lord Selkirk's agent, the Attorney General, Mr Johnstone, to rent Lot 10 where we hope to obtain timber to build our ship.'

'Forbes will supervise our team of French lumberers there,' he added.

Forbes had smiled when Donald had happily described the Lot 10 contract with his nephew. Lord Selkirk had generously agreed to be paid a small deposit followed by instalments out of the proceeds of the sale of the cut trees. Lot 10's timber was not bountiful but who would notice if the lumberers strayed occasionally into the neighbouring Lots thought Donald. After all, this had been common practice over the last twenty or thirty years. Boundaries between the Lots were not always easy to discern.

Ignoring Jane, Donald had then appealed directly to his brother: 'William, you know our timber trading depends on obtaining favourable terms from shippers. In the meantime, immigration from Liverpool and London to America and Canada continues to rise. Timber one way, people the other. Nothing has changed. But to realise large profits we must own our own big ship capable of carrying hundreds of people and tons of timber.'

Jessie took up the reins again: 'And the trade in rum and sugar from the West Indies has dwindled as the US now grows more of its own sugar and makes its own whisky.'

But Jane folded her arms and said: 'No Donald. I will not permit it. Your brother will not take on any more loans.'

There was a pause in the discussion as everyone digested the words of this heated exchange.

Then someone spoke slowly and calmly: 'Mother, Father I regret I must agree with Aunt Jane.'

The MacKay gathering was shocked. This was the first time Donald's son, William, had spoken out in public against his parents.

'Yes, we all understand the business reasons but this proposal is too risky. We could lose everything, our farms included.'

And then quietly and painfully: 'Barbara and I want no part of it. We have troubles enough with our proprietor demanding more rent. To take on the added burden of a loan to build this ship would be too onerous.'

Donald and Jessie were dumbfounded by the lack of filial loyalty shown by their son. They had only planned to ask William and Barbara to take on part of the loan as a last resort in case Jane and William had refused to take on half. And now even that option had been summarily removed.

The meeting had ended unsatisfactorily: Donald and Jessie had been forced to borrow much more money than they had anticipated. And relations between Donald and his son were beyond repair. Despite the major setback, the construction of the new vessel went ahead.

There had been some discussion between Donald and Jessie about the name of the new ship. They had contemplated *Jane II* as a sweetener for William's wife, but her rejection out of hand of taking on half the loan changed their minds.

'No, we are paying for nearly all of this ship. So it will take the name of *my* wife,' said Donald.

Donald now stared with justifiable pride at the ship whose construction he had master–minded from start to finish. Jessie had played her usual role of raising the finance. He smiled as he saw Forbes chatting to people, making last minute checks of the cradle and its wedges which would shortly be hammered away to allow the ship to slide along the greased wooden rails.

'I name this ship *Jessie*.' No bottle of champagne was available nor would have been wasted in this manner to mark the occasion. Donald's wife simply cut a ribbon and spoke out loud and clear in Gaelic and then repeated the words in English. Forbes slapped the backs of a team of horses which started to pull the ship down the slipway and then pulled the team away as the Jessie gathered momentum and slid smoothly, stern–first into the river.

About a week later, Donald was proud to read in the island's newspaper, *The Register*, which reported: 'On Tuesday last, a fine brig was launched from the Yard of Messrs. D. MacKay & Co. – A great concourse of ladies and gentlemen were present, and we are happy to say, she glided into her destined element to the delight of the spectators and the satisfaction of those enterprising gentlemen and their builders.'

By the year's end the *Jessie* was ready for sea. On Christmas Eve 1824, the *Jessie* set sail from The D. MacKay & Co shipyard near Georgetown in Three Rivers for Pictou across the narrow Strait to load the rest of her cargo of timber. Donald sailed across to Pictou separately and joined her on Christmas Day after enjoying a hearty lunch with a merchant trading partner, John Campbell. His host had found it odd that Donald MacKay, who usually had money to spare in his pocket, had asked for a £300 loan in cash. Shrugging his shoulders, Campbell had gladly proffered the money. The merchant had done a lot of mutually profitable business with MacKay over the years so he was confident the loan would be repaid.

That afternoon, the Jessie left Pictou and set sail out into the Gulf of St Lawrence, bound for Glasgow's River Clyde with her cargo destined for Scottish shipyards.

Donald was in high spirits. He had enjoyed excellent whisky and wine at Campbell's table. He confidently expected a good profit from the sale of timber in Glasgow and the return passage of about three hundred emigrants. The £300 in his wallet would enable him to pay the crew and fit out the *Jessie* quickly for the return leg. Unknown to anyone but Donald and Jessie, there was an additional £100 in notes sewn into the lining of his coat.

Also only known to Donald and his wife was how close D. MacKay & Co was to bankruptcy. The repayments for the loan to build the *Jessie* were crippling the business. Cash might become essential to tide the company over until the profits from this voyage were realised.

Two days later, when the twinkling Christmas lights of Pictou were but a pleasant memory, the *Jessie* was in the Cabot Straits and had started rounding Cape Breton. The weather had been poor and the ship was making heavy going, tacking against a headwind. Through the grey dusk Donald looked towards the dark mass of the headland and remembered sadly how George must have drowned near here.

'A dangerous coast, MacAlpine,' Donald observed to the weather-beaten face of the *Jessie's* captain, who had strolled easily across the rolling deck in an experienced sailor's gait to join his ship's owner at the railing 'Aye, Mr MacKay,' replied the sailor, a man of few words, typical of his breed.

Realising what must be occupying MacKay's mind, MacAlpine grunted, not unsympathetically: *'The Grenville* sailed too close to the cape, Mr MacKay.'

MacAlpine puffed on his sailor's corncob pipe: 'A common enough mistake when wishing to avoid St Paul's Island.

'I prefer to take a course closer to the island,' MacAlpine added, jerking the stem of his pipe in the opposite direction over his shoulder.

MacAlpine was a good captain and knew the shores well. But even the most experienced sailor could be caught out by the capricious winter elements around the Newfoundland shores. And so it proved to be the case once more. There was suddenly a lull in the wind and the *Jessie's* empty sails flapped and the heavy ship slowed.

Donald grasped MacAlpine's shoulder and pointed towards a low dense cloud, so black that it was still distinct despite the falling night, hurtling across the sea towards them.

The blinding snow storm hit the *Jessie* with a rapid wind shift which refilled the ship's sails but shoved her sideways. The *Jessie* became rudderless while the gale pushed her bow around and set the ship off on a course at right angles to the one she had been sailing not five minutes ago.

The strength of the wind and the almost complete loss of visibility meant MacAlpine could not see, let alone send anyone aloft to furl the sails. Sensing the danger, Donald and MacAlpine rushed across the stern deck through the stinging snow to where they knew the helmsman must be.

'Hard a starboard,' MacAlpine bellowed at the dazed, terrified helmsman. The three men grabbed the wheel spokes and turned them as hard as they could clockwise. They could feel from the wind on their faces but not see through the blizzard that the *Jessie's* bow was starting to come around agonisingly slowly. By now the ship was sailing swiftly under gale–driven, full sail. Suddenly after a few minutes their fears were realised when there was a scraping, snarling crescendo underneath the keel as the copper hull was ripped apart. The ship shuddered to a halt as she smashed into St Paul's Island.

Such was the momentum of the *Jessie* that she had ridden up over a reef bordering a cove and wedged her prow firmly between rocks close to the shore. All those on deck were thrown down by the violence of the vessel's abrupt halt. Waves started to roll in across the stern deck as the heavily–laden *Jessie's* keel cracked and then broke in two. The main masts snapped like matchwood and smashed down on the deck. Men were killed instantly underneath or drowned in the tangled mess of rigging and sailcloth.

Grabbing whatever handhold they could, those who survived waded desperately through the onrushing sea, scrambled up onto the groaning bow and jumped onto the rocks, which provided a lucky escape route for Donald, Captain MacAlpine and about eight of the crew. Luckily someone had had the presence of mind to have grabbed a storm–lantern whose candle he had kept alight. Terrified and shivering the survivors managed to reach the cove's sandy beach where they managed finally to light a fire from some wreckage and warm themselves.

They thanked God for their deliverance and eagerly anticipated rescue.

Chapter 18: Jessie's Cove

Donald took 65 days to die. He was the last one. The others, he noted in a diary, slipped away day–by day, leaving him alone, an emaciated, pricked balloon of a man: 'I started with the most ample girth and the thickest coat,' he wrote with gallows–humour in the barely readable, weak, grey pencil marks of his last entry.

The *Jessie's* owner wrote how the survivors had lit fires in the hope they would be seen on the mainland but after a few weeks the wood from the ship's wreckage ran out. Their initial optimism at safely surviving the ship wreck slid gradually into despair as they realised nobody could see them and they were doomed.

Donald's writing meandered along with his thoughts as starvation took over his cold, comatose senses. He devoted some time to apologising to his brother William for his gamble to build the *Jessie*. He declared his love to his wife and urged her to rebuild her life once he was gone. He mentioned Jane just once: 'You were right and I was wrong,' he wrote simply and added, 'the ocean has not been kind to us MacKays.'

By May 1825 there had been no reports back from Glasgow of the *Jessie* nor had there been any wreckage sighted. The D. MacKay & Co's creditors were becoming restless.

But they did not press Donald's wife too hard. There was still faint hope that the *Jessie* would appear. Bad weather might have driven her so far off course that it could take two months or more to have any storm damage repaired and finish her return voyage to the Clyde.

One June afternoon, Jessie was shopping frugally in the Three Rivers store when she saw someone, out of the corner of her eye, wearing a large, impressive overcoat. She turned inquisitively only half–recognising what the man was wearing.

Then she gasped and screamed: 'Where did you get that coat?'

Betrayed by his guilty face, the stranger turned to run away but other shoppers grabbed him. Jessie pulled the coat open and sure enough she saw the initials DM which she had sewn.

The man confessed that he had taken the coat from a body on St Paul's Island. He was part of a fishing boat crew which had landed in

126

May, as was common practice, to see if there was any salvageable material on the island. The captain of the fishing boat had taken the cash he'd found in a wallet in the coat's pocket. He remembered that there was also a book with writing but as none of them could read it had been left behind. Yes, there were other bodies, one of them wearing a captain's coat, but most of them were not much more than skin and bones. The eyes had been pecked out by birds.

There were no fainting vapours from Jessie. Donald's tough widow swiftly arranged for a boat to take her, Forbes and a party of men to St Paul's Island with two coffins: one for Donald, the other for Captain MacAlpine. On the island the party carefully placed the men's remains into the coffins and buried the other bodies as best they could. Jessie found her husband's diary preserved between a couple of rocks where it had been carelessly tossed by the fishermen. Once alone she read her husband's diary. She made known to the others the gist of what Donald had written but let no one else read his journal.

Once she was alone with Donald's coffin in the small ship's cabin, she wept with her face pressed hard against its polished wood, keening for her husband. Forbes heard Jessie mourning but did not dare go to her. Jessie would be too proud to accept comfort, even from her nephew.

The story of a ship owner's widow sailing to St Paul's Island to collect his body had captured the imagination of Charlottetown. Now news spread quickly along the waterfront and into the town centre that she had returned. The boat, with flags at half–mast, sailed gently into the Charlottetown harbour. A large crowd had gathered and murmured sympathy as she and Forbes stepped ashore.

Her head held high, back straight and with a firm voice, Jessie told all within earshot that the two coffins would be brought ashore in the evening. She was going forthwith to the church to make arrangements for a speedy funeral. Everyone would be welcome to attend.

The church had been packed with fellow Presbyterians from New London, who had made the trip from the other side of the island, friends and relatives of all the dead and the many business associates of Donald and Jessie from the island and across the water from Pictou.

The last–named group included those to whom money was owed by D. MacKay & Co.

'Dear Mrs MacAlpine, if any good can come out of this tragedy, let it be a means of warning future mariners of the menace of St Paul's,' Jessie said to Captain MacAlpine's widow on the steps of the church as they exited after the funeral service.

'Will you join me in petitioning the Governor to have a lighthouse built on that accursed island which has robbed us of our husbands?' Jessie asked.

Like her husband, Mrs MacAlpine was a person of few words. But, like Jessie, she knew how to get things done. The widows' campaign was quickly supported by hundreds of others and a petition submitted to the Governor and parliament. And in due course a lighthouse was promised at what became known as Jessie's Cove.

The manner of Donald's death broke his brother William's heart. He was already saddened by the news of his two youngest sons: Hugh and William. Once it became clear that John and Sybella would inherit the farm, the younger brothers, in their early twenties, had decided to go to sea. They did not last long. Barely three months elapsed before they died after signing up for their first ship which turned out to be riddled with smallpox. Not for the first time Jane felt her fears about the sea and the MacKays were justified.

Nobody had tried to persuade the two boys to stay: William and Jane's farm would simply not be able to support another two families. The departure of younger male sons was an increasing trend on the island as the constraints of the small island's size and diminishing timber resources forced young men from large families to seek a livelihood elsewhere.

Chapter 19: Bankrupt

A week after Donald and Captain MacAlpine's funeral, Jessie and Forbes greeted D. MacKay & Co's creditors in the company's Charlottetown office. All her guests had glum faces: they feared the worst. After expressions of sympathy had been proffered and politely received, Jessie told the meeting: 'Gentlemen, I find this a painful and embarrassing thing to say, but I regret I must disappoint all of you.

'My husband's company has very little means of meeting its debts.'

'I have been advised that the estate of Donald MacKay must be declared insolvent,' she continued.

Jessie cleared her throat and stated clearly, so there would be no misunderstanding: 'My husband was the sole director.'

Insolvency was a criminal offence so Jessie looked around the room to make sure her words had been understood.

There followed a painful pause during which the group of creditors glanced at each other and wondered what should be the next step. For most of them, this was their first experience of bankruptcy.

Lord Selkirk's agent and the island government's attorney general, William Johnstone, coughed impatiently and rose. He inclined his head towards Jessie and said unctuously: 'My dear Mrs MacKay, on behalf of all of us, please accept our sincere condolences. Provided my fellow creditors agree, may I suggest I be appointed administrator of the estate?' Johnstone turned and was greeted by relieved nods of agreement from the dozen or so merchants and suppliers present.

Jessie stood up and said firmly: 'Thank you Mr Johnstone. I shall, of course, cooperate with you as best I can to bring this distressing matter to a conclusion.'

Johnstone raised his eyebrows: it was clear that Mrs MacKay considered the meeting was at an end. Forbes opened the door and politely ushered the visitors out. One by one the creditors left, repeating their condolences. Some of them were sincere. But all sincerely regretted lending Donald MacKay money.

Events moved swiftly thereafter. Johnstone appointed bailiffs, who seized anything of value in the MacKays' Charlottetown office and Georgetown shipyard. The surveyor, Johnstone had dispatched to inspect the Lot 10 logging business, returned with a disquieting report. Not many trees on Lot 10 had been felled. It seemed more trees on the adjacent Lots had been harvested.

Johnstone summoned Forbes to a meeting at Ravenwood House, his sumptuous country estate near Charlottetown to answer some difficult questions.

'I had no knowledge that the French team of lumberers were taking trees from anywhere else apart from Lot 10,' protested Forbes. Both men knew that was a lie. They also knew that taking timber from adjacent Lots had been standard practice for the last twenty or thirty years. But those free–booting days were over as timber became ever scarcer on the island.

'You must have visited the site to oversee operations, Mr MacKay? Surely you could see that the amount of cut timber exceeded the felled trees on Lot 10?' Johnstone continued angrily.

In fact the Attorney General could not care less about the source of the timber. He was furious that the fruitless contract with Donald MacKay would greatly embarrass him because he had recommended its generous terms to Lord Selkirk.

Johnstone was after revenge and was determined that the MacKays should be punished. He knew that Jessie MacKay, whose haughtiness had irked him, would be perceived as a defenceless, grieving widow, and was therefore untouchable. But her nephew who, similarly showed scant guilt, was a suitable target.

'And what of the money from the sale of the timber, Mr MacKay? Come now, answer me, what have you done with that?'

Forbes took his time to answer. He looked around Johnstone's spacious office and at the acres of green lawns outside. 'You hypocritical bastard,' Forbes muttered under his breath. It was common knowledge that the attorney general had pocketed funds from a number of clients and was being pursued by several of them. Money that no doubt helped build this mansion, reckoned Forbes.

Johnstone glared, reading the younger man's thoughts.

'There was no money received, Mr Johnstone,' replied Forbes steadily, looking at the lawyer straight in the eye.

'All of the cut timber was used in the building of the Jessie,' he added in a flat tone.

This time Johnstone believed that the young Scot was telling the truth.

The Attorney General, put on his most censorious legal tone and curtly dismissed Forbes: 'Thank you Mr MacKay. That will be all.'

'For now,' he added as he flicked a finger towards Forbes, as if the young MacKay were an annoying fly.

Johnstone ignored Forbes' proffered hand and waved a hand to his servant to see his visitor out of the building.

The attorney general remained at his desk fuming. He knew that to mount a case against Forbes MacKay meant he would have to obtain evidence from the foreman of the French lumberers. But that should not prove too difficult, he realised. The French lumberers stuck together. He knew where they drank. Threatening the foreman with jail unless he agreed to testify against Forbes MacKay should obtain the desired result. He drummed his fingers on the desk. Yes, within a month he should be able to issue a warrant for Forbes' arrest. He smiled thinly at the prospect. At least he would be able to proffer a face–saving, satisfactory outcome to Lord Selkirk.

Aware of the danger posed to him by the island's most powerful lawyer, Forbes did not dawdle in Charlottetown but headed off to catch the next boat destined for French River.

A small stone rattled on the window pane of John and Sybella's bedroom window. Alarmed, John grabbed the musket by his bed. Stealing food was not unknown in French River. The culprits were usually seamen who had jumped ship at the Yankee Hill Jetty.

Even though he was aware he looked ridiculous, he opened the front door and strode out barefoot onto the verandah clad only in his nightshirt: 'Who's there?' he demanded.

The answer came softly in Gaelic: 'It's me, your brother.'

Forbes slipped carefully out of the shadows into the soft lamplight shining through the open door.

The brothers embraced. The loss of Hugh and William had made them become even closer. They were now the only two remaining children of William and Jane.

In answer to John's puzzled expression, Forbes beckoned his brother to follow and entered the front room. For fear of waking Sybella, the two brothers walked as quietly as they could into the kitchen where there were always fire embers glowing.

John followed, placed a lamp on the kitchen table and sat down facing his elder brother, his heart pounding. What more could possibly go wrong with the family's fortunes?

Forbes whispered: 'I don't want Father, Mother or Sybella to know what I am now going to tell you John.'

Glancing at his brother's face, Forbes said: 'I am in grave trouble. Lord Selkirk's agent, the attorney general has it in for me. He is furious that Uncle Donald died insolvent and Lord Selkirk is out of pocket for the timber I used for the Jessie.

No doubt the crafty little shit hoped to swindle some of the money for himself,' he added bitterly.

'One of his surveyors has inspected the land at Lot 10 where we had been felling trees,' Forbes continued.

'I am accused of permitting our team to steal timber from the adjoining Lot.'

John looked at his brother, fearing and half–guessing what was coming next.

'Of course our French lumberers were not over–scrupulous as to where they felled trees. It has always been thus on the island.'

John nodded but they both knew that times had changed. Turning a blind eye was not so easy these days. Forbes could go to prison, John realised suddenly.

'What will you do, Forbes?' he whispered.

'I must leave the island. I have thought about the mainland. But that is too close. Even in the United States Johnstone might hear of me.'

Forbes slouched forward, his hand over his mouth, staring wildly at his brother.

'I need to go far away where nobody has heard of me.'

Forbes stiffened himself and placed his hand on his brother's shoulder: 'I spent the trip from Charlottetown considering what to do.'

The older brother took a deep breath and said: 'John, I have resolved to go to New South Wales.'

Forestalling his brother's alarmed reaction, Forbes continued quickly: 'Listen to me, I have read that the colony is growing quickly. Men with building skills are required. And grants of good land are available with free convict labour,' Forbes continued.

There was silence while John absorbed his brother's decision.

'This is for the best,' – Forbes stuttered – 'I..I shall work my passage. I already have First Mate papers.'

Pain and some shame now registered on the older brother's face: 'John, I hate asking this. I know times are difficult.' Forbes swallowed: 'I will need some money in Sydney to help me make a start. Little Brother can you lend me some?'

John did not hesitate: 'I will give you what I can.'

Forbes placed both hands on his brother's shoulders and leant forward to stare into his sibling's eyes: 'I know my departure will leave you to care for Mother and Father by yourself. I swear'– he took a deep breath and repeated – 'I swear by Almighty God that I will repay you one day.'

Not long after Forbes told John of his intention to flee to New South Wales, Jessie visited her now empty Charlottetown office. Anything of value had gone. There were dusty marks on the walls outlining where the grandfather clock had once stood and the painting of a ship called *The Grenville* had hung.

Jessie sighed as she looked around and then spoke out loud: 'Oh Donald, my dearest what times we had! We dared to dream and our dreams came true. But misfortune dealt us cruel blows.'

Jessie bowed her head and started to weep but managed to recover her composure after a few minutes.

She looked around the office again, remembering how it had been a focus of activity and excitement as she and Donald had planned the expansion of their business.

But now she forced her thoughts to turn to that nice, well–to–do, widower, Mr Holland, who had made his interest in Jessie quite clear. Her would–be suitor was the son of the man who had first surveyed the island. His family belonged to the first rank in island society.

She would insist on a minimum period of mourning after which an engagement could be announced. She had to admit 'Mrs Holland' had a certain ring to it. Donald would approve and might even chuckle at her opportunism. Donald's widow decided that her time as a MacKay was coming to an end. She walked steadily to the office door and closed it firmly behind her. Jessie did not look back.

A sheet of D. MacKay & Co letterhead, disturbed by the sudden draught from the open door, floated down from a window sill and settled gently on top of the muddy footprints left by the bailiffs.

Part 3: New South Wales, Australia

At last we anchored within Sydney Cove, we found the little basin, containing many large ships & surrounded by Warehouses. In the evening I walked through the town & returned full of admiration at the whole scene. It is a most magnificent testimony to the power of the British nation: here, in a less promising country, scores of years have effected many times more than centuries in South America. My first feeling was to congratulate myself I was born an Englishman.

The Voyage of the Beagle, Charles Darwin, 12th January 1836

The whole population, poor and rich, are bent on acquiring wealth: the subject of wool & sheep grazing amongst the higher orders is of preponderant interest.

The Voyage of the Beagle, Charles Darwin, 22nd January 1836

Chapter 20: *The Orpheus*

The tropical South American sun shone down on Lieutenant Jonathan Warner's fraying straw hat. Under its shady, damp brim he was forced to squint as he stared into the brightness. Every way he turned his eyes gorged on the bright purples, yellows and greens of the fruit and vegetables swaying past on the heads of turbaned, sashaying women. And then, one hand on hip, the other on their basket, the women would sit down, elegantly upright, on their heels and lower their basket onto the wharf. Not a single mango, fig or banana fell.

Every human colour and feature was on display in the port of Rio de Janeiro: African, mulatto, native Indians, Arab, Chinese, Latin and North European. Above the swarm of humanity was a hubbub of thousands of voices selling, buying and haggling for ships' supplies and personal consumption of food and cooling drinks. Bare, brown shoulders of women glistened with sweat as they served customers. Male porters flicked their dripping brows, pushed their trollies and shouted at the crowd to make way.

Warner had served in Portugal under the Duke of Wellington in the Napoleonic wars where he had picked up a smattering of Portuguese. He looked forward to showing off his linguistic skills to his two companions, his fellow army officer, Lieutenant William Bell, and *The Orpheus'* first mate as they wandered around the market, looking idly for a souvenir.

'I say, I fancy that new hat,' Warner exclaimed.

The stall–keeper smiled, happy to accommodate the Englishman's desire to chat and negotiate in a foreign tongue.

Forbes MacKay grinned inwardly at Warner's obvious pride in his Portuguese. He wondered if the Englishman would be surprised to learn that *The Orpheus'* first mate had learnt English as a second language.

Warner fixed his new hat at a jaunty angle and gazed around. Through the hazy melee of travelling carts, carriages, horses and pedestrians on the harbour quay he spied the word Taverna on a whitewashed wall above a faded awning. No, no, he insisted on buying the other two a drink to celebrate his new hat. A feeble excuse but the men had been on board *The Orpheus* for about a month. They had become friends. Shore leave was a time to let off steam and enjoy oneself.

The three settled back into their chairs under the awning as a waiter poured glasses of cachaca, the local strong rum.

'Here's to the Royal Veteran Corps and all who serve in this glorious regiment,' Warner grimaced.

As Forbes started to raise his glass to his lips, he felt a wobbly paunch shove into his back followed by a hearty, hail–fellow–well–met thump across his shoulders.

'Damnation,' swore Forbes as he was jolted forward, spilling his drink. Looking round he saw a bewhiskered, red–faced man whose dirty shirt was open to his hairy, fat navel.

'Sergeant Hopkinson, I might have known.'

A slurred, 'Good afternoon, First Mate' was followed by a friendly, but, nonetheless, sarcastic, unsteady salute towards Warner and Bell, 'And good afternoon to you, Sirs.'

'At ease, Sergeant,' replied Bell with faint weariness.

'We would be honoured if you gentlemen joined our party inside,' Hopkinson said, almost falling over as he gesticulated towards the depths of the taverna.

The sergeant struggled to get his words out just in time before a long, loud belch exploded through his flapping lips and soggy moustache, spraying spittle and rum onto the table.

The sergeant giggled: 'Beg your pardon, Gentlemen.'

A wave of raucous, drunken English laughter from watchers deeper inside the taverna shadows engulfed the tables under the awning. Men guffawed; women cackled hysterically.

The three raised their eyebrows. They had no wish to join in a drinking spree with the men and their wives from the 32 military complement on board *The Orpheus*.

'Thank you kindly for your *de profundis* Hopkinson, but we have some business to discuss with Mr MacKay,' Warner declined as jovially as he could.

The sergeant smiled uncertainly, saluted once more, and staggered back towards his friends.

'I suppose we are lucky he didn't fart,' Warner sighed.

Forbes shrugged his shoulders. What could he say? The company of soldiers on board *The Orpheus* had turned into an insoluble problem.

Following the end of the war with France, the United Kingdom found itself with thousands of unemployed former soldiers and seamen. Social unrest and crime rose. Disgruntled former soldiers who knew how to shoot and organise themselves raised concerns among the authorities. The Royal Veteran Corps was an attempt by officialdom to prevent revolutionary movements festering. Recruits were offered a two year service in Australia after which they would receive a grant of land.

Many who returned to the colours were determined to enjoy the free food and accommodation on board before arrival in Sydney. And alcohol smuggled onto *The Orpheus* had created an unruly company of men who were difficult to control. There would be plenty of time to be merry on the journey from England, calling at Rio and Cape Town before Sydney.

'The attitude of Captain Robison makes things worse, Forbes,' said Warner bitterly.

'Um, I don't find Robison too bad,' said the first mate, non–committedly.

'I grant you he can be charming,' admitted Warner.

'But that's because he's not your commanding officer,' the lieutenant added.

'Unlike your Captain Duff who is a decent old cove and has common sense.'

Bell joined in the complaints: 'He insists on trying to drill us as if we were going to fight the French again. But what's the point? We will only be guarding convicts or being policemen. And, I hear, the natives only have spears and clubs.'

Bell downed his drink and smacked his lips as the fiery liquor took effect: 'We won't be fighting Boney's Imperial Guard, for God's sake,' he snorted.

'Christ, I saw the carnage at Waterloo myself,' the young officer said bitterly.

Bell signalled the waiter for a refill while his two friends fell quiet, knowing their companion had lost many good friends in the slaughter on the Belgian battlefield where the British defeated Napoleon.

The voice of an exasperated wife floated into the taverna from the edge of the crowd, filling the void: 'Jonathan, Jonathan. There you are. I might have known.'

Warner smiled ruefully and stood up: 'Excuse me chaps. Duty calls.'

The other two shrugged their shoulders in bachelor–sympathy to the departing husband and happily called for another refill.

Bell inhaled deeply on a cigar: 'The men don't flagrantly disobey us, Forbes. Most of them aren't so bad. But they're old lags. They know how to make it impossible for the junior officers like us to enforce the orders they don't like.'

Bell broke off, sensing he was being stared at. He glanced across the tables to where he saw a garishly–dressed, young woman, twirling her necklace, trying to catch his eye. She smiled coquettishly, leant ever–so–slightly forward and squeezed her bare shoulders together, accentuating her cleavage.

Through the cigar smoke Bell's muddled, fuzzy head took a few seconds to grasp the invitation. His genitals swirled: 'Christ Forbes, I need a woman. Do you mind, dear boy?'

Not for the first time, the first mate observed how the language of English officers could sound affected. Forbes puffed his cigar and nodded: 'Enjoy yourself, William.'

The first mate chuckled as his friend knocked his chair over in his haste to stand up.

'If I don't go now I'll stain my trews,' Bell gasped.

The officer followed the prostitute out, mesmerised by the contrast in the colour of her shimmering white necklace against the nape of her shiny, dark brown neck. He was followed by loud whoops of: 'Fix bayonets, lads' and 'Charge' from Hopkinson and friends.

Left alone, Forbes became melancholic. He swirled his drink while his thoughts took him back to Prince Edward Island. Autumn would be starting soon in French River. The harvest would have been gathered and the MacKay families would be stocking up food for the winter. He rubbed his brow disconsolately and doubted if he would ever see his parents again and prayed he would be reunited somehow one day with his brother, John.

Only a few months previously Forbes had managed to slip unnoticed on board a ship bound for England. The captain knew the MacKays from as far back as the Quoddy smuggling days and didn't ask questions. Once in London, the freemasonry among ships' commanders soon meant a personal recommendation gained Forbes a position on one of next ships sailing for Sydney.

Another burst of laughter interrupted Forbes' black–dog mood. *The Orpheus'* first mate gulped his drink down. He was not keen to receive another invitation from the sergeant.

A few unsteady steps from the taverna, Forbes stopped and stubbed his cigar out. Left unexpectedly alone by Bell's sudden departure, he pondered on what he should do next. Wander around the market? Back to *The Orpheus*? A drink in another taverna?

He felt a delicate squeeze on his elbow. Forbes spun round and saw the shrewd, inviting face of a teenage boy. Forbes stared uncomprehending at first and then felt himself harden involuntarily. The boy now grinned confidently, noticing the white man's bulging reaction. Sweating, Forbes looked around to see if anyone was watching.

The boy had moved away and threw a quick glance back over his shoulder. *The Orpheus'* first mate followed him into a grubby alley, sunlit at its entrance, fading into twilight and then an impenetrable blackness.

The boy now led Forbes by the hand.

Chapter 21: Roaring Forties

'Sunshine, a following breeze and gentle waves always make for a happy ship, Gentlemen,' Captain Duff observed to his first mate and one of the ship's passengers, Lieutenant Colonel Dumaresq. Four weeks out of Rio, the *Orpheus*, its sails curved tightly with steady Trade Winds, was nearing Cape Town. At any moment the look–out, high aloft, hoped to sight Table Mountain.

Most of the ship's passengers, soldiers, wives and children, were on the main deck enjoying the clement weather, promenading, chattering and eagerly anticipating a two–day break in the colony's capital.

The pacific mood on board had been greatly helped by the tacit truce which had developed between Robison and his command: the captain would not lose face by issuing orders to his company which would not be obeyed.

Dumaresq turned to Forbes as Duff strode off to supervise the hourly measurement of the ship's speed: 'Lieutenant Warner speaks highly of you, Mr MacKay.'

Forbes politely half–shrugged his shoulders.

'Unfortunately we have not had much opportunity to converse while I have been tending my wife,' continued the army officer.

'I hear she has regained her sea legs, Colonel?'

'Yes, thank you. Each morning her constitution improves.'

The first mate was wary of talking to the colonel, the brother–in–law of the governor of New South Wales, Lieutenant General Ralph Darling. Dumaresq was en route to take up the post of private secretary to Darling, a role he had already performed during his brother–in–law's previous post as governor of Mauritius.

Forbes knew the far flung British Empire could be surprisingly efficient in sharing information among its colonies. Dispatches to London from Sydney could easily be forwarded to Prince Edward Island, if something suspicious had been observed by one of its senior officials.

'Lieutenant Warner is very generous, Colonel,' Forbes said lightly, concealing his unease. Dumaresq was clearly in the mood to pass the time of day in gentle conversation.

142

'He tells me you have experience in the timber and building trade in Prince Edward Island?'

'Yes, that's right, Colonel. My family was engaged in trading with America and the West Indies.'

Dumaresq's face encouraged Forbes to go on.

'We felled trees, sold timber, farmed and sailed our schooner down to Jamaica and back,' he said with pioneering pride.

'Why did you leave?' Dumaresq asked with genuine curiosity.

Forbes had thought about this moment for a long time. He knew one day someone would ask the question. And he knew his answer would have to be a plausible lie.

He mustered his composure and looked at Dumaresq as steadily as he could: 'The profitable timber on our land has run out Colonel. In the not too distant future we will have to rely solely on farming produce for our livelihood.'

Forbes bowed his head gently and added quietly: 'And my brother is to inherit my parents' farm.'

'Ah, I see,' Dumaresq nodded in sympathetic understanding of the universal fate of the younger son who had to seek his fortune elsewhere.

Dumaresq smiled beneficially at Forbes: 'Well, Mr MacKay, I'm sure a bright future awaits you in New South Wales.' The colonel was always happy to be perceived as a felicitous instrument of the British Empire.

A slightly embarrassed Forbes paused, thinking on how best to respond to the implicit compliment.

'Land ho,' the shout from above wafted down through the billowing sails and brushed aside the two men's conversation.

'Excuse me, Colonel. I must go aloft to see where we have arrived,' Forbes said hastily, gratefully seizing the opportunity to terminate their discussion

Captain Duff grunted with the satisfaction of a competent navigator as his first mate shouted down that Table Mountain could indeed be seen from high above the deck. Only a slight adjustment to the ship's course was required. The crowded deck rushed forward to try and catch their first glimpse of the British colony at the foot of Africa.

By mid–afternoon the *Orpheus* was tied up for two days, loading supplies for the final and longest leg of its voyage, across the Indian Ocean to the colony of New South Wales.

A day later out of Cape Town, south of Latitude 40 degrees, the prevailing Roaring Forties wind blew the *Orpheus* along at a fair old rate towards southern Australia.

Then, in the blink of an eye, the wind strengthened to gale force and took the *Orpheus* in a banshee–howling grip. Forbes had to order the main sails to be furled. The bare masts bent forward and their supporting back stays became so taut that they screeched like vortex–shedding violin strings.

Although the *Orpheus* was now only under one reefed foresail, the ship still ploughed quickly up the sides of the mountainous waves to their foamy summits where, for a tantalising, terrifying second or two, she see–sawed and the few on deck could glimpse all around the spray–drenched, alpine peaks of hundreds of other huge waves. And then, in the nick of time, gravity grabbed the bow and the ship surfed down into the deep valleys.

On his watch, Forbes lashed himself and the helmsman to the wheel. He had experienced storms around Nova Scotia but had never seen such enormous waves. Water regularly came over the bow, surged around the deck and leaked through the hatch covers and door frames. After a drunken soldier's wife, vomiting over the side, was washed overboard, Captain Duff limited deck visits to small groups of men. Eating at tables became impossible and the cabin passengers confined themselves to their quarters. The stench of sea–sickness permeated everywhere.

In the confined space below in steerage, the mood of the Veterans turned ugly. Brazilian rum and cards led to vicious fights which the junior officers wisely allowed the sergeants to manage and deliberately concealed from their commanding officer.

Captain Robison brooded in his small cabin, annoyed that the weather forced him to stay inside for most of the time. Bored and irritable with his own company his mood blackened.

Then as speedily as it had arrived, the wind moderated to a stiff breeze and the waves gradually calmed to a majestic, metronomic swell. Forbes ordered the mainsails one by one to be unfurled. Under full sail once more *The Orpheus* surged onwards, hatches and windows were opened, decks scrubbed clean and fresh air revitalised the fetid cabins.

The first Sunday after the weather had improved, the Veterans company was parading for inspection on the main deck before the morning religious service. The three officers and two sergeants stood smartly dressed in front of the company. In contrast, the ranks of the scruffy troops reflected the poor quality of cloth of their uniforms. Trousers once white were dirty brown and grey, the stitching was coming apart in their blue jackets, and once cylindrical shakos were badly dented and their plumes scraggy. The difference in standard of clothing between officers and men was causing resentment. The surly answers to the roll call revealed four men missing from the thirty-strong force.

'A high number of absentees, Sergeant?' Robison queried.

'Yes, Sir. Several of the men fell ill during the storm. Some have not yet recovered,' replied Hopkinson.

Robison pursed his disbelieving lips: 'I see.'

He motioned Warner and Bell to carry on with the inspection and, brushing past the sergeant, he muttered: 'I shall check for myself.'

Followed by Hopkinson, Robison slithered down the gangway into the steerage, his scabbarded sword clattering behind. His eyes took several seconds to adjust to the light and shadows from swaying lamps, hanging from the roof beams. From behind bunks and timber columns curious women's faces stared at him. A small boy peeped from around his mother's skirts and poked his tongue out. Someone giggled.

Near the cooking stove Robison could see a table with three chairs. Another lay rocking on the floor. On the table were some scattered playing cards and some half–empty glasses. He could smell the rum.

'You, why are you not on parade?' Robison glared at one man in his bunk nearby.

'He's not well,' a slatternly–looking woman replied protectively, placing her arm around his shoulders.

The captain had to admit the soldier was pasty–faced and sweating.

He spun around looking for the other men he suspected of malingering.

All three protested they were unwell. The smell of rum on their breaths suggested otherwise.

'Sir, I think it might be best if you let me deal with this,' Hopkinson said as diplomatically as he could.

'I can get to the bottom of the matter and punish those who have disobeyed orders,' the sergeant added softly.

'Very well, Sergeant. See that you do,' Robison said reluctantly.

'Fucking idiot.' The words, although whispered, were heard by the officer. Twisting around at the foot of the stairs, he stared at the bunk whose occupant was grinning insolently.

Robison's patience snapped: 'Sergeant, arrest that man immediately. Swearing at an officer is a flogging offence.'

'But I didn't hear anything, Sir,' Hopkinson said truthfully. Years of canon fire had impaired his hearing.

Robison glared at the sergeant, turned back and started to run up the stairs. After three steps he tripped over his scabbard and had to grab the stair handles to stop himself falling down.

The officer climbed through the hatch, his face ashen grey in fury as he heard the barely suppressed laughter following him from below.

Robison ignored the parade and his junior officers and marched straight towards the poop deck where the ship's captain was chatting to Colonel Dumaresq.

'Duff, I need your assistance with a disciplinary matter,' he interrupted without any preliminaries.

Both men turned in surprise at Robison's peremptory tone.

'I would appreciate it if you addressed me using my rank of Captain,' the ship's commander responded coolly.

There was awkward silence. The haughty, former cavalry officer felt it beneath him to apologise to a civilian sailor.

Masking his annoyance, Duff asked: 'How may I help you, Captain Robison?'

'I need a man flogged.'

'Why so?'

'That is not your concern.'

Duff hesitated, and then responded calmly: 'Captain Robison, you are aware that I command here. No man on board will receive corporal punishment without my approval.

'I suggest you reprimand your man by other means unless you can convince me that his crime merits a public whipping.

'This is not the Royal Navy. I spare the lash and maintain discipline by earning the respect of my men.'

'Something, if I may say, you appear unable to do,' Duff added cuttingly.

Robison's face reddened. He spat out: 'I shall complain that you have undermined me, Sir.

'I shall report this matter to Governor Darling immediately upon our arrival in Sydney.'

The captain turned to Dumaresq: 'Colonel, you will bear witness that Duff refused my instruction for one of my men to be flogged?'

'I shall certainly confirm you requested the punishment,' the colonel replied guardedly.

He regarded the flushed–faced, officer trembling in front of him: 'If I may suggest, you should compose yourself and finish your parade. The matter can be resolved in due course.'

Robison looked in frustration at Dumaresq but eventually nodded curtly and turned back to his parade.

'That young man is a trouble–maker,' observed Duff quietly as they watched the commander of the Royal NSW Veteran's Company depart.

'Quite so,' Dumaresq frowned in agreement.

Both men looked in silence towards the bow as the *Orpheus* thundered on, rolling and pitching due east towards Australia.

Chapter 22: Not a Darling boy

True to his word, within a day of his arrival in Sydney, Robison had stormed into Governor Darling's office and protested vehemently that the *Orpheus'* captain had refused his demand to flog one of his soldiers during the voyage out to New South Wales.

The governor gave Robison short shrift: 'A ship's captain is in sole command of his vessel. You must surely have known that?'

What was worse, Dumaresq, who was also present refused to support the angry young officer.

To cap it all, Darling now informed Robison that the soldiers under his command were to be dispersed around the colony.

'That Sir is out of order and not the conduct of an officer and, er, a gentleman.' Robison could not help keeping the hesitation out of his voice as he glared at the governor of New South Wales. Darling knew what Robison was implying: that he, the governor, was one of a minuscule band of senior British Army officers who had started their careers as privates, the lowest rank in the army. Darling therefore could not really call himself a gentleman.

The general showed not a scintilla of emotion. Years of jealous rivals' insults as he received promotion after promotion had inured him to snobbish jibes.

Robison made one last attempt: 'Sir, the War Office appointed me to command all the mounted soldiers in the Veterans' Corps, police and your own escort.

'General Darling, you must surely realise that to go against their wishes is highly irregular and against the King's Regulations?'

The governor regarded the captain for a moment: 'Robison, the security situation has deteriorated in the colony since those orders were issued.'

Darling pointed to the map of New South Wales on his desk, which showed the colony's nineteen counties, its limits of location, the large area in which colonists were officially permitted to settle: 'I have decided that it would be better to relocate your men and place them under the command of officers and magistrates who have more local knowledge.'

Darling paused once more and stared, this time with irritation, at the younger officer: 'I have considered carefully your objections. But I have to say that I am confident that the War Office will support me in this matter.'

Angered by Robison's expression of superior disdain, the governor said coldly: 'I must also add that the drunkenness and mutinous behaviour of your Veterans is so appalling that it is our view that it would be better if they were, in effect, partly disbanded.'

Robison flushed at the explicit criticism of his capabilities as a commanding officer. He realised that this was the main reason for Darling's decision. He turned to Dumaresq and sneered: 'Thank you for your support, Colonel.'

Darling banged the table with his fist: 'That will be all Captain Robison. Return to your quarters and await further orders!'

Once again Dumaresq watched the departing back of the furious junior officer who felt himself unjustly treated by his superiors. Robison stamped out of the door which he slammed behind him.

'Ralph, that fucking idiot will start a vendetta,' Dumaresq sighed.

'If he does, I will destroy him,' the governor snorted, sitting back into his chair and crossing his legs calmly. Robison had already disappeared out of the governor's thoughts.

Dumaresq regarded his brother–in–law with affection and respect. Such was Darling's ability he had risen swiftly to the rank of Lieutenant General. He had been rewarded with the military governorship of Mauritius. The French colonists came to detest him because of his success in stamping out their illegal slave trade and the way he trampled on their council. Darling ruled as a British dictator of a conquered French outpost.

As an efficient private secretary, the freshly arrived Dumaresq had already taken soundings among Sydney's leading citizens as to the challenges that faced the new governor. Although his brother–in–law's performance in Mauritius had pleased his masters in London, Dumaresq was beginning to suspect it might not have been the best training for the colony's complex range of issues and diverse population. Dumaresq counted one blessing: his deeply religious sister,

Elizabeth, Darling's wife, twenty–seven years younger than her husband, whose charm would surely win many admirers.

Darling leant forward and rubbed his forehead: 'Now, how far had we got before that fool, Robison, disturbed us?

'Ah yes' – the governor clicked his tongue in exasperation and looked up – 'You've read the latest edict from those bloody idiots in London?'

'Yes, I have.'

'Well Henry, I warn you that our settlers will now believe they have carte blanche to shoot any native. That's how they will interpret permission to meet force with force.'

Darling drummed his fingers on the map for a couple of seconds and then pointed to the northern part of the map: 'Look, this is the Hunter Valley leading inland from Newcastle, which is about 100 miles north of here. We send recidivist convicts there. It takes days on horseback but can be as quick as 12 hours by coastal cutter. The convicts mine coal at the river mouth and inland there is timber and fertile land for crops and grazing.'

Darling paused to gather his thoughts before continuing his briefing: 'Last year there was guerrilla warfare along the valley between the Aborigines and settlers.'

Henry nodded, remembering his time fighting small military engagements in Spain.

'Although only a series of skirmishes, each involving less than 50 blacks, in the context of a colony of about 25,000 people, dependent on agriculture for its wealth, the security of isolated rural settlements is a major issue.'

Darling stood upright and began pacing the room: 'And damn it, the settlers make matters worse with their heavy–handed retaliation to thieving. I wish some of the larger land owners lived on their estates rather than appoint superintendents, often ex–convicts who have been brutalised by their penal servitude.'

Darling stopped pacing and threw a frustrated hand in air: 'To make the situation worse we have escaped convicts forming bandetti – bands of bushrangers – robbing settlers and violating women. Some of the blacks have helped the police as trackers so the bushrangers shoot any aborigine on sight. Capturing the bushrangers is made more difficult because the convict field hands warn the bushrangers when the mounted police are in the area.'

Darling spun round: 'So you can see how important it is for us to have people who we can trust and are loyal to me in the Hunter Valley. This is why I'm glad you've recommended Lieutenant Warner. I shall appoint him as a district magistrate. In due course he will be granted some land.'

Darling sat down before continuing: 'One reason convicts are escaping is that Newcastle gaol is in a state of disrepair. The prison hospital has no roof. The previous superintendent of public works was incompetent and probably corrupt. We need to find someone who can train convicts to fell cedar trees, cut them to size and steer the log rafts downstream to Newcastle.'

Darling rested his chin in his hands. For a moment he wished he was back in Mauritius. Dealing with recalcitrant French colonists had been comparatively easy.

The governor scratched his chin despondently: 'And then this person needs to supervise the convicts as they repair the jail and hospital.'

Darling clenched his fist to signify the additional and equally–important criterion for the candidate: 'He must be loyal to me.'

Darling noticed the optimistic smile on his brother–in–law's face: 'What, you know someone who fits the bill?'

'Yes, I believe I do. I met him on the *Orpheus*.'

'Who is this man?'

'His name is' – Dumaresq paused – ' his name is Forbes MacKay.'

Chapter 23: The Ultimo conspirators

Ultimo House had history as a meeting place for conspirators. Following a dinner party there, Captain William Bligh, a previous governor of New South Wales, was sent packing by disgruntled soldiers and wealthy settlers. That was the second time the strict–disciplinarian Bligh had faced a mutiny. The first had been on his ship, HMS *Bounty*. Now history was repeating itself: Ultimo House was becoming a focal point for dissent against another governor who sought to rule in a strict military style.

The two–storey mansion was one of Sydney's grandest residences. Its 30 acre grounds were laid out in the style of an English country seat. The local bush had been transformed into parkland grazed by imported Indian deer. The small home farm supplied the kitchens.

The rented house and its grounds were now a suitable home for the colony's second most important judge, Mr Justice John Stephen, and his large family. One Saturday evening, the judge's wife had organised a small reception – she preferred to call it a *soirée* – for the colony's *bon ton*.

A major domo barked out the names of arrivals as they entered the grand drawing room where they were offered refreshments by white–gloved waiters. Surrounded by a gaggle of admirers, one of the judge's daughters was playing Mozart on a pianoforte in a corner. In England one would have been forgiven for assuming that Stephen was a wealthy man who could afford several servants. In Sydney all the judge's servants, waiters, and cooks cost virtually nothing – all were convicts.

'Welcome Captain Robison,' said a tall, well–built man who extended a firm grasp to the young officer as he was announced.

'My name is William Wentworth.'

Robison had started to walk across the room to where the Stephen family was grouped but he stopped to shake the distinguished–looking man's hand. Who hadn't heard of Wentworth in Sydney? Although the colourful family background of Sydney's foremost political figure had ceased to be gossip in the colony, it still proved fascinating to newcomers. Wentworth's wealthy, land–owning father, D'Arcy

Wentworth, a relation of the English aristocrat, Lord Fitzwilliam, had been an impecunious surgeon in London who had topped up his coffers with spells as a highwayman. Arrested four times, the charges somehow never stuck. D'Arcy, perhaps wisely, decided to make his fortune in the colonies and left for Sydney. On the voyage out he seduced a seventeen–year old convict girl who eventually gave birth to William. The couple never married. D'Arcy sent his son Home – to the mother country – to be educated at the Greenwich school of a liberal scholar, Dr Alexander Crombie. Later on William returned to study at Cambridge University and train in London's Middle Temple as a barrister. England had polished a colonial diamond into a glittering polymath: poet, explorer, author, orator, and lawyer. Although a loyal disciple of Britannia, Wentworth had become a fierce advocate for more self–rule for the country of his birth, anathema to the staunch monarchist, Governor Darling.

D'Arcy had died in 1827 and Wentworth was now one of the colony's richest men. But the illegitimate son of a convict mother was not welcome in the homes of Sydney's more polite society. However, as a lawyer and a strong proponent of an independent judiciary and trial by jury, coupled with a refined wit, he was appreciated as a guest at Justice Stephen's home where he could mingle freely with his more liberal–minded peers, many of whom opposed the governor's dictatorial rule.

'I hear, Captain Robison, you have fallen foul of our dear governor?' Wentworth quizzed.

'That is correct, Mr Wentworth,' Robison replied curtly, his face colouring, annoyed at further confirmation that his predicament had become common knowledge in Sydney.

'You are not alone in your status, my dear Sir,' said an emollient voice joining in the conversation.

'Ah, well timed,' Wentworth said. 'Captain Robison, allow me to introduce Mr Robert Wardell, editor of our colony's first newspaper, *The Australian.*

'Robert and I have been friends since Cambridge. Like me, Robert is a lawyer but nowadays enjoys the court of public opinion just as much as his legal practice.'

Another guest nearby, overhearing the conversation, joined in: 'Permit me to introduce myself also, Captain Robison: I am Edward Smith Hall, the publisher of *The Monitor*. Like these two friends of mine I have also fallen foul of Darling.'

Robison smiled at the editors: 'It is a pleasure Gentlemen. I obtain great enjoyment from your newspapers.'

Whereas our Caesar does not, Captain Robison. In fact he is trying to muzzle us,' said Hall.

'Fortunately our independent judiciary will not permit his despotic presumptions,' Wentworth added.

'To what do we owe the pleasure of your company in Sydney, Captain Robison?' asked Wardell.

'I have been recalled from Bathurst, Gentlemen. This follows my official complaint to Governor Darling about the improper conduct of the commanding officer of the region, who is using convict labour to enrich himself.'

The three colonials managed with difficulty to conceal their amusement. Nearly all officers of the Crown took advantage of free convict labour. Ultimo House itself was one such example.

'I hear that the governor has been particularly churlish and has not offered you a grant of land yet?' queried Wardell.

'Yes, that is correct. He has singled me out for unfair treatment,' Robison confirmed.

'Unlike your colleague, Lieutenant Warner,' commented Wardell dryly.

Robison looked blankly at the editor.

'Ah, you haven't heard? Well, it is no secret. Warner had been appointed a magistrate in the Newcastle district. And the first mate of *The Orpheus*, a Mr MacKay, has been made Superintendent of Public Works in charge of rebuilding the town's jail and hospital. I understand both men will receive generous grants of land.'

Robison's hand suddenly clenched his wine glass in such fury that the stem broke and the remainder of the glass fell and smashed onto the parquet floor narrowly missing an expensive silk, Indian carpet.

There was a startled hush for a moment until a couple of waiters bent to clean up the mess.

A young woman hurried over and placed a hand on Robison's arm: 'Robert, whatever is the matter?'

'Nothing, my dear,' Robison said as he turned to reassure Justice Stephen's daughter.

'No, I will not have it. You look so red and angry. Come and sit down with me over there by the window.'

'Excuse me gentlemen. Captain Robison clearly needs to recover from his long journey,' sniffed the young woman, blaming the three men for Robison's discomfiture.

Wardell, Wentworth and Hall watched as Robison was ushered off.

'Well, well there you have it. I had heard a rumour that Robison was betrothed to Sibella Stephen,' Wardell said.

Wentworth looked wistfully at the back of the judge's daughter as she led the officer away and sighed inwardly in bitter agreement: Sibella Stephen belonged to the exclusive class of women into which he felt entitled to marry. But he knew from which he would be forever barred.

'William, what do you make of Robison?' asked Wardell.

Wentworth mulled over the question and took a sip from his glass.

'William?' nudged Wardell.

'I think he is a naive fool. Quick to take offence. A poor brain.

'Hardly a Cambridge man,' he added drily.

'And he has already made an enemy of Darling,' said Hall.

Wentworth swallowed his wine and smacked his lips: 'D'you know my dear chap, I really do believe kind fate has placed at our disposal a weapon which we can use to bring Darling down.'

Wardell smiled: 'Precisely my thoughts.'

Hall nodded.

The trio looked across the room to where Robison was sitting next to Sibella. Catching the officer's eye, the chuckling conspirators raised their glasses as if they were offering Robison good cheer.

Chapter 24: Nelsons Plains

Forbes MacKay had been primed to expect trouble. The letter in his pocket from the governor thanked his Superintendent of Public Works for the rapid progress in repairing Newcastle's public buildings. Darling's letter went on to say that Captain Robison was being posted to Newcastle to take charge of the detachment of the Royal Company of Veterans guarding the prison and its convicts. This was because it seemed there was no satisfactory accommodation for him and his wife on Norfolk Island, New South Wales' harsh prison for its worst recidivists, located in the Pacific Ocean, half way to New Zealand. Any posting for an army officer to Norfolk Island was considered as a punishment in itself.

Forbes was instructed to provide Robison with appropriate accommodation. 'But do not allow him to demand quarters above his station. He is, after all, a mere captain and not a senior officer,' the letter had instructed.

'Robison is dangerous,' Darling had added, 'Take care.'

Along with nearly all the other grateful landowners in the lower Hunter Valley, Forbes supported Governor Darling in the public, political quarrel he was having with his enemies. In Forbes' case, in addition to his job, he had managed to establish a small but profitable dairy farm on his grant of land, not far from Newcastle on Nelsons Plains. In Sydney Wentworth, Wardell and Hall attacked the governor repeatedly using Robison's allegations of excessive, illegal maltreatment of some malingerers. The situation grew worse as Robison took his case to his allies in the London parliament.

Back in Sydney the dispute had become ugly enough for Colonel Dumaresq to call out Wardell to a duel. Shots were fired, nobody was wounded but honour was satisfied.

Captain Robison and his wife, Sybella, arrived in Newcastle in late 1827. Any hope that the polite relations on board the *Orpheus* between Forbes and Robison would be resumed were quickly dashed. The captain took one look at the quarters which had been assigned to him by Forbes and snapped: 'MacKay, the Watt Street cottage is inadequate.

'I note that your quarters are larger and more pleasant. And you are but one person.

'Kindly relinquish them to me at once. That is an order,' Robison snapped.

The haughty English soldier received a frosty response from Forbes: 'I am in charge of all public works here. I, and only I, allocate the living quarters. You will have to be patient. As building continues I have every expectation that your quarters will increase in size.'

Robison was furious. He knew he could not count on the loyalty from the men in the Veterans to eject Forbes out of his rooms. He was a figure of ridicule to those who remembered the bumbling martinet from *The Orpheus*. And everybody in Newcastle knew he had become the deadly enemy of the governor.

In retrospect Forbes' letter, written shortly after Robison arrived in Newcastle, to his brother in French River was hubristic. The joyous letter had told John that by the grace of God he had arrived safely. Furthermore, he had had the good fortune to make the acquaintance of the governor's brother–in–law on board his Sydney–bound ship. This had resulted in him being put in charge of rebuilding the convict facilities in Newcastle.

Forbes had written: 'John, my work replicates much of our endeavours in French River. After I train the convicts to fell and cut the trees, we float the lumber on rafts downstream. I then supervise the building works. I have been awarded a small grant of land for which I used the money you gave me as a deposit. My convict labour has built a tidy dairy and provided me with workers to tend and milk my cows. I am now making a useful profit selling my milk and butter.'

Robison fumed and bided his time. The captain did not have to wait long before he noticed men from the Veterans also guarding convicts who were working on Forbes's dairy farm without official permission.

Robison lodged a complaint to Darling's office that the Superintendent was abusing his position. The captain raised the matter again months later after the governor had tried to ignore the letter. Eventually Darling felt he was unable to ignore a complaint from someone now married to the daughter of the colony's second most senior judge. An enquiry was eventually held and Forbes MacKay was found guilty and dismissed from his post.

Lieutenant Warner, Forbes' friend from the *Orpheus*, now a local magistrate, reassured the former superintendent: 'The governor is aware of the good work you have done here in Newcastle. He does not forget those who are loyal to him.'

'He can count, of course, on you to be a witness in the forthcoming court–martial of Robison?' Warner raised a querying eyebrow.

Forbes needed no persuading. He would gladly help in Robison's downfall.

And indeed, Newcastle's former Superintendent of Public Works was generously rewarded for his loyalty to the governor. In 1829 he was awarded a grant of 640 acres along the fertile Williams River, a tributary of the Hunter River, near a hamlet called Dungog. Later in the same year he was permitted to use 4,500 acres of land adjoining his own land. In the following January he received permission to graze his stock on a further 5,000 acres.

Forbes had taken John's reply, which arrived six months later, to one of Newcastle's many public houses. He had taken a quick glance and knew he would have to sit down and digest his brother's news, accompanied by a large tot of rum.

Forbes sipped his drink carefully. He lifted the letter and quickly scanned John's opening pleasantries until he reached the paragraph in which his brother told him the sad news of their father's death. William had died peacefully in his sleep for which everyone had been grateful.

'Father had been slipping away for some time. As you know, he felt the death of our Uncle Donald keenly, coming as it did so soon after the loss of our dear brothers, William and Hugh.

'Our mother has been magnificently stoic in the face of adversity. Her Christian faith has been of great comfort.'

John had not mentioned that William's spirit had been utterly crushed once he had learnt that Forbes had had to flee from Prince Edward Island and he would never see his elder surviving son again.

The date of his father's death leapt out from the page: the same day as Forbes had arrived in Sydney: the 29th September, 1826. Forbes' hand trembled at the malign coincidence.

He ordered another drink and thanked God he had a younger brother who could look after their mother, Jane, in her old age. Forbes pledged once more to repay John when he could.

Part 4: Sold out

Thus what the Mackays held through sunshine and storm for about twenty generations, was at last miserably frittered away in 1829 by a degenerate son who accidentally got the power to do so.

The Book of MacKay, Angus MacKay, 1906

Chapter 25: The traitor

At about the same time as Forbes MacKay in Williams River was reading his letter from his brother, John, thousands of miles away from both of them, back in Strathnaver in the Scottish Highlands, Eric, the 7th Lord Reay, clan chieftain of the MacKays, sat slumped in his chair in Tongue's Ben Loyal Inn.

Reay, quill in his hand, was steeling himself to sign the stiff parchment document lying on the drink–stained table in front of him, its contents well–lit by a fresh candle.

Written at the top of the document's front page was: *Disposition of Sale of the Reay estate by Lord Reay to the Marquis of Stafford, the husband of the Countess of Sutherland, for the sum of £300,000, dated 15th April, 1829*

A sudden, sharp gust of cold evening wind, blowing down the Kyle of Tongue, straight from Iceland onto the most northerly shores of Scotland, rattled the windows of the inn. Opposite Reay, a latch screeched, metal against metal, as it fought the elemental pressure to force the obstinate window open.

Glad of the excuse to delay, Reay glanced up and, through the fetid, draughty mist of tobacco and peat smoke, he could make out his reflection in the glass window pane. Although distorted by its uneven surface and rivulets of condensation, the chieftain could still discern his face. He saw a portrait of a middle–aged man vainly trying to conceal shame and guilt.

Sitting opposite him, Patrick Sellar coughed softly, flat hand in front of his mouth, a face saving gesture of pretence that he was not trying to hurry Reay along.

'My Lord?' he prodded.

'A moment, Sellar,' Reay mumbled, pouring another tot of whisky into his glass.

'Let me ponder a few minutes yet.'

Sellar hid his impatience. Although no longer directly employed by the Countess of Sutherland, the Clearances had enabled him to become one of her largest sheep farm tenants. And he wanted still more land.

Much was riding on this matter. Reay still owned extensive tracts of Strathnaver, among the few remaining areas left to be cleared.

It was a betrayal of a chieftain's duty to his clansmen. But Reay faced debtor's prison after failing to meet the interest payments on the £100,000 loan he'd received from the wily, old Countess.

In front of him writ large, was the agreed sum of £300,000 for Strathnaver. Large enough to pay all his debts, still enjoy a comfortable life, and generously dower his illegitimate daughter for a suitable aristocratic marriage. His brother and inheritor, Alexander, an army officer in the regiment of Gordon Highlanders, would have to make the best of a bad hand.

Reay grimaced. While still sober he was able to feel pangs of guilt about his behaviour. 'After all,' he muttered to himself, 'I'm not the first one.'

A previous Lord Reay had indeed borrowed money from the Sutherlands. But this predecessor had managed to safeguard the estate for his descendants. Desperate for money, Reay had employed lawyers to unlock Strathnaver from the historic legal conditions which prevented him from using it as surety for a loan.

At the bar two big men were standing, a tacksman and his brother, clay pots held firmly in their hands, watching suspiciously. Although their clan chief had his hunched back to them, the men could sense his discomfort. Alarm turned to despair as they guessed the reason.

The older one hissed in Gaelic: 'Look at him. That's Sellar, I'm sure of it.' There had been rumours flying around Strathnaver for weeks that Sellar was searching for Lord Reay. Now it seemed he had tracked his quarry down in one of Reay's favourite haunts during his infrequent visits away from London or Paris. Most of the clan's tacksmen knew about the loan from the Sutherlands but surely their chieftain would find a way to resolve the matter without betraying them?

Since the Year of the Burnings, Sellar had become infamous throughout the Highlands as one of the most ruthless instruments of the Clearances, a man who did not hesitate to raze buildings to the ground and watch his gangs indiscriminately manhandle the screaming

166

young and tearful elderly out of their burning homes, forcing them to flee and fend as best they could on the muddy sheep trails, which served as tracks between the glens.

Although dampened by the room's roughly–hewed stone walls and peat roof, Sellar lifted his eyes guardedly when he heard the native tongue. Accustomed to being a target for hostility, Sellar looked over Reay's shoulder warily towards the source of the foreign sound, the language of people he dismissed as no better than sheep–stealing bandits. He saw two tall men framed by the roughly–layered stone pillars supporting the roof, their ruddy faces reflecting the flickering peat fire as they sipped beer and sucked furiously on corncob pipes.

Ignoring their vicious gaze, Sellar smirked inwardly at the prospect of yet more grazing land. He was well on the way to becoming rich. Very rich.

The quill moved across the carpet of parchment, the split nib flicking droplets of ink forwards on its uneven way, seemingly in a vain attempt to render Reay's signature unrecognisable. But at last it was done – Reay had signed – and he now buckled back into his chair, his knuckles white as he clenched the armrests.

Sellar wasted no time with a man well–known for his dissolute habits. After a perfunctory handshake he left Lord Reay alone with a modest advance payment to seal the contract. The final payment would be a month later in the London office of the Marquis' agents. Sellar swiftly exited the tap room and jumped into his swaying carriage, its springs groaning under each gust of wind.

'Dunrobin,' he ordered the groom towards the Sutherland's castle in the town of Golspie, still at least a day's hard travel away even on the good Highland roads built by the British Army to regulate the Highlands.

About twenty minutes after Sellar had left Reay stood up, the bottle empty and the candle wick whispering in a soft circle of spent wax. Unsteady on his feet he twisted clumsily around and felt himself being stared at by the two men at the bar. Recognising one of them as Angus MacKay, a tacksman and a local figure of importance, he started to move forward and raise his hand in greeting. He stopped, barred by an impenetrable wall of contempt shooting from the blazing eyes of his clansmen who now banged their half–empty pots down on the bar and barged past Reay, hardly bothering to make space. The tacksman suddenly turned back and, within one pace, grabbed Reay by his lace cravat. Twisting the material noose–tight, Angus MacKay spat accurately into Reay's eyes: 'Traitor,' he snarled.

Reay was too shocked to move, could not, dared not look the outraged man in the eye. 'Forgive me,' he gasped in panic, fearing a blow, staring down at the floorboards. But there was no need. In an instant the two men had already gone.

With translucent, salty tears of self–pity dripping down onto his expensive silver–buckled shoes, the 7th Lord Reay stood with his head bowed, trembling for several minutes before he had composed himself enough to shuffle away.

The innkeeper and the few remaining customers had watched the incident. But they all ignored Reay, as if he were a leper. They knew a terrible deed had been done.

Elizabeth, the Countess of Sutherland permitted herself a smile of satisfaction as she regarded Patrick Sellar who was sitting in front of her in Dunrobin Castle's enormous, drawing room. The countess had judged the 7th Lord Reay correctly. She had persuaded her husband, to lend Reay the money on one of their trips north to visit their Scottish estates. 'He's a wastrel, George. He will default on the interest. Mark my words. He inherited the Reay title almost by accident and has little regard for Strathnaver and his people.'

Sure enough, after some haggling with Sellar, Reay had accepted £300,000, a sum which cleared his debt to the Countess but was sufficiently low for profitable running of sheep across that part of the Highlands where the MacKays had farmed since about 1200 AD.

'Excellent Mr Sellar. I congratulate you on bringing the matter to a timely conclusion.'

The countess beamed in the knowledge that after five hundred years of intermittent feuding and fighting with the MacKays, the Sutherlands had at last gained control over all the MacKay country.

Strathnaver would be expunged from all maps. Forever.

... the payment of rents has been resisted; the sheriff has been assaulted....'

The Statement of the Escheat Question in the Island of Prince Edward and the Remedies Proposed, George R Young Esq, London 1838

Chapter 26: An ill wind blows nobody any good

The commonplace name of the vessel, *Richard Smith*, was at odds with its important symbolism as the wooden boat entered Charlottetown's harbour in 1830. The key to this statement was the smoke from its funnel and stern–mounted revolving paddles as the craft chugged steadily along against a headwind towards the wharf.

Among the spectators watching the first steam–powered boat to enter Prince Edward Island were two MacKays: John and his cousin, Uncle Donald's son, William. Since the tragic shipwreck about six years ago of the *Jessie* and the death of William's father on St Paul Island, the French River MacKays visited Charlottetown infrequently. On this occasion the two men had sailed the day before from the Yankee Hill jetty to collect a cargo of seed potatoes expected from Boston.

To the sailors on the wharf a steamboat was no longer a novelty. The craft was now common in coastal waters from Halifax to Liverpool. But to those who had never seen one before, the *Richard Smith* was an unwelcome intrusion of the threat steam posed to wind power and possibly their livelihoods.

The optimists in the timber and ship building industry on the island pointed out that ships still had wooden hulls and there were no steam–powered ocean–going vessels sailing across the Atlantic. Surely sail would continue to dominate and demand for timber hulls, masts, spars and decking would remain? The pessimists averred that it was only a matter of time before steam–power became viable for the Atlantic. The optimists shrugged their shoulders and pointed to the commercial failure as far back as 1818 of the American hybrid sail and steam paddle ship, *Savannah*. But both optimists and pessimists knew that the amount of timber on their small island was steadily dwindling and would one day run out.

John and William jumped; startled by a loud noise they had never heard before: the approaching boat's loud steam whistle as it neared its berth.

The cousins laughed awkwardly, embarrassed by their gauche nervousness.

John eyed the *Richard Smith* suspiciously: 'What do you think William? Will steam eventually mean the end of the timber trade?'

William grimaced, 'I think the golden age of timber is already over.'

He shrugged his shoulders at his cousin: 'Everywhere and forever.'

'Not just because of steam power but also iron,' he added.

'We are in the middle of a revolution. Some call it the Industrial Revolution.'

'Look John,' William gestured towards the Richard Smith, 'I would wager that much of that boat's internal frame is made from the metal.

'And it won't be too long before ships' hulls will also be made of iron.'

John frowned. After D. MacKay & Co. had been wound up, for a short while he had continued to dabble in the timber trade. He had hoped to augment his Yankee Hill farm income. But with no family ship, he was forced to operate as a middleman between growers and shippers. Then the price of timber had collapsed. In 1824 pine timber was making £1 per ton but the following year the price had crashed to 15 shillings per ton. The repercussions for the island were grim. Families like the MacKays now had no choice but to make a living solely from the land.

John sighed in frustration but, spying out of the corner of his eye the swaying sign of the Crossed Keys inn, said: 'Come, let us take a drink and eat some food. We need some good cheer.'

William's face reddened in embarrassment but before he could decline the invitation, John put his arm protectively around his cousin's shoulders and led the way towards the hostelry: 'Do not fret William, I shall pay.'

By chance the two men sat down at the same table where Jessie and Donald had entertained his brother and his family, including John, fresh off the *Elizabeth & Ann* in 1807.

John looked around the room, remembering the day well. He smiled as he recalled his boyish delight at how food had never tasted so good after the months crossing the Atlantic. The room had been crowded as it was today. But the ambience in the Crossed Keys had changed. Gone were the sea dogs swapping yarns, the lumberers quaffing rum, and the ship builders boasting about the size of vessels they hoped to construct. But one thing remained the same: the saloon was still crowded with immigrants. But this time Irish rather than Scottish Gaelic dominated the hubbub.

'Where will these people work?' wondered William aloud. 'Our population already numbers 30,000. There are no jobs on the farms and only a few places on the fishing boats.'

John remained silent. He had no answer. He vaguely remembered the poor, itinerant Highlander field hands who had worked on the family's farm until he and his siblings were big enough to take over.

'John, how fares my Aunt Jane?' asked William, changing the subject.

His cousin took a swig from his beer, ignoring the vestigial feeling of guilt he always had when consuming alcohol, as he imagined his father glaring down at him from above.

'Her spirit remains strong. But my mother pines for my father and my brother.'

William knew better than to ask about John's brother, Forbes. His whereabouts was simply not discussed. After his brother had departed rapidly, John had been the sole beneficiary in his father's will. In turn he had become a proprietor and had only a small annual quitrent to pay the government.

John looked at William and his eyes softened in sympathy. He knew times were difficult for his cousin. William's father, Donald, had chosen the farm more for its timber than the quality of its potential fields. This is why John gladly let his cousin and family share the work and harvests on his Yankee Hill farm.

William sighed: 'We are always late to pay our rent to our proprietor, John Collings. If it were not for your farm, we would find it almost impossible.'

Both men fell into a few moments of depressed silence.

'Have you observed that the number of large proprietors is getting smaller, John?' William mused, idly staring into his mug.

His cousin nodded: 'Yes, I see that about half a dozen have been buying out the others and now own half the island.'

John continued quietly: 'I know that Samuel Cunard is one of them. I wonder if he knows the hardship he is causing to the family of his former shipmate, my brother, George?'

William broke in impatiently: 'We all know they are willing to speculate that the value of the farms will increase as their tenants continue to improve the land, while they demand more rent but refuse to invest in fences, roads and mills. Most of them live like fat pigs in London, and contribute nothing.'

William had drunk most of his beer and, now red–faced, almost spat: 'The situation is intolerable, John. It must change.

'Surely London must see the only course is escheat: to compulsorily purchase the proprietors' lots and sell the land to us tenants?'

John put his empty glass down and looked patiently at his cousin: 'William, I agree that change is in the air. The Catholics have even been given the vote. Thank God my father did not live to see it,' he added *sotto voce*.

'And it seems likely that slavery will be banned throughout the Empire and more people allowed to vote in the elections for the London Parliament.

'Even so, I do not store great hope that change will occur in the island's system of land ownership.'

His cousin sat staring at the table, his mind in a turmoil.

'Well, well Mr Mackay, I trust life treats, you well?' a rough Cockney voice suddenly growled.

William looked up sharply at a corpulent, red–faced man who was swaying above the MacKays, one fist clamped around a pewter tankard.

Before William could reply, the man leant forward to balance himself and jerked a thumb at John: 'Who's this then?' he grunted.

'This is my cousin, John MacKay,' replied William, reddening at the man's boorishness.

The man nodded slowly and turned to John: 'Ah yes, I have heard you are a small proprietor, Mr MacKay' – the word small was sarcastically emphasised.

'You will understand then why I take a dim view of tenants who do not pay rent on time.'

'Who are you and what is your business sir?' responded John sharply, observing that William's fists were slowly clenching in anger and a vein was turning a vivid red in his cousin's temple.

'My name is Simpson. Your cousin knows well enough what I do,' replied the man tersely, turning to confront William whose face, contorted with hatred, was starting to stand up. Aggression was provoking a furious reaction. Violence was imminent.

'Careful Mr MacKay,' said a slow, calming voice, as its owner placed a restraining hand on William's shoulders. John had noticed that their tense, heated conversation had attracted the attention of someone standing at the bar. As the man approached, John recognised the rolling gait of someone who had spent many years at sea.

Simpson glanced at the newcomer and pushed reluctantly away from the table.

'Mr Cooper?' he sneered.

'You should leave Mr Simpson. Your company is unwelcome,' snapped John, intervening.

Simpson looked slowly and deliberately around at the three men, took a deep draught of beer and wiped his lips with the back of his hand.

'Of course, I might have guessed. This is a meeting of the jolly revolution of rent rebels,' he jeered as he sauntered off.

John inspected William Cooper with interest as the former ship's captain and Lord Townshend's land agent sat down at the MacKays' table. Cooper had been appointed by Townshend after his previous agent had been killed by an angry tenant who had resisted an attempt to seize his horse, in lieu of unpaid rent. The new appointee proved an able manager and invested money in improving Townshend's property and the lives of the tenantry. While times were good, Townshend was amenable to his agent's efforts. But as the economic situation in the late 1820s deteriorated, the absentee landlord begrudged his agent's investment policy and Cooper was fired.

Cooper's experience in managing Townshend's property had led him to believe that there should be a compact between tenant and landlord: the former would work the land efficiently and the proprietor would facilitate production. And there would be a fair division of the financial rewards. His beliefs and high reputation for enlightened land management led Cooper to become gradually the champion of the island's tenantry and smaller merchants who were demanding land reform. Soon the erstwhile agent of an absentee landlord found himself the leader of the Escheat Movement.

'Your cousin attended our public meeting a few months ago in Princetown,' Cooper explained to John.

'He made an impressive contribution to the debate and helped draft our public demand for reform.'

'Yes, I read the outcome of your meeting in a pamphlet,' said John, nodding.

'But I had no idea of your involvement, William,' he added as he took a drink from his tankard.

'You are not annoyed, I trust?' William asked cautiously.

'No, on the contrary, I support your cause,' John replied. 'I assume Simpson is a rent collector?'

'That is correct Mr MacKay,' replied Cooper. 'He is also a bailiff. One who is cruel and heartless and gives every impression of enjoying his work as he seizes possessions and evicts families from their homes.'

'If he tries that with me, he will sorely regret it,' said William fiercely.

John pursed his lips and studied his cousin. He remembered his family's home in the Old Country and his parents' arguments. Their decision to emigrate had proved prescient as the subsequent Year of the Burnings had shown.

'To oppose the proprietors' bailiffs will require courage,' John added softly.

'We are ready Mr MacKay,' said Cooper softly. William's eyes flashed in agreement.

178

Chapter 27: Justice

About three years later in 1833, William MacKay and seven other friends and neighbours assaulted a bailiff during a riot near French River. It was not until 1834 that the perpetrators were arrested and incarcerated in Charlottetown's jail pending their trial. Shortly before the case was due to come to court, the island's governor, Aretas William Young, was holding his annual dinner to celebrate the King's birthday. The ladies had retired to the drawing room in the magnificent new Government House, leaving about a dozen men to their port and cigars.

Chuckling through the blue haze, Young told his incredulous guests an amusing story: he had heard that the chief of the remnants of the island's indigenous tribe, the Mi'kwaq, was apparently drawing up a petition which he intended submitting to the governor, praying for a grant of land to his people, which he represented as consisting of five hundred souls.

Some of Young's guests had never even seen a Mi'kwaq. One of them snorted derisively: 'Five hundred? More likely a fifth of that number.'

The conversation became animated as the men around the table discussed the attributes of the natives on the island compared to those on the mainland.

Sitting next to the governor's left was the island's Chief Justice, Edward Jarvis. Sensing an opportunity, the governor passed the decanter, leant forward and said: 'A word in your ear, Edward, if you please, my dear fellow.'

'Of course, Aretas.'

Young took a deep draw on his cigar before he began: 'I take it you know the lawyer, Mr Robert Holland.'

The governor tilted his chin towards where the subject of his question was sitting. Jarvis glanced briefly down the table: 'Yes, but only a passing acquaintance. There are several lawyers on the island now.'

Young continued: 'His wife is the widow of that unfortunate merchant, MacKay, who was shipwrecked on St Paul Island. You recall the incident, what, ten years ago, now?'

The Chief Justice nodded.

'Mrs Holland is still a fine–looking woman, even though she will not see sixty again.'

Jarvis nodded in agreement. He had observed Mrs Holland while she had been sitting next to her husband. He sipped his port and wondered where the conversation was heading.

The governor paused before saying: 'She came to see me last week.'

The chief justice could see from the involuntarily smile on the governor's face that his meeting with Mrs Holland had been a pleasant affair.

'Mrs Holland has a son by her previous marriage.'

Ah, thought Jarvis to himself: here comes the nub of the matter.

'His name is William MacKay,' continued Young.

The judge looked blank.

'He is one of the eight men accused of assaulting a bailiff in New London,' the governor prodded.

'Yes, of course. The case is due to come before me shortly,' Jarvis replied, recalling his thoughts. Surely the matter was straight forward? A sentence of at least five years would be an appropriate punishment he had considered. After all assaulting a bailiff, riot and prevention of the execution of legal process were serious offences.

'I, naturally, told Mrs Holland that the law must take its course but I would pass on that she begs you to show some clemency,' the governor said, looking his chief justice in the eye.

Jarvis swallowed, playing for time, keen not to be perceived as too malleable.

'There is another matter, to consider in this case,' the governor pressed on.

'The Escheat Movement goes from strength to strength. They now have a sizeable number in our House of Assembly. And their leader, that damn fellow Cooper, keeps making a nuisance of himself.

'Anything other than a light punishment would make the men seem like martyrs to their cause and could provoke major disturbance.'

Young fell silent, raised his glass and looked around to reassure himself that he could not be overheard: 'And quelling a widespread uprising would be difficult with the few troops I have at my disposal,' he added quietly.

The governor let the chief justice absorb his words for a moment.

'So it might be politic to give this due weight when you reach your decision?' Young pressed on, raising a quizzical eyebrow.

'Ah yes, I take your point Governor,' Jarvis said, capitulating. 'You can rely on me.'

Pouring more port into their glasses, Young smiled, already anticipating a pleasing second conversation with Mrs Holland. Yes, a handsome woman of good taste he thought. After all she had found it difficult to conceal that she found him attractive, hadn't she?

William Mackay and his friends got off lightly: the highest tariff was four months. The Escheat Movement expressed surprised relief at the light sentences but carried on with its rural, sometimes violent, protest of rallies, proclamations, pamphleteering and rent strikes.

Chapter 28: The call of Williams River

In Yankee Hill, French River the glad tidings of William's light sentence reached John's home at about the same time as the latest letter from Forbes in New South Wales arrived.

Because John was still in Charlottetown after William's trial, John's wife, Sybella, had given the letter to her mother–in–law to read. Forbes always wrote painstakingly in Gaelic. Even though John's brother had fled seven years ago, he was still wary of his letters falling into the hands of Anglophonic officialdom. Sybella's Gaelic was rusty. Even Jane, fluent though she had once been, now needed time to read her mother tongue.

Jane took Forbes' latest missive to her seat overlooking Grenville Bay. She liked to read her elder boy's annual letters on the bench he had made for her more than twenty years ago. The seventy–eight year old woman walked slowly, leaning heavily on her stick and sat gratefully down onto her well–worn seat, its comforting wood warm from the afternoon sun.

Jane read the letter three times, placed it down on her lap and looked out across the bay and its twinkling blue waves. Much had changed since the MacKays had arrived. The dark forests that had lined the shores were almost completely gone, replaced by the bright yellow and green of wheat and potato crops nearing harvest. And on the other side of the bay there were now double the amount of buildings in the fast–growing settlement of New Cavendish. She had heard too from her grandchildren that the lobsters and crabs in French River were now proving hard to catch.

Looking back over the ups and downs of her family's fortunes she wondered for an instant whether the MacKays would have done better to have remained in Strathnaver. 'Tsk, tsk,' she chided herself at even entertaining the thought. The clan had been crushed and was a pale shadow of its former self. She knew that it had been the right decision to emigrate from the Old Country. But it was true that the current times on the island were depressing and the outlook bleak. The family had never fully recovered from the loss of the *Jessie* and the end of their timber trading. Jane looked down at Forbes' letter. Her forehead's muslin–thin, translucent skin crinkled as she pondered its contents. At last she decided what she should say to John and her daughter–in–law, Sybella. She knew she would have to choose her moment carefully.

Jane groaned as a sudden severe pain shot through her chest. She became dizzy and almost slumped off the bench onto the ground. The blue bay turned a gloomy grey. She knew, she just knew her time was coming: the pains had become more and more frequent over the last month. But she was not scared. On the contrary, she looked forward to joining her dearest William in Heaven. 'But dear Lord, please let it be quick. I do not want to be a burden to my son,' she prayed aloud.

A pale–faced Jane waited until her strength returned sufficiently, struggled to her feet and walked falteringly back to the house.

One evening after John had returned, while Sybella was tucking the children into bed and helping them say their prayers, Jane judged the moment right to discuss the letter from New South Wales with her younger son.

'John, my dear, we need to discuss Forbes' letter.'

John hunched forward in his chair and looked down at his feet. His mother was forcing him to confront a thorny issue, again.

Jane stretched out her hand and stroked her son's curly, thick grey hair. The years vanished – she was once again a mother tending a small boy. She said softly: 'My dearest John. I only have two children left. They are very precious to me. I desire only what is best for them.

'I know, Mother,' John replied, 'But Sybella..'

John left his unfinished sentence hanging in the air.

The years returned and Jane was again the matriarch: 'John, consider this. We have little more than six hundred acres here. More than many, I grant you, but Forbes already has 2,500 acres and writes he has permission to use another 4,000!

'His land near the Williams River he writes is fertile and he has convict field hands which cost him nothing.'

Jane stopped talking for a moment before broaching a delicate family matter: 'Forbes, fine man though he is, we all know he will never have children.'

John brushed his hair back in a motion he adopted whenever an awkward fact had to be addressed.

'Yes, Mother,' he replied wearily, knowing what was coming next.

'How many children do you have? Jane said charging on determinedly.

'Mother, you know how many,' John replied patiently.

'Yes, I have six grand–children already. Four boys and two girls. 12 year old George is the eldest,' Jane said without waiting.

'And Duncan Forbes who was only born a month ago – may I remind you – was named after your brother in New South Wales.'

Jane paused before adding: 'John, our farm is not big enough to be shared among your four boys. And you can expect more.'

'I understand this, Mother,' her son replied, barely concealing his impatience.

'Listen John' – ignoring the pained expression on her son's face, his mother continued – 'Forbes now warns in this letter' – Jane waved it in front of her son's face – 'that if, God forbid, he dies there will be no MacKay to take over his farm.'

John interrupted: 'Mother, I've already told you. Sybella does not wish to leave. Her mother and the McKenzie family are our neighbours.'

Jane pulled her son's arm urgently towards her: 'Do you remember all those years ago how Uncle Donald wrote letters to your Father urging him not to leave it too late to emigrate to this island?

'And how I resisted Donald's call? But in time I came to realise that we should go?'

Jane stared into John's eyes: 'Do not let Sybella make the mistake that I almost made.

'Promise me, for the prosperity of this family that you and Sybella will consider carefully what Forbes suggests.

'Promise me and I shall go to my grave above your Father a contented woman!'

John patted his mother's arm: 'Of course I promise Mother. Now please no more talk of graves. You have many good years left.'

Jane smiled tightly to mask another pain shooting through her chest.

True to her word, Jane died a few weeks later with a peaceful smile on her face, confident that John would convince Sybella that the case to emigrate to New South Wales was overwhelming.

After the crowd of more than a hundred mourners who had attended Jane's funeral, conducted by New London's Reverend Keir, had paid their respects, Jane's coffin was lowered down to rest above her husband. Their grave was next to where Hugh and William were buried. After the service, John, Sybella and their children stood alone, praying around the fresh grave. The baby Duncan Forbes, his name already shortened to Duncan, was cradled in his mother's arms. Sybella's mother and the rest of the McKenzie family stood nearby.

John bowed his head and read aloud from the new headstone:

'This mound contains the remains of William MacKay Esq and Jane Scobie his wife who together with their two sons Hugh and William Emigrated to this Island in the year of our Lord 1806.

Erected to their memory by John MacKay their son.'

John stepped back from the grave satisfied. He knew instinctively that the man who dishonours his parents, dishonours himself.

John glanced sideways at Sybella but she was already standing next to her mother, who was rocking their baby Duncan with the exaggerated care of a doting grandmother.

Chapter 29: Chaos

If the chaos theory had been postulated in the 19th century, a proponent might have claimed that the violent eruption of a volcano in north west Nicaragua started the 1837 economic depression in Britain and North America, which lingered on for seven or eight years. He or she would have claimed that the atmospheric ash from the explosion of the Consiguina volcano on January 22nd 1835 led to a poor wheat crop in England, a consequent price rise, and a surge in imports of the cereal. The Bank of England, worried about possible inflation, hiked its interest rate. The developing US economy was heavily dependent on British banks, such as Baring Brothers, for the finance of canal and railway projects. The Anglophonic economies were already sufficiently interlinked to force the U.S. banks to follow the Old Lady of Threadneedle Street and raise their interest rates. The economies of the U.S., Canada and Great Britain began to crash.

Because of Consiguina, the late winter of 1835 was severe and prolonged in Prince Edward Island. A carpet of crunchy snow covered New London and its Frozen French River. One March evening there was a heavy banging on the front door of William MacKay's farm. His wife Barbara, well–known for her medical skill, was urgently needed at their close neighbours, the Cousins, where one of the children was seriously ill. Believing she would have to stay the night, Barbara picked up her suckling baby boy, Donald, left William and their older children behind and followed the Cousins boy who had been sent to accompany her on the short twenty minutes' walk between the homes. It was a clear, bitter–cold night. A bright moon and blazing stars left a trail of crisp, glinting footsteps.

Barbara's treatment worked better than expected and within a couple of hours she felt able to return home. After about ten minutes or so of retracing her tracks, a snow storm struck. Nearly halfway back Barbara decided to press on. But fresh, drifting snow swiftly covered the trail. She lost her sense of direction and unknowingly began to walk in large circles. In the grey, swirling gloom, blinded by snowflakes melting in her eyes, she ploughed on against the now knee–high snow. After half an hour, exhaustion and hypothermia made her stumble and finally collapse. Barbara managed to sit up but had no energy left to stand. She cradled her child and hunched her shoulders, desperately trying to provide the infant with some shelter. The snow soon gripped her up to her chest. Barbara sobbed with the despair of a mother who realised her child was in mortal danger.

The stiff, frozen torso of Barbara huddled under her shawl, desperately trying to shield Donald was found the next morning by William, about fifty yards from their home. Her white face and the icicles hanging from her forehead made Barbara look like a marble statue of a weeping Madonna, vainly trying to protect her baby.

Calamity followed tragedy.

The following summer in 1836 along the North American Atlantic seaboard was almost as cold as The Year without Summer, twenty years previously. The harvest was poor and many tenants, including the recently–widowed William MacKay, could not pay their rents. Once more William had to depend on his cousin, John. This time he needed financial support as well as food.

The families in New London were forced to join together to share food during the winter. By the Spring of 1837 food stocks were running low but the Good Lord seemed to answer their prayers as sunshine returned and crops were sewn. But come early September a frost of unprecedented severity damaged much of the potato and cereal crop.

Hubristic tragicomedy now followed in French River. Years later John would look back in amazement at his madness. Why had he ignored his mother's warnings that the sea was never kind to the MacKays?

It was his neighbour, John Sims, who seduced John with an opportunity seemingly too good to miss. Sims was weathering the recession better than most – certainly better than John MacKay. Shrewd investment had meant he had still managed to squeeze a profit from timber trading. To settle a bad debt a schooner, aptly called *The Two Farmers*, fell into his hands at a knockdown price. Sims' plan was to load the boat with what grain and potatoes could be harvested and sail for Chaleur Bay on mainland Canada's northern shore, whose

187

inhabitants were desperate for food. A good profit was assured. John still had enough money to become a part–owner. More importantly he was confident enough that he could act as the schooner's Master.

The Two Farmers was loaded at the Yankee Hill jetty and set sail in the autumn. A sudden wind shift hit the ship before she had gathered enough speed to be steered. John MacKay's rusty seamanship meant he tried to fight the wind instead of allowing it to speed up the *Two Farmers.* John lost control and the schooner ran aground on Grenville Bay's eastern shoal where she began to break up. Sims had bought a leaky old tub. It was fortunate she did not make it into the open sea. The crew had just enough time to launch their tender and row back to the Yankee Hill jetty.

A furious Sybella blamed her husband for the family's misfortune and the onset of dire financial problems. Her anger turned to frustration as Forbes' latest letter arrived full of good news of bountiful harvests and the prospect of more fertile fields, as his convicts cleared more bush. 'Come now to Williams River,' Forbes urged.

Economic depression, hunger and cold foment revolution and Canada was no exception. Would be republican French–speaking colonists rebelled in Lower Canada in 1837, followed by a smaller number of British rebels in Upper Canada. Although both revolts were quashed, they added to the Escheat Movement's confidence that their time was coming. In 1838 the movement's leader, William Cooper, went to London to lobby the British government but was rebuffed. No meeting was offered. Instead the government was swayed by the island's proprietors and ordered the island's governor not to entertain any thought of escheat. Hope among island's tenantry for land reform sank and the movement began to disintegrate.

Sybella had to admit finally that the future for their children on the island paled in comparison with what Forbes seemed to offer. She agreed with John it was time to join his brother in another land.

John Sims agreed to pay a reasonable sum for the MacKay's house and farm which made up for the *Two Farmers'* disaster and paid for a passage to New South Wales.

William MacKay, still injured by the loss of his wife, Barbara, took the decision by his cousin to leave the island badly. Although he tried, William could not hide his feelings of hurt and betrayal.

Similarly Sybella's family grieved. Her mother had been particularly close to her daughter. But, in time, they came to accept John and Sybella's decision. After all, the MacKays were not alone; there was now a steady trickle of emigration from the island to other British colonies, mainland Canada and the United States.

On the morning of their departure, John was the last of the family to leave their home. As he stepped out onto the porch, he turned and looked up at the carved MacKay coat of arms. Although much of the wood was weather–beaten and faded, he could still make out the motto: *Manu Forte*. John winced: he certainly did not feel he had a strong hand. He knew his mother would approve of the decision to abandon French River. But his father? It was with a heavy heart that John joined Sybella and the children and started to walk along Cape Road down towards the Yankee Hill jetty.

There was a large gathering of family and friends, kith and kin, waiting at the jetty to say goodbye as the family caught the ferry across Grenville Bay to New Cavendish.

Halfway across the bay John was hit by utter sadness as he looked back at the Cape. So much effort had gone into making the family's thirty–two years on the island a success.

A distraught Sybella had broken down on the ferry, weeping in the knowledge she would never see her McKenzie family again. John gripped the ferry's iron railing as he fought off sudden severe doubt: the MacKays had been so successful for a while. If they stayed, wouldn't the good times return? But the die had been cast: the family's next adventure was starting.

On the other side of the bay, the baggage was loaded onto a hired cart for the journey south across the island to Charlottetown. The MacKays were accompanied by their friends, John and Jenny Macleod, to help with the children and baggage and see them off on their ship to the port of Liverpool in England. After three hours they arrived in good time and ate a picnic lunch by the quayside until passenger boarding began.

In a scene John still remembered from Thurso when he was a small boy, the ship's purser checked the family names against his list of paying passengers: the parents John (38) and Sybella (36) followed by the children George (16), Jane(13), William Hugh (12), John Kenneth (10), Jesse Johanna (7), Duncan Forbes (4) and Charles Boyce (1).

'John, Sybella,' a lady in widow's weeds suddenly called out through the noise of the bustling quay.

'Aunt Jessie?' John asked doubtfully, half–recognising the voice. Since her wedding to Robert Holland, there had been little contact with Jessie. The MacKays, particularly her son, William, had not approved of the marriage so soon after his father, Donald's death, even though they had all been pleased to hear that Jessie had used her influence to obtain a light sentence for her son.

'Robert died six months ago,' Jessie explained as she pulled her veil to one side.

'I'm sorry to hear your sad news, Aunt Jessie,' said John truthfully. 'If I had known I would have visited you to express my condolences.'

'Thank you John. But it is of no consequence.' There was a brief silence as aunt and nephew looked at each other. John realised that Jessie had not yet informed her son, William, of his step–father's death.

'I only discovered by chance this morning that you were preparing to embark,' said Jessie.

'Here, I want you to have this,' she said, pressing a sealed, thick package tied with string into John's hands. 'Don't open it now. Wait until your ship has sailed,' Jessie ordered.

'How is my son?' she asked after a moment, her voice betraying a fraction of motherly concern.

'William is finding life difficult, Aunt Jessie. Our decision to leave has saddened him. He fears for the future. I must admit to some guilt that we are leaving him in the lurch.'

Jessie looked at her nephew: 'John, do not worry about William. I shall ensure his security. After allowing for his children, Robert did his best for me in his will,' she added.

'What will you do now, Aunt Jessie?' asked her nephew.

'I am returning to Tongue,' Jessie replied quietly.

'I have decided that I wish to die in the Old Country, in Strathnaver,' she said in response to John's startled expression.

'Yes I know I came here more than thirty years ago. But I am an old woman now. This island has too many sad memories for me.'

Jessie smiled softly, her eyes moist and her voice trembling slightly: 'Besides, the governor has, at last, built not one, but two lighthouses on St Paul Island. One of them is not far from where your uncle, my darling Donald died. I shall always think of it as a memorial to that dear, impetuous man.'

Jessie stepped forward and hugged John and one by one Sybella and all of the children.

Her last words to the departing MacKays were: 'Godspeed. I shall pray that New South Wales is kinder to you than Prince Edward Island.'

A few days later Jessie went by herself to Donald's grave. With a small garden trowel she bent down and dug a small hole in front of the headstone. With her old bones creaking, Jessie stood up and looked around. The graveyard was deserted. Jessie bent down and tenderly placed Donald's diary in the hole. After she had filled the hole up, Jessie placed a small pot of flowers to hide the freshly dug soil.

Stepping back, Jessie brushed her hands clean in the manner of someone who has completed a task satisfactorily.

In an unsteady voice she said: 'Farewell Donald. You were the only man I truly loved.'

Jessie turned around and walked purposefully away. With her head up and measured stride, someone watching her from afar would have admired her widow's stoicism. But anyone closer would have seen a sheen on her cheeks and tears dripping from her chin like a slowly melting icicle.

Not long out of Charlottetown, John and Sybella opened Jessie's package and found a short letter wrapped around a thick wad of cash.

Jessie had written in Gaelic: 'Please accept this small gift from me. I hope you will also think of it as part–atonement for the financial misfortune Donald and I caused our family by insisting we build that cursed ship named after me.'

John and Sybella counted the notes surreptitiously for fear of being observed by their fellow steerage passengers. The total was £500.

Part 6: The Williams River Valley

One of the first and most essential government services was the administration and maintenance of law and order. In view of the vast distances, the wild nature of the pioneering stage of society, the large convict population and the blacks made hostile by the loss of their lands, this proved a difficult task, and usually lagged behind the spread of settlement.

Theme Five, The Early Government Influence, Dungog Historical Society

Chapter 30: The serial emigrants

John Hooke was an authentic English country squire who could trace his lineage back for hundreds of years. Tall, fair–haired and handsome with a square jaw and masculine mutton–chop whiskers, he looked the part too. His ancestor, Robert La Hogue, sailed across the English Channel with the Norman duke, William the Conqueror, who successfully invaded England in 1066. It took the Norman conquerors about three hundred years for English – regarded as the primitive language of serfs and artisans – to become fully their mother tongue. At some point the family anglicised their name to Hooke – the more accurate translation of Hog was considered too coarse.

Family legend had it that another Robert saved King Edward III's life at the Battle of Crecy in 1346. After his French relatives were routed, a grateful king wished to knight Robert on the field. But his faithful subject refused the honour, begging instead for Edward to give him his sword and shield so that Robert could always defend the king's lands. For some reason the sword and shield eventually ended up in Westminster Abbey.

John Hooke lived on one of the family's estates, Normanton Hall, near the city of Sheffield in the north of England. The squire had two passions in his life: thoroughbred horses and, unusually, silver. For the latter he collected plates, knives and forks, and bright ornaments. There was no woman in his life so jewellery did not figure large in his collection.

That all changed one day when he visited, Bielchovsky's, a Sheffield silversmith. The owner happened to be out and had left the shop in the care of his daughter, Miriam. Hooke was immediately smitten by the olive–skinned, dark–eyed beauty. The feeling was reciprocated. John was mesmerised by the difference between the exotic Miriam and the pale English roses his widowed mother considered as suitable candidates for a marriage. For her part, Miriam was exhilarated by the difference between John and the business–minded Jewish merchants and apprentices her parents were putting forward as potential suitors. Clandestine, whispered meetings followed one after the other until the pair announced they wished to marry.

All hell broke loose. John was accused by his furious family of wishing to pollute the family bloodlines with a Jewess. Miriam's parents were equally horrified. Allow their daughter to marry a goy and waste the precious female Jewish line?

To appease the Hookes, Miriam Bielchovsky anglicised her name to Mary Ann Beale and renounced her faith. In cosmopolitan London marrying a Jewess might be acceptable, if she were rich. But society in the provincial shires was less amenable. Besides, Mary Ann's silversmith father was not wealthy.

After it became clear that the marriage was inevitable, John's brother, Richard, reluctantly agreed to be a witness in the family's small chapel in Crook's Park, the family seat in Gloucestershire.

Mary Ann's family now cut the apostate off. John's widowed mother refused to receive her son's wife and entreated the gentry for miles around to ostracise the newly–weds.

In short, it was a scandal which fuelled salacious and snobbish gossip at grand dinner tables, noisy public houses and hushed servants' quarters for miles around.

Fortunately the new couple were able to insulate themselves financially. As the elder son, John had inherited most of his father's estates. In fact, John was wealthy, so wealthy that he hardly bothered with financial matters, leaving them to his factors, housekeepers and stewards. But socially they were pariahs, shunned by Christians and Jews alike.

After about four years, John's patience at being ostracised was wearing thin.

'If England will not have me, by God, I will not have England,' he vowed one day after being cut by an acquaintance in Sheffield. He and Mary Ann decided to emigrate to Argentina. It was a disaster. If only John had done some research first, he would have realised that a Protestant married to a Jewess was even less likely to be welcome in the rigid society of a conservative Roman Catholic colony than in England. Besides, it transpired that the natives, that is the Spanish colonists, did not speak much English. The couple returned to England. John pondered awhile and then decided that their next destination should be the Australian colony, Van Diemen's Land, which was as far away as one could get from England, but where English was still spoken. John was attracted by reports that the colony's new governor, George Arthur, wished to encourage the immigration of English land–owning classes who would be guaranteed a liberal supply of free convict labour. If Argentina had proved disastrous, Van Dieman's Land was doubly so. John, Mary Ann and their four boys settled on 400 acres of fertile land about 50 miles north of the colony's capital, Hobart, not far from a settlement called Oatlands. At first everything went swimmingly. John built a comfortable home and employed an ex–convict overseer who put his gang of about a dozen convicts hard at work clearing fields for wheat and pasture for sheep and the thoroughbreds John intended to import. Woe betide any settler who did not enforce hard labour on his convicts. Governor Arthur's police inspected regularly and settlers who did not obey would be relieved of their free labour.

In the summer of 1824, John, Mary Ann and the boys were sitting contentedly on the front verandah, chatting before the evening meal was served by their convict servants. The family fell silent as they suddenly heard the sound of a musket shot.

'Look Father', one of the boys said, pointing at a plume of smoke rising from one corner of the field where their first crop of wheat awaited harvest. Almost immediately they heard the sound of a horse galloping up the drive towards them. Everyone sprang up as the overseer came into view, whipping the sides of his sweating mount with the reins.

'Mr Hooke, Sir. You must flee', the man shouted as he reined in his horse.

The overseer took a deep breath and gasped frantically: 'The blacks, Mr Hooke. They've set fire to the field and speared half the men.'

Twisting around in his saddle, the man looked back and stared in disbelief at the crackling blaze sparking skywards and, fanned by the wind, rushing towards the house.

In what came to be known as the 'Black War', the Hookes were early victims of the first major, bloody resistance by Australian Aboriginal tribes to the invasion by British colonists of their lands.

The Hookes managed to hitch up a couple of horses to their trap and escape with what they could carry. They heard later that their new home was burnt to the ground and that for months afterwards pieces of melted silver were still being found amongst the blacked ruin by gleeful escaped convicts and bushrangers.

With little cash left, the family arrived in Sydney and waited for a ship to return Home. While waiting for a passage, John took the time to travel around the capital of New South Wales. His gloom at his experience in Van Dieman's Land was gradually dispelled as he viewed Sydney's impressive progress. He found the fertile area of Parramatta, inland from Sydney particularly attractive. All the more so when he was reliably informed that all the wild blacks in the area had been dispersed. He knew that Mary Ann would take some convincing but, after he took them on a tour, they realised Parramatta was no longer a frontier town, unlike their recent home near Oatlands.

'Yes, we could live here, John', Mary Ann agreed eventually.

Once back in England, John Hooke's financial affairs at Crook's Park took four years to recover. The abortive expedition to Van Dieman's Land had been expensive. Finally John came to an agreement with his brother, Robert, for the sale of his estate. Once sold there would be no turning back.

During their stay in England Mary Ann produced two more sons, James and Theodore, the latter dying a few months later. Shortly afterwards John booked a passage for the family back to Sydney. Such was John's hatred of the land of his birth he wished to take Theodore's body for burial in Australia. But the captain refused – like most sailors he was superstitious.

John Hooke impetuously cancelled all their bookings, forfeited the passage money and chartered his own ship, a brig called the *Courier*. The Hookes arrived for the second time in Australia on March 2nd 1828.

Based on their experience in Van Dieman's land, the *Courier* was filled with everything the Hookes considered necessary for their second expedition to Australia. There was furniture, more silverware, a carriage, merino sheep, purchased from an agent of the King of Spain, cattle and horses. He had paid 800 guineas for one of the carriage horses which survived the voyage until the entrance to Sydney harbour but then promptly died. Fortunately John Hooke's blood horse, Chilton, survived the trip.

One of the family's first acts upon arrival was to bury Theodore who had been pickled in brine for the voyage and had had pride of place in the hold next to Chilton.

The family settled in some splendour at Bayly Park in Parramatta, a mansion with gardens, cultivated grounds and pasture of about 2,500 acres.

John was content. Sydney society was more receptive to his beautiful wife – it was rumoured she was Spanish and they had met in South America – and approved of the wealthy, jolly English country squire who established himself as a leading horse breeder and winning jockey. Much to Mary Ann's exasperation, John was always vulnerable to hard–luck stories by visiting sprigs of English gentry who needed funds 'just to tide me over, Mr Hooke, Sir'. She was forever having to pursue those who failed to pay the money back.

One discordant note and malign harbinger was set by a tutor, employed to teach the Hooke children, who forged John's signature to obtain money. Fortunately his crime was detected and he was brought to court.

John employed as his agent a man named Hickey. If only, if only John had left behind in England his seigneurial indifference to financial matters. One day, under the guise of routine papers to be signed, Hickey presented a Deed of Gift in his favour of Bayly Park. John signed in the presence of a lawyer and two witnesses.

At the New South Wales Supreme Court, the judge, James Dowling, made it clear that although he believed John had been swindled, his hands were tied.

'Mr Hooke, I bitterly regret that I am forced to find in favour for your agent Mr Hickey and dismiss the action you have brought against him.'

Hickey gained possession of nearly all the house and livestock. And John Hooke became the laughing stock of Sydney. There were a few animals which the Hookes retained, among them, Chilton. John wept as he was forced to sell the thoroughbred to pay the legal fees. He obtained a fair price for the magnificent animal, even so the family had not been left much over to furnish their next and final expedition.

John Hooke had also been promised a grant on the Williams River about 50 miles north west of Newcastle near the hamlet of Dungog. With the disaster of Van Dieman's land still fresh in his mind, John had not taken up the grant in country which was still on the frontier and where some of the Aborigines were still wild. Hearing of the family's plight and not wishing a gentleman to suffer unjustly, Governor Darling readily acceded to John's belated request to take up the grant of 2,500 acres.

From the day of Judge Dowling's judgement onwards, Mary Ann vowed that she would oversee all family financial matters and not allow John to make decisions independently. In time she advised her daughters to take a similar attitude to their husbands, an emancipated view which was not always welcome.

Even though the paucity of their possessions meant they only needed one cart, pulled by a team of four horses, it took the Hookes about three weeks to travel overland along the new Great North Road from Parramatta towards their new home on the Williams River.

Mary Ann's heart sank as she viewed the tumble–down shack left behind by the previous unauthorised occupant. The family's new residence consisted of wooden slab walls and a rickety, bark roof enclosing a single room. Next to their new dwelling was a stinking, fly–ridden privy and a rusty, hooped barrel to collect rainwater. She knew also that they only had a couple of weeks' supply of salt pork and flour. Cleaning up their new home might have to take second place to finding more food.

The whole family was silent, sunk in deep depression, as they compared the hovel to the splendour of Bayly Park. They hardly heard the dusty, clip–clop of an approaching horse. A stranger pulled up and nodded at the new arrivals.

'Hardly a welcoming sight is it?' he said, leaning forward in his saddle to ease his back.

Sunk in a slough of despair nobody replied.

The stranger studied the Hookes for a few seconds. He noticed the husband was utterly careworn and exhausted but his wife exuded determination not to be crushed by adversity. That was fortunate, he thought – as the first white woman on the Williams River, she would need all her strength of character.

Mary Ann stared closely at the man on the horse, not in a hostile manner, but determined that he should realise she was not a woman who could be trifled with. Disconcerted by Mary Ann's gaze, the man waved an imaginary fly away from his face. Mary Ann was used to men looking at her but she noticed this man's eyes did not show sexual interest, rather an empathy with her family's plight. She instinctively felt he could be trusted. She smiled faintly, encouraging the man to continue.

'There is much work to be done before this wretched place is made fit for you. My home is not far from here. There is plenty of room for you and your family.'

He paused and smiled at Mary Ann, acknowledging that she commanded her family: 'I would be honoured if you accepted my invitation to be my guests until your new home is made sufficiently comfortable by my men.' John was reassured that the man spoke educated English, furthermore his mount was passably well–bred and his clean clothes and demeanour indicated he was a man of some substance. He was comforted too by the sight of a well–oiled flintlock pistol in a saddle holster and a gleaming scabbard from which the butt of a polished musket protruded. He stepped forward and extended his hand upwards: 'My name is Hooke, John Hooke.'

Too polite to mention that the snide gossip about the Hookes had already reached as far as the Williams River, the man simply doffed his hat and leant down, revealing a full head of dark wavy hair: 'Forgive me. I am not often in polite society these days.

'My name is MacKay' – a welcoming smile lit up his hitherto stern face – 'Forbes MacKay.'

Mary Ann walked up to shake Forbes hand and said: 'Thank you Mr MacKay. We would be most grateful if you could assist us until we are self–sufficient.'

The Hookes climbed wearily back into their cart and followed Forbes down a track through the woods. Presently they glimpsed a house through the cedar trees. The view became clearer and they halted outside the front of a sprawling stone building with glass windows and a wooden shingle roof. There was a large barn next to the house and a simple wood slab hut for the convicts.

Forbes MacKay wheeled his horse round and smiled: 'This is my home. It is not a grand mansion like some others down the Hunter Valley towards Newcastle. Nonetheless it is comfortable and there is plenty of room for you and your family. I have a dairy and a bakery so you will not want for food.'

Mary Ann's lip trembled with relief and she was forced to dab a tear from an eye before she managed to say: 'Mr MacKay, we will be forever grateful.' She paused to recover her decorum and asked: 'What is the name of your lovely estate?'

'I call it Melbee, Mrs Hooke.'

Chapter 31: The demise of the Gringai

Civilisation in the form of a magistrate's court came to the Williams River in 1833. The first magistrate was landowner George McKenzie and the clerk of the court was Forbes MacKay. Before a Dungog court house was built under Forbes' supervision in 1835, the court would meet in private homes.

As the number of farms around the Williams' River increased, so their plump cattle became tempting targets for absconded convicts–turned–bushrangers. Rustling became widespread. The larger landowners, including Forbes MacKay and a Lawrence Myles, formed themselves into the pithily–titled: An Association for the Protection of Stock on the Upper Districts of the Patterson and Williams Rivers. In 1834 William Burke had been appointed by the association as their ranger with the grand title of 'Protector of Stock'. Within a year Burke had success. In one of the first cases in Dungog's new court house, Thomas Skeefe was tried for shooting with intent to kill William Burke. Skeefe was hanged. The well–organised rustling continued but more carefully.

Rustling was not the only problem facing the Williams River settlers. The arrival of the Hookes, and other families like them, increased the friction in the early 1830s between the Aboriginals living along the river – the Gringai tribe – and the encroaching British settlers with their wheat fields, livestock and convicts.

About ten miles down the Williams' River from Forbes' Melbee home lived a group of about forty member of the Gringai tribe. Their leader's name was Wong–ko–bi–kan. He was also a respected tribal elder. Early one April morning in 1834, Wong–ko–bi–kan sat outside his simple bark shelter, looking through the autumnal mist floating lazily through the cedar trees. Apart from a possum skin cloak, under which he slept at night, he was naked, as was the Gringai custom. His sharp eyes were suddenly drawn upwards towards a white kookaburra with a black snake in its beak. The member of the kingfisher family had just landed on a bough, high up in a tall tree. The bird shook the snake vigorously and let it fall to the ground. Wong–ko–bi–kan knew this process would be repeated until the reptile was dead and could be eaten.

The elder now frowned as he spotted through the trees a herd of sheep slowly grazing their way towards a nearby creek. The white men had told him – they had called him Jackie – that these sheep belonged to their chief, a man called Mossman. Wong–ko–bi–kan shook his head in puzzlement. He could not understand how anybody could own animals, or land for that matter. He looked back bitterly to the time, it seemed only a short while ago, before the white men had come to the narrow valley. Food had been plentiful: kangaroos, wallabies and emus. Now the newcomers' sheep and cattle were driving the Gringai's traditional meat supply away. Even the possums had virtually disappeared, making it impossible for him to replace his cloak with their fur. Worse still, some of the Gringai women had started living with the ghosts, as many of his tribe called the white men. A number of women got sick and died. Others drank the white men's water and behaved as if they were mad. Wong–ko–bi–kan had no compunction in killing the babies spawned by this union of Gringai women and white men. No Gringai man would want a woman who already had a child in tow.

The tribal elder also thought it was just that his tribe could kill the white men's animals for food. After all, the sheep had replaced the kangaroos. Of course the white men guarding their animals and food in their huts had to be speared sometimes, if they tried to stop Wong–ko–bi–kan and his hungry warriors.

Earlier that morning, while Wong–ko–bi–kan was still asleep, two of Mossman's convicts, one of whom was called John Flynn, had walked the seven miles to Underbank, the neighbouring property owned by McKenzie, Dungog's first magistrate.

Flynn shook the shoulders of one of the sleeping men in the rough, wooden slab convict hut close to the substantial stone–built McKenzie house and hissed: 'Thomas, Thomas wake up!' The startled man jerked upright, rubbing sleep from his blood–shot eyes.

'John? What are you doing here?' Thomas Rodwell gasped, slowly recognising one of Mossman's men.

'We was robbed last night by Jackie's blacks. I reckon the bastards will be back and kill us all if we don't chase them off. I think I know where they're camped. We need more men and muskets.'

A former convict and now overseer, Rodwell was also one of McKenzie's police constables. He slowly stirred and then stumbled out of bed. Liz, the young black woman, who had been lying next to him, groaned in deep slumber but did not wake. The room reeked of sweat, unwashed bodies and cheap, illicit grog.

Roused from his sleep by the constable, the magistrate quickly ordered two more of his men to join Flynn and Rodwell and supplied the group with guns and ammunition.

'Take Lumpy,' McKenzie ordered. Rodwell nodded. The young mixed-race boy from a different tribe lived safely at the Mckenzie place. He was good at tracking, even in the dark, and had no love for Jackie and his men. Two more of Mossman's convicts joined the group en route. Dawn had broken as the seven–man party crept towards the Gringai camp. The band divided into two. One, guided by Lumpy, went straight on. In an attempt at a pincer movement, the second, led by Flynn, followed the easier and quicker route along the river bank. His attempt at surprise was thwarted by a flock of sulphur–crested cockatoos, which took sudden squawking flight.

Wong–ko–bi–kan immediately spotted the two groups of white men and reacted swiftly. The women and children were woken and sent off into the deeper bush. The twenty–odd Gringai men split into two platoons. Wong–ko–bi–kan led the first towards the river. The other, led by one of Wong–ko–bi–kan's most trusted lieutenants – called Charlie by the white men – crouched down waiting to ambush Rodwell's advance.

Wong–ko–bi–kan stood up to confront the first white man. It was Flynn. The convict raised his musket and took aim. But before he could shoot, the aborigine threw his spear which pierced Flynn's rib cage. The convict fell to the ground. The remainder of Wong–ko–bi–kan's men threw a shower of spears, none of which hit their targets. Flynn's group fired their muskets and charged after the retreating and now weaponless Aborigines.

205

Rodwell's men were alerted by the sound of Flynn's muskets. They managed to dodge the spears and boomerangs thrown by Charlie's platoon and fired their weapons at the Aborigines, who were now running back into the wood to receive their next orders.

Wong–ko–bi–kan gestured to his men, some of whom were wounded, to follow the women and children. Satisfied nobody was left behind, the Gringai leader turned to flee himself but a rough arm gripped him around his neck and threw him to the ground.

'Got you, you fucking black bastard', said Rodwell.

Flynn was the only white man injured in the attack. His wound did not appear at first too severe. He managed to pull the spear out himself and was helped back to the McKenzie settlement but he deteriorated. The spear had lacerated his lungs. Flynn was put in a cart which set off for the nearest doctor, twenty miles away in Paterson. He survived as far as The Settler's Arms, a small pub next to the Paterson River. A naked Wong–ko–bi–kan was brought before the magistrate's court, convened in McKenzie's home and recorded by Forbes. The accused was sent for trial in the colony's capital. He was manacled hand and foot by Rodwell and taken by cart towards Newcastle for a boat to Sydney. The chafing leg irons soon began to rub the skin off the prisoner's ankles. Blood dripped onto the road. Nobody noticed Charlie shadowing the cart or could see his eyes fill with hatred when he saw his leader's blood on the track.

Wong–ko–bi–ban was finally given some clothes before his court appearance and given a translator: the Reverend Thregold, a Newcastle–based missionary. Although the trial judge, Justice Dowling, thought the attack on the Aborigines was provocative and felt some sympathy towards Wong–ko–bi–kan, the jury found the bewildered Aboriginal guilty of manslaughter. The defence lawyer requested that he be allowed to address the jury on Wong–ko–bi–kan's behalf because it was obvious that taking an oath was not understood by the defendant. Justice Dowling refused because he could not find a precedent and sentenced Wong–ko–bi–kan to transportation for the rest of his life to the harsh gaol in Van Dieman's land.

By the end of the month Wong–ko–bi–kan died in the Hobart hospital. Before his miserable death, Wong–ko–bi–kan's dazed mind wandered back to the white kookaburra and the black snake he had seen on the morning of the attack by the white men. He sobbed as he realised that his people were doomed. Even a dangerous black snake would not win against a patient, laughing white kookaburra.

In Dungog the only repercussion of note was that constable Rodwell was dismissed by McKenzie for being intoxicated. But McKenzie still retained his former constable to manage his convicts – competent overseers were thin on the ground.

Led by Charlie, the killing of sheep and cattle by the Gringai continued. In July 1835 a furious Forbes wrote to the Paterson mounted police for assistance: 'the Blacks have again commenced committing serious depredations in the neighborhood,' including spearing cattle in the bush opposite his own residence.

From time to time in the evenings Rodwell saw Charlie in the distance watching the white man and his black mistress. The overseer chuckled to himself, realising that there must be a link between Liz and a jealous Charlie. Rodwell had seen Charlie running off into the bush after Flynn had been speared and knew that the Gringai warrior must be involved in the ongoing killing of livestock.

One day, by chance, the overseer glimpsed Charlie scouting a flock of sheep. He managed to creep up and knock the Gringai warrior unconscious with his musket. Charlie woke up and found himself in front of a jeering group of five drunk white men. One of them was Rodwell, who had an arm around Liz's shoulders and was fondling her breasts. The overseer took a swig from a bottle and dangled a talisman he had ripped from Charlie's neck.

'Watch this, you piece of nigger shit,' Rodwell snarled as he slowly ripped it apart. The overseer had realised the talisman was important from Liz's horrified reaction when she saw him snatch it from Charlie's neck. The white men and Liz went on carousing and eventually staggered off to bed leaving a bleeding Charlie prostrate on the ground. He recovered sufficiently to crawl away unnoticed into the bush.

Upon hearing Charlie's tale of the outrage, the Gringai elders were in unified agreement. The destruction of the talisman, called a Mura–Mai, warranted a penalty of death against the perpetrators.

It was easy to kill the five convicts. Charlie and his fellow Gringai waited patiently for the one day that the white men did not work. They knew the convicts would start drinking by midday. Sure enough, as dusk fell the men and Liz started to sing drunkenly around an open fire. Clubbed on their heads and speared, the white men were dead in less than two minutes. Only Liz was spared. The Gringai trotted swiftly back to their camp. Charlie's decision not to kill Liz proved his undoing. Her loud wailing woke the McKenzie household up.

'Who did this Liz?' demanded McKenzie as he chucked water over her head and repeatedly slapped her face to sober her up.

In the dark, a petrified Liz had only recognised the single Gringai who had grabbed her hair and stopped himself, at the last second, from clubbing her to death.

'Charlie', she sobbed.

The chase took two weeks but Lumpy finally managed to track the Gringai down in the hills known as the Barrington Tops not far from Dungog. Charlie was arrested and taken away by two police troopers, accompanied by McKenzie and Forbes. After the magistrate and his clerk had departed, the whispered gossip around Dungog was that the remaining Gringai were shot and pushed over a cliff. Mass killing reprisals of Aboriginals had become common throughout the colony's frontier areas. Provided no witness was willing to testify what they had seen, the perpetrators would get off scot–free.

Charlie was tried in Sydney. But this time, as was the custom in an English and Welsh court, Justice Dowling donned a black cap and sentenced the accused to death. Fearful that the concerted attack on the McKenzie property was tantamount to a declaration of war by the Gringai and determined to deter further killings, Governor Darling intervened and ordered that Charlie should be executed in Dungog.

Forbes MacKay had supervised the building of the gallows by a team of his convicts and now watched a short man with a deep scar on his face, grinning as he swung on the gallows rope and landed nimbly on the wooden platform.

'You've done a good job, Mr MacKay,' the man said, rubbing his hands in satisfaction.

Forbes regarded Alexander Green, a former circus tumbler, convict and now the government's hangman with morbid curiosity. Forbes had been sent the official drawings only a week ago; he'd pushed his team of convicts hard to build the gallows on time.

'I hear you were once Superintendent of Convicts at Newcastle?' Green asked. Forbes nodded reluctantly.

'Ah well, that explains why these gallows are so sound.'

Green looked at the half a dozen or so shacks and Dungog's most substantial building: the lock up – also built by Forbes.

'I enjoy these country trips, you know,' grinned Green. 'I can tell from their faces that people are fascinated. In Sydney town the crowd has grown used to hangings.'

The executioner looked up at Forbes: 'Close on fifty every year, Mr MacKay. One a week, just about. That's what you wanted to know. Everybody does.'

Green laughed dryly: 'Governor Darling is a good customer.' And I'm well paid the hangman thought to himself. I get £60 a year for work I enjoy.

He had cheerfully described the execution procedure: Charlie would be led up the steps onto the wooden stage, his chains replaced with leather straps around his feet and his hands tied behind his back. A white hood would then be placed over the condemned man's head.

'The ladies find it distressful to see their faces as they get strangled', Green had explained, smiling to himself.

Forbes and the other onlookers watched fascinated as the hangman finished his final testing, tying a noose around a hessian bag full of soil. The executioner jerked a lever quickly and a trap door in the middle of the stage swung immediately open. The bag shuddered as it jerked violently to a stop in mid–air.

'All set for tomorrow then,' Green said, rubbing his hands.

The Dungog magistrate and his court clerk stood in front of the large crowd who had come to watch the hanging early the following day. All the families from near and far were represented. The wives and children of the landowning class were absent but there were several convict women and their offspring, looking forward to the show.

The crowd's eyes swivelled as the door of the lock–up creaked open. The hand–and–foot manacled prisoner was frog–marched by two red–coated soldiers between two lines of fellow soldiers, leading towards the gallows. The soldiers faced outwards, bayonets fixed. They needn't have bothered. There was not another member of the Gringai tribe in sight.

On the wooden platform Green knocked the chains free with practised ease and tied Charlie up with the leather straps. He flipped the noose over Charlie's head and tightened the knot around the Aboriginal's neck.

During the few seconds before Green pulled the white hood over Charlie's head, Forbes and the Gringai's eyes met. The Scot saw the fury of a man who was losing everything, his dignity and very soul. There was something else: Charlie glared at the clerk as if the white man were a thief.

With a sudden flash of recognition Forbes thoughts were transported back to Prince Edward Island and Strathnaver. Of course, Forbes realised, Charlie's anger was the same as that felt by the MacKay clansmen who had suffered from their chief in Scotland, and the settlers in Prince Edward Island from their proprietors. Land rights were at the root of these bitter disputes.

The crowd hushed as Green put his hands on the trapdoor lever. The hangman glanced quickly around. He always enjoyed increasing the suspense. Green pulled the lever and Charlie dropped.

Forbes looked around at the red–coated soldiers and the stern, determined faces of the white crowd as they watched Charlie's tied feet writhe in agony. The military, settlers and their convicts were united in their determination that their law should be imposed on the blacks.

Only the Reverend Threlgold, who had read Charlie his last rites, showed some compassion.

'This is our land now', Forbes muttered. He exhaled slowly, staring at Charlie's body, now swinging gently like a pendulum: 'You poor, ignorant, bloody fool. This is the British Empire. You had no idea of what you were opposing.'

McKenzie overheard his clerk and chuckled in Gaelic: 'Aye laddie, a mosquito on an elephant's arse would have had a better chance.'

McKenzie watched as the soldiers took Charlie's body down and dumped it casually into a rough coffin: 'He killed five of my men. The murdering savage got what he deserved.'

The attacks on sheep and their shepherds continued but their frequency decreased. By 1837 Williams River was relatively peaceful. Those Gringai who behaved well received blankets from the government to protect them from the winter's cold. The possums may have gone but the laughing white kookaburras remained.

Chapter 32: Myall Creek

'Do you not see Mr Hooke, if my men had allowed those black savages to get away with spearing my cattle and murdering seven white men on my neighbour Mr Łanarch's property, it would be open season on all our cattle and sheep. Not to mention our very own lives. Have we forgotten the McKenzie murders already?

'That bloody idiot of a new governor does not understand that we are the wealth creators of this colony. Not those whining lawyers in Sydney.' The words were spat out from a well–built, bombastic man. His name was Henry Dangar, famous or infamous, depending on one's point of view, throughout New South Wales

There were murmurs of empathy from the gathering of about a dozen prosperous Williams River settlers that John Hooke had kindly hosted in his Wiry Gully home for Dangar.

In 1823, as a government assistant surveyor, Dangar had mapped out Newcastle and surveyed the Hunter Valley where he was granted land. His further work led to his discovery of new fertile lands in the unsettled territory further inland. In 1825 he was found to have abused his public office by misappropriating about 7,000 acres to his family and had been sacked by Governor Darling. Despite failing to clear his name in London, Dangar's ability as a surveyor meant, upon his return, he gained employment with the large Australian Agriculture Company. He eventually returned to his Hunter Valley property and started accruing more land. One big parcel of land he acquired was Myall Creek, in the frontier country outside the 19 counties of the ever–expanding British colony, which was inexorably invading more and more Aboriginal lands.

Furious with the blacks spearing cattle and murdering white men, in June 1838 Dangar's convict stockmen, including one black African, accompanied by others from adjacent stations, had taken advantage of an absence of the property's overseer to round up a group of twenty–eight mainly women, children, babies and elderly blacks. The Aborigines were living peacefully on Dangar's station. Their menfolk were absent. The stockmen were determined to create a deterrent of such frightfulness that it would prevent further transgressions by the local blacks. With pistols and swords they butchered the defenceless group and set fire to their bodies. News of the massacre eventually reached the new governor, George Gipps. Eleven convicts were arrested and sent for trial in Sydney.

Dangar's audience nodded in agreement with Dangar's words. They all resented how the shop keepers and merchants of Sydney seemed oblivious to the fact that their prosperity and very existence depended on the wool, beef, corn and wheat of Williams River settlers and others like them.

'And how do they reward us?' Dangar asked.

'The bloody fools wish to abolish transportation and the supply of free convict labour. The very foundation of this colony's success,' Dangar replied bitterly to his own question.

Having obtained apparent unity in the face of Sydney's foolishness, Dangar proceeded confidently, his English West Country accent becoming more pronounced as he raised his voice: 'Now, gentlemen, I would be most grateful if you joined our Black Association, the body which has been established by me and my associates to fund the defence of these unfortunate men who are being accused of murder by those idiots in Sydney. As if one could murder an ignorant black savage, indeed!'

There was an uneasy silence as the settlers waited for someone to speak for them. Some looked down and shuffled their boots uneasily. They knew that Dangar must have heard the rumours of the killing of a large number of Gringai in the Barrington Tops, the hills near Dungog.

But now relations between the two races around Dungog had been relatively peaceful over the past couple of years. The declining numbers of blacks seemed to have accepted their lot. Nobody wished to alert Sydney's new governor to investigate Dungog's recent history.

'Mr Dangar, none of us here is a stranger to the natives, or bushrangers for that matter, killing our livestock and the risk they pose to our own lives.'

There was a murmur of relief around the room that someone would respond on their behalf. Dangar looked keenly at the source of the Scottish accent. He'd heard that Forbes MacKay had been of great assistance to John Hooke in helping the naive English country squire recover from his financial disaster.

'I have also in the past requested assistance from the police troopers to disperse any of the Gringai around here who were proving a problem.'

Dangar snorted: 'Mr MacKay, if I may say so, that is hypocrisy. We all know what dispersing can entail. Those drunken Irish troopers often shoot the blacks without hesitation.'

Forbes flushed. He knew Dangar spoke the truth.

'Nonetheless, Mr Dangar it is surely better to have some law, however imperfect, rather than none at all.'

Forbes chose his next words carefully: 'And, if I am correct, your Myall Creek property is outwith the colony's limits and you were therefore not able to request support from the troopers?'

Forbes felt no need to add that the Queen's Writ ran over all Australia, in or outside the colony's nineteen counties and, in theory, applied equally to all her subjects, irrespective of skin colour.

'I also hear your overseer is prepared to testify to the guilt of the men?' Forbes asked. Dangar nodded reluctantly.

'I do not know if I speak for everyone here', Forbes continued, 'But I, for one, regret that I do not feel able to join your' – Forbes hesitated deliberately – 'Black Association, and support these men who are accused of a murder of such magnitude.'

Dangar could see that Forbes MacKay's words had struck a chord with his neighbours.

'I agree with you, Forbes. This is a frightfully rum business.'

Dangar frowned and raised his eyebrows at the patrician English tones of a person unknown to him who had just joined in the conversation.

'Dowling, Vincent Dowling, Sir,' said the young man who briefly inclined his head as he introduced himself.

Ah, yes, Dangar thought to himself. Justice Sir James Dowling's boy who managed his father's property. He would have to tread carefully. Dowling could be the judge in the forthcoming trial.

Henry Dangar looked around at the group's now doubtful faces and realised that it would be most unlikely that he would recruit new members in John Hooke's house. Perhaps the Black Association name he'd invented in jest together with his friends was not so funny after all?

Come the following December, Forbes MacKay sat every day in Sydney's Supreme Court and listened to the second trial of the nine men accused of the massacre. The first trial had found the accused not guilty because the evidence presented was too flimsy. A second was reordered. Henry Dangar's outrage at the trial of the white men was shared widely throughout New South Wales; its leading newspaper, the *Sydney Herald*, had declared that 'the whole gang of black animals are not worth the money the colonists will have to pay for printing the silly court documents.'

In Forbes' pocket was a tear–stained letter from his brother, John. Forbes kept repeating its words: 'Dear brother, we will be leaving Prince Edward Island within six months. We have booked our passage to Liverpool. And we have had confirmation of our passage on the *Earl Durham* to arrive sometime in late December or early January 1839. Thank you for arranging this. I understand you will receive the government migrant bounty of £400 for sponsoring us.'

Forbes heart had pounded when he received the letter. Each day he prayed for his brother and his family's safe arrival. He had left Melbee's fields and convict labour in John Hooke's hands and now, every morning, he joined the throng jostling to read the notices posted outside Sydney's post office announcing the expected arrival time of each ship which had been sighted offshore, heading towards Sydney's enormous natural harbour, Port Jackson.

Sitting in the soporifically–hot, mid–summer courtroom, Forbes' thoughts sometimes wandered away from the bewigged lawyers, sweating in their wigs and black cloaks, arguing some arcane point in front of Judge Dowling. Together with the other settlers along the fertile, alluvial soil next to the William's River, Forbes had prospered during the 1830s. His convict labour had worked hard. Melbee's crops and wool had sold for good prices. And over the years he had become

215

good friends with John and Mary Ann Hooke. Forbes taught the Hookes farming and they taught Forbes about horse breeding. The Hookes joined the exclusive club of prominent land owners near the growing town of Dungog. Not long after he had received John's letter, Forbes had managed to snap up a land grant of another 2,500 acres. Forbes smiled: the reunited MacKays were well placed to prosper even more in the forthcoming 1840s, weren't they?

Towards the end of December, Sir John Dowling had donned his well–worn black cap before sentencing seven of the accused to death by hanging. The remaining four prisoners were released. Their conviction had depended on evidence to be supplied by an Aboriginal youth. Mysteriously, the young man, by the name of Davey, had disappeared. No trace was ever found of him again. Rumour had it that Davey had been killed on Dangar's orders.

Chapter 33: Sydney Cove

Paddy Brinkworth was a seeker for a steam tugboat called *Surprise*. His job was to spot ships which would need to be towed into harbour. Paddy was one of Sydney's best. The teenager took up his position at the crack of dawn two or three mornings a week on the southern side of the windswept Heads, the bulbous headlands marking the entrance to Port Jackson. Given the Heads meaning in the nautical world, it always seemed amusing to Paddy that he started his mornings by having a pee. In one of his pockets he had a list of the ships expected to arrive that week. Armed with his powerful telescope he would sweep the horizon looking for approaching sails. On any morning there could be up to a dozen young lads like himself watching for ships. Once he spotted sails he would wait until he was certain he had identified the ship. Paddy could expect a thrashing from his skipper if he raised the alarm only to find out the boat was a nimble coastal packet, in no need of a tow. No, Paddy was only interested in sizeable ships – 300 to 400 ton vessels.

On the 2nd January, 1839 Paddy gazed up from sketching an intriguingly shaped puddle with his fountain of urine. Squinting, he noticed two specks far out to sea. Through his telescope he soon recognised both of them: one was the *Earl Durham* and the other the *Eden*. Both large ships were regular visitors from London. The former carried immigrants. The latter transported convicts to the colony and then would work as a whaler, returning eventually to England with a cargo of valuable oil to grease the mother country's mills – a profitable round trip for its owners.

Muttering that the ships were not prospects for tows and making the excuse that he needed a shit, Paddy sidled off to where his horse was hobbled. He quickly mounted and galloped off. Wise to his tricks, Paddy only had about a five minute start on his competition. But he also had one of the fastest horses so by the time he arrived, half an hour later at Sydney Cove, where all the tug boats were moored, most of them already gently simmering like kettles on a hob, he was at least a precious ten minutes in front of the other lads.

Paddy knew where his skipper was: in bed with his favourite whore in one of the area's many brothels. Most of the *Surprise's* crew were in the adjacent rooms. They were still sleeping off a drinking spree which had started on New Year's Eve. The *Surprise* was one of Sydney's most profitable tug boats and its crew correspondingly well–paid.

'We'll go for the *Durham*', panted his skipper, cursing as he fumbled with his fly buttons. The immigrant ship would need a two way tow: first into the port and then, less than a week later, out to start its return journey to England, full of wool. The *Eden* would need longer to convert itself from human cargo to a working whaler. Its captain knew the harbour well and would wait until a favourable wind to depart with only a short, cheap tow at the start of its whale hunt.

By the time the *Surprise's* half–dressed men had stumbled on board, shovelled more Newcastle coal into the boiler and cast off, their lead had nearly vanished. The more abstemious crew of their principal competition, the *Hero,* left the quay only a couple of minutes behind. The race was on to reach the *Earl Durham* first. The two tug boats steamed east at full speed towards the warm, rising sun, chasing the smoke from their funnels, blown ahead by a westerly breeze, heading seawards, straight down the harbour.

The MacKay family were among the crowd on the top deck as the *Earl Durham* nosed its way between the Heads, not far behind the *Eden*. It was an already hot, humid mid–summer's morning. There was an expectant hush followed by excited chatter as the passengers caught a first tantalising glimpse of a wide expanse of water, stretching for miles into a hazy inland.

The moment was marred by Duncan who wrinkled his nose and asked: 'What's that smell, Father?'

John hesitated, looked down at his son's enquiring eyes and pointed to the Eden: 'That ship is transporting convicts, Duncan. The conditions can be dirty.'

Pre–empting Duncan's next question, his father said: 'Convicts are people who have been expelled from England because they have been caught stealing. They are lucky. Instead of prison back Home, here they work for people like Uncle Forbes.'

'Will they work for us too, Father?'

Before John could answer, the small boy's puzzled interest was ripped away by the blast of two large steam whistles. The *Surprise* and *Hero* suddenly appeared round the bow of the *Eden*, racing for the *Earl Durham*. The *Surprise* was still slightly ahead but the *Hero* seemed to be gaining. Above the noise of their steam engines at full throttle and the staccato slap, slap of their frothing side paddles, the *Earl Durham's* passengers could faintly hear the competing crews shouting insults as they shook fists at each other. Suddenly the *Surprise*'s whistle screeched again and veered starboard – a course which would place it directly in front of its competitor. The *Hero's* skipper spun his wheel hard–a–starboard and avoided a collision by no more than a couple of feet. The race was over. The *Hero* turned slowly around and headed back to the *Eden*, the jeers of the foolhardy *Surprise* loud in their ears. The *Hero's* skipper cursed under his breath and vowed that there would be a settling of scores later that day in The Fortune of War, the favourite drinking haunt of sailors in Sydney Cove.

As the *Earl Durham*, towed by the *Surprise*, overtook the heavier, waddling *Eden* and its straining *Hero*, the new Australians began to admire the unfolding vista in front of them. The immigrants had marvelled at Rio de Janeiro and Cape Town, with their majestic backdrops of Sugar Loaf and Table mountains. But the portal to New South Wales had a different kind of beauty. Sydney's harbour was laced by a series of coves, bays, beaches and jutting promontories. The immigrants from England's West Country were struck by the similarity of some of the quiet coves to those they had left behind in Devon and Cornwall. The rocky headlands reminded some of their native Scotland. In the strong sunshine, rarely experienced in the Old Country, the wet sandstone rocks glistened and the silica in the sandy beaches flickered a welcome to the new arrivals. The immigrants had fallen quiet as they became mesmerised by the grandeur of the harbour and the varied nature of its shoreline. But as windmills and buildings began to appear, excited voices began to point out the features of Sydney town.

To the east were elegant villas which gave way to government buildings including an army barracks. In front of them now was the busy port of Sydney Cove which was full of ships from small to large. The swinging bodies of the seven men executed for the Myall Creek massacre had been taken down from the walls of the gaol overlooking the harbour only a few days before. They glided past a rocky headland and turned into an inlet enclosing a new harbour on the west side of Sydney. Stretching along the shore, an embankment and protruding jetties were still under construction. At the shallow end of the inlet, steam rose from an engine house next to a textile mill. *The Earl Durham* was now carefully tugged alongside a new quay. Thin ropes were first thrown by the crew which the dockers on shore pulled in and then heaved and tied the larger mooring ropes around the cast iron bollards.

On the quay the loud, welcoming crowd presented a novel spectacle to the newcomers. Prosperous merchants and settlers were dressed in plum–coloured swallow–tailed coats and rankeen tights. Poorer settlers, dungaree–men, were clad in cheap blue Indian cotton. Convicts in canary–yellow prison uniform were watched by musket bearing red coated soldiers. And mingling throughout was a motley collection of men in every sort of jacket and headgear from straw beaver to kangaroo skin.

Among the heaving, shouting mass was a tall, well–dressed man standing by himself. He was visibly trembling. Oblivious to the sympathetic looks he was attracting, under his broad–brimmed hat he started to weep. The man made no attempt to wipe his eyes. Tears dripped off his nose as he began to wave. It was Forbes.

Chapter 34 : The Jew Boy Gang

The MacKays were in a jolly mood. It was a Sunday morning in August 1839. After disembarking from the *Earl Durham* in January, earlier that year, John, Sybella and their children had joined Forbes, living in Melbee. The co–habitation went well. Forbes built separate bachelor living quarters but joined in the family meals.

They had all just worshipped in St Anne's Scots kirk in Paterson, about ten miles from their home near Dungog, before going to Sunday lunch at the Hooke's Wiry Gully property. Seventeen–year old George had been left behind to watch Melbee and its convicts.

This was the first time for the new MacKays in Paterson. At first they had joined Forbes worshipping in friends' barns around Dungog, but now felt well enough established to attend the area's only Presbyterian church – though there had been talk of building a kirk in Dungog, nothing had been realised. Forbes had contributed to the cost of building St Anne's on a rocky outcrop close to the Paterson River. Tall, slim, stained glass windows in a gothic–revival style emphasised the church's austere high brick walls, capped by a neat shingle roof. The gentle background sound of the flowing river complemented the overall effect of a simple, tranquil building with intrinsic inner beauty.

After the service, the worshippers lined up to thank the Reverend William Ross who had thundered out a sermon, which brooked no deviation from the Bible.

Outside in the late winter sunshine, Forbes introduced his brother and wife to other Presbyterians from Paterson, Maitland and Clarencetown, keen to meet Forbes' relatives. Young boys, released from religious duty, ran around excitedly. Fathers kept a watchful eye. Girls held their gossiping mothers' hands before they ventured away to play.

A small, excited fist suddenly punched John's thigh; he had no need to ask who it was. Six–year old Duncan was the most exuberant of his children and enjoyed any rough and tumble.

'Father, I want to go and play by the river', the small boy demanded.

'No Duncan, it's too dangerous,' his elder brother Kenneth admonished, running up behind and pulling his brother away.

John looked at his sons and, not for the first time, wondered how two brothers could be so different. Unlike his elder brother had at the same age, Duncan showed little interest in books and rarely spoke unless he needed to. The family suspected that the small boy of few words would become a man of action. Whereas, Kenneth, now aged eleven, to his parents' delight, was already reading adult books, articulated clearly and had refined manners.

Forbes watched his brother, Sybella and their children and sighed contentedly. This is how he had dreamt it would be. His family together again in the Australian sun. He puffed on a cigar, slapped his brother's shoulder and said in Gaelic: 'You know, John, at one stage Reverend Ross' fire and brimstone took me back to when our father used to preach to us in French River.'

'No, Forbes, Father was louder and banged the lectern much harder,' chuckled John.

'Yes, you're right. He certainly used to scare me. But there was one thing which was different today,' Forbes paused and then added sadly, 'there were only a few words in Gaelic.'

'Yes, my children are forgetting our old language,' John observed.

'And their children won't be able to speak a single word. They probably won't even consider themselves Highlanders, let alone Scots,' Forbes said.

'Will they think themselves British, though?' asked a slightly bemused John.

'Yes, but they will think of themselves as Australians first. This country is growing and the drum of independence is beating louder. Sometime in the future our descendants will cut the ties with the motherland and won't even call themselves British.'

John's thoughts strayed back to French River and what might have been. If they had decided to stay, the family would have become Islanders and Canadians eventually. Well, does it matter? We are all God's children, even misguided Catholics, as his Father would have said, John reminded himself, squeezing his bible.

'John, John, stop day dreaming,' called Sybella. 'It's time to leave. We don't want to be late for the Hookes.'

About an hour later the happy, chatting family cart, after it had been ferried across the river on a punt, was trundling along the track to Dungog. They had left the river flood plain behind them and entered a more hilly, thickly wooded section of the road.

Seven pairs of eyes hidden in the trees studied the cart carefully.

'Slim pickings, I'd say.'

'Yes,' an authoritative leader's voice agreed, 'but let's follow them for a while. You never know, they might lead us to something valuable.'

One rider went on carefully ahead to track the cart, the others followed some distance behind until their intended prey had disappeared down the track leading to the Hookes' home, Wiry Gully.

Forbes pulled the horses up, John jerked the squeaky brake and the cart rolled to a stop.

'Hooray, they're here,' the Hooke children shouted as they raced outside to greet the MacKays, who were looking forward to some food and drink after their dusty one hour journey from Paterson.

The two families mingled outside the front verandah for a few minutes while the younger children tried impatiently to pull their parents inside for the meal. Sybella hugged Mary Ann gently. The mother of the Hooke family was pregnant. The two families eventually turned to step up onto the front verandah, when Sybella suddenly screamed, her hand on her chest, as she looked back.

Lined up outside were seven mounted men, all of them pointing muskets or pistols at the Hooke and MacKay men and older boys. Incongruous ribbons fluttered from their horses' bridles and their riders wore colourful cloaks.

The adults knew instantly this must be the gang of bushrangers who had started robbing people about a year ago, gaining a Robin Hood reputation for giving some of their plunder to their victims' convict servants. Some landowners had been whipped if they were known to have mistreated their convicts. The gang had been attacking people closer to the coast and, until now, nobody further inland along the Williams River had been robbed.

'Ladies and gentlemen. No harm will come to anyone, provided you do what I say,' said the gang's leader.

'I will ask you to stand over there,' he pointed with his pistol to a corner of the front yard, 'while my men go inside and help themselves.'

There was something about the gang's swarthy leader which stirred Mary Ann's memory. His London accent had a patina of something from her buried past. Without pausing to think of the baby in her womb, she ran forward and stood in front of his horse. The years fell away and now it was an irate, Miriam Bielkovsky who glared up at the rider and hissed: 'Feh! Schaeme dich! She caught her breath and this time screamed: 'Schaeme dich.'

The startled horse took a step backwards and snorted in fear. The bushranger was astonished to shouted at in Yiddish by a furious, woman, clearly with child, that he should be ashamed of himself. She reminded him uncomfortably of his own mother. He fumbled his reins in embarrassment and muttered, shamefaced in the same language: 'I'm sorry, Madam. We shall leave you and your family in peace.'

Pointing his pistol at the rest of the group on the verandah, he warned : 'Do not try to follow us.'

He lowered his weapon, tugged his horse round and galloped away, followed by the rest of his men. Dust and cedar tree leaves swirled up from the track as the drumming of their horses' hooves gradually died away, leaving a strained silence behind.

The Hooke and MacKay families stood dumbstruck. What was the strange language Mary Ann had spoken? What had she said to the bushrangers' leader which had caused him to leave so quickly?

Although, in time, everyone present realised that Mary Ann must have been originally Jewish, the subject was never spoken about.

Back on the Dungog road, the gang's leader reined his horse in: 'Sorry boys. Something was not quite right about that place. Call it what you will. A sixth sense perhaps,' he lied.

One of the gang spat tobacco juice in an arc towards the ground and wiped his lips with the back of his hand: 'I don't believe you Teddy. That Jew bitch scared you off. Fuck knows what she said in that cursed Hebrew language of yours.'

'You hold your Irish tongue, John Shea. I command here,' ordered his leader.

The rest of the gang was silent. They sided with their chief. Trying to rob an angry, pregnant woman was not an attractive prospect.

Edward Davies was the leader of what came to be known as 'The Jew Boy Gang'. He was the son of a dishonest solicitor's clerk and, ironically, his brother was the chief constable of Penrith, a village near Sydney. The members of his gang, all escaped convicts, had been forced to swear not to kill anyone. Davies fancied himself as a chevalier of the road and dressed his recruits accordingly. In reality, his recruits were vicious criminals – rapists and thieves – happy to indulge their leader's fantasies because he was adept at planning and carrying out raids. Their lair was less than an hour's ride from the MacKays and Hookes in the sandstone hilly country around the 1,000 foot high Pilcher's Mountain. This is where they secretly rested between raids and stashed their booty.

The Jew Boy gang made a round trip every month, swooping down on isolated farms around Paterson, then swiftly on to the Maitland area, robbing homes, and then skirting Newcastle down the coast to Gosford. Their raids were so dramatically swift and with such overpowering force that their victims had no time to resist. Homes were stripped of plate, jewellery and cash. Sometimes the gang locked the occupants up and spent the day feeding, drinking and loading their pack horses, which were led back to their mountain hideout.

In September 1840 the gang attacked the home of a Mr Pilcher – ironically the man after whom Pilcher's Mountain was named – near Maitland. Money and jewellery were taken from a party of visitors but someone sneaked off and alerted the nearby police troopers. A pitched battle ensued. The gang fled chased by a posse led by the ebullient, local magistrate, Major Denny Day. The major was a fearless veteran of the British Army in India. This was the same man whose high reputation had led Governor Gipps to entrust the magistrate with the arrest of the men accused of the Myall Creek massacre.

With the posse on their heels, the gang headed back to their lair to hide their loot and recuperate. It was early morning at Wiry Gully when Major Day and his men galloped up the track and skidded to halt in front of the Hooke home.

The major bellowed: 'Hooke, Mr Hooke where are you sir?'

John Hooke and his boys tumbled out of bed and ran out through the front door, still half dressed. John and his older boys had grabbed muskets, fearing another attack by The Jew Boy Gang.

Day grinned at the alarmed reaction his shouting had caused: 'I take it I am addressing Mr Hooke?' John nodded, his attention inadvertently drawn to a fresh bullet hole in the moustachioed–man's broad brimmed hat.

'Forgive me, Sir. I must make haste. I am the Maitland magistrate, Major Denny Day. We are chasing The Jew Boy, Edward Davies, and his gang. They seem to be heading towards Pilcher's Mountain. I'm told you know the area well and could help us track them?'

John nodded: 'Yes, major. We all know the land well. But my son, Henry, knows it best.'

Day hesitated: 'How old?

John pulled Henry forward: 'He's twenty, Major.'

The major's piercing eyes quickly sized up the young man and nodded: 'He'll do. As quick as you can, gentlemen.'

The posse headed off with Henry at the front next to the major followed by his father and two of his brothers riding with the rest of the posse. Henry soon picked up the gang's tracks where they had left the Dungog Road and led the posse into the maze of gullies, caves and boulders around the mountain.

Tracking was difficult and Henry, expert bushman though he was, had to dismount and lead his horse on foot. After a couple of hours he stopped and looked up at the major: 'They've left, Major.'

'What do you mean?' shouted the exasperated magistrate.

'They must have seen us coming. These are fresh tracks about three hours' old. Seven horses and two pack animals, travelling light. I'd say they are heading back to the Dungog road.'

The major frowned: 'The pack horses are light, you say?'

Henry nodded. Day reckoned the gang must be short on provisions. A store robbery to stock up on food was likely to be the bandits' next move.

The frustrated posse quickly picked up the trail again on the Dungog road and headed west. The Hookes went home. Their local knowledge no longer needed. Still, Henry had established for the major that the numerous old tracks from the same horses meant Pilcher's Mountain must be the gang's main hideout and where they had stashed their now two years' worth of loot.

The hot–tempered John Shea was the cause of Edward Davies' downfall. In the town of Scone, while robbing a store owned by one of the Dangar family, a shop assistant, John Graham, fired a shot at Shea and his accomplice. The young Englishman, not long off the boat, missed. A furious Shea chased after Graham, shot him in the back and killed him. At the same time Davies and the rest of the gang were robbing the St Aubin Arms, the town's hotel and public house. The game was up: in New South Wales an escaped convict murdering a free settler was akin to a black runaway slave killing a white man in the U.S. There would now be a relentless hue and cry until the perpetrators were captured.

The gang fled north, hoping to disappear into the vast, open, inland plains. But Day's rested and freshly replenished posse, reinforced by some outraged citizens of Scone, cornered them in Doughboy Hollow near the hamlet of Murrurundi. A long, blazing gunfight followed which stopped only after the bandits ran out of ammunition. One of the gang managed to sneak through the posse and escape. The others were hauled off in irons to await trial in Sydney.

Edward Davies was the only one of the gang to be represented by a lawyer – paid for by his brother. The lawyer pleaded that Davies' life should be spared because he had not been present at the scene of Graham's murder. Davies' police brother implored the governor to show mercy but it was in vain. The court judge, Sir James Dowling, yet again, put on his now fraying, black cap and passed sentence.

At 9am on the 16th March 1841, Alexander Green put on another grand show when the six men were executed on the public gallows towering above Old Sydney gaol's walls in front of a large, excited crowd. During his last moments Edward Davies was comforted by a rabbi. On the same day, his brother, John Davies, resigned as Penrith's chief constable. The bodies were handed over to surgeons for dissection in the aid of medical knowledge.

The Jew Boy gang refused to reveal where they had hidden their loot. Despite intensive searches of the caves around Pilcher's Mountain it was never found.

Chapter 35: The land of the long white land grab

Three men, two Maoris and a Pakeha – a white man – were looking across the broad flood plain of the River Piako in New Zealand's North Island. One of the men, dressed in a cloak of kiwi feathers, was the local Maori chief, called Koenaki, who shook the hand of the tall, lithe white man called Cormack. The chief had come to know the Pakeha well. A few days ago, Koenaki had agreed the sale of 6,000 acres with Cormack, acting on behalf of a man called McKinley who lived in a big town called Sydney, across the sea in the rest of New South Wales. Koenaki had rubbed noses with Cormack on several occasions. The chief didn't mind 'selling' the land. For him this didn't mean losing the land, only that others might be allowed to live there. The money he received would be used to buy muskets in the tribal fights he and his people were having.

This time the chief's translator explained that Cormack was buying the six thousand acres for three other white men who all had the same name: MacKay. The chief was a little uneasy about this. Were the MacKays a tribe? he asked. Cormack chuckled and replied that indeed they were a tribe but owed allegiance to Queen Victoria. Koenaki was reassured: he knew that the English queen was the paramount chief of the white men's tribes. Besides, the chief had already 'sold' this land to another Pakeha. More money, more muskets.

Cormack looked across the flat land towards the river and picked up a handful of soil. He rubbed it between his thumb and fingers and was struck by the similarity between the rich, alluvial soil with that of, Coorei, his recently sold property along the Williams River where, a couple of months ago, he had stood talking to the MacKay brothers, Forbes and John.

'Conditions here are perfect for growing fine tobacco,' Cormack had gestured with his hand across the lush fields, groaning with tall, swaying plants, stretching down from his farmhouse to the banks of the Williams River.

'I have found them very profitable,' he had continued.

'How many convicts do you need to work the land and process the crop, William?'

'I find six is sufficient.'

Forbes and John had glanced half–heartedly at each other as they tried to concentrate on the commercial possibilities of buying Cormack's farm across the other side of the river from Melbee.

Cormack had come first to his MacKay neighbours when he had decided to sell up and move to Auckland in the New South Wales dependency of New Zealand. By coincidence, the tobacco farmer had first met Forbes in Prince Edward Island, where he had done business with Donald MacKay. W.E. Cormack had become famous in the British North American colonies when he was the first white man to explore the interior of Newfoundland. Like many explorers, Cormack was an energetic, restless man. A bachelor who disliked being too long in one place. After he settled in William's River, he had renewed his friendly acquaintance with his fellow bachelor, Forbes MacKay, and visited his neighbour frequently. They had become close friends. But since the arrival of Forbes' brother and family, the frequency of the visits had to be reduced. Cormack knew it was time for the next episode in his life.

The MacKays did not need to ask Cormack why he was going. The British government was planning to make New Zealand a separate colony. The native chiefs were still amenable to selling land to British settlers at cheap prices, but once New Zealand was recognised as a colony in its own right, the country's remaining land would be controlled by the government in London. A speculative land rush had started with hundreds of well–off colonists in Australia scrambling to buy property from the Maoris in New Zealand.

'William, we thank you for giving us first refusal on the sale of your farm. Frankly, we do not believe we have the expertise to harvest and dry the crop, which we have seen is not a straightforward affair,' John said.

'But we would be interested in investing in New Zealand land,' Forbes added, smiling at the tobacco farmer, knowing full well that was the real reason Cormack had invited the two brothers to visit his farm.

'Yes, we would be delighted if you could act as our agent and purchase land in the name of myself, John and his eldest son, George, who is now seventeen,' Forbes added.

Cormack nodded: 'That will be in order, Forbes. I am delighted to have the MacKays as clients.'

In early 1840 the Maori Chiefs in New Zealand's North Island signed the Treaty of Waitangi which recognised Maori land ownership but gave the sole right to the British government to purchase land. The British now proclaimed sovereignty over all New Zealand: the North Island by treaty, the South Island by discovery.

Realising the treaty had not yet been signed by the Maori chiefs in South Island, the shrewd, ever–entrepreneurial, William Wentworth, ferried the southern chiefs across to Sydney and persuaded them to sell South Island at a knock down price to a consortium, which he headed. Wentworth was now the largest landowner in the whole of the British Empire, the U.K. included.

But Wentworth's avarice had gone too far. Governor Gipps was furious and thundered his condemnation in New South Wales' Legislative Council: 'If all the corruption that has defiled England since the days of the Stuarts were gathered into one heap it would not make such a job as the one Mr Wentworth now asks me to perpetrate; the job, that is to say, of making him a grant of twenty millions of acres at the rate of one hundred acres a farthing.'

The council blocked the purchase and Wentworth was humiliated. The South Island chiefs signed the Treaty of Waitangi and within a year New Zealand was a separate colony. A Land Commission was set up to review all purchases of property before the treaty. Something was clearly amiss because the acreage of land 'bought' from the Maoris was greater than the whole area of New Zealand.

At about the same time Cormack wrote to the MacKays: 'My dear Forbes, I am delighted to confirm that I have bought on your behalf six thousand fertile acres bordering the Pikou River, two thousand acres each in the names of Forbes, John and his son George. I am confident that our purchases will be recognised.

'You may be interested to know that the natives here are fierce and are using the money from land sales to purchase weapons for their tribal wars. Like some of the Australian aborigines they also practise cannibalism. They tend to eat the bodies of their opponents who have shown courage.'

Cormack's confidence that his land purchases would be recognised proved misplaced. The Land Commission did not recognise Forbes and John's claims and only recognised 25 square perches of land – a derisory seventh of an acre – in George's name, and that only by 1864.

The MacKays lost six hundred pounds in their attempted New Zealand land grab. Although, at the time, they dismissed the loss as part of the ups and downs of commerce, the money would have proved a great boon in the coming years.

Chapter 36: Boiling down the 1840s

The swirling edge of the financial storm which had struck Great Britain and North America in 1837 was just starting to ripple onto the shores of New South Wales and its still booming economy at the beginning of 1839, when John and Sybella MacKay and their children disembarked in Sydney.

Later that year Governor Gipps decided to increase the minimum price of land in the colony from 12 shillings to £1 per acre. In an example of how increasing a tax can have the opposite of the desired result, the government revenue from this source plummeted from £316,000 in 1840 down to £15,000 two years later. In 1840 Gipps began to withdraw money from deposits in Sydney's banks to meet the government's £1m commitment for grants for immigrants. The banks were forced to curtail and review loans. And the already hard–pressed financial institutions in the City of London stopped lending money to the colony. The price of wool had already slumped in England.

As a tragic overture to what shortly followed, the MacKay's second eldest boy, William died in the summer of 1840. He had cut himself with an axe and the wound refused to heal. Later the same year a financial tsunami rose up on Australia's beaches and swept inland, drowning the colony's agrarian–based economy. The property bubble burst, companies went bust and many people became bankrupt. Sheep worth 60 shillings in 1840 might sell for one shilling in 1841. Farmers deserted properties and livestock was abandoned. Horses fled inland to the wide, grassy plains and thrived among the kangaroos and emus on the, as yet, uncolonised Aboriginal tribal lands. New South Wales faced ruin.

If financial problems were not already bad enough for the Williams River pioneers, their prospects became even bleaker. Despite furious opposition from farmers and major landowners like William Wentworth, and lesser fry like the MacKays and Hookes, metropolitan Sydney finally had its way and on the 22nd May 1840 the transportation of convicts to New South Wales was ordered to cease. Later that year, the *Eden* unloaded in Sydney the colony's last human cargo of convicts, or government–men as some preferred to call them, more genteelly.

Showing admirable chutzpah, Sydney was declared a city in 1841 and in the same year gas lamps appeared on its streets – the majority of them outside public houses. Although transportation to New South Wales had stopped, the families along the Williams River still enjoyed free labour from their convicts serving out their sentences. The 'system', as it was called, would go on until the last convict had spent his or her time.

In the summer of 1842, a grey–haired woman came out of the door of a large, wooden building on the edge of Dungog and sat wearily down on a bench. She was dressed respectably although her clothes and boots were dirty. She wiped her brow with a greasy hand. Her forehead was deeply lined with sadness and she reeked of dead animals and tallow. Even under the grime it was still possible to discern she must have been beautiful as a young woman.

A few minutes later, Forbes and his younger brother, John MacKay, walked out of the same building behind her, which was belching smoke from a brick chimney and sat down on a bench next to the woman. Like her they stank. She poured water from a pitcher into tin cups. The two heavily–perspiring men drank deeply and gratefully.

'Well, you were right Mary Ann', said John after a few moments, licking water onto his dry lips.

'Your boiling down works will prove our salvation.'

A few minutes later, the group was joined by Mary Ann's husband. The English squire, John Hooke, was, for once, not impeccably turned out. He was wearing a butcher's smock which was dripping blood.

A year previously, the Hooke family matriarch had first heard how boiling sheep and cattle bodies for tallow could help farmers survive the economic nightmare, which had gripped New South Wales. She had first experimented on a small scale. From what she had read in a week–old *Sydney Morning Herald*, it seemed easy enough: all she needed was a large pot full of water and wood for a fire. Mary Ann had persuaded Forbes to butcher half a dozen worthless sheep, remove their intestines and chop off their heads and legs. Each sheep's meat and bones were shoved into the pot, boiled and the fat skimmed off. Tallow was made simply enough by gently boiling the fat. Mary Ann got confirmation from a Mr King, who had started his own boiling down works in Maitland, not far from Newcastle, that her product was of a standard high enough for export to England for use in candles, greasing machinery, and cooking. Mary Ann calculated her sheep were now worth six shillings each, a tenth of their boom time price but much, much better than nothing, and enough for a viable business.

A determined Mary Ann pushed on: she built a larger plant with four pots on Melbee land, conveniently close to Dungog's slaughter house and the Williams River. The four pots were replaced after a year with two industrial scale boilers. The equipment was cheap and easy to obtain from Sydney merchants desperate for sales. The slaughterhouse owner, Mr Finch, was keen to collaborate. His business was on the point of collapse. Slaughtering livestock for Mrs Hooke's project offered him hope.

Inside the building two Hooke boys, both in their twenties, were stirring the pots and feeding the fires. The other two grown up Hooke boys, trained in butchering by the MacKays, were now helping Finch slaughter and prepare animals for boiling down.

The woman and the three men leant back and, in the manner of tired people, looked down at their footwear to clear their minds. Laced up, calf–length boots for Mary Ann, once fashionable and shiny–new but now caked in animal fat and charcoal; heavy–duty, hob–nailed boots for the MacKay brothers and John Hooke, just as filthy. All four of them became lost in thought, dwelling on the tumultuous events of the last few years.

Mary Ann now lent back on the bench and looked up at the bright blue sky. She was conscious that her husband threw her a guilty, sideways glance. She sighed silently to herself: whenever financial matters were discussed, she knew her husband avoided looking straight at her in the eye.

Without Mary Ann's knowledge, John had put a thousand pounds deposit on Dingadee, a 2,000 acre property north of Dungog, belonging to an absentee landlord, Lawrence Myles. John had shook hands on a sale price of two thousand pounds but, after the depression struck, had been unable to find the final instalment. Myles foreclosed and the Hookes reined in their operations to their original property, Wiry Gully. They were badly in debt. Apart from the money they owed Myles, as with nearly all farmers, they had borrowed in advance to buy livestock and equipment.

Guilt finally did for John Hooke. The spirit of the proud but financially incompetent English squire suddenly snapped in 1845. His last words as he died in his wife's arms were: 'Forgive me.'

Forbes had been even worse hit. In 1841 he was forced to sell his largest 2,560 acre holding at a knock down price. Even so, he was, in effect, bankrupt. Like John Hooke he owed Lawrence Myles money. In Forbes' case £700 for a mortgage on Melbee and another £200 to a bank for all his 1,400 cattle. Myles had not foreclosed because he knew that he would only get a pittance for a high–quality property. To be fair to the man, he was also reluctant to throw Forbes and his brother John's family out onto the street. No, he would bide his time and wait until the good times returned.

Mary Ann's boiling down works at Melbee was profitable from the start. The Hookes and MacKays were soon killing about forty cattle and many more sheep a day. The waste from the plant ran straight into the Williams River which soon ran red with blood and stank of offal and rotting intestines. Protests from people living downstream were ignored.

The boiling down works continued at a high rate of production which meant after a matter of months the number of sheep and cattle around Dungog began to run out. Within a year, their remaining convict labour had been trained to run the operation enabling the Hooke and MacKay men to fan out north and west to buy more animals and drive them back home. They found ready sellers among destitute settlers and, further inland, abandoned herds of cattle, sheep and horses. They kept some of the best for themselves. 'Are we reivers now?' John asked Forbes in Gaelic so that his sons would not understand. His brother shivered as he remembered the rustler his father had shot long ago on the drive to Caithness in the Old Country.

'No John, these animals have been left to fend for themselves. Look, they are not even branded.'

Listening to his father and uncle, eleven–year old Duncan shrugged his shoulders at his older brothers, seventeen year old, Kenneth, and twenty–three year old, George. Duncan only understood a few words in Gaelic learnt at his school in Maitland; his elder brothers not many more. They were used to their uncle and father speaking in their mother tongue when they did not want to be understood by the younger MacKays.

On their travels inland the Dungog men encountered a trickle of destitute settlers, heading southwards, who had been scared off the northern, sweeping plains, outside the official area of the colony, by fierce, 'wild blacks' who threatened to spear white men and their livestock. This was when the MacKays first heard the name of an area called Moonie River.

Despite the warnings from the settlers fleeing southwards, the oldest of John MacKay's sons, George, was sorely tempted by the talk of wide, empty space, there for the taking. After all, he reasoned, the Gringai had been tamed easily enough around the Williams River.

One lazy, warm evening, the MacKay family was sprawled out, sitting and chatting on Melbee's verandah, George broached the subject: 'Father, this economic malaise will not last forever. There must be an opportunity to lay claim to large areas of country, further north and profit when the good times return.'

John looked at his son. He knew George was right. The success of Melbee's boiling down works meant the family had arrested the decline in their fortunes. Although they still had loans to pay off, they now had some money in the bank. There were enough MacKay men and women to supervise the few remaining convicts, serving out their time, if George left to explore the north. But it could be dangerous, even if only half the stories of the hostile blacks were true.

'John, we should let George go,' Sybella said quietly from her rocking–chair on the verandah.

Surprised, her husband turned around to stare at his normally cautious wife.

Sybella smiled: 'This is not a risky venture out to sea like the *Jessie* was in Prince Edward Island. We do not have to borrow money to finance a reconnaissance.'

Forbes agreed: 'Yes, Uncle Donald over extended himself with that damn ship. This is different.'

He waved his cigar around: 'But like it was in Prince Edward Island, all the good land around here is now taken.'

Forbes looked at his brother, John, and his wife: 'Some of your boys will have to seek their fortune elsewhere. I have every confidence that George knows how to avoid trouble from the blacks, wherever he goes. He can ride and shoot as well as any man.'

The rest of the family had been listening intently, none more so than one of the youngest boys, Duncan, who pleaded: 'Father, please let me go with George.' Ignoring the smirks from his older brothers, he stuck out his chin pugnaciously and pushed on: 'I am the family's bestest and fastest rider. And I know how to shoot.'

Forbes looked affectionately at his nephew: the young lad was right. He had grown up quickly on the cattle–buying forays.

John looked around at all the family: 'Aye, I agree George is right.' Then he smiled and tousled Duncan's long, wavy black hair: 'But I, not you young man, will go with George. I'm sorry. You will have to stay and help look after your mother and sisters. Be patient, your time will come.'

Duncan's father looked up: 'If we discover empty land which has potential we might become squatters.'

There was a short silence while the rest of the family digested John's decision.

'What is a squatter, father?' piped up one of the daughters.

'Why Johanna, it's simply somebody who goes to live – to squat, people call it – outside the official limits of the colony on some land which nobody is using.'

The thirteen–year old girl frowned: 'Is that lawful? Doesn't the Queen own all the land?'

'Yes, you are correct. Even we pay a small rent for Melbee to her. More precisely to the governor who acts on her behalf.'

'But you are right to ask Johanna,' her father reassured her. 'The governor turns a blind eye to squatters. In fact, he has recently started issuing licenses to them provided they stock the land with animals. We all know that the colony is growing and that someday soon the boundaries will have to be pushed outwards.

'Those people who are squatters will surely have first claim on how the land is to be allocated.'

Johanna nodded. She understood her father but now hesitated before asking her next question: 'What about the natives, Father? Don't the blacks have some rights to the land?'

John chewed his lower lip. This was an unexpected question from his daughter.

Her uncle broke his brother's short embarrassed silence: 'No, Johanna. They do not.'

In answer to Johanna's puzzled face, Forbes continued: 'When we British arrived we couldn't see any difference between the nomadic tribes or find any chiefs with whom to agree a treaty.'

Forbes shrugged his shoulders: 'You know how primitive the blacks are?'

Johanna nodded doubtfully.

'So we declared the land to be *terra nullius*.' Forbes pre–empted his niece's next question: 'That is Latin for nobody's land.'

Now all the children looked blank: 'Territory which can be claimed by men from the first 'civilised' country discovering it,' he explained.

The family could see that Johanna was not convinced.

Forbes ploughed on: 'By contrast, in New Zealand we found distinct tribes and chiefs among the Maoris so we negotiated a treaty which recognised their land rights.' Forbes thought it best not to confuse the issue for Johanna by mentioning that the New Zealand Aborigines had been persuaded that they should only sell their land to the British government. Something, he remembered ruefully, which had caused him and his brother to lose money a few years before.

But Johanna was determined to have the last say: 'But, Father aren't the blacks a bit like those MacKay clansmen whose rights were ignored by Lord Reay?'

239

The awkward question was left hanging in the air. John felt a pang of regret in telling his children about their family's history.

Hearing of their expedition, a neighbour, Sam Cobb, asked to join them. Sam was the younger brother of George who had inherited Anambah, a property not far from Melbee. With no inheritance and money Sam had nothing to lose and plenty to gain if the foray northwards succeeded.

Within a week the three men headed into the unknown lands far to the north of Dungog. They set a course for the Moonie River.

'Walker and his force soon established themselves. He tamed the natives, saved the whites, and made the country comparatively safe', *The Queensland Native Mounted Police*, Sergeant A. Whittington, 1964

Chapter 37: A declaration of war

Four men, two children and one woman fled towards the front door of the wooden slab hut. A spear thudded into the ground narrowly missing one of the children. The door was slammed shut and barricaded with a plank of thick timber suspended between two metal hooks on its frame.

'How many?'

George MacKay squinted through one of the narrow gun ports which had been sawed through the building's wooden walls.

'About two hundred, Father.'

John swore silently to himself. He had half–expected an attack from the blacks on the settlers on the Moonie River, about three hundred miles north of Dungog. But he was surprised and alarmed by their large number.

Not long after the three men had left Dungog and headed north, the government's Surveyor General, Thomas Mitchell, had started in 1845 on an expedition to ascertain whether there was an overland route from Sydney to the continent's northern coast, some 1,000 miles from Sydney. After leaving the nineteen counties of the colony, Mitchell passed the isolated homesteads of squatters. The further north he travelled, the number of homes dwindled away.

Mitchell reached the Moonie River and its rolling fertile plains in 1846. The surveyor had met only a handful of Aborigines whose curiosity appeared aroused by such a big party of white men. The natives had kept their distance. To his surprise, so far from Sydney, Mitchell found that there were already squatters along the river. Three of them were John and George MacKay and Sam Cobb.

When they had arrived the year before, the Dungog squatters had worked fast to cut the initials JM into tree trunks along the banks of the Moonie to establish the limits of John MacKay's claim. They built a solid wooden slab hut, which they called Ningan, on the other side of the river from the home of a squatter family called Roach. The watching Aborigines appeared indifferent.

Leaving Sam Cobb behind to protect the claim, John and George had returned to Melbee and paid their squatter's licence fee to the government agent in the Hunter Valley. They returned within three months with three hundred head of cattle to stock their new property.

Unknown to the settlers along the Moonie River, every three years thousands of Aborigines from different tribes travelled from hundreds of miles around to gather on Mount Mowbullan, the highest peak in a range of mountain forests of bunya pines, at a massive corroboree – a festival of competitions, dancing, music and eating. The majestic bunya, which can grow to a height of 120 feet, flowers every three years when its football–sized cones, with their delicious kernels of fruit, crash to the ground. Putting aside their usual antipathy, the tribes feasted together on the fruit, sang, and competed in spear and boomerang throwing. In 1841, and then again in 1844, the tribal elders angrily discussed the increasing advance of the white man from their coastal settlement at Morton Bay who threatened their traditional sources of food supply and molested their women. Their fury increased after 1842 when poisoned flour had been left behind by shepherds at a place the white man called Kilcoy.

After the corroborees the elders sent the tribes home with the grim order to ambush and slaughter every white man and their flocks and herds until the land was free from the invader. These more northerly tribes had yet to learn, as the southern tribes around Sydney already had, that behind the few white men they had encountered would be thousands of others armed with deadly weapons, which rendered their traditional spear and throwing stick obsolete.

The inland tribe around the Moonie River was the Kamilaroi. They had previously warned off some of the white men entering their territory but, unlike the tribes nearer the coast, they had perceived little threat from the few who remained. The Kamilaroi's relative indifference to the white incomers was about to change.

Mitchell had sent word back to Sydney about his discovery of new land of grazing potential around the Moonie River and further north. The government decided to open up the new territory for settlement and regularise the ownership of land. From 1847 onwards squatters' licences would be dispensed with and any settlers would have to apply for leaseholds. George MacKay was one of the early applicants. A land rush started. Hundreds of settlers trekked north.

The reaction from the blacks was swift and brutal. One morning a man staggered, leading his horse, into the Ningan station. They were both covered in red dust, exhausted and thirsty. Over gulps of water the man gasped he had been forced to flee for his life from a large cattle farm – a station – recently started to the north at Mount Abundance. The blacks had killed several fellow stockmen and the sheep. He looked over his shoulder: 'Mr MacKay, I recommend you join me in abandoning your home.'

The man was still trembling in fear. He looked around at the group who had gathered to hear his news: 'You risk your lives if you stay. There are too many.'

But stay they did, the men from Dungog. They somehow beat off several attacks.

In 1848 John managed to get a letter to the Sydney Morning Herald in which he complained vehemently that not only did the Aborigines 'kill our cattle but our horses are speared and ourselves are in danger every time we go out. Unless the government give us some protection this part of the Moonee will have to be abandoned.'

The seemingly inevitable bloody cycle of Aboriginal killing of livestock and white men, followed by mass reprisals by the settlers began. At one stage every homestead in the region came under attack. The few police troopers in the territory proved powerless against the high numbers of the fierce tribes.

John MacKay's letter to the newspaper had been noticed. In 1848 Governor Fitzroy decided to act and sanctioned the establishment of a detachment of mounted native police for which he allocated the sum of £1,000. Allocating money in a budget is not the same as spending it. The settlers around the Moonie and neighbouring MacIntyre River had to dig into their own pockets to help fund the new police.

Under the command of Frederick – 'Filibuster' – Walker, the force was recruited deliberately from four southern tribes – tribal hatred would be given full rein. Walker respected his black troopers but he was brutal in putting down 'wild blacks'. He also advocated a divide and rule policy of breaking up large groups of Aboriginals and forcing them to live in smaller numbers on the settlers' stations. He threatened not to help settlers who did not conform. Walker was therefore not universally popular with his white compatriots.

Although numbering no more than about one hundred and twenty men at the end of its service, the native police became one of the most vicious instruments of the invasion of the northern districts of New South Wales. They combined Aboriginal tracking skills with a high degree of horsemanship and carbine sharp–shooting. Not for the first time settlers wondered why (and thanked God) that the hostile tribes had not embraced horses and guns in their resistance to the British.

Two native troopers and Walker's second–in–command, Lieutenant Richard Marshall, were billeted at Ningan. The black troopers slept in their humpies outside; Marshall was inside. The small number of blacks at Ningan had melted away after the native police's arrival. After the evening meals prepared by Mrs Roach, Marshall was not reluctant to describe the new force's operations and its commanding officer.

'If I may be frank, Mr MacKay: Captain Walker likes a drop or two. He is – how should I express it – sometimes overcome with enthusiasm to stamp out the hostile blacks.'

'Our black troopers are not restrained', Marshall coughed awkwardly, 'and they are allowed to take matters into their own hands.'

John MacKay had already heard that Walker was overseeing a merciless campaign of murder, kidnapping and rape. John was also guiltily aware that his father, William, an elder of the kirk, would have been against any inhumane behaviour.

Marshall noticed John grimacing: 'This is war Mr MacKay. When our fathers' generation fought the French, it was kill or be killed. And these are savages. They kill with impunity.' The lieutenant downed a tumbler full of brandy which he carefully replaced down on the table. John noticed the police officer's hand was trembling. 'Besides, they sometimes eat the dead.'

Marshall fell silent for a moment.

He picked up the bottle of brandy and looked at John: 'May I?'

'Of course.'

Marshall grinned thinly as he looked at the four squatters: 'When we commence our dispersals I ride at the back of my troop. Do you know why?'

'Trackers always go first,' observed George MacKay, shrugging his shoulders with an obvious answer to an obvious question.

'Yes,' Marshall nodded. 'But I allow the whole troop to go in front. I am last by a good way.'

The officer put his glass down again: 'If I am ever asked I will be able to say truthfully that I saw nothing untoward. And we all know that an Aboriginal's evidence is inadmissible in an English court of law. That is unless the savages become Christian and can swear truthfully on the Bible.'

John turned away from the conversation, his mind full of doubt. George looked up: 'Father, I believe the governor prefers to ignore that we are fighting a war. Now that he has had to send reinforcements to New Zealand to fight the Maoris he has no soldiers to help us. We are on our own.'

John nodded. He rationalised his concerns that in times of war desperate measures were required. They all knew the local Kamilaroi and Bigambul warriors along the Moonie and MacIntyre rivers were tough adversaries. More numerous than the Gringai had been in Williams River, the district's tribes posed a dangerous threat to the settlers. Although the British government policy accorded Aborigines rights to stay on leasehold land, this was more observed in the breach than in the observance. Walker had injudiciously described in his official despatches to the Colonial Secretary in Sydney a pitched battle with some hundreds of Bigambul, following the killing of a number of white men. In a moment of frankness he had written: 'I much regretted not having one hour more of daylight and I would have annihilated the lot, among which were six murderers and all the rest living solely on cattle …'. According to William Telfer, a drover who later worked in the area, 'nearly one hundred perished under the sword and bullet of the white man' on that occasion.

Rumours of atrocities against the Aborigines filtered back to Sydney but officialdom found it impossible to gather sufficient evidence to substantiate the whispered allegations. A conspiracy of silence – omerta – was maintained by the settlers and the native police officers, accompanied by downright obstruction. The lessons of Myall Creek had been learnt: no more white men would swing for killing blacks.

Walker's campaign was successful: his troopers killed and harried most of the hostile blacks and forced the survivors to retreat inland into the 'back country'. The settlers along the Moonie and MacIntyre began to establish viable enterprises. The Mackay men left in Dungog would take supplies up to the Moonie and drive cattle back down to Melbee for boiling down.

And then something momentous happened in 1851, which was to drain the Moonie of many of its white men. But before that the MacKay family was struck with tragedy at Melbee.

Chapter 38: The stroke

Saddle–sore and filthy, Forbes, Kenneth and Duncan MacKay closed the gate of the cattle pen next to Melbee's boiling down works, into which they had just herded about two hundred head. The men had returned home after a month in the saddle from the Moonie. They slid wearily out of their saddles down onto the ground.

'What's happening? Is it an earthquake?' Forbes' strained voice suddenly demanded as he staggered on his feet, swaying from left to right, as if drunk.

'Uncle Forbes, are you alright?' his two frightened nephews shouted.

Kenneth and Duncan stared at Forbes' face in horrified fascination; the right hand side had drooped. The side of his mouth collapsed and he started to dribble.

A puzzled Forbes shook his head. Some sparks had suddenly appeared in his eyes. He tried to lift his right hand to rub them away but it had become as heavy as a cannon ball. His right leg buckled and he collapsed to the ground.

'Dear God,' a terrified Forbes just managed to blurt out in a heavily slurred voice.

'Quick Duncan, ride as fast as you can and fetch Mrs Hooke immediately,' Kenneth ordered his younger brother.

But a desperate Mary Ann could do nothing.

'Forbes, dear Forbes can you understand me?' she gently asked, staring closely into Forbes' eyes, his head cradled on her lap.

Forbes gurgled back, his eyes flashing wildly at a shocked Sybella who had rushed outside.

After about twenty minutes Mary Ann gave up. She looked up sadly at Sybella: 'It's no use. He has lost his mind. I fear I can do nothing.'

'No I haven't,' Forbes screamed. But no words came out of his mouth just more meaningless, bubbling gibberish. In a furious panic Forbes lifted his left hand and struck Mary Ann as he shouted: 'You stupid bitch. Can't you hear me?' But to the listener it was just more mad, frothy gurgling.

Kenneth moved to restrain Forbes who wrestled back and kicked his nephew hard with his left leg. Mary Ann, helped by Kenneth and Sybella, held Forbes down and tied his legs and hands. Forbes frothed at the mouth even more. He had a nightmarish realisation that he was now trussed up as securely as the Gringai, Charlie, had been at his execution.

Sybella and Kenneth took a restrained Forbes down to Newcastle and then by steamer to Sydney. Sybella wept as she got confirmation from two doctors in Darlinghurst Gaol that her brother–in–law had become deranged – legally a dangerous lunatic. Subsequently confirmed by a judge, Sybella handed Forbes over to the care of Tarban Creek Lunatic Asylum. She made sure the warders had enough money to look after Forbes properly and promised that someone would return regularly to visit their new inmate.

'No, no,' Forbes screamed at Sybella and Kenneth as they departed.

Forbes was taken out of his cell once a day when he was wheeled around the exercise yard where the other lunatic prisoners gathered. Some were wailing, some sat slumped next to the wall. Others were in wheelchairs. And some were manacled with chains around hands and feet. It was a madhouse.

'Mr MacKay is it not?' a short man with a scar face cackled at Forbes one morning.

'You remember me Sir? Course you do. I hanged that black bastard, Charlie, on those stout gallows you built in Dungog.'

Forbes eyes flashed in recognition. Yes, the little man was the former public executioner, Alexander Green. Was it God's punishment that the hangman and the gallows builder were now incarcerated together in a living Hell, Forbes wondered despondently.

'Get out of the way, Green,' the warden pushing Forbes chair ordered warily. The hangman had a reputation of being unstable and capable of sudden violence – he had received a short sentence for being drunk and disorderly. Green had been sent to Tarban Creek for his own safety. In Darlinghurst Gaol he would have been lynched. The short man hopped aside and grinned: 'You recognised me. I know you did, Mr MacKay. You can't be that mad after all.'

Forbes' head slumped forward and his mind slipped back into that dark, abyss that only those who are trapped in their bodies unable to communicate can understand.

'God forgive me for my past sins,' Forbes prayed.

The warden jeered: 'You sound like a baby gurgling.'

Forbes was wheeled back to his cell where he was stripped and his faeces–ridden night gown taken off. He was given a short wash and then a clean gown was put on him. He would be washed and changed again in a week.

The MacKays at home in Melbee often thought of Forbes and his horribly quick transition from a vibrant, big man into a gibbering, violent idiot. Sybella prayed every night that Forbes' suffering would be short and he would be released quickly from this world before her husband, John, visited from the Moonie. She did not look forward to being forced to tell him of his brother's plight. At the start Sybella or Kenneth tried to visit Forbes every month. The frequency of their visits declined quickly. What was the point, Sybella asked herself, when her visits seemed to upset Forbes. His mad eyes flashed as he waved his left arm wildly and lashed out with his left leg furiously.

Then, another man, purely by chance, going about his work, recognised Forbes in the exercise yard. His name was Robert Dixon who was a government surveyor. Their paths had crossed near Dungog when Dixon had been preparing maps of the Hunter Valley. The surveyor had been entertained at Melbee. Now Dixon was carrying out some survey work of the asylum. Saddened by Forbes' unfortunate condition, the surveyor wrote to the MacKays and offered to visit Forbes regularly and check he was being well looked after. A grateful Sybella wrote back, accepting Dixon's kind offer.

It was 1849 and Forbes was aged fifty–seven. After a year of purgatory, sitting alone in his cell, Forbes was praying. Like his younger brother, every day Forbes beseeched the Lord to forgive his sins and allow him to die. Forbes sighed and began to subside into an uneasy stupor – half sleep, half coma. As he was drifting off a vision of his brother's face floated across his closed eyes. Somehow Forbes managed to say something faintly intelligible; he croaked his brother's name: 'John, John.'

Forbes clenched his left hand in excitement at the sound of his voice enunciating a word. Dear God: would he, after all, be able to speak again? His emotion reached fever pitch as he now also sensed, rather than saw, an imperceptible twitch in his right hand. From then on, while alone, Forbes practised speaking and moving his right hand every day. He did not want to attract the warders' ridicule. His progress was minuscule, nonetheless progress it was.

While Forbes was imprisoned in his cell, John had left his sons in the now pacified Moonie, enabling him at Melbee to grow crops for the family's food. All their convicts had now served their time and left, forcing John to do much of the work himself. One day in January 1851, sweating in the fierce mid–summer sun, John was ploughing. His experienced team moved quickly and smoothly through the soft alluvial soil. Suddenly a large tiger snake slithered across the ground in front of the horses. The panicking team shuddered to a halt and reared in the air, desperate to crush the reptile with their hooves. John's momentum carried him rapidly forward onto the plough's protruding handle. He felt a rib crack, fell to the ground in agony and passed out. The horses bolted, dragging the plough on its side. Sybella screamed as she saw the unattended plough, zigzagging crazily along the ground, pulled by a straining, hysterical team of horses.

Once again Mary Ann Hooke was sent for: 'He has a broken rib, Sybella. I can bind the bone in place. But I fear he has internal damage which I cannot treat. He needs a surgeon.'

John flitted in and out of consciousness. He began to cough blood.

'We must get him to Newcastle, Sybella,' Mary Ann advised.

'There is a surgeon there who has experience of war wounds.'

She put a comforting hand on Sybella's shoulder: 'It is his best hope.'

John was made as comfortable as possible in a cart and taken the fifteen miles to Clarencetown, the upper navigable limit of the Williams River, where he was gently lifted aboard a steamer for Newcastle.

On board the boat and semi–conscious, John had a vision of Forbes speaking to him. He clenched Sybella's hand and sat up with a start. He whispered urgently to his wife: 'Sybella, you must tell George to fetch Forbes.'

'Hush dear. Of course we can fetch him together when you are better.'

But John died in his weeping wife's arms at the Newcastle dockside.

The family buried John in the Presbyterian graveyard in East Maitland near Newcastle. The simple inscription on the headstone read: 'To the memory of John MacKay native of Tongue, Sutherland, Scotland, who emigrated from Prince Edward Island to this colony AD 1838. Died at Newcastle January 20th 1851 aged 51 years.

Another year passed before Sybella could summon herself to dwell on her husband's death and repeat John's last request to their eldest son, George.

Back in his stinking cell, Forbes continued to improve slowly. By early 1851 he even dared dream of the day he would be able to extend his right hand in welcome to his younger brother and say: 'Take me home to Melbee, John!'

Part 8: Boom times again

'This is a memorable day in the history of New South Wales. I shall be a baronet, you will be knighted, and my old horse will be stuffed, put in a case, and sent to the British Museum!'

Edward Hargraves, 1851

Chapter 39: Gold

'Put it away, Mr Clarke, or we will have our throats cut,' the governor, Sir George Gipps, had said in 1844 to the Reverend William Clarke when the clergyman and keen amateur geologist had shown him particles of gold he had discovered near the inland town of Bathurst. Gipps shivered: 'The last thing we need is men deserting the farms in a wild goose chase for gold.'

'Sir George, my traces of gold merely confirm what others have found before. It is surely only a matter of time before a large discovery is made.'

Gipps regarded Clarke morosely. The governor was part of the technocratic intelligentsia which had begun to dominate the senior ranks of the British Army as a result of the Industrial Revolution. After being commissioned as an officer, Gipps trained as an engineer at the British Army's Royal Military Academy, in the Woolwich suburb of London, whose graduates were prone to regard the civilian products of the older universities as dilettantes. Like the perpetual thorn in his side, William Wentworth, Clarke had attended Cambridge University. A black mark as far as Gipps was concerned. Jealous officers who had bought their officer's commissions and fearing fewer promotion prospects, because they had not attended Woolwich, sneered that its graduates were 'mad, married or Methodist'. Quite why this was an insult was never clear. Perhaps it was because the army's more traditional upper class generals would never have dreamt of entering anything other than a Church of England and their knowledge of physics was scanty, at best.

The governor had enough problems already without having to consider gold mining. New South Wales was virtually bankrupt. He wished the Reverend would return to tend his church flock or resume his headmastership of The Kings School Parramatta – the academy for the sons of the colony's elite. Politely Gipps stood and ushered Clarke to the door. The governor sighed as he sat down again in front of the large pile of paperwork on his desk. He picked up the latest file and forced himself to read its petition from the settlers living around Dungog, appealing against his decision to impose a tax on them to help fund their constabulary. Well, if the people living in the Williams River valley wanted police protection, they would have to help pay for it Gipps told himself.

Blast that man, Clarke, muttered Gipps, as his thoughts, against his better wishes, wandered back to the mention of gold. The governor forced himself to concentrate on his administrative tasks.

But events eventually overtook Gipps' apathetic reaction to Clarke's prediction. Five years later able young men in New South Wales started, at an alarming rate, to sail away and join the 1849 Californian gold rush. Gipps remembered Clarke's words and obtained London's approval to allow a search for gold.

The man who first found viable deposits of the yellow mineral was a big bear of a man who had returned to Sydney from California. Edward Hargraves was his name. He had been unsuccessful in America but had mastered techniques for gold prospecting. In 1851 he found gold near Bathurst. His discovery was recognised by the governor in February 1852 and Hargraves was given a £10,000 reward.

Gold fever erupted. As Gipps had feared, men deserted town and country, lured by stories of easy gold. And a torrent of men started to pour into Sydney Harbour from every part of the British Empire and many other countries.

Men from all walks of life hurried west from all over the colony: servants, farm labourers and absconding convicts, still serving out their time. Suppliers of tools and services soon followed. Butchers and hardware stores hastily erected crude shops and opened their doors. Owners of dance halls and brothels erected marquees. The number of people on the once bustling streets of Sydney began to dwindle. The Williams River farms were hit hard by the steady disappearance of their remaining farm labour.

Then welcome good news arrived for the farmers around Dungog. Prospecting was heavy work. Although cheap, illicit alcohol – called sly grog – slaked the thirst of the miners – diggers as they became known – food was in short supply. Prices of beef and mutton rose swiftly. The Williams River settlers were quick to notice.

Sitting in Melbee's large kitchen one morning, two widows regarded each other affectionately over their tea cups. Both were well into their fifties. Already firm friends, Sybella MacKay and Mary Ann Hooke had become even closer after their husbands had died.

'More tea, Mary Ann?'

'Thank you, Sybella,' Mary Ann smiled.

Both women watched Sybella's daughter, Jessy Johanna, as she gently poured the milk first and then tilted the pot carefully to avoid spilling any tea. Sybella's expression was a mother's mixture of love and anxiety. Her daughter was already twenty. Eligible young men were scarce around Dungog and getting scarcer, as the gold fields lured them away.

Sybella thanked God that she'd managed to marry off her eldest daughter, Jane, to Sir James Dowling's boy, Vincent, a couple of years ago. The judge had died of exhaustion six years before and Vincent had inherited his debt–free, Canningulla estate and its convicts. The family's Sydney home had gone to his younger lawyer brother. Sybella had sighed with relief that Vincent had been besotted with Jane, despite her age of twenty–four. Now she fretted about Jessy Johanna. Thankfully, it was far too early to worry about her other two girls, Amelia and Louisa.

Mary Ann empathised with Sybella's transparent emotions. Although her elder children had been mainly boys, she now had two teenage daughters, Emily and Leonora, with a third, Adelaide, following shortly behind. She too foresaw matrimonial challenges ahead. Even without the rush to the goldfields, there had been a lack of eligible men in the William's River and all places around. Eligible meant sufficient money to keep a wife and raise a family in comfort. It also ruled out anybody whose family was stained by convict blood.

The two matriarchs were firmly in charge of their respective families. Melbee belonged to Sybella and Wiry Gully belonged to Mary Ann. And their children knew it. George, the eldest MacKay son fretted that his mother would divide Melbee up too generously between him and his siblings. The eldest Hooke boy, John, named after his father, shared similar fears for Wiry Gully.

There was a slight tremble of excitement in Sybella's hand as she placed her cup and saucer down on the table: 'Dare we believe, Mary Ann, that the good times might be returning?'

'I believe that could well be the case,' Mary Ann nodded.

'It would be a blessed relief to close our boiling down works,' she added wearily.

Mary Ann and Sybella had already discussed the possibility of driving sheep and cattle down the 200 odd miles to Bathurst. Sybella was pleased that George, who had rushed down from the Moonie, leaving Sam Cobb in charge, would be able to lead the drive. The news that the lawless, debauched goldfields might be morally dangerous to their sons had also figured in their thoughts. But, as Sybella remarked: 'Our young men have dealt with thieving bushrangers and blacks. I have confidence they will manage whatever they would encounter near Bathurst.'

'They will have to leave as soon as possible. Winters can be cold on the central tablelands,' warned Mary Ann.

Safety in numbers dictated the MacKay and Hooke boys should team up, agreed their mothers. Hearing of the decision by the MacKays and Hookes to drive cattle to the goldfields, Sybella's son–in–law, Vincent Dowling, joined the enterprise with his stock. The plan was to take about 1,000 head to the goldfields and then cut out the middle men – butchers – and set up their own butchery. They would then sell the cuts direct to the diggers, maximising their profits.

Three weeks out from Dungog, heading south, nearing Bathurst's Ophir goldfield, Vincent Dowling gestured towards a hill about a mile ahead with his expensive telescope, before handing it to his younger brother–in–law, seventeen–year old, Duncan. The two young men were riding point about half a mile ahead of the mob of cattle. 'Have a look young Duncan. Do you see the rider up there watching us?'

Duncan squinted one eye, looked through the telescope and adjusted its focus. He saw an unkempt, bearded man on a horse. The rider was holding a musket across his chest. The man leant back in his saddle and let his horse bend its neck down to chew some grass.

Duncan could now see two saddle pistols and a sword handle at the man's side.

'He looks like a bushranger, Vincent!'

Vincent nodded. The thirty–five year old polished and privileged son of a judge had taken a shine to his much younger companion. True, Duncan could run wild and behave selfishly but Vincent envied his young brother–in–law's enthusiastic, youthful belief that anything was possible. His own upbringing had been more constrained by his father's admonition that book learning was the foundation of success. The judge had been disappointed that Vincent, unlike his younger brother, had showed no aptitude for the law.

'You're right. The bastard is scouting us. I caught a glimpse of him about an hour ago and thought he was just passing by.'

The following morning the crew breathed a sigh of relief. There had been no attempt to steal cattle during the night. Perhaps the rider had been scared off by the sight of the well–armed, eight–man crew? The day passed off without the rider being spotted again.

But an attack came at about two o'clock the following morning. The crew had been lulled into a false sense of security. Most were asleep. Only four men, Vincent and Duncan, among them, were out patrolling.

'Hush, Vincent,' Duncan whispered as he pulled his horse up. Yes there it was again – the sound of a horse gently easing forward into the herd, pushing lowing cattle aside. Through the gloom they could now just about see the outline of four riders about one hundred yards ahead.

'Who goes there!' Vincent shouted and urged his horse forward followed by Duncan.

The duffers – rustlers – were now in the herd skilfully separating the animals they intended to steal. As Vincent and Duncan came closer the rustlers shouted and whipped about twenty head of cattle away. One of the duffers fired his pistol into the air. The main herd nearby bellowed and shied away in fear. Vincent and Duncan galloped on until they stopped next to the milling cattle. Suddenly out of the shadows one of the duffers came close to Duncan. The man lifted his pistol and took aim. Duncan took a deep breath – he had no pistol and his musket was in its scabbard. But he lashed out with his stock whip and slashed the rustler across his face. The man snarled and tried to take aim again but this time another pistol flashed and a ball smashed into the man's shoulder, almost unseating him. Cursing, he recovered his seat, wheeled his horse and galloped off after the rest of the gang.

'Are you alright Duncan?' Vincent asked coolly, trotting over, a smoking flintlock pistol in his hand.

'Yes, thank you,' Duncan replied, the stock whip trembling in his hand.

'I saw what you did. You were very brave.'

The rest of the crew had galloped up by now and were busy soothing the herd. A stampede was just avoided.

'Hold your horse Duncan,' his elder brother, George, ordered sternly, observing that his younger, impetuous brother was full of excitement and frantic to go after the rustlers.

'But if we don't chase them now they'll escape,' his younger brother shouted.

'Listen to your brother,' ordered Henry Hooke the eldest of his family.'

'Shut up, retorted Duncan. 'You Hookes are damn cowards.'

Duncan had gone too far. Henry kneed his horse up close to the young MacKay and punched him hard in the nose. Duncan had to be restrained by Vincent from retaliating.

'Apologise at once you bloody idiot,' George shouted.

'Do as you're told Duncan,' Vincent said calmly, relaxing his grip on his friend's arm.

'I apologise,' Duncan said unconvincingly, blood dripping into his mouth.

Henry Hooke glared, still furious.

'Now listen everyone,' George said. 'We've only lost about twenty. If most of us chase after them, we leave the rest of the herd unprotected.'

Duncan and Henry calmed down. George was right. The drive continued at its leisurely pace the next morning. Duncan avoided the Hookes for the rest of the journey. The incident was never spoken about again. But it was never forgotten.

'Blacks', warned Vincent a few days later, pointing with his whip at some specks across the undulating tableland. 'Fear not. I've checked; they're not wild.'

The crew realised they must be getting close to the goldfield as the small band of Aborigines slowly overtook the herd. The half a dozen or so men and women were dressed in badly–fitting European clothes. Most of them were mixed race. Two big kangaroos were hanging from wooden poles.

'White fella want eat,' their leader said in answer to George's question.

'Plenty money', he added. His sad eyes flickered a faint spark of happiness as he looked up at the white man looming over him from his saddle.

The group trudged on silently towards the latest incomprehensible manifestation of the British invasion.

One late afternoon a few days later, as evening was falling, George halted the drive and signalled all the crew to ride with him to the brow of a hill.

'Look boys. Have you ever seen anything like this before?' asked George, twisting in his saddle to grin at everyone. He gestured theatrically, his hand unfolding the panorama before them.

In the gentle valley below was a city of white sun–bleached tents. The crew was mesmerised by the activity. The ground was honeycombed with trenches at every stage of excavation. Thousands of men were digging, some in new holes, barely scratching the ground. Others were out of sight in deep holes, only their shovels regularly appearing and disappearing as they threw dug soil up into the air, their loads thumping onto the dusty ground. There was a continuous background noise of mechanical washers and rockers down by a stream.

A large, prominent tent was flying a Union Jack. They guessed this belonged to the government commissioner who was responsible for collecting the hated mining licence of 30 shillings a month from each digger. The official coffers in Sydney gratefully swallowed the lifesaving income. The commissioner's police troopers had the almost impossible and unpopular task of maintaining a semblance of law and order.

The crew jumped in their saddles and their startled horses stepped back as a large gun next to the commissioner's tent was fired. This signalled approaching nightfall and the end of the day's work.

The goldfield fell silent. One group of short men with pigtails, wearing strange clothes and caps trudged off from their own section of the field to a separate camp. These were the first Chinese the men had seen.

Through the gently settling dusk camp fires, as far as the eye could see, began to twinkle like fireflies. The spellbound crew had never seen anything so beautiful before. Then the sound and smell of thousands of men cooking over burning wood and eating in metal cans clinked and wafted its way up to the riders. Eating was followed by singing. Here and there Welsh, Gaelic, German, Italian and French voices competed with rowdy, dominant English.

The large tents on the edge of the field began to fill up with men and a piano honky–tonked through the air. Female shrieks of laughter infiltrated through raucous, masculine shouts. A drunken brawl broke out. A shot was fired, a woman screamed and a man, lit up for an instant by an open tent flap, staggered out and collapsed. The crew gasped, shocked.

Dismounted, they went on watching until the tent fires were doused one by one. The dance hall music stopped. This was followed by the constant popping of firearms, emptied each night for careful reloading by anxious diggers ready for any robbers or claim jumpers. The last pinpricks of lantern light were extinguished. A dog barked and exhaustion took over the diggers, slumped on the ground in their tents.

'Have you ever seen such a thing?' George repeated himself quietly through the now misty, smoky night.

Nobody disagreed. In the days to come the drovers from Dungog sensed instinctively nothing would be the same again in New South Wales. The discovery of much more gold shortly afterwards in the sister colony of Victoria led to a massive influx of a greater number of immigrants. Over the next ten years about half a million people flooded into Australia. Within a short period of time free men outnumbered convicts and their descendants. Australia was rapidly changing, for sure. But nobody was certain what those changes would bring.

The next morning a large pond of coagulating blood lay in front of the mob of cattle. The crew had begun the work of butchering. The first fully laden cart, dripping red, was driven by Vincent and George down to the goldfield and halted next to one of the dance halls. They did not need to announce their wares. Within five minutes there was a queue of about fifty men. And then one hundred. They sold out after twenty minutes. All day, for the next five days, the Dungog men slaughtered their cattle, filled their cart and sold the butchered meat. Cattle that had been bought at a knockdown price of £1 each for their boiling down works now had a value of £6 each. By doing their own butchering the MacKays and Hookes made even more money. Their windfall profits were very high.

On the last evening George and Vincent rode down to the gold field to see if they could buy some supplies. The crew was short on tea and flour.

'Vincent, let's take a look,' George grinned and pointed to a dance hall after they had loaded their horses. Inside the large tent's gloomy, candle–lit interior two girls immediately approached and put their arms around them: 'Why, hello boys. You handsome gentlemen don't look like common diggers.'

'More like bush rangers,' the other one giggled, half–heartedly adjusting her shoulder strap which had slipped down, exposing an ample bosom. The women smelt of cheap scent which failed to mask the smell of strong alcohol and body odour.

This was the first time the two men had met prostitutes. Flustered, they were unsure how to behave, George nodded to the barman when the girls asked for a drink. And then another.

A few rounds later, Vincent excused himself. He swayed outside to take a pee. As he relieved himself between the dancehall and the next tent, he overheard two men.

'Take a look at the fellas inside with Jill and Flo. I recognise them. They're the butcher boys. They had that mob on the hill. Christ knows how much money they must have on them.'

Vincent heard heavy footsteps leave and then quickly return.

'I only saw one. Maybe the other's gone off with Jill for a quick fuck? He won't be long,' a hoarse voice chuckled.

'Can we get Flo to lure them outside and take them? What do you think, Bill?' the other voice replied.

'Not by ourselves. They've got pistols.'

'Well then, let's get Fred and Dick.'

The two men slid off into gold field camp. Vincent slipped quickly inside the dance hall and grabbed George by his neckerchief.

'Damn it, Vincent! What the hell are you doing?' his startled friend blurted, spilling his drink.

'We must leave immediately,' Vincent said urgently, keeping his voice down so not to attract attention.

But George was very reluctant. By now his shirt was unbuttoned and Jill and Flo were stroking his chest.

'Oh, please don't go, my darling,' Flo breathed heavily, kissing George on the cheek as one of her hands fluttered down near the heavy money pouch attached to his belt.

Vincent tossed a generous number of coins on the make–shift counter. The barman raised his eyebrows in disapproval. He chucked some more and the barman nodded begrudgingly.

Vincent pushed Flo away, grabbed one of George's arms and pulled his brother–law outside. He half–carried George to their horses. Out of the corner of his eye, Vincent saw four figures running towards them. He raised his pistol and fired a warning shot. The men paused long enough for Vincent to lift George, now half–sober, onto his saddle. Grabbing George's horse's reins, Vincent trotted the two horses away from the gold field.

The crew stood up in alarm as Vincent and George, now galloping, rode into the camp.

'We'll need to post more guards tonight, lads,' Vincent said briefly before he had dismounted.

'We might have visitors.' He looked around at the puzzled faces. 'They're after our money this time.'

The Dungog men left for home at daybreak. They travelled swiftly and began to relax after two days without attack. They were home within a week.

The MacKays and Hookes drove cattle down to Bathurst the following Spring. Other gold rushes to places closer than Bathurst meant shorter cattle drives and a quicker turnaround. A stream of money began to flow into the families' coffers.

'It's a shame that Uncle Forbes and Father cannot see our return to good fortune, Mother,' George said over the family evening meal as the winter in 1853 brought the droving season to a close.

Sybella nodded and began to speak but halted. Her family looked quizzically at their mother; she was not normally stuck for words.

'George, just before your father died I promised him that I would send you to see his brother.'

Sybella's voice cracked: 'It was his dying wish.'

She paused and dabbed her eyes with a handkerchief: 'I have been unable to speak about this until now. Our circumstances are now more favourable and I think it would be timely for you to visit Uncle Forbes.'

Sybella gulped uncertainly: 'I think you should take your brothers too.'

She looked at George, Duncan and Charles: 'Kenneth will warn you what to expect. When we last heard from the Dixons, Forbes was still no better.'

Sybella looked at the floor, her eyes swimming as she remembered glumly how happy her husband and his brother had been after they had been reunited in Sydney, oh what was it, twelve years ago?

Life at Tarban Creek had not changed for Forbes. He had continued to conceal the improvement in his speech and movement from the warders and Robert Dixon and his wife. But there was one person who had noticed: Alexander Green, the public hangman. The sharp–eyed former acrobat had been showing off with some crazy cartwheels in the exercise yard and had accidentally bashed into Forbes' wheelchair.

Forbes had inadvertently sworn under his breath and his right arm had twitched. The warder had not noticed but Green did.

'Ah, getting better are we Mr MacKay? Trying to keep it a secret?'

Green tapped his nose: 'Don't worry. Mum's the word,' he whispered in Forbes' ear. With that he backward somersaulted away. Green had no idea why the big man would want to hide his recovery. But a secret in a gaol was a valuable thing. Who knew when it might prove useful? Besides, perhaps he had found someone with whom he might one day be able to have a conversation? Nobody else in the exercise yard seemed capable of chatting and the warders shunned him.

'Wake up Mr MacKay. You have visitors.' The warder gently shook the tall grey–haired man's shoulder. It was fortunate that the lunatic had been washed only a few days previously and did not smell too much.

A dozing Forbes woke with a start and stared at the three young men in front of him.

He recognised George instantly.

Delight at the sight of his nephew was followed by instant concern: 'Where's my brother, John?' he managed to whisper, one word at a time.

'By Christ, Uncle Forbes, you can speak!' George yelled, his voice reverberating around the cell's cold, sandstone walls.

He rounded furiously on the warder: 'Why were we not told?'

'Not his fault. I kept it from them,' Forbes panted at a snail's pace, his fists clenched and face turning red with the effort of forcing out each syllable: 'I wanted to surprise your father.'

There was silence as the three MacKay brothers looked sadly at Forbes. George bent down on one knee in front of Forbes: 'Dear Uncle, our Father died one year ago. He had an accident when he was ploughing.'

George held Forbes' twitching right hand while his uncle wept soft tears into his scraggy grey beard.

'We're taking you home now, Uncle Forbes. Home to Melbee.'

Forbes was washed and dressed in clothes George bought from the warders and lifted into a cart and taken down to the docks. The sea trip to Newcastle put colour back into his face. Forbes' prison–grey complexion began to disappear. He laughed for the first time in three years as he felt cold, salty spray on his face. Their uncle sat on deck between Kenneth and George, listening spellbound as they told him everything which had happened during his time in the lunatic asylum.

Among Tarban Creek's inmates only Alexander Green noticed Forbes' departure and felt sorry. Who would he talk to now?

Chapter 40: Inheritance and matrimony

Back at Melbee Forbes received two things which transformed his life. The first was a brand new tricycle wheelchair. With its padded seat and back, Forbes reclined in comfort like a king on his throne. The second was a young Scottish nurse called Marnie who spoke Gaelic and only some English. Forbes became a fixture on Melbee's verandah where Marnie would read to him – his eyes never recovered sufficiently from his illness. Then they would chat in Gaelic. For some reason, Forbes found revising his mother tongue helped improve his English speech and, incredibly, the movement in his right hand and leg. Gaelic also helped Forbes relive the many happy and difficult times he'd experienced from Tongue to French River and then New South Wales.

Their uncle watched with pride as the next generation of MacKays began to restore the family's fortunes. Gold had brought money to Dungog and the Moonie River. The prices of meat and wheat soared. The boom times of the 1830s started to return. The MacKays and Hookes began to pay off their debts.

Forbes' nephews would join him on the verandah and regale him with stories of life on the trail to the various goldfields. Eighteen–year old Duncan quickly became his favourite. The young man found a willing audience in his uncle who would sit back contentedly, puff on a cigar, sip a whisky and listen to his nephew describe his hopes for the future. Once, larking around, Marnie helped Forbes stand and Duncan hopped into his uncle's wheelchair.

'Look Uncle Forbes, it's almost as if it's made to measure for me. It's really comfortable,' Duncan chortled.

Sybella joined Forbes one quiet evening on the verandah and sat down in a comfortable rocking chair. She was quiet for a few moments. All her sons were up at in the Moonie mustering cattle. Forbes guessed his sister–in–law wished to raise a sensitive family matter. Sybella was grateful for the interlude caused by a flock of fruit bats which suddenly flew over and disappeared behind the gum trees, the setting sun illuminating their big, black whooshing wings.

'Forbes I have decided to leave Melbee to George. He is the eldest,' she said finally.

Sybella looked at her brother–in–law's face to gauge his reaction. If one did not know, the tall, handsome man with a head of steel–grey hair and matching grey eyes appeared in good health. Only when he tried to move or speak was it evident that he had suffered a devastating blow.

She pressed on, her voice betraying some nervousness: 'You made Melbee over to John some years ago. When he died I inherited it. Now the time has come to name our eldest as my successor. George is my eldest and is already thirty. A good marriageable age.'

'You are right to do so, Sybella,' Forbes replied slowly. His voice still sounded as though he was speaking through a mouthful of marbles.

'Thank you for your blessing Forbes. I also wish to sub–divide Melbee,' Sybella continued.

'I would like to convey some of our home to Kenneth. He has undertaken to pay his share of the small sum of money that we still owe to Lawrence Myles.'

There was a short silence while Forbes digested Sybella's intention, bowing his head in discomfort at saddling the family with debt.

Sybella gently squeezed Forbes' weaker hand, despite knowing that it always, like a baby, clamped on to anything its fingers felt, and said happily: 'He intends to call it Cangon.'

Ah yes, Forbes recalled. That's what the Gringai had called the land closer to Dungog by a billabong. With its own source of water, Cangon should be viable.

'The other boys?' Forbes mumbled.

'That is more difficult,' Sybella acknowledged.

'Melbee is not large enough to split it up for Duncan and Charles as well.'

Forbes knew from their numerous happy talks that Duncan was well aware, as one of the younger sons, he would have to fend for himself one day.

271

'Duncan reminds me of Uncle Donald,' Forbes rasped suddenly. He raised his eyebrows at his sister–in–law and forestalled her: 'I mean that in a good way.'

Sybella frowned remembering back in Prince Edward Island how Donald MacKay's stubborn determination to build the *Jessie* had cost him his own life and severely damaged the family's finances.

Forbes smiled and pushed on: 'Sybella, Duncan has dreams, big dreams, and a boundless confidence that anything is possible. I know he can behave badly but I believe the boy will go far.'

'Yes, he can annoy people,' his sister–in–law agreed. She knew that Duncan could irritate his elder brothers and the Hookes thought Duncan was too wild.

Sybella hesitated for a brief second and then said: 'I've given the matter much thought. I've decided to give John's claims along the Moonie to Duncan. I'm pleased to say that George will also give up some of his claims to Duncan as well. However unlikely it seems now, who knows, perhaps the Moonie land might become valuable some day?'

Forbes nodded: 'I think that is a possibility. Whatever happens, I know Duncan will be thankful for your generosity.'

Sybella looked at Forbes and gently moved the subject on to her next son.

'And what am I to do for Charles? He's fifteen now,' she said wistfully.

Forbes fell silent. Sybella's youngest boy had very poor eyesight. At one stage the family thought he was almost blind. But a pair of expensive new powerful spectacles bought recently from Newcastle's first optician seemed to have improved her youngest son's life dramatically. Even so, Charles would need some family support for some years. He would have to be taught to ride a horse, shoot and read.

It would help, of course, if the two younger boys could marry women with reasonable dowries. Sybella slowly peeled Forbes' fingers off her hand. Her thoughts turned to matrimony once she had settled the property issue in her mind. The improvement in the Hooke and

MacKay families' fortunes meant George and Kenneth had become eligible bachelors with the prospect of inheritance. And dowries had made the Hooke daughters attractive. She and Mary Ann Hooke had already talked about pairing the rest of their children.

'After all, Sybella, we are among the leading families in these parts. How satisfying for future generations if we started a MacKay – Hooke dynasty,' Mary Ann had said.

'I know my John would be proud that his bloodline would be joined with the MacKays.'

Sybella had nodded in enthusiastic agreement. Nonetheless she had kept her eyes fixed on her lap, knowing that Mary Ann was acutely sensitive about her Jewish background. The subject had never been discussed after the incident with the Jew Boy Gang. Even in the less hidebound colonial New South Wales, many people still frowned on a marriage between Christian and Jew. Mary Ann's daughter, Leonora, had inherited her mother's dark complexion and was severely reprimanded if she ever forgot to wear a hat in the bright sunshine.

Sybella felt she had let Mary Ann down when she had had to tell her friend in late 1851 that George had set his heart on Alice Cooper, the young widow of one of the few doctors in the area. In her mind, Sybella had reserved George for sixteen–year old Emily Hooke. Sybella's reluctance to the marriage was offset by the size of Alice's inheritance from her former husband. The fact that Alice was distantly related to an English duke also helped assuage her guilt.

But the two matriarchs' well–intentioned scheming eventually succeeded with Kenneth and Emily who married a year later and took up residence in Cangon. Two years further on Sybella's daughter, Jessy Johanna, married Sam Cobb's elder brother George, who had inherited the fertile Anambah estate, which was now prospering again. Mary Ann's son, Augustus, was the same age as Jessy Johanna but both mothers agreed twenty–three was a bit too young for a man to marry.

The two family weddings crystallised Duncan's decision to leave Melbee which would shortly belong to George. He knew that in due course he would be given George's share of the Moonie land but in the meantime he wanted to travel. To sow his wild oats as Uncle Forbes laughingly described it. None of his brothers or his mother tried to dissuade him. They all knew that Duncan would never be content to pick up the crumbs from his elder brothers' tables.

'Where will you go, Duncan?' Forbes asked.

'I hear the Dumaresqs are looking for drovers to move a mob to Samaurez, their property upcountry.'

His uncle nodded, his mind flooding with grateful memories of his former benefactor, Henry Dumaresq, Governor Darling's brother–in–law, who had been granted about two thousand acres at St Helier's in the Hunter Valley. Further inland in the wider open spaces of New England, Henry had been granted 100,000 acres which he had named Samaurez. Yes, Darling had always been very generous indeed to his family and supporters.

Forbes sighed: Henry had finally died in 1838 as a result of the wound he'd received at the Battle of Waterloo. His properties had been inherited by his wife, Sophia, and were now overseen by his brother, William.

'After that I will take whatever opportunity comes along, Uncle Forbes. I have enough money to make a start in whatever takes my fancy. I'll head north to the Moonie eventually.'

Duncan gave his uncle a winsome grin: 'Mother has been generous.'

Apart from the promise of the claim to Moonie land both uncle and nephew knew Duncan had been given little by his mother. Cash was still in short supply. Most of the money from supplying the gold fields was still going to paying off Forbes' debts.

'Or perhaps I should go north to the Moonie now?' Duncan said, rubbing his new beard speculatively.

'No Duncan, wait until Walker's native police have fully cleared the area. Sam Cobb is doing a good job holding the fort for now. You're young. Go and experience some life elsewhere.'

'You know Uncle, I've heard Walker is encouraging small groups of the 'tame blacks' to live on the stations. They are proving to be good stockmen. And they don't demand high wages like the white men around here.'

Duncan shrugged his shoulders: 'We no longer have convicts. Perhaps the blacks will replace them up north?'

'Aye, you might be right,' agreed his uncle, blowing cigar smoke away and sipping some whisky.'

Duncan noticed his uncle's Scottish accent was always more pronounced after a dram or two.

There was a steady stream of visitors who came to wish young Duncan goodbye. Vincent Dowling trotted over from his Canningulla property to give Duncan a present. Vincent brushed away Duncan's polite refusal when he tried to hand over his telescope.

'If you are travelling by yourself it could save your life. It belonged to my father. The judge would have been happy to see it put to good use rather than remain an ornament on my mantle shelf.'

Duncan was touched by the generous gift: 'Thank you. I will repay you some day.'

'I'm sure you will,' smiled Vincent, gently punching his young friend's shoulder.

Chapter 41: Eureka

People don't often die quickly when they are clubbed over the head. Once unconscious, about another half a dozen blows to head and several kicks are usually needed to complete the deed. This is what happened late one night to a Scottish digger – gold miner – by the name of James Scobie who, together with a friend, had tried to break into the Eureka Hotel in the goldfields town of Ballarat in New South Wales' neighbouring colony of Victoria. Earlier that evening, the two diggers, already drunk, had lurched up to the Eureka's bar and demanded more rum. It was early October 1854.

A group of stockmen, newly arrived with a mob of cattle to sell to the town's butchers, had watched in some amusement the efforts of Scobie to order drinks. The crew were slaking their own thirst. They had just finished driving two thousand head of cattle about three hundred and fifty miles down from the New England tablelands in New South Wales. Among them was a striking young man with long, black wavy hair slicked back to reveal a forehead, mahogany brown from months of driving cattle. It was Duncan MacKay who had left Melbee about six months ago.

To judge by the barman's face, Scobie must have said something insulting. In the hubbub of noise from card tables, a bowling alley and shrieks from whores, Duncan and the rest of the crew could not make out the exact words.

The atmosphere in the pub was already heated. Resentment against the government's expensive mining licence of £2 every three months and its aggressive collection by police troopers was widespread. Disgruntled men at tables were formulating demands for the removal of the licence and, more seditiously, the right to vote in state elections. Englishmen motivated by their compatriot reformers, the Chartists; Irish Fenians dreaming of a free Ireland; and Americans to whom British colonialism was anathema. The pub was a babble of different accents and languages.

Duncan stared at a table of black Americans. He'd overheard someone saying they had recently arrived from California. Duncan was staring, not because of their skin colour, rather what was strapped to their waists. Noticing Duncan's interest, one of the Americans drew out of its holster a new type of pistol which Duncan had never seen before. Catching Duncan's eye, the American grinned and spun the revolver's well–oiled six chambers around.

Duncan's gaze was diverted by the sight of three barmen frog–marching Scobie and his friend and throwing them outside. There were catcalls and shouts of protests from many in the Eureka. Everyone knew the owner of the pub was in cahoots with the local magistrate and police troopers to fleece the diggers. The mood in the bar grew ugly and violence seemed imminent.

The crew's boss, Tony Wightman, ordered his men to follow him out the pub's door.

'C'mon lads, there are plenty of other places to get a drink around here.' The crew eased their way through the agitated crowd of diggers.

Later that night the two drunken diggers tried to get into the Eureka again. Alerted by the sound of a breaking window, the publican and his men gave chase to the drunks. The next morning the bloody mess of Scobie's body was discovered alongside his unconscious companion.

The publican and his accomplices were arrested. Despite the strong evidence of their involvement in murder, they were promptly released by the local magistrate. This infuriated the diggers, five thousand of whom rioted and burnt the Eureka to the ground. The atmosphere on the gold field grew even more ugly and mutinous.

Tony Wightman and his crew were already about 100 miles from Ballarat on the way back to New England when the goldfield rebelled against the government.

Twelve thousand diggers built a wooden stockade and vowed to fight the government if it did not agree to dispense with the licences. Named the Eureka stockade, the diggers ran up their own flag –a white cross with the stars of the Southern Cross against a blue background – and openly challenged the British governor's rule.

The stockade did not last long. Early one Sunday morning in November, while most diggers were in their tents sleeping off the previous night's revels, redcoat soldiers and police troopers stormed inside, overpowering the mere 120 defenders. The fight was swift, brutal and bloody and all over in 20 minutes. Many of the police troopers went berserk, bayoneting and shooting wounded diggers. The soldiers had to protect some of the digger prisoners from the police. Five British troops (including a captain) and 22 diggers were killed or later died of their wounds. The strong protests in the state capital of Victoria, Melbourne, and even as far as London, against the excessive use of force led eventually to the governor agreeing to the diggers' demands. The licence was replaced by an annual tax on earnings from gold, payment of which was rewarded by the right to vote for the state parliament. Despite many who had regarded the diggers' rebellion as an uprising by outsiders who were exploiting the country's resources and refusing to pay their fair share of taxes, the Eureka stockade's plucky resistance to British colonial authority became seared into Australian folklore.

Duncan had arrived at the Samaurez station – ranch – at the end of the drive from the Hunter Valley. His services had been quickly snapped up by the Dumaresqs' station manager, Tony Wightman. Mass desertion to the goldfields meant experienced stockmen were thin on the ground. Duncan was well paid. The Dumaresq property was a model enterprise with comfortable living quarters and fair wages. Even former convicts, now old in the tooth, who had served their time, stayed on. By and large Duncan kept away from alcohol and the shacks where prostitutes plied their profitable trade in country areas where white men outnumbered women by at least twenty to one. Free board and lodging meant Duncan saved money. After another year of droving for the Dumaresqs and, despite Wightman's entreaties, Duncan left Saumerez and headed towards the northern frontier. Duncan judged he had seen enough of life outside his family circle – the Moonie was calling. With a tidy sum of money, plenty of ammunition and food in his saddle bag, a good horse, one of the new six–shooter revolvers and a rifled musket he felt confident he could deal with whatever challenges he would meet as a single traveller. More than once he felt himself being watched and stalked. Vincent's telescope proved itself useful several times as he evaded his shadowy would–be assailants.

Duncan travelled northwards from station to station, sometimes staying up to a week, paying for his board and lodging by helping with mustering, branding and breaking in brumbies – wild horses.

He eventually hit a trail which he recognised –the one which the MacKays used to drive their cattle from the Moonie district, south west towards Williams River. He paused. Should he turn right and head home to Melbee or left and continue to ride towards Ningan in the Moonie where he expected Sam Cobb to be living. Even though he particularly wanted to see his mother and Uncle Forbes again, he realised that he would now be a guest in Melbee, now the home of his elder brother, George. Duncan turned left.

As darkness fell Duncan made camp, well–screened by scrub and trees. He lit a fire and made some damper, Australian soda bread, and drank some billy tea laced with a gum leaf. Unusually for Duncan he was in a reflective mood, looking back on his life. Happy in the company of men from whatever background, he suddenly realised, unlike his brothers, he did not have any close friends his own age. In fact his best mate was his Uncle Forbes. A black dog of depression seized him as he realised he would see much less of Forbes now that he had decided to base himself in the Moonie. Duncan chewed his salt beef jerky despondently. He reached for a bottle of brandy in his saddle bag. Never usually a heavy or solo drinker, Duncan took a swig, followed by another. And then another.

He fell into a drunken stupor and slipped onto the ground. His fingers relaxed and the empty bottle rolled across the ground, leaving a snake–like track on the red soil. The fire smouldered on and the water in the billy can gently boiled off. The supporting tripod of sticks turned to charcoal, collapsed and the hissing can clattered onto the ground. Startled by the noise, his horse whinnied and pulled against its tether.

Duncan's bushman's keen senses would normally have heard even the most stealthy of steps creeping up on him as dawn broke and the

Southern Cross faded into morning's bright blue sky. But not on this occasion.

Waking up with a bad hangover is never pleasant. It is even worse if one is staring down the barrel of a Colt revolver.

'Who are you?'

Duncan groaned, his temples throbbing in pain as he forced himself up onto his elbows. He managed to prise open his sleep–glued eyes and gradually focused on the speaker, peering down on him.

'Who are you? Answer or I will blow your damn head off,' the man demanded again, his authoritarian tone as threatening as his steadily–held pistol.

'Duncan MacKay.'

'Where are you from? And what are you doing here?'

'I'm from Dungog in the Hunter Valley. I'm on the way to our homestead in the Moonie.'

'Name a family from Dungog'

'Er, the Hookes'.

The man frowned at the unrecognised name.

'Vincent Dowling – the judge's son,' Duncan next said hopefully, guessing from the man's clipped English accent that he was a former British Army officer and had something to do with the law.

On cue, two rifle–wielding police troopers appeared out of the surrounding scrub.

'No other tracks Mr Bryden,' one said, his Irish brogue washing over the tense atmosphere.

Sounding slightly disappointed, the man slipped his pistol into his holster, reached down, grabbed a hand and helped a prostrate Duncan to his feet.

'Allow me to introduce myself: Hugh Bryden, formerly of Her Majesty's Indian Army, now magistrate around these parts.'

'We've been chasing a couple of duffers – rustlers – but we lost their tracks. I hoped you were one of them.'

Bryden shook his head reprovingly: 'We smelt your fire about half a mile from here as night was falling. I thought we might ambush you at first light.

'It is not a good idea to let your fire burn too long. Bushrangers and wild blacks would have made short work of you. But I suspect you know that already?'

Duncan nodded ruefully, his head gradually clearing.

'Oh well. We won't catch the duffers now.'

The magistrate took in Duncan's clothes and fine–looking horse. He'd welcome some civilised conversation.

'You look a respectable chap. Breakfast?' he asked jovially.

To each other's surprise they talked for over an hour. After the troopers had finished eating, Bryden ordered them to return to the district's lock–up.

The two men found they had common ground. They were both younger brothers who had left their families to try their luck elsewhere. Bryden had been wounded fighting Afghans on India's north west frontier and had been invalided out of service. After his recovery, rather than return home to a cold Britain he'd fancied his luck in warm New South Wales. A contact in the governor's office had led to his appointment as a magistrate – a common destination for former colonial British army officers with action experience and who could be trusted.

'I'd welcome the chance to visit the Moonie. I've heard there are several duffer gangs up there. I might pick up some intelligence.'

Duncan was happy to invite Bryden to accompany him up north.

During the final stage of the journey, the two men became close friends. In fact, over the next couple of years, best mates.

They reached the Moonie River a couple of weeks later. They were hugging its lazy bends, their thoughts straying as they watched the muddy river slowly flowing, rather than keeping on the trail. Suddenly they came upon a tumble down, abandoned homestead, nestling in a curve of the river separated from the water by a large sandy mound. Duncan and his new friend were by now about 350 miles from Dungog and still a day's ride from MacKay's Ningan station. The layout of the house reminded him of Melbee. It was spread out and had outbuildings for workers and horses. He could see where there once must have been a large garden and fruit trees, which were now growing out of control. Not far from the property, separated by a collapsed fence, he could see a camp of Aborigines' humpies – small wood and bark shelters.

Both their mounts snorted in surprised alarm as a horse trotted out from behind a bush. Its rider was black. Duncan's right hand involuntarily searched for his new revolver but he relaxed when he saw he had been greeted with a wide grin by a man dressed in stockman's working clothes and, like Duncan, wearing a wide-brimmed, slouch hat. A long stock whip was coiled around his saddle's pommel. This was another feature of his travels that Duncan had noticed. The number of Aboriginal stockmen had started to increase the further north he went. He had already worked with some and had admired their horsemanship and droving skills that he had heard about previously.

'Hello, white fellas ', the Aboriginal said.

'Hello, black fella', Duncan replied, smiling. Bryden nodded, his hand still on his revolver.

The three riders stopped after a few minutes. The same thought had crossed their minds simultaneously.

They reined in their horses, twisted around and each held out a hand.

'Me, Jonathan.'

'I'm Duncan.'

'And I'm Hugh.'

With a sudden shock, Duncan realised Jonathan was the first Aborigine whose hand he had shaken. The same thought occurred to Bryden.

Jonathan chuckled in similar amazement: Duncan and Bryden were the first white men whose hands he'd shaken.

The tall black man grinned again, eased forward in his saddle and pointed towards the run-down homestead: 'Bullamon.'

'White fella run away from here from black fella,' he added.

He pointed to humpies: 'My friends. I have holiday.''

'You are Kamilroi tribe?' asked Duncan.

No, me Bigambul.'

Jonathan reined his horse and turned to look Duncan in the face.

'Bigamul and Kamilroi run away from Walker. Now Walker go. They come back. Bad for white fellas again.'

Walker's gone? Duncan thought to himself.

'Where do you work?'

'Ningan,' replied Jonathan pointing north along the river.

Duncan smiled: 'We are heading that way.'

Sam Cobb was mightily relieved to see the three men at Ningan the following day.

'The wild Kamilroi are back and roaming around. I could use some more pistols if they attack us here.'

He spat tobacco juice on the ground: 'They've killed two of our cattle. The bastards slit their bellies and took their livers.'

Sam glanced wearily at Jonathan, as if to blame him partly for the dead cattle.

The black stockman merely shrugged his shoulders: 'Black fella like fat more. White fella like meat more.'

'I know, I know, Jonathan. I'm not really blaming you.'

Sam stepped forward and held Jonathan's horse: 'Now go and get something to eat from the cook. I'd like you to go out and track them so we know where they're headed.'

The three white men watched Jonathan's back as he loped off towards Ningan's kitchen.

'He's my top stockman,' Sam said. 'I'd trust him with my life, you know,' he added.

'No, really', he said in reply to Duncan and Bryden's surprised looks

'We've had close calls with duffers but Jonathan's always managed to make sure I haven't been ambushed.'

He shook his head in admiration: 'I don't know how he does it, but sometimes it's almost as if the bush is speaking to him, telling him where to go. Even at night. Something that we white men will never learn.'

Sam noticed Hugh's eyes had narrowed at the mention of duffers and looked quizzically at Duncan.

'I'm sorry Sam. I'm forgetting my manners. This is Hugh Bryden. Magistrate of the Mooree district.'

Over lunch inside the homestead Hugh asked: 'I'd welcome any intelligence you can give me about duffers heading towards my jurisdiction.'

Sam nodded: 'I'll make sure Jonathan keeps his eyes open for tracks heading south.'

He turned to Duncan: 'How long are you here for?'

'I'm here for good, Sam,' Duncan replied carefully, worried that Sam might react badly to the news that he would no longer be in charge of Ningan.

But Sam, who had already heard that Duncan was to inherit most of the MacKay property, just smiled genuinely: 'Welcome, I can do with some help. We've got about three thousand head now. I've got a crew of four drovers plus Jonathan and another couple of blacks.'

He swilled some water around in his tin cup: 'It's a pity. You've just missed Kenneth and Charles. They were here last week. They've taken about 500 head down to Melbee along with a couple of drovers.'

'Charles?' blurted Duncan.

'Yes, wearing the biggest pair of spectacles I've ever seen. Still, he can ride a horse now and crack a whip.'

'But you'd be risking your life if you gave him a pistol', Sam chuckled.

'Did they say how things were at Melbee?' asked Duncan.

'Everything seemed much as it was when you were last there,' answered Sam.

Knowing that Duncan was close to his uncle, Sam hesitated before he said: 'They did mention that Forbes had fainted.'

'But he was only out cold for about ten seconds,' he added swiftly to dispel the look of alarm on Duncan's face.

But Sam's optimism was misplaced.

Chapter 42: Our MacKay land

Forbes suffered a major seizure in 1859. His brain was sucked, screaming and protesting into a dark, jagged vortex full of sparks and cackling demonic shadows. His jaw became slack and his eyes as dull as lead. There would be no recovery this time.

Duncan had hurried down from Ningan to Melbee after he had heard the news. The family took Forbes back to Sydney for medical examination knowing full well what the result would be. The poor man was re-incarcerated. He did not last long. In less than a year, Forbes was dead.

Duncan wept more than his brothers at Uncle Forbes' funeral in St Stephen's Church in Sydney's Newtown. The widow of the surveyor, Robert Dixon, had kindly offered the MacKays a space to bury Forbes in the Dixon family grave near the church's front door.

After Duncan's father, John MacKay, died in 1851, as well as a good friend, Forbes had become a father–figure to his nephew. As the Church of England vicar led the funeral service, Duncan, through his tears, remembered the warm sunny evenings on Melbee's verandah when his uncle had listened attentively to his nephew's dreams for the future – grandiose visions chuckled at by his elder brothers. But Forbes had offered the young man encouragement and advice.

'You are just like Uncle Donald. You dare to dream,' Forbes had said more than once. He'd mesmerised Duncan with stories of colourful family life in Prince Edward Island which Duncan had been too young to remember. Of ships, wrecks, rum, timber and smuggling. The ups and downs of the family's fortunes.

'*Carpe diem*, Duncan. Always grasp the opportunity when it arises.'

Oh, how Duncan wished Forbes could have been present upon the family's return to Melbee after the funeral to hear his report on progress at Ningan, along the Moonie.

Duncan politely helped his mother pull up a chair in the dining room next to the table on which he proudly unrolled a map: 'Mother, I know I haven't been home for a couple of years. I have just been too busy. I hope what I now say will reassure you that I have not been wasting my time.'

Transferring a cigar to his left hand, he pointed to a thick line which snaked its way through rectangular blocks of land from the top to the bottom of the map: 'This is the Moonie River. 'I' – Duncan hastily corrected himself – 'we now own most of the properties along the Moonie River from here in the north at my home, Ningan, down to here,' Forbes stabbed a number on the map which showed the location of surveyor Mitchell's old camp number 86.

'We only need to get Bullamon,' he thumped the map on the next property south, 'and we MacKays will have control of all of the lower Moonie.'

Duncan looked at his mother: 'Our land will then comprise some 320,000 acres. Not all of it suitable for grazing, of course, nonetheless we are accumulating a sizeable holding.' And that will be just the start, he thought to himself.

Duncan ignored the sharp collective intake in breath when he mentioned the number of acres, blew his cigar smoke sideways and said casually: 'Bullamon is owned by an ex–convict called Dunn. He got a bit lucky on a gold field. I'll winkle him out soon enough.'

Sybella regarded her second–youngest son with some awe. Her boy had grown into a tough, twenty–six year old man who oozed swaggering, self–confidence. Any sense of a wild youth had gone. His jet–black, wavy hair was slicked down firmly with hair oil, accentuating his broad forehead and his penetrating grey eyes. Forbes had been right: there was definitely something impressive about Duncan that reminded one of Uncle Donald.

'Are the blacks under control now, Duncan?' asked a doubtful George who remembered very clearly fighting for his life together with his father. After he had ceded his share of the Moonie property to his younger brother, he had not visited Ningan again.

'By and large yes, around the Moonie. Further north and west they are still troublesome.' Duncan shrugged and said dismissively: 'You remember that's where James Hooke tried and gave up a few years ago.'

Duncan cleared his throat: 'After we stupidly fired Walker in 1855 and disbanded his native police, the wild blacks started to return and attack us.'

He rapped his fingers on the table: 'They wanted their land back. Understandable, but it's ours now.'

Duncan rolled his eyes towards the ceiling: 'Those idiots in Sydney set up a new force but didn't provide enough finance. What's more,' Duncan shook his head in disbelief, 'they even recruited local blacks who, of course, turned out to be spies.'

Duncan looked around the room and said quietly: 'The Moonie's just become part of the new state of Queensland. We've had to start our own unofficial force.'

'By and large we've been successful getting rid of the wild ones and training the others. Sam and I have quite a few black stockmen now. I'd trust one of them, called Jonathan, with my life.'

Duncan could see his brothers were doing sums in their heads.

'We should not entertain selling any land at the moment. Because of the blacks, the Moonie's reputation is still regarded as evil. Land values are correspondingly low.'

Duncan turned away from the map, one hand in a pocket, the other holding his cigar, very much the chairman of the meeting: 'The prices of beef and wool show no sign of dropping. I intend building viable businesses and using profits to accrue more land. It will not remain cheap forever.'

Sybella smiled and nodded. Although Duncan was to inherit most of it, much of the land was still in her name. If she agreed, that was the end of the matter. Apart from Duncan, only Kenneth had a share. It began to dawn on George that perhaps he had been too hasty in agreeing to give up his Moonie share to Duncan?

'That was well put, Duncan,' Sybella said, linking an arm firmly with her son and leading him into Melbee's drawing room, leaving the rest of the family behind.

Duncan looked around at the comfortable furnishings of what was now George and his wife's home.

'George lives well, Mother.'

'Yes he does. He has a lovely wife and already two children. And they look after me very well. I am very happy here.'

Sybella turned and grasped both of her son's arms: 'I truly believe you have great prospects, Duncan. It is now time for you to think of starting your own family.'

'Should I take that as an order, Mother?' smiled Duncan.'

Sybella returned her son's smile: Yes, you should.'

She took stock for a second and said seriously: 'We will call on the Hookes.'

Duncan grimaced. Ever since the incident droving down to Bathurst, he had avoided visits to their neighbour's home. Nonetheless, like all the children in both families, he was well aware of their mothers' matrimonial scheming.

'Perhaps when I next come down from the Moonie?' he suggested hopefully.

'No, we will visit Wiry Gully tomorrow,' Sybella said firmly.

Duncan raised his eyebrows – disagreement was pointless.

Chapter 43: The bride and groom

Frances Leonora Hooke's hand was steady as she raised the delicate Wedgwood cup to her lips while she coolly observed the young man who had come calling with his mother. She had seen Duncan before at various birthdays, weddings and funerals but not since he was a small boy at her family's home, Wiry Gully. There had always been some plausible reason for Duncan's non–appearance, whether work or health–related. Nora knew her brothers didn't care for him which was probably why he also kept his distance at those social functions that both families attended.

The day before, a servant from Melbee had ridden over and delivered a note to her mother, Mary Ann, who had hastily scribbled a reply. Nora had not paid much attention. She guessed the message was about a luncheon invitation or maybe somebody's birthday celebration.

Nora had been working with her mother on the financial accounts of Wiry Gully. Even though Mary Ann had conveyed the property to her eldest son, Henry, not long after her husband's death nine years ago, it was on the understanding that Mary Ann would continue to oversee Wiry Gully's financial affairs. Her daughter who was the most adept of her children at figures had become her assistant.

From her adjacent desk, Mary Ann had watched her twenty–three year old and second youngest daughter as she worked diligently with her new steel pen manufactured in Birmingham, England by a company called Myers. Nora had caused some family laughter when she had speculated on what sort of person made steel pens. Was Mr Myers an impatient, lovelorn writer who had perhaps become frustrated with his slow quill? Or had serendipity led him to pen nibs after researching a new tooth pick?

'Nora,' her mother had said quietly.

'Yes, Mother?' she'd replied patiently, guessing that the messenger from the MacKays would be the subject of the conversation.

'I've invited Sybella for afternoon tea.'

'That should be pleasant, Mother. You haven't seen each other for a month or so?' Nora said, only listening with one ear.

Mary Ann cleared her throat to emphasise what she now had to say: 'Sybella will be bringing her son Duncan with her.'

Nora cursed her clumsiness under her breath as her pen nib slipped, turning a number one into a seven. To gain some time she carefully corrected her mistake with some blotting paper. Despite her startled red face, she steadied herself enough to turn and face her mother.

'Yes, they are coming here tomorrow,' Mary Ann repeated, holding her daughter's gaze.

'Tomorrow Mother? I, er...'

'Nora' – Mary Ann reached out and held her flustered daughter's hand – 'this is purely an informal visit. Of all the MacKay boys, I know Duncan the least. I will never force you to do something like this against your will.'

Mary Ann squeezed her daughter's hand. 'You know that, surely?'

Nora nodded uneasily: 'Yes, of course Mother.'

Duncan Forbes MacKay – Sybella introduced her son using his full name – felt awkward. Very awkward. At ease in the company of men, the twenty–six year old young man was unused to being in a minority of one surrounded by women. Worse still, despite the womanly politeness, he knew he was being inspected and examined. Just like a bull at a cattle sale, he thought ruefully.

The unfortunate death of Forbes occupied the start of the meeting – because, in truth, a meeting was what it was and a business one at that. Mary Ann expressed genuinely sincere condolences. The Hookes would never forget the kindness and support Forbes had provided when they had arrived in 1829. They would visit his grave on their next visit to Sydney.

After a respectful pause, Mary Ann turned to the main item on the agenda: ' How long are you staying at Melbee, Duncan?'

'Only a few...'

Seated next to her son on a large comfortable sofa, Sybella smiled and quickly patted her son's thigh: 'Only a week or so.' Her jolly manner contrasted with the mourning, dark colour of their clothes.

Duncan caught a glimpse of an empathetic smile flitting across Nora's face. Her face? He darted a look at her again. Yes, she was pretty, striking even. He shouldn't have been surprised: Squire Hooke, as the MacKays affectionately had called him, had been a handsome man. And Mary Ann had been a well–known 'beauty'. Even now, aged sixty–six there were still glimpses of what she must have looked like as a young woman. All the Hooke children had inherited their parents' good looks, including Emily, his brother Kenneth's wife.

Nora observed Duncan was well dressed in an expensive velvet jacket, corduroy trousers and a silk cravat, although they seemed a bit on the tight side. She guessed correctly that his clothes were borrowed from one of his brothers.

'Tell me Duncan, I understand you are managing the MacKay venture in the Moonie?'

'Yes, that's right, Mrs Hooke.'

Sybella prodded Duncan: 'Tell Mrs Hooke about the extent of the property we already control.'

Duncan stared at Mary Ann: 'I reckon about 500 square miles, 320,000 acres,' his vestigial, Scots accent coming more to the fore, as it instinctively became more in tune with his mother's voice.

He flicked a glance at Nora, conscious of her close gaze.

'And there are other opportunities. At least 500,000 acres should be possible if one is determined and shrewd enough,' Duncan said shortly, annoyed to be spoken to like a boy.

'You manage all this yourself?' asked Mary Ann.

'No, I am assisted by Sam Cobb.'

Mary Ann glanced at Sybella: 'Oh, Mr Cobb has a stake in the MacKay venture?'

'There is a gentleman's agreement, Mary Ann, that Sam will be fairly rewarded. But there is no formal contract,' Sybella said quietly.

Ah, thought Mary Ann. That should pose no difficulty. Sam's elder brother, George, was married to Sybella's daughter, Jesse Johanna.

'Are the natives not dangerous? My brother, James, says it is still too dangerous up there for white men?'

Duncan turned to Nora who had asked the question, surprised that she had spoken without being invited to by her mother. At the appropriate juncture he had expected her mother to say something like: 'And what do you think, Nora?'

He chose his words carefully: 'There have been major depredations by the natives, certainly. But around the Moonie they have now largely been dispersed.'

The code word 'dispersed' did not cause any of the women's eyebrows to rise. Provided there was no participation in atrocities by their menfolk, it would be remiss not to profit from the pacification of the emerging frontier areas. Furthermore the disquiet over the harsh treatment meted out to the blacks, evident in Sydney government circles, was not shared by many settlers whose lives had been personally threatened.

Duncan thought for a moment before continuing: 'The danger is still there and precautions must be taken. But I believe the situation is now no worse than what it was when our families first came to the Williams River. The frontier is moving north and west, pushing the wild blacks out. The tame ones who remain behind make excellent and cheap stockmen. I employ about a dozen. Of course, I never allow them in the house.'

'In any case, we now face greater trouble from duffers. Our property runs about ten miles along the river and twenty five miles inland on both sides. They steal our cattle and hide them in the scrub away from the river banks.'

While Duncan had been speaking, Mary Ann had been searching for any signs of weakness or doubt in his voice or mannerisms. Thus far she had seen nothing to concern her; indeed much to impress her had been in evidence.

'Do you intend staying long in the Moonie, Duncan?'

'Yes, Mrs Hooke. The properties – runs, as we call them – are already profitable. I shall invest the proceeds in more land. Prices are depressed because of the perception the area is too dangerous.' Duncan shrugged his shoulders: 'Once values increase, who knows?'

'By how much do you think they might rise?'

'If they begin to approximate Hunter Valley prices, perhaps by as much as fifty times.'

Mary Ann had heard enough. There would need to be a Hooke family gathering to discuss the next steps.

The meeting became more social, the two matriarchs gossiped about neighbours and the weather. The two young people continued to eye each other up. Nora was not shy Duncan realised. And Nora, like her mother, had been impressed by the young man's resolve and bearing, more like a man ten years older. The MacKays departed. Duncan and Nora did not notice the almost imperceptible nod Mary Ann gave Sybella as she was helped into the surrey carriage by her son.

'That went well, dear, don't you think?' said Sybella with a satisfied sigh, her hands folded neatly in her lap.

Duncan did not reply, deep in thought. He flicked the horse whip and the carriage drew away. His mind was on Nora's pretty face.

'No mother, I will not allow it.' Henry thumped the imported, mahogany dining table hard. Not once but twice: 'Duncan MacKay is not a suitable husband for Nora.'

Mary Ann's eldest child, now 39, his face red with anger continued: 'He is rude and wild.'

'I agree with Henry. Besides, he lives in the most dangerous part of the colony. I should know. Totally unsuitable for a white woman,' her second eldest son, 35 year old James almost spat.

Mary Ann studied her two elder boys. Prosperity meant that these two admirable characters had become risk–averse and set in their ways. Obviously Duncan MacKay had upset them – perhaps it was something he'd done nine years ago on the cattle drive down to the Bathurst gold field? She knew they had hardly spoken to him since the event which marked the revival in the family's fortunes.

She cast her mind back to the family ruptures caused by her own controversial marriage to John. Would it really matter what Nora's siblings thought if she married the young Duncan? As the family matriarch, still steering its finances, she believed it was her duty to consider business opportunities. She knew in her heart of hearts that her two boys would never have contemplated started a boiling down works. And James, bless him, had decided to abandon the Hooke property near the Moonie, rather than stay and fight. By contrast, Duncan MacKay, at the comparatively young age of 26, was staking his future on a project which might, despite encouraging signs, not succeed. Anyone who had survived the 1840s knew nothing could be taken for granted.

'Would you like to know what I think?' Mary Ann asked her sons.

They nodded reluctantly but respectfully.

'Duncan MacKay might well have been a wild boy but my impression is that he has matured into a sound young man.'

She pursed her lips: 'And I am a good judge of character.

'He comes from a family who we know well and to whom we owe a great deal.

'Without the MacKays we would never have established a toehold in Williams River and the boiling down works might not have succeeded.'

Her mind was made up: 'In my view he is an acceptable suitor for my daughter.'

Mary Ann looked at Nora sitting next to her, facing her siblings.

'Now Nora, tell the boys what you thought of Duncan.'

Her daughter thought for a moment, her mind searching for the right word: 'He seemed very determined.'

Mary Ann's face was impassive. She had trained her daughter to make her own mind up and did not wish to be seen by her sons as placing pressure on Nora.

'Would you receive further visits from Duncan MacKay?'

Nora did not hesitate: 'Yes Mother, I would.'

It was not a match made in heaven. Nor was it devoid of emotion. Duncan and Nora got to know each other better and felt a growing attraction. Duncan found himself enthusiastically describing his dreams in the same way he used to for Uncle Forbes. Nora began to share them but insisted in any marriage she would want some oversight of the financial affairs. Without being disloyal, she referred obliquely to the hardships her family had endured because of her father's mistakes. Henry and James eventually realised that if their mother and Nora wished the marriage to proceed, they could not prevent it. Nonetheless they persuaded their mother that Nora should remain at Wiry Gully until their sister's safety in the Moonie could be reasonably assured.

The final item in this union of a MacKay and Hooke was sensitive: the amount of the dowry. The two matriarchs met. Both looked forward to the negotiation, spiced by what they considered to be their personal attributes of a Scot and a Jew, respectively.

Sybella suggested £4,000. 'I fear that might be too much,' replied Mary Ann. 'It would be difficult for me to get Henry's approval for this figure. I had in mind £2,500.'

'For my part, George would consider anything less insufficient.'

The women paused, their faces blank but their eyes betraying faint amusement. They knew that their respective eldest sons would do what their mothers told them. In the end after offer and counter–offer, a figure of £3,000 was agreed.

There was one unusual condition insisted on by Nora: the dowry would be in the form of a loan from the bride to the groom which would have to be repaid at some stage. Mary Ann informed Sybella proudly that the bride was determined that she would not be taken for granted in financial matters. This proved a sticking point for a short while but Sybella quickly realised that Nora would not allow her mother to compromise on this matter.

With the dowry settled, Duncan was not overly concerned that his bothers felt snubbed when he announced that he had invited a Hugh Bryden, a stranger to them, to be his best man.

With her Myers' pen, Nora wrote neatly in the family bible: 'The marriage took place today, the 14th June 1860, between Frances Leonora Hooke and Duncan Forbes MacKay at Wiry Gully near Dungog. The service was performed by the Rev. Whitmore Carr DD of the Church of England. Witnesses: John Hooke and Hugh Bryden.'

Nora's eldest brother, Henry, refused to be a witness, preferring his younger brother to sign the marriage certificate.

Duncan was not overly concerned by Henry's disapproval. He and Nora enjoyed a honeymoon of about a month. By the time Duncan returned to the Moonie, Nora was already pregnant.

Part 9: A new home

Although the district was now mapped out on paper, it was still wild country. According to an old bushman... who was familiar with this district in the early 1860s, the Moonie 'was a very stronghold of duffing (rustling)'

Before the line – The Thallon District before 1911, Melanie O'Flynn, 2011

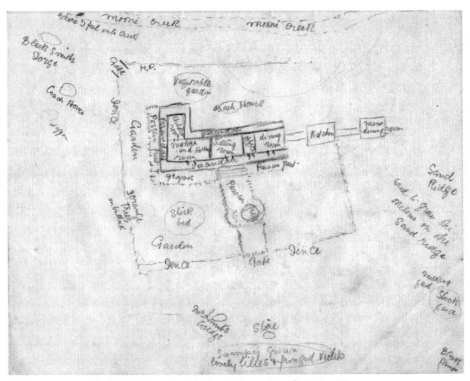

Bullamon, sketch by Mary Annie MacKay

Chapter 44: Bullamon

'No, we will have to leave. Damn you, I will not live here so close to that...that hotel.'

Nora MacKay was furious. She had arrived in the Moonie only a few weeks ago, together with the couple's two children.

She glared at Duncan: 'And you know why.'

Duncan could not meet her gaze. He knew why.

They had been married for about four years. Until now Nora had lived in the Hooke family home, Wiry Gully, near Dungog where her husband had visited every four months or so.

In early 1864, news of a great flood in the Moonie area had swiftly reached the *Maitland Mercury*, the newspaper read everywhere in the Hunter Valley, including Dungog. The *Mercury* carried a report that Duncan Forbes MacKay had lost 4,000 head of sheep.

'The thundering idiots,' exclaimed Duncan to the relieved Hookes and MacKays, not long after the waters had receded and he had headed south to Wiry Gully. 'We've only lost about 200.'

Duncan explained that his land had fared much better than others. There was sufficient high ground to protect most of the livestock. Many people in the Moonie had been ruined by the floods. But the value of the flood–resilient MacKay property could only improve.

Eventually alone with Nora in her bedroom, Duncan sat on the edge of the bed in his underclothes. He lit a post–coital cigarillo, which usually lasted much longer than sex with his wife, and looked at Nora in her night dress under the bedclothes.

'It is time my dear. The natives are far less troublesome. The rains have gone. As a rule of thumb, we won't have another flood for another seven years.'

He lazily blew smoke into the air: 'Once the mess from the flood has been tidied up, I would like you to join me.'

Nora did not require any persuasion, although she was still deeply grieving for her mother, Mary Ann, who had died recently. Nora knew her brother, Henry, now wished his sister gone, together with her two children and disagreeable husband.

'Yes, Duncan, we shall come.'

Nora sat up, plumped a pillow behind her back and swept her long blond hair away from her face: 'Ada is now three but Forbes is not yet a year. Give me a few months to get him strong enough for the journey. We would not want him to come to any harm.'

Duncan nodded quickly in agreement. He had been overjoyed when his first son was born and had insisted the baby would be christened using Uncle Forbes' full name, the same as his own: Duncan Forbes.

Later that year, Duncan escorted his family up to the Moonie to the new Nindigully Hotel, known by everyone as the 'Gully, while his home, Ningan, was prepared for its extra occupants. The new pub was only a few miles upstream and had been converted from a disused sheep shearers' shed on one of Duncan's properties. The publican, Thomas Bradbury, and his wife were immensely grateful to Duncan for his generosity in providing the property and for his signature on the licence application form.

Mrs Bradbury had greeted a weary Nora warmly after Duncan had left his wife and children in her care while he had to ride off on urgent business.

The publican's wife, in her mid–thirties, looked the part. Bright rouge, red lips, excessively coiffured hair and an impressive cleavage were guaranteed to attract thirsty men along the now busy, dusty track leading northwards to the expanding frontier. It was rumoured too that she was occasionally generous with her affections, if a man were lucky enough to catch her fancy and had several shillings in his pocket.

'Ay up ducky. Welcome to the 'Gully. Nice it is to talk to another white woman,' she said in a jolly, broad English midlands' accent. She gave Nora a deep hug and planted a sweaty, friendly kiss on the new arrival's cheek.

'I'm Bridget but everyone calls me Biddy'.

The young Mrs MacKay failed to repress a shudder as the older woman wrapped her in a warm embrace, her ample bosom squashing against Nora's chest. But she was not the daughter of a long line of English squires for nothing. Over familiarity with the lower orders was unacceptable. Especially with one who was sluttishly–dressed and sounded as if she might have once been a young English convict?

She stepped back and said sternly: 'Thank you Mrs Bradbury. I would be grateful if you could show us to our room.'

Biddy was nonplussed for a second. Nora's standoffishness and accent took her right back to the terrifying time when she was transported from her English village, barely in her teens, for stealing some freshly–baked bread. The baker had demanded that the magistrate impose a harsh penalty on the hungry girl.

Nora looked pointedly at her valise. After a few moments' hesitation, Biddy picked it up and muttered: 'Follow me.' Under her breath she mouthed bitterly: 'My Lady.'

Burning resentment in Biddy's mind towards the system which had expelled her from England at a cruelly young age flared into an overwhelming desire for revenge on its personification.

Biddy carefully placed Nora's valise on the floor, turned as if to leave but tarried by the door. Her lips formed a half–smile but her eyes were frozen: 'We are very grateful to Duncan', she said, emphasising the first name of Nora's husband.

'He's such a lovely man.'

Biddy paused and glared at Nora, before ever so slowly slipping in an acid–tipped stiletto: 'Such a loving man.'

Biddy turned away, fluttering her eyelids, one hand clasping a new necklace on her heaving breast.

She murmured, barely audibly, as she put her other hand on the door handle: 'Oh yes, such a loving *and* generous man.'

Nora's face reddened as Biddy slowly disappeared behind the door, leaving a poisonous smirk dripping in the air.

Nora and the two children left the Nindigully Hotel the next day.

At first flustered by his wife's rage Duncan was fortuitously rescued by events. He had at last persuaded an ailing Robert Dunn to sell his property, Bullamon, not long before the old squatter had died. Nora's £3,000 would come in useful to complete the purchase.

'We could use your dowry to quickly buy Bullamon. You remember the place, about twenty–four miles south of here, downriver. We stopped to buy some stores on the way.

'The house is a handsome property, ideal for a family,' he suggested, unsure of Nora's reaction.

'That could be acceptable,' his wife snapped, 'provided the property is in my name.

'And you repay my loan – not dowry – in due course.'

Nora's first impression of Bullamon close up was mixed. She could see that the property, like a medieval castle, used the river to protect itself from attack on one side. The main house was on high ground. It would not take much to do it up. Some of the outbuildings would need to be demolished but a few were still serviceable. In a way she was grateful that she would have a project to get her teeth into and help put behind her mother's death and the comforts of life she had left behind in Wiry Gully. Troubling though was a camp of about one hundred blacks nearby.

But Duncan's stockman, Jonathan, was reassuring: 'Good blackfellas, Mrs MacKay. My friends. No danger.'

The relationship between Nora and Duncan, cool at the start of their life at Bullamon, gradually warmed again. Nora tolerated Duncan's visits to her bedroom. She knew it was her wifely duty. Biddy Bradbury's name was never mentioned.

It was unfortunate that within a year Nora's next baby was born at Bullamon while Duncan was away with Sam Cobb, mustering some cattle.

'Are you sure you will be alright alone with the children, Nora?' Duncan had asked his wife over breakfast before he left.

'Yes of course, I will,' Nora had replied irritably, rubbing her lower back, her protruding belly scraping the kitchen table.

'There's no sign anything will happen today.'

But Nora was wrong. Her contractions started mid–morning. She didn't panic. Nora knew what was coming. When she was a girl she had rushed off with her mother several times, responding to urgent pleas for help with difficult deliveries. And her mother had helped her daughter with her first two births. Now the third was imminent. But her mother was dead and could not help her this time.

Nora calmly prepared a picnic for Ada and Forbes and sent them out of the back door towards the sandy mound overlooking the river.

'Ada you are a big girl now. Four years old. Go on now, take your brother onto the hill and play there until I call you.'

Ada nodded doubtfully. She had heard her parents talking and knew a baby was coming. It had been expected a week ago. And Mother's stomach was very big. Ada took two–year old Forbes' hand and led the puzzled toddler to the top of the sloping river bank. At the top she turned to wave uncertainly to her mother but Nora had already gone inside.

Nora was now lying on her bed The gaps between contractions were short. She lay sweating with her knees in the air and pushed for an hour. But this baby was obstinate and refused to appear. Exhausted and racking her brains, she suddenly remembered what her mother had done with one difficult birth.

Nora stood up and tugged her sweaty night gown off. Naked and groaning she put her hands on her knees and began to squat down and stand upright again. Almost at once mucus and a rush of water splashed onto the floor between her feet. With one hand she felt a little, slimy head easing out. She pushed harder and screamed in pain. The baby slithered down into her frantically, catching hands.

Nora placed the baby girl onto the bed, quickly cut the cord with some kitchen scissors and washed her with a wet cloth. The baby started crying but quickly stopped as she took to her mother's breast. One–handed, Nora managed to half put on a dressing gown and walked with the suckling new born to the back door to call Ada and Forbes back. But they were already standing in the kitchen.

'We heard the new baby, Mother,' Ada said simply.

Nora smiled, her black–ringed, tired eyes crinkled as she bent down: 'Look Ada. Look Forbes. You have a beautiful new sister.'

Tears welled up in Nora's eyes and began to drip down onto the new baby's shiny tummy.

'Why are you crying Mother?'

Nora took a deep breath and recovered her composure.

'Because I am so happy.'

Forbes looked up at his mother confused. He recognised the word happy but had never associated it with crying before.

'We are going to call your sister' – Nora paused to bite her lip to prevent herself from sobbing again – 'we are going to call your sister the same name as my mother. You remember what that was Ada?'

'Mary Annie?'

Nora laughed: 'That is close enough my darling. It was actually Mary Ann but, yes, let's call your new sister, Mary Annie.'

When Nora had moved into Bullamon she had quickly taken charge of its refurbishment. Overruling Duncan's objections, the new chatelaine spent money and began to create a large, comfortable residence befitting an increasingly prosperous pastoralist –rancher – and his family.

The living room was furnished with fine furniture bought in Dungog by Nora's brothers and carted up to Bullamon. She decorated the walls with prints of the famous French artist, Doré. A children's room and one for a maid and a nurse were eventually provided. Nora would never have to give birth by herself again. Husband and wife had separate bedrooms. There was a dairy below ground at the end of a large verandah. Grape and passion fruit vines thrived and an orange tree was planted over the grave of dead sheep. Good fertiliser, Duncan explained.

A building with a dormitory for shearers and stockmen was erected not far away in which a separate room was installed for a tutor engaged to teach the first two children to read and write. An outside bathroom with a shower was built. In time Bullamon expanded to include a blacksmith's forge.

The blacks' camp was about 50 yards away on the other side of a stout wooden fence. Only Jonathan, was allowed into the garden, but never the house. Everyone knew even a tame black could suddenly turn violent for no apparent reason.

While Nora was recovering from the birth of Mary Annie, she realised that Duncan must be sleeping with other women because it was a good six months before they had sex again. She turned a blind eye because Duncan was discreet – in fact she welcomed the respite.

305

Chapter 45: Captain Thunderbolt

Hugh Bryden was drunk. Some men are happy drunks; some are sad. Bryden belonged to the latter category. He was sitting by himself in the 'Gully' pub gloomily looking down as he swished his drink around. Bryden refilled his glass from a bottle of beer fetched from the pub's cool cellar.

A friendly hand tapped him on the shoulder: 'I thought you might be here, Hugh.'

Bryden twisted round, spilling his drink: 'Hello, my dear fellow.'

Duncan MacKay sat down opposite his best friend and waved his hand towards the bar: 'Biddie, lassie, bring me a bottle of beer too, if you please.'

The publican's wife disappeared into the pub's cellar and returned as quickly as she could before Duncan changed his mind. She knew that he almost invariably drank brandy. Beer was much more expensive. The carting costs from Newcastle on the coast were high.

'Damnation, why did I do it, Duncan?' Bryden slurred.

His friend sighed to himself. Duncan had heard the story several times already. Hugh had met up with some old army pals in Sydney. They'd gone out on the 'razzle dazzle'. The tipsy magistrate had become infatuated with a barmaid in The Fortune of War pub and had married her after a whirlwind romance. Before this Duncan had always looked forward to his friend's regular visits but lately Hugh had begun to change. He drank too much, became maudlin and bemoaned his stupidity that he had married 'beneath himself'.

'Now she wants money to set up house in Sydney and expects me to join her,' Bryden groaned, wallowing in the depths of self–pity.

Deeper in the shadows of the bar, hidden by the milling evening crowd of drovers, shearers, and carters were three men drinking with their shoulders hunched. With their wide–brimmed hats it was impossible to see their faces. This was not uncommon in the 'Gully' where suspected duffers did not want their faces too well–known.

'Fred, have you seen the two men drinking beer near the door?'

The target of the question craned his neck and threw a quick glance through the crowd. He glimpsed two well–dressed men. One looked like a prosperous squatter; the other, clearly worse for wear, wore a smart, if faded, ex–military jacket.

Fred shook his heads: 'Who are they?'

'The one on the right is the magistrate, Hugh Bryden.'

Fred's face tightened and his hand instinctively began to reach for his pistol, its holster covered by his overcoat. Bryden and his police troopers had cornered him and his gang a couple of years ago in northern New South Wales. He hadn't seen Bryden's face during the furious gunfight but had seen the magistrate fire his pistol with deadly accuracy.

'You mean the one who killed Jonny?'

His mate nodded.

'What's he doing over the border?'

'He's best mates with the other one –Duncan MacKay – the squatter who owns all of the Moonie run.'

Ah yes, Fred thought to himself. He'd heard of Duncan MacKay and his family. His partner, Mary Ann Dubb's father, had a small holding down near Dungog, which he'd managed to buy from the MacKays during the 40s' slump. Now Mary Ann was holed up in their camp caring for their baby son, Fred junior, who was feeling poorly.

The bushranger was relieved to see a few minutes later MacKay leading a stumbling Bryden out of the pub's front door. Even a drunk magistrate might have recognised Fred from the picture of the man on the Wanted Dead or Alive poster for the notorious bushranger, Captain Thunderbolt.

Bryden woke the following morning in the Bullamon stockmen's hut not long after day break. He swayed outside and splashed his face in the horse trough. After a pee around the side of the hut, he forced himself up onto his horse. After a bender he usually went for a solitary ride, delaying the embarrassment of talking to Duncan and his family while helping clear his sore head.

The sun was still low in the blue sky and the shadows of the trees bordering the muddy, brown river stretched long on the rich red soil. Bryden reined his horse in to take a long swig of warm water from his saddle bottle. He frowned as he noticed some still–fresh signs of three horses heading inland. All of Duncan's men were still in bed. These suspicious tracks must have been made by strangers last night.

The magistrate pulled his horse round and started to follow the hoof prints. At the edge of some scrub after about half an hour's gentle trot, he stopped when he smelt a breakfast fire. Dismounting he began to creep up a ridge.

'Put your rifle down, Mr Bryden' a soft voice said from behind him.

'Very slowly', the man continued.

'We saw you coming from a mile away,' the voice added.

The magistrate was disarmed and his arms tied behind his back by two other men who slipped out of the shrubs.

'Let's shoot the bastard, Fred,' one of them growled.

'There's no witnesses around here.'

Bryden suddenly realised his captor must be Fredrick Ward, the gentleman bushranger, known as Captain Thunderbolt.

Ward walked to the front and looked at the magistrate, holstered his pistol and folded his arms imperiously, as if a judge addressing a defendant.

'Mr Bryden, if I were captured by you I would be taken by you to Sydney for trial.'

The bushranger sucked his teeth and spat out a piece of salt beef.

'I would be hanged, wouldn't I?'

The magistrate nodded, knowing he had just signed his death warrant.

It took a good ten minutes to find a tree bough high and strong enough for a hanging. Ward's accomplices were growing impatient, their fingers near their triggers, itching to finish Bryden off until, at last, their leader found what he was looking for. The magistrate was bundled onto to his now bareback horse and a noose placed around his neck.

The magistrate was calm, his face impassive. The gang were disappointed. They had been hoping for some last minute grovelling plea from Bryden for them to spare his life.

'I congratulate you sir. You are clearly a man of courage. Do you have any last request?' Ward asked.

'No, damn you. You will not be long behind me,' the magistrate spat.

Ward slapped the rear of the horse and mercilessly watched his victim swing, face contorted and legs kicking. The horse galloped off wildly in a panic. They cut the hanged man down and tossed him on the ground – no longer a person, now just a sack of flesh and bones.

Ward wedged Bryden's saddle into a fork in the tree trunk.

'I want people to find him and see that justice can be wrought on those who dispense it too liberally,' Ward said.

His accomplices looked perplexed. Fred was always using highfalutin words. They didn't care. They were satisfied with the revenge for their mate who had been shot by the magistrate.

Duncan was distraught. His friend's horse had eventually found its way back to Bullamon, its muzzle flecked with foam, almost on its knees. He'd ridden out desperately to search but a heavy rain shower had obliterated any tracks. He would have carried on looking but he knew Nora had received an urgent letter from her sister Emily, his brother Kenneth's wife.

Emily had demanded Nora make haste and return to Dungog because the Duke of Edinburgh, Prince Alfred, was to visit Maitland, not far from Dungog.

'You must come Nora. Our husband's eldest brother, George, is on the welcoming committee. There will be an agriculture show, horse races and a ball! Kenneth is sure one of Cangon's horses will do well. Imagine, we will get the opportunity to be introduced to our Queen's son!'

The weekly mail meant that there was no time for a delay. The journey south with all the family would take three days. The MacKays set out in some style in an American covered wagon, laden with camping equipment and the children, with a buggy for Duncan and Nora. For the first leg there was a drover for the wagon and Jonathan scouted ahead. The second day would be by a Cobb & Co stagecoach and the last leg on the steam train on the Newcastle line.

On the first night out, the MacKays and the wagon driver were sitting comfortably around a camp table. Jonathan interrupted their meal, suddenly walking into the firelight: 'Rider coming.'

Duncan warily pointed his carbine at a man who slowly led his horse up to the edge of the camp.

'Sir, I mean you good people no harm. We are camped no more than ten minutes from here. My little boy has been taken poorly. His mother fears for his life. Have you some food you could spare?' he said out of the half shadows.

Nora stood: 'Of course we have some food.

'I also have some medical knowledge, Sir,' she added politely, the stranger, whoever he was, had good manners.

'I would be happy to accompany you and help your wife.'

Nora and Duncan left the children with their wagon drover and followed the man in their buggy. As they walked towards the stranger's camp fire, Duncan thought he detected a faint flash of recognition from the man. He also noticed there were more horses tethered than were needed for two adults. But there was no sign of other riders. Something was not quite right. Duffers? His eyes crossed the stranger's and this time, even through the flickering firelight, he was convinced the man had recognised him. There was something else too. Was it a flash of guilt?

Nora took charge immediately, her nursing skills coming to the fore.

'Here, let me, my dear,' she said cradling the boy's head, feeling his forehead and looking into his eyes.

'He has a bad fever. Nothing more. You must make sure he drinks a little but often. 'Keep him wrapped up. He is young and strong. When his fever breaks, which I'm sure it will by tomorrow morning, he will need food. We will leave you this bread and salt beef.'

'Thank you, thank you,' the mother gasped in relief, her hand squeezing Nora's arm in gratitude, her eyes looking at Nora's face and smiling.

Nora stood and looked down at the small boy, his sweating head now resting in his mother's lap.

'He will recover soon. Trust me.'

On the way back Nora observed: 'Do you know, I fancy that poor woman recognised me, Duncan.'

'And I had the same feeling about him.'

Duncan handed Nora a pencil–written note: 'I noticed him scribbling this before we left. It's too dark to read now. I wonder what it says?'

Nora squinted in the faint day–breaking light: 'I suppose he has written to express his thanks. He did seem very polite.'

Her husband returned the unread note to his pocket and thought no more of it until the family were jolting southwards in the stagecoach.

At a horse change stop, he fished the paper out of his pocket and read: 'Thank you Mr MacKay. Your cattle will never be touched by me. Yours etc. Captain Thunderbolt.'

Duncan returned home from Dungog as soon as he could on a swift horse he bought from his brother, Kenneth who understood why Duncan felt he had to leave as quickly as possible to try and find his friend Hugh Bryden's body.

Their father hugged and kissed his children goodbye and stiffly gave his wife a peck on the cheek.

'Say hello to Prince Alfred from me,' her husband said to Nora in an attempt in jocularity.

Nora smiled in assent.

Duncan eventually found Hugh's saddle and a rope hanging from a bough. He never told anyone about the rope. His gut instinct told him instantly that the murderer must have been Captain Thunderbolt. Only someone of that ilk would have had the audacity. He swore he would kill the bushranger at the next opportunity. But Duncan never had the chance. Frederick Ward was eventually gunned down by a sergeant police trooper.

And Duncan never found his friend's body. Wild dogs – dingoes – ate the meat and crunched the bones, leaving no trace of the former magistrate.

In time, the next MacKay boy born at Bullamon was christened Lewis Bryden – called Lou by everyone – in memory of Duncan's friend.

Down south in Dungog, the two sisters, Nora and Emily, giggled as they began to try on their outfits for the Royal Ball. For Nora, it was the first time she had worn crinoline. She had found the fashion of hooped skirts and petticoats wildly impractical and too restrictive for life on a frontier homestead.

'Both of you deserve to be the belle of the ball,' Kenneth said when the two women paraded themselves in a dress rehearsal.

'Prince Alfred will be overwhelmed by your beauty,' he chuckled.

Chapter 46: A right royal bastard

Prince Alfred, the Duke of Edinburgh was Queen Victoria's second son. Like his elder brother, Bertie, the heir to the throne, he was a compulsive womaniser, drank and smoked too much, gambled and enjoyed shooting. The Prince of Wales introduced Alfred to Parisian brothels including the exquisite Le Chabanais, which housed Bertie's famous *siege d'amour*, love seat. This sex–aid enabled its royal owner to enjoy two women at once.

Unsurprisingly Alfred was bored by the civic duties that he was supposed to carry out under his parents' plan to make their family a model to be admired by the people and thereby diffuse republican tendencies. He found the cutting of ribbons and unveiling of plaques to commemorate the opening of civic amenities tiresome. Pretending to be interested in talking to provincial dignitaries and local politicians wearied him.

But he loved the sea and became a competent naval officer. His first command was the frigate HMS *Galatea*, a combined sail and steam–powered vessel.

Alfred was sent out on the *Galatea* to Australia and New Zealand in 1867. The news of the visit, the first by a royal, was greeted with enormous enthusiasm by the British colonies and extravagant receptions were planned. In Victoria's capital, Melbourne, the early experience was mixed. The illuminations were magnificent. An Australian cricket eleven defeated a rest of the world side. But later that evening a sectarian riot erupted between Orange and republican Irish. Shots were fired.

The Duke of Edinburgh's attention turned at night to one of his favourite sports in which he excelled: whoring. The prince shouted he wanted 'girls' and that was what he got. Melbourne's chief police commissioner and former army officer, Captain Fredrick Standish, a scion of English gentry, was also a bachelor and no stranger, professionally and personally, to Melbourne's *demimonde*. Diggers fresh from the goldfields and made rich overnight had demanded sex in Melbourne. And plenty of it. Brothels from luxurious to sleazy sprang up to satisfy the burgeoning market.

Standish proved a willing guide for the prince. Bordellos were graced by royal visits from the prince and his aristocratic entourage. During Alfred's visit the city's leading newspaper, *The Age*, maintained a loyal silence about the prince and his friends' behaviour. After their departure it was less restrained and asked whether 'the wise and experienced gentlemen of the Reception Committee would like their sons to be exposed to the dissipation and the temptation to which they have treated the Queen's son during his six weeks' stay.'

Not to be outdone by its sister colony, New South Wales also planned extravaganzas to entertain the prince. One such was a visit to the colony's second most important metropolis and its environs: Newcastle and the Hunter Valley. The prince was greeted by the customary fanfare at the town's port and was only mildly surprised to be led by the local merchants under a welcoming arch of coal, the local valuable mineral. The prince was, no doubt, relieved to escape Newcastle and be transported by steam train into the country by a committee which had planned a day at an agricultural show with horse races followed by a ball at Maitland, twenty five miles from Newcastle.

This time Alfred and his friends were pleasantly surprised and indeed impressed by the quality of the horses bred by the local landowners. The noble animals were not the only creatures attracting the prince's attention at the races. The wives and daughters of the local landowners and breeders drew admiring glances from him. Some of the younger girls blushed, so obvious was his ogling. The prince placed bets, won and lost, and enjoyed himself, free from the need to make a speech or cut another ribbon. In the winners' enclosure he was introduced to a Kenneth MacKay, his wife Emily and her sister Leonora MacKay, whose husband was detained by essential business on their property a great distance away.

The prince expressed great admiration for Mr MacKay's winning horse. The two men discussed the finer points of breeding the noble animals. Kenneth MacKay, not one to stand on ceremony, invited the prince to visit his stud farm.

'We live about an hour's ride from here. Our property is called Cangon, near the village of Dungog.'

'Thank you Mr MacKay. Unfortunately my days are full of official functions. Perhaps another time?'

The prince's disappointment was sincere. Nothing would have pleased him more than to have another period free of his duties. He was also interested in Leonora MacKay, a striking woman with an exotic olive skin.

Alfred had found it more difficult to procure women in Sydney than Melbourne. There was no police commissioner with intimate knowledge of the city's brothels to show him the way. In fact New South Wales' governor had already given the royal visitor a dressing down for consorting with undesirable people. Yes, the prince was feeling distinctly in the mood for female company.

After the races the royal party repaired to Maitland's Northumberland Hotel for a grand luncheon after which a ball was to be held. The prince talked about horse breeding with people who were even more knowledgeable than him and his companions. Horses from England had been imported and bred to suit local conditions. Forty regiments of British cavalry in India were desperate for mounts after a major rebellion by native soldiers in the north of the country, dubbed the Indian Mutiny. The cavalry particularly favoured those from New South Wales' Hunter Valley and had given them the name of Walers.

Alfred noticed the affluent landowners in the Hunter Valley he spoke to were more at ease in his company than the business and professional classes in Sydney and Melbourne. Their manners and speech less stilted in his company. The Australian accent, which his foppish companions openly sneered at, was a barely perceptible, pleasant patina. His entourage was informed, with only mild exaggeration, that the fertile Hunter Valley had been settled mainly by the most superior of colonists: English gentry and officers from the British army and navy. Their women too seemed intriguingly less deferential towards him.

After several glasses of champagne his royal highness needed to urinate. Alfred could not be expected to use the communal smelly, outside privy so he climbed up the first flight of stairs and made his way along the corridor towards his room where he would find a chamber pot. Not watching where he was going and slightly unsteady on his feet, he barged into a young woman coming in the opposite direction, just outside his door. The two of them clashed heads. Alfred felt himself go giddy and grabbed his door handle. The door flew open and the prince and the young woman tripped over each other onto the bedroom floor.

The prince had the good grace to apologise immediately. As he scrambled to his feet he said: 'I am most awfully sorry, Madam. I was not watching where I was going.'

Alfred bent down and pulled a hand to help her up. He put an arm around her waist. Alfred quickly saw a wedding ring. If anything this was an encouragement: finding aristocratic wives at the London court happy to oblige him, discreetly of course, was not too much of a challenge. He glanced at her face and recognised the attractive woman from the winners' enclosure. Alfred smiled to himself, keeping her close to his chest. The day was very warm and both of them were sweating profusely.

The prince quickly dabbed his silk handkerchief in a bowl of water on the dressing table: 'Here, allow me,' he said wiping her forehead before she could refuse.

'Is it always as hot as this in Sydney?'

'Sometimes, your royal highness,' she replied, holding his gaze.

'And this is Maitland, not Sydney, she added, matter–of–factly.

'Forgive me, I recall we were introduced previously, but could you please remind me of your name?'

'My name is Leonora, your royal highness'. She paused: 'Leonora MacKay.'

'I think we can dispense with excessive formality, Leonora,' the prince said with the mildest exasperation.

'Yes sir.'

The prince stared into Nora's eyes.

'Your name is Scottish but you sound English?'

'My father's name was Hooke.'

317

'Hooke of Crookes Hall in Gloucestershire,' she added proudly.

'Ah, by Jove, a country squire, no less. An unusual address though,' Alfred said jocularly, failing to keep a patronising tone out of his voice.

'Yes sir. But *our* family can trace its lineage back to William the Conqueror.'

Alfred knew what the colonial minx was implying: his father's minor royal German family – Saxe–Coburg Gotha – was *parvenu* by comparison.

'So you are really English?'

'No. My father was but I am Australian.' She paused and thought for a second: 'But I am proud to be British too.'

There was a heavy silence for a few moments. Nora averted her eyes from the prince's over–familiar gaze, his face still close to hers. She began to pull herself free: 'I must return to my family, sir.'

Alfred ignored her and on an impulse leant forward to kiss her on her lips.

'Please don't.'

The prince ignored Nora and kissed her cheek, once then twice and then gently on the lips. Nora had never been kissed so softly before. The sensation was enhanced by the prince's clean–shaven cheek, so unlike her husband's prickly beard. She was flattered too by the advances of a handsome son of the Queen of the British Empire. Her attempt to push Alfred off was half–hearted, influenced further by an inexplicable recognition of his *droit du seigneur*.

Now the prince's tongue was searching out hers. Apart from her husband she had never been kissed by a man in a sexual manner. In fact Duncan hardly ever kissed her on the mouth and had never used his tongue. Sex with her husband had always been brief and on his terms: pleasure for him and children for her.

Alfred kicked the door shut.

Nora closed her eyes as the prince softly caressed her breasts through the silk material of her dress. Nora realised that she was in the hands of a dangerous lover. Her body wanted more but her head screamed: 'Dear God what am I doing?'

She feebly tried to press him away but he refused to budge. Now Alfred picked her up and sat her on the bed. Even consensual sex with a lady wearing a crinoline outfit was a difficult undertaking. But the prince was an expert. He carefully raised the steel hoops up above Nora's waist, lay back on the pillow and placed Leonora on top, her knees straddling him.

Nora tried to speak but no words came out of her mouth. Alfred was now doing things with his fingers she had never felt before. Although aroused, she also felt vaguely ridiculous. Her hooped dress and petticoat were tucked up under her breasts blocking her view and imprisoning her arms.

Down below penetration was comparatively easy. Alfred smoothed her split crotch drawers open, lifted Nora up and slid in.

The prince grabbed Nora's buttocks and moved her up and down. Although the position was completely new to her, she quickly realised she controlled the tempo. Slow, fast, slow and fast again, Nora felt him inside her moving up and down. Alfred lay back and thought of Australia for a couple of minutes then groaned in relief.

After a brief moment he lifted himself onto to his elbows and looked up into Nora's eyes and smiled in amusement: 'Thank you, your prince is truly grateful.'

She said nothing and stared back, her face a mask.

Mistaking her silence for alarm at the possible consequences, he said: 'Fear not Leonora. Your honour is safe with me.'

Alfred chuckled: 'Perhaps I should visit that stud farm of Mr MacKay's after all? I have enjoyed myself so much in Australia I believe I shall return.'

He smiled at Nora: 'It would be pleasant to renew acquaintance?'

Nora did not reply.

The second in line to the British throne lifted Nora off, pushed himself away from the bed and stood up. He pulled his trousers up and twanged his rubber braces, the latest thing in menswear, over his shoulders.

He smiled down at Leonora and stepped away buttoning his coat: 'I would much rather stay here with you, my dear. But, I fear I must return to the party and make jolly, small talk. But before then, please excuse me, I am desperate!'

Alfred almost ran into the adjoining bathroom. Leonora could hear him peeing.

The prince washed his hands and reappeared. He walked back to Nora and kissed her hand.

He smiled briefly: 'Ach, du bist sehr huebsch, Leonora.'

Nora guessed the German words meant she was beautiful or something similar.

Alfred bowed and clicked his heels in mock formality: 'Goodbye, Leonora MacKay.'

His head peering back around the bedroom door, Alfred added: 'I suggest you remain here for a spell. We should not be seen coming down the stairs together. I shall see you are not disturbed for at least half an hour.'

Nora had been surprised that the prince had complimented her in German. But why should she be? How ironic, she thought, the royal family of the British Empire – the biggest empire the world had ever seen – was, in fact, German.

Nora sat on the edge of the bed washing her thighs with Alfred's silk handkerchief. Out of the corner of her eye she caught a reflection of her face in a dressing table mirror. She did not look distraught; her face was calm. She regretted giving in to Alfred's advances but she felt no shame. After all she knew Duncan was regularly unfaithful. Besides, she was shocked to admit, she had enjoyed the brief encounter.

Downstairs Alfred enjoyed drinking more of the local wine. After an hour he gave his apologies to the committee. He had been taken unwell and would have to leave. Perhaps he was suffering from the heat? Everyone could see he was red–faced and perspiring.

Peering through the throng Emily MacKay caught a glimpse of Alfred's back. She turned to her sister: 'Oh, Nora, what a shame. I hear the prince has had a funny turn. I expect his English constitution has not yet become accustomed to our climate.'

Leonora nodded, her thoughts elsewhere: 'Yes, I expect you are right.'

Duncan arrived back at Cangon after another week. At the evening meal with Kenneth and Emily, Leonora made sure her husband did not drink too much. As soon as it was polite, she allowed Duncan to lead her off to bed.

Alfred returned to Sydney where his tour ended in a disaster which almost cost him his life. At a public picnic, a mad Irishman, Henry O'Farrell, who fancied himself a Fenian rebel, shot the prince in the back. The bullet was diverted away from Alfred's spine by his snazzy bracers. Alfred was badly wounded but survived. He left on the *Galatea* leaving behind a Sydney mortified with shame and simmering with anti–Irish feeling. O'Farrell was tried and sentenced to death. Despite Alfred's pleas that his life be spared, the deranged man was executed.

Two days after Christmas in 1868 and nine months after the prince's visit to Maitland, Nora gave birth to a baby girl.

Duncan's wife wrote in a red wax–sealed envelope to Prince Alfred care of Government House in Sydney. Anyone opening the envelope would have read that on his next visit to Sydney, the prince was cordially invited to visit Mr Kenneth MacKay's stud farm on the Williams River. The letter's author, Mr MacKay's sister–in–law, mentioned that there had been an addition to the farm since the prince had met Mr MacKay in Maitland. The letter was worded in such a way that a casual reader would assume that a prize mare had given birth to a foal.

Within a year, Prince Alfred returned to Australia. It was a private, unofficial visit and caused far less comment in the newspapers. Few wished to be reminded of the shameful end to his first visit. Some thought it odd that he would return so soon to the country where he was almost murdered.

Also surprisingly, he returned once more in 1870. Given his interest in horse breeding, the prince decided to visit the Hunter Valley's leading stud farms. At Cangon he was greeted by Kenneth MacKay and shown around the property. After afternoon tea, he was re–

introduced to the ladies of the house and the group took a turn around the property's well–known, beautiful gardens.

'Your highness, you might recall my sister–in–law, Leonora MacKay? You met briefly at the Maitland races?'

'Yes of course, I remember clearly, Mr MacKay.'

The prince coughed nervously: 'I see you have been blessed with another child, Mrs MacKay, since we last met?'

'Yes, I have Sir.'

Kenneth and Emily had moved aside, allowing the prince to stoop down and inspect a small girl, little more than a baby sleeping in her pram.

Nora pushed away a lock of hair from her daughter's face. Yes, Alfred could see a family resemblance. Fair–haired, a broad mouth and a light skin. *Verdammt noch mal!* he swore silently to himself in German, she looks just like my mother.

'We have christened her, Agnes, the pure one. My husband who is, alas, absent once more is quite delighted with her.'

There was a silence as Nora stood up and said quietly, looking steadily at Alfred.

'As am I, Sir.'

Alfred nodded, relieved. The last thing his ghastly, dictatorial mother would want at the moment was another scandal. Not long before, Alfred's brother, Bertie, had almost been named as a correspondent in a divorce. He realised that Leonora had only wanted him to have the opportunity to see his daughter.

The prince looked around at the cultivated roses and shrubbery:

'This is a beautiful garden. Like an English one but more lush.'

'Things grow more quickly here than at Home,' Nora said.

Alfred cocked his head: 'You still call England Home?'

'Yes, strange isn't it? I suppose one day we will cut the ties that bind us.'

Two small children, toddlers, were playing on the lawn in front of them. Unlike their mother, they had peaches and cream complexions. Alfred smiled ruefully as he looked at them: 'Yours?'

Nora nodded.

'I envy them their childhood.'

He sighed: 'Mine was far too regimented.'

Behind a bush a peacock suddenly crowed and walked into view, its plumage opening in a magnificent sunlit display. The prince's pensive mood was broken. He bad polite farewell to the MacKays. Alfred never visited Australia again.

There was always something different about Agnes compared to her siblings. She hated being kissed and cuddled. She enjoyed dressing up in her brothers' clothes. Agnes never married. In later years she became more mannish and took to wearing tweed and sensible shoes. She enjoyed breeding dogs.

From time to time Nora would watch the young Agnes from out of a window and wonder how many other illegitimate royal children Alfred had fathered around the world.

Chapter 47: Goodbye to the Moonie

Bugger, shit, bloody,' the words suddenly spewed for no reason out of seven–year old Mary Annie's mouth as she sat down for breakfast.

The reaction by Nora was instantaneous: a hard slap on her daughter's cheek. Mary Annie ran outside crying from Bullamon's kitchen. She ran half angry, half ashamed up the sandy mound next to the river – the refuge for the MacKay children when they wished to get away from the adult world. She slumped down disconsolately on the bank and threw sticks down into the muddy Moonie. Watching them float away on the endlessly moving stream was strangely comforting. Mary Annie knew she had been naughty but for some odd reason she had been unable to stop the words coming out of her mouth.

Even though Mary Annie was a bit fey – she'd recently landed in a bowl of cream, trying to fly like a bird down the steps into the dairy cellar – her siblings at the breakfast table had listened to their sister's outburst in astonishment. They recognised the words: the Bullamon stockmen, drovers, shearers, carter and blacksmith all swore loudly and frequently. The MacKay boys knew to expect a thrashing from their father if they were heard copying the men. The girls quickly learnt that it was unladylike to use foul words. And to be unladylike was one of, no, was the worst possible thing in their mother's eyes.

Their father's heavy riding boots fractured the stunned silence in the kitchen as he strode in from the outside privy – the dunny.

'What's the matter with Mary Annie? Why is she sitting up on the mound by herself?' he asked the family over his shoulder, washing his hands.

'She used bad words, Father,' the oldest boy, Forbes replied disapprovingly, failing to disguise a faint note of glee in his voice.

'Nora?'

'Forbes is right,' sighed his wife. 'I don't know what came over her.'

Nora stopped and made a shamefaced grimace: 'And I slapped her.'

Duncan raised his eyebrows. Nora did not often lose her temper with the children. He chewed his bread and jam slowly and cut a piece of salt beef, uncertain how to deal with the family disagreement.

With all the grown–up confidence of the eldest child, eleven–year old Ada sniffed: 'I think Mary Annie's upset you have sold our home.'

She looked nervously at her parents, aware she was treading on adult ground.

'The blacksmith told us,' she added.

Duncan looked around the table and saw the troubled young faces.

He took a mouthful of sweet tea: 'Forbes, fetch Mary Annie. You all deserve to be told.'

Duncan looked at his children sitting around the table and Nora standing behind them. He felt justifiable paternal pride. His eyes met Nora's. He turned his gaze away. It was at close family moments like this that Duncan regretted his peccadilloes and wished things could be better between him and his wife. He began by telling the children that, yes, somebody had wanted to buy Bullamon but he had not offered enough money. The blacksmith had got it only half–right.

Duncan didn't mention it but he knew there was at least one other person interested in buying Bullamon. He was confident that if he played his cards right, their home would get a very high price.

'Mary Annie: that means we won't be leaving immediately,' Nora said gently, putting her arm around her daughter, who suppressed a sob.

'But you mean we will be leaving sometime soon, Mother?' Ada asked uncertainly.

Nora glanced at Duncan before she admitted: 'Yes, we will be leaving.'

She held up her hand to forestall Ada's next question: 'The boys are getting to an age when they need proper schooling. And you girls need better tuition than we can arrange here.'

Nora took a deep breath: 'We will leave for Sydney in about six months.'

Mary Annie started to cry: 'Mother I don't want to leave. I love Bullamon.'

'I know my darling but you will love Sydney even more.'

Through her tears Mary Annie wailed: 'What's Sydney?'

Ada laughed: Don't be silly Mary Annie. Sydney is a city. Lots of houses where lots of people live.'

'That's right Ada. We won't stay too long in Sydney though. We will return to live not far from the Hookes and MacKays in the Hunter Valley,' her father said.

'Will we have our own home, Father?'

'Why yes, my princess. And it will be a beautiful palace which you can name.'

Are you staying with us in Sydney, Father?' asked Forbes, noticing his father looked distant.

Duncan hesitated and then replied slowly: 'Yes, but before I can, I have to ride north with Vincent to view some properties we might buy.'

Forbes' face lit up: 'Father, please, please let me come. You know I can ride and shoot.'

Duncan smiled affectionately at his pleading ten–year old, remembering how he had asked his own father exactly the same thing, twenty years ago when his father left for the Moonie with his eldest son, George.

'No you are too young, Forbes. Be patient, your time will come.'

Duncan was keen to get away. The trip with Vincent Dowling had been planned for some months. Vincent was the son of Duncan's old friend who had christened his son with the same name. The younger Vincent had been sent by his father to Bullamon to learn property management 'from the best' as his father had described Duncan.

The frontier war against the wild blacks had continued but was now far from Bullamon. In the areas which were still dangerous there were properties which could be snapped up cheaply from hard–pressed squatters who could not hold out for more.

Like a string of pearls, Duncan's grand plan was to own properties from the far north of Queensland down as far south as the Hunter Valley. Cattle would be driven down south from property to property until they would be near enough to be fattened for the markets in Newcastle and Sydney.

A few days after their father and Vincent had ridden off, the six MacKay children were sitting on the sandy mound, lined up like a flock of galahs – Australian parrots.

Ada had the youngest, baby Alma, on her lap. Forbes had a firm grip of a reluctant three–year old Agnes, who was trying to wriggle away. Mary Annie held five year–old Lou's hand.

They hadn't planned to gather; it just seemed to happen. Lou had seen Ada carrying Alma. He'd followed and then Forbes appeared too. The children were silent. Each child, apart from the baby, was wrapped up in their memories of what had been the only home they had known, and their concerns for the unfamiliar future.

Their reverie was broken by Mary Annie: 'Do you remember when I fell in there from the boat?' – she threw a stick towards the spot on the river bank – 'I was fishing and Vincent had to save me from drowning?'

They all nodded.

'And when Jonathan had to swim and save me when the boat capsized during the floods?' Forbes said.

And how those bad men had been cross jus' cos Father won all the horse races on Julian?' Lou added excitedly.

They all smiled wryly at that: Father had brought the horse up from Uncle Kenneth's Cangon stud down in Dungog. Some of the local drovers and other squatters had cast black looks at the MacKays for unfairly 'importing' a top horse from outside the district.

They carried on swapping their memories and giggling until the shadows began to lengthen and Nora called them in for supper. Mary Annie was last. She had started sketching a plan of Bullamon on a piece of paper and vowed she would never forget her first home.

What had at first seemed a casual gathering of siblings became deeply imprinted in their memories. So much so that whenever they were asked in later years about Bullamon by the next generation of MacKays, the first thing that sprang to mind was that day sitting by the Moonie watching the muddy river flowing softly by. It was the happiest and saddest day of their lives.

Within six months, the MacKays had left Bullamon for Sydney. The boys were sent to a leading private school, Sydney Grammar, and a tutor hired for the girls.

Not long after Duncan, Nora and the children had arrived in Sydney, Sybella MacKay collapsed. Her children and their families began to gather at Melbee to bid farewell. Duncan and Nora hurried up from Sydney with their children. They were the last to arrive.

Duncan's mother looked like a tiny doll in her deathbed. Her hair had been brushed and spread out over the pillow behind her. She smiled weakly when Duncan, Nora and the children tip–toed into the bedroom.

'Hello Mother,' Duncan whispered on one knee as he kissed her finely wrinkled forehead. It felt cold. Sybella's youngest son shivered as he realised his Mother was quickly slipping away.

Sybella smiled again: 'The Moonie?'

Duncan squeezed her hand gently: 'You were right to let me take the risk, Mother. Our venture will pay a very handsome dividend'.

'Aye, laddie, I'm not surprised. Your father would have been so proud,' Sybella whispered.

She strained her neck sideways and looked at Nora, her voice fluttering in her throat: 'Your mother, Mary Ann, would have been proud of you too. I know you have endured many hardships.'

Sybella panted and forced herself to focus beyond her daughter–in–law: 'Your children are thriving, my dear.' Her exhausted eyelids shut slowly. The intervals between each laboured, shallow breath shortened.

Duncan bent forward and caught Sybella's last words: *'Gabh mo leisgeul.'*

Duncan vaguely recognised what his mother had said but looked up uncertainly at the Presbyterian minister, the Reverend White, who squeezed his shoulder.

'God bless you, is what she said, my boy.'

Duncan kissed his mother's forehead and squeezed her hand. He realised with a pang of unexpected, deep sorrow that his mother was the last of the MacKays who spoke Gaelic as a first language.

They took Sybella's body down the Clarence River to Maitland and buried her next to her husband, John. It was 1873.

The next year was a dry year but, as with the times of flood, Bullamon proved resilient. Duncan ensured that the stock was husbanded carefully with adequate rations of food and water. Unlike other properties in the Moonie area, stock losses were few. The prospective buyers saw major potential for modern irrigation in the pastures away from the river. Bullamon was sold for a large sum of money, so large that it was not revealed.

Even after paying Kenneth his share and Sam Cobb a fair sum, Duncan and Nora were rich. Extremely rich.

Duncan headed north again and bought property. Hearing of the Palmer River discovery of gold he decided to drive 500 head of cattle north to Cooktown from one of his new properties, called Tilpal, near Rockhampton, halfway up the Queensland coast. Duncan was at his most happy driving cattle in the company of mates. And in the arms of laughing women in the pubs along the trail. They did not answer back.

The track became rough and narrow as it began to head towards the coast. They lost at least fifty cattle to repeated attacks from the tallest and most fiercesome blacks Duncan had seen. They almost turned back after one particularly heavy ambush but Duncan was determined not to be defeated. He never had been beaten, nor would he ever be, he swore to himself.

In crowded, unruly Cooktown the profits were good. The Chinese butchers paid top prices for the beef. In a Cooktown pub, savouring a celebratory French brandy with Vincent, Duncan noticed that his legs had become stiffer than normal. He shrugged it off as saddle soreness. He was no longer young and his muscles were not so supple.

The gold rush town was dangerous for men with money in their pockets. Shootings were commonplace. Duncan decided not to tarry long.

Two hours out from Cooktown trotting on the return journey they saw a group of spear-waving blacks ahead, standing over somebody whose life seemed in danger.

Duncan, Vincent and Jonathan charged.

Chapter 48: The Chinese cook

Not long after the MacKays had departed the Moonie, thousands of miles away a young Chinese teenager, Li Hejun, and his two elder brothers left the Guangdong province of China. They were bound for the New Gold Mountain, as the goldfields in Australia were called – California was the first Gold Mountain. News of the latest rich discovery by an Irishman, James Mulligan, on the Palmer River in northern Queensland persuaded them to leave their poverty–struck home to try their luck in the search for gold.

The brothers were Hakka Chinese. Life was tough in their home village following the bloody clan wars with the Punti Chinese living in the same area. Li's peasant family had fled to the hills leaving the fertile plains behind. The fourteen year–old had been trained by their mother to be a good cook, eking out their meagre rations. Li's culinary skills might prove useful which is why his brothers said the eager youngster could join them on their trip to Australia.

Li's elder brothers, who had no money, had previously joined the secret Hung League to obtain mutual aid and safeguard their livelihoods. The organisation arranged the three brothers' travel to the coast and their passage on a ship to Australia owned by the league. The brothers now owed the secret organisation a considerable sum and would have to work hard to clear the debt and interest. But the stories of instant wealth on the new goldfield had filled them with confidence and enthusiasm that they would quickly make their fortunes.

The ship was crowded with happy men. All of them were optimistic they would be rich soon and be able to send money home to their poor families. Li would often sit with a group which was learning English. Their teacher was a wily old sailor who took money for passing on the few words of broken English he knew. Li learnt to say, pointing proudly to himself: 'Me, cook'. He repeated the words happily, as if they were a passport to a new, happy life in a kitchen.

The ship arrived at last in 1875 at a port the gweilo – the white ghosts – called Cooktown. Almost overnight a tent town of stores, banks, bars, brothels and gambling and opium dens had sprung up in Cooktown since the gold discovery inland the previous year along the

Palmer River. People from many nations in the world mingled in the streets. Over the next few years the number of Chinese grew to almost 20,000, outnumbering all the others put together on the goldfield and in Cooktown. The rapid Chinese influx, its different working practices and success led to calls among the British colonials that only whites should be allowed into Australia.

Any thoughts the brothers had of quickly walking to the Palmer River were dashed as soon as they disembarked. Cooktown's Hung League boss accompanied by a gang of tough–looking thugs quickly herded the league's debtors to a quiet area on the quayside.

'Welcome brothers,' the boss said.

'After you have rested and eaten a meal provided by us, I will explain to you what the league expects.'

All the newly–arrived were told they would have to work as coolies – labourers – until their debts was paid off. Nearly all of them would join a team of five hundred earlier arrivals delivering food and equipment to the goldfield and returning with the league's hidden gold, much of it to be smuggled out of Cooktown, away from officialdom's eyes. The period of indenture depended on the amount of debt. To their dismay, given the large amount they owed, the three brothers found out they would have to serve for at least a year before they would be released to search for gold for themselves.

The newly–arrived coolies were told by the old hands that the sixty–mile trek from Cooktown to the Palmer River was hard–going and dangerous. There were no horses and carts. Everything would have to be carried in the baskets hanging from poles balanced across the coolies' shoulders.

'Stick together and don't wander off the track,' their new team mates warned.

'Otherwise the gwai – black ghosts – will capture and eat you.'

At first the brothers laughed at the joke. But they quickly learned the warning was meant to be taken seriously.

The track to the goldfield followed the Endeavour River from Cooktown and then turned left towards the hills. The path narrowed as

331

it rose upwards until it became a narrow gap through rocks, ideal for ambushes. This became known as Hell's Gate.

It did not take long for Li and his brothers to get used to the week-long trek to Palmer River. They were still moderately fit from their hard work on the family's small holding back home.

During the first month they saw more evidence of violence on the Palmer River goldfield than along the trail. Fights in the evening among drunken gweilo were common. Disputes between Chinese groups about rights to claims spilled over into gang fights. Murder was frequent. The detested gweilo goldfield commissioner, Thomas Coward, and his black troopers regularly rounded up Chinese suspected of not paying their licences. Raids on illegal gambling and opium dens occurred frequently but the fines were easily paid by the Hung League goldfield boss – the league's cut of diggings on the goldfield was hefty.

During the six month tropical wet season the goldfield closed and the coolies had more time off. Ships still arrived in Cooktown and the three brothers worked hard in the oppressive humidity and high temperatures, warehousing goods and equipment ready for the following dry season.

In May, the monsoon stopped and the back-breaking trek to the goldfield recommenced. On the brothers' first day back on the track, about half an hour after they had passed through Hell's Gate, Li experienced severe stomach cramps. Not wishing to soil his trousers he scuttled between some rocks. His two brothers sauntered on for a couple of minutes, wandered a few steps off the path and sank down onto their haunches, grateful for the short rest. A small group of gweilo, not far in front, slowly disappeared around a gentle bend.

Hungry eyes hidden by a clump of trees stared at the travellers. A band of half a dozen fierce warriors from the local Merkin tribe had considered ambushing the white diggers. The Merkin had been on the point of rushing the whites before they had a chance to use their pistols and rifles. But then they saw Li's two brothers. Li, himself, had not been spotted diving into the rocks. Unarmed Chinese were a much easier prey. And they tasted less salty than the whites.

Li was pulling his trousers up when he heard his brothers' cries of alarm and terror. The last words he caught were: 'Run Li, run!'

The scared teenager peered through a crack between the rocks. He saw four tall, muscular, copper–coloured men smeared with white paint attacking his brothers with wooden clubs. It was all over in less than two minutes. The young Chinese were hit over their heads and carried off, half–unconscious.

Li fell to his knees, fighting for breath as panic took hold of his brain.

After a minute he managed to regain his composure and crawled out of the rocks. He caught a glimpse of his brothers being carried like sacks of rice, disappearing into the bush. Li followed far behind, out of sight.

A fire was already burning at the Merkin camp in the middle of a small ravine as the party of warriors arrived with their prey and were greeted by their womenfolk and children. One of Li's brothers was dropped on the ground and his knees smashed with clubs. He would not be able to run away. The second was tied from a tree bough by his pigtails.

The brother on the ground was hit again on the head. Blood seeped from his cracked skull. Completely unconscious, his clothes were ripped off. He was lifted carefully onto the fire. His pigtails caught on fire first as he began to roast. After half an hour meat was carved from the sizzling body and devoured by the waiting Aboriginals. The rich smell of cooked human flesh wafted up to Li hidden in some bushes, watching helplessly. More wood was thrown on the fire which glowed brightly in the oncoming dusk. Li put his hand over his mouth to mask the sound of his retching.

By now Li's other brother had regained consciousness and started to wail as he saw the fate of his brother. He began kicking his feet and frantically trying to untie his pigtails. The biggest warrior walked over and calmly ripped the clothes off the hanging man and cut him down. He fell with a thud onto the ground. With three heavy blows he smashed the young Chinaman's head to pulp.

Some older women walked over and helped the chief lift the naked body and place it gently in the fire next to the bubbling remains of his brother.

Li could not watch any more. Night fell as he stumbled away back towards the track. Shadowy black rocks and strange shapes distorted by the bright moon would ordinarily have terrified him. But not now. He was in a traumatic, comatose state, completely desensitised.

Unaware at first he gradually realised that he had lost his the way. He stopped and desperately looked around and decided to follow a rough, moonlit path, which wound its way through rocks and hanging scrub. On and on Li went for hours. He tripped over stones and roots several times and cut his head as he tumbled down onto hard ground.

The sun rose and an exhausted, thirsty Li blundered onwards. A flock of birds called out. Yes, there it was again, the sound of a flock of unfamiliar birds which seemed to be following him. But now the birds were accompanied by excited human voices. Li gasped in terror: the gwai must have spotted his tracks and were hunting him.

The young Chinaman sped up but it was no use, the hunting party was gaining rapidly. The voices were laughing now, the confident hunters closing in on their quarry. Panic–stricken Li tripped again and rolled down a ragged rock slope onto a track. He lay panting, face downwards, utterly spent, a bundle of torn clothes and blood.

The warriors were around him now, shaking their spears in triumph and shouting in glee at the capture of their next meal.

Li was lucky though.

Loud bangs from pistols rang out. Bullets whizzed past the hunting party. One warrior fell. The blacks looked at their chief. Should they stay and fight? After all they had speared many whites before. This time though, the attackers were on horseback and charging through pistol smoke, two abreast down the narrow track. The chief decided to retreat. His stomach was still full from last night's feast. Why risk more loss of life? The dry season had started. There would be plenty of the strange, little men with pigtails on the trail to the river where they dug holes in the ground for some mad reason.

Li felt galloping horses thunder to a stop near him. Spurred boots approached and his shoulder was pulled by a strong hand to roll him over. He screamed as he looked up into a black face.

'Good God, the little Chinaman *really* is scared of you, Jonathan.'

Li's eyes swivelled to the sound of a voice from a gweilo on horseback.

Managing to catch the white man's eye, the young Chinaman whispered desperately in English: 'Me, cook', tapping his chest feebly before he fainted.

Li was doubly fortunate. Not only had his life been saved but Duncan MacKay was short of a cook for the journey back to Tilpal. The Chinaman's cooking proved to be tasty. So good, in fact, that Duncan kept him on at Tilpal in charge of the kitchen.

Chapter 49: Iffley

Eighteen year–old Lou MacKay picked up the brand–new Colt single action army revolver and fired off four rounds. Every one of them hit the middle of a mango tree about 60 feet in front of him. He turned his aim to a couple of hanging fruit and squeezed the trigger twice. The fruit exploded into pulp. Lou holstered his weapon, sauntered over and picked up their stones. He threw one into the shrub and absent–mindedly pocketed the other.

His elder brother, Forbes, looked on in admiration, tinged with slight jealousy. He was used to being better at most things than Lou. At rugby football and athletics at their school, Sydney Grammar, because he was older he had grown accustomed to beating his younger brother. Forbes, himself, was handy with a revolver. But Lou was a crack shot, he had to admit.

'Good shooting, Lou,' his father nodded approvingly.

'I thought you two would like the latest Colts.'

Both the boys had also been given Winchester rifles. Duncan himself had brought along a treasured Martini Henry – capable of downing an elephant. The MacKay men were well–armed.

Duncan and his two sons were at their Tilpal property, about fifty miles north of Rockhampton. They'd just had lunch. The boys had at first turned their noses up at the food. The smell of the sauces was new to them and there were too many vegetables. But Duncan ordered them to eat what was put in front of them. They'd carried on and after a few mouthfuls they had to admit the food was delicious. The fresh beef had been sliced into thin strips and covered with a brown sauce and onions.

'You like?' Li, the Tilpal Chinese cook, asked, beaming that his boss' sons approved.

Li's English had improved in the eight years he had worked at Tilpal after Duncan had rescued him near the Palmer River goldfield. He had revolutionised the production of food at the station. There was a large kitchen garden producing salads and vegetables. Grape vines, passion fruit, mango trees and bananas were grown and carefully tended to produce maximum fruit. Of course, the rich soil and tropical climate helped. Chickens ran free during the day laying eggs and eating maggots. To one side he grew herbs with funny foreign names.

One thing hadn't changed. Li was still terrified of blacks. Even though there weren't many left around Tilpal, he wouldn't leave the house unless there was a white within sight. The drovers and stockmen on the station would chuckle as they watched Li scuttle outside to the privy or to his room in the shed where the employees slept.

Duncan looked at his boys with pride. They were both handsome young men. But they had inherited his wildness. Too much money, drink and girls had put paid to twenty–one year old Forbes' medical studies at Sydney University. And Lou was showing every sign of following in his brother's footsteps. Nora blamed her husband for spoiling them. Of course she was right, he sighed.

Duncan had decided he'd take them with him on the journey up to the Gulf of Carpentaria – the large shallow sea enclosed on three sides by northern Australia – to view a huge property which was for sale.

He had been approached by a property agent, Jones was his name, who had made a speculative visit to Minimbah, which Duncan had bought from Sam Cobb's family.

'Ah, Mr MacKay, I'm delighted to make your acquaintance, Sir. Please forgive my intrusion but I happened to be in conversation with the Bank of New South Wales manager in Newcastle and he mentioned that you might be interested in an investment opportunity in northern Queensland?'

Duncan had tugged his beard thoughtfully but said nothing. He knew how to negotiate. Raising his eyebrows was sufficient to encourage the agent to continue: 'Iffley is a very fine property, Mr MacKay. Not far from Normanton on the Gulf. About 1,000 square miles in all. Fine country, Sir.'

Duncan spoke: 'But still dangerous?'

The agent paused, conscious he had a faint nibble: 'No, if I may correct you Mr MacKay. Compared to other districts, Iffley is largely clear of wild blacks these days. Inspector Urquhart has been very successful with his Native Police.'

'Nonetheless, I hear the Kalkadunje are fiercesome warriors?'

Jones looked startled for a second: 'I see you are well–informed, Mr MacKay. Yes, I have heard them described as the elite of the native tribes. But even they are no match for rifles and pistols.'

'Why do the Walshes wish to sell, Mr Jones?'

Again the agent was surprised: obviously Duncan MacKay knew more about Iffley than he expected.

Jones replied cautiously: 'The current Mr Walsh is unwell. I understand his son would rather live in Brisbane.'

Duncan had heard a year ago that Iffley was on the market. He knew that land values in the Gulf were low because of the continued resistance of the blacks. Even so, after his purchase of other smaller properties, he knew he might have to borrow money to buy such a large asset. But if, as Jones claimed, Iffley was now largely pacified, perhaps the timing was right to invest before others became interested?

He stubbed his cigarillo out: 'Yes, Mr Jones, I would like to inspect the property. I trust Mr Walsh would find that acceptable?'

Unable to keep the enthusiasm out of his voice, the agent gabbled: 'Yes, of course, Mr MacKay. I shall write to inform him immediately. When should he expect you?'

'About a month from now.'

Jones looked surprised again: taking the steamer from Rockhampton around Australia's most northerly point, Cape York, into the Gulf of Carpentaria would only take about a week.

'I intend following the stock routes from Rockhampton, Mr Jones. I wish to see for myself how easy it would be to drive cattle from Iffley down south to the Hunter Valley.'

Two days after their target practice, Duncan, his two sons and three spare horses headed due west from Rockhampton for a week and picked up the main stock route north at a place called Barcaldine. They made good time and met with no incidents. The eyes of any white bushrangers and wild blacks took one look at their weapons and decided attack would be foolhardy. Forbes and Lou took it turns to use their father's precious telescope, which he called Vincent, to keep watch as they rode along.

They continued north towards Julia Creek where they would be within a few days' ride of the Iffley boundary.

'Blacks!' warned Forbes suddenly, handing Vincent to his father.

Squinting through the lens, Duncan inspected a group of about twenty blacks about a mile away. The men were tall and well built.

He handed the telescope to his other son: 'What do you see, Lou?'

'One, two, three..,' Lou started to tally the numbers up.

'I'd say nearly ten big blacks, about the same number of lubras – women – and half a dozen piccaninnies,' he finished.

'Who's in front?'

'There's an old man.'

Lou looked more closely: 'That's funny, he looks as though he's singing.'

'So maybe it is true,' Duncan mused.

'What do you mean, Father?' asked Forbes.

'I know it sounds strange but,' Duncan shook his head pensively, 'Jonathan told me that's how they navigate around the bush.'

'What, by singing?' snorted Lou.

'Yes,' replied Duncan. 'He said they sing something like,' he hummed a tune, 'walk two hundred paces and turn left at the hill which looks like an emu.'

'Look, the one behind the leader is learning the map,' he added, looking again through the telescope.

The two brothers looked quizzically at each other: unspoken between them was a dawning realisation that perhaps, just perhaps, the blacks were not as primitive as they believed?

Duncan looked at the map and checked his compass. Keeping a wide berth from the blacks they trotted off towards Iffley, across the rolling downs of Mitchell and Blue grass. The sale price included two thousand head of cattle. By the time they arrived at the station two days later Duncan reckoned Iffley could take 25,000 cattle and two hundred horses. They'd proved to his satisfaction the viability of the stock route from Iffley, in the north, down to the southern cattle markets. Provided the price was right, he'd buy.

The deal was done quickly. The Walshes knew they would not get more. And Duncan was confident the land value would rocket once the Cape country was completely pacified.

As Lou mounted his horse for the long ride south, Lou felt the mango stone in his trouser pocket which he'd picked up after his target practice at Tilpal. He casually tossed it in front of the Walsh's home. Helped by the tropical rain, sun and fertile soil, the stone germinated and a bountiful mango tree sprang up over the years.

But by the time the MacKays had ridden back to Tilpal, Duncan found it difficult to dismount. 'Damn it,' he swore softly to himself. Although he tried to laugh his difficulty off to his sons as 'old man's legs', he had the first inkling that he might have an illness. His legs were becoming stiffer by the month.

The three men then caught the steamer from Rockhampton, south to Newcastle, at the mouth of the Hunter River, to rejoin Nora and the girls inland at Minimbah, the property Duncan had bought from Sam Cobb's family. Although Minimbah was pleasant enough, Duncan had decided he wanted something grander, befitting his rank as one of Australia's biggest pastoralists – ranchers.

Part 10: The palace

In Xanadu did Kubla Khan
A stately pleasure–dome decree:
Where Alph, the sacred river, ran
Through caverns measureless to man
Down to a sunless sea.
So twice five miles of fertile ground
With walls and towers were girdled round:
And there were gardens bright with sinuous rills,
Where blossomed many an incense–bearing tree;
And here were forests ancient as the hills,
Enfolding sunny spots of greenery.

Kubla Khan, Samuel Taylor Coleridge, 1816

Chapter 50: Dulcalmah

Revenge gave added impetus to Duncan's decision to build an enormous 45–room Italianate mansion. He was furious after the neighbouring Dangar family had refused to invite the MacKays to a grand party, reportedly because of Nora's Jewish blood. To rub salt into the wound, he'd bought the plans from the Dangars' architect when his client had backed out of a project for a new grand house. It had cost Duncan and Nora a fortune to build – £30,000, but worth every penny.

The vast U–shaped building was surmounted by a gleaming white tower. Duncan had wanted a look–out to identify anyone approaching the property – there was still a risk of bushrangers. French windows opened onto a wide verandah on three sides. Internally, Australian cedar panelling was complemented by a rosewood staircase hand–carved in Germany. Stained glass windows, colours ablaze from the Australian sun added bright reds and blues on the floors and walls. The latest plumbing served the bathrooms and lavatories, the drain pipes leading to a large brick cesspit, well away from the house. All the thousands of bricks were made on the site. Nora, of course, had meticulously kept a record of expenditure on Dulcalmah's construction. Although he'd never taken it seriously, he'd finally been forced to pay her back the £3,000 marriage loan not long after she'd come across a bill from the Dulcalmah builder for a little townhouse, 33 Gipps Street in Newcastle. He'd stupidly thought that it would not be noticed amongst all the papers for Dulcalmah.

'I know what you are getting up to in that dirty little bordello,' Nora had seethed.

Relaxing outside on Minimbah's verandah, sipping a post–breakfast cup of tea, Duncan had idly picked up a two–month old copy of the *Illustrated London News*, a magazine which was regularly posted to Nora and eagerly read by the girls for news of the latest fashions. Duncan had flipped through the pages and was about to toss it aside when a name jumped out at him: Sutherland! The article was from London and described Dunrobin Castle, the seat of the Sutherlands, as 'a magnificent fairy–tale confection, 'remodelled at vast expense in

1845 by Sir Charles for the 2nd Duke and his Duchess. God damn the Sutherlands! Duncan had shouted inwardly – his father, John, had handed down enough hatred of the treachery of Lord Reay and the brutal Clearances perpetrated by the Sutherlands. Built with money from sheep grazing on land robbed from the MacKays, no doubt. He had grimaced in gallows' humour at the pun of the castle's name: 'Done robbing, more like', he thought and had resolved there and then to call the MacKays' new home in memory of his clan's purloined homeland: Strathnaver.

Ada joined her father after breakfast and cantered across the mile or so to inspect progress on their nearly–completed new home. Closer to the building site, Duncan and Ada reined in their horses as they quietly watched two perspiring labourers sliding clay brick moulds into a fiery kiln. Duncan smiled in satisfaction as he looked up the drive. The imposing mansion oozed wealth and power. Even his brothers would be impressed.

Ada tugged at Duncan's sleeve, leaning over from the side saddle on her horse, the expensive cloth of his jacket soft to her touch, the silk lining smoothing down over his rough knuckles: 'Father, what shall we call our new home?'

Unaware of her father's reawakened hatred of the Sutherlands, Ada pulled at his arm again, this time more gently, perplexed by the look of anger on her father's face and his clenching fist. 'Father what did you have in mind for a name?'

Duncan had looked at his eldest daughter and realised from her wistful, eager expression that she actually wanted to name the house herself. Of course, he remembered now, he had promised in Bullamon to let Ada name their new home. He sighed, torn between anger and love for his daughter. Well, he admitted reluctantly to himself, what was the point of foisting old, half–forgotten enmity on a different generation in a new country? After all, he was part of Australia's new aristocracy, soon to be living in one of the country's grandest seats. He smiled with satisfaction as he reminded himself that he now owned more acres than the Duke and Duchess of Sutherland. He derived further enjoyment in the knowledge that mountains of wool from

Australia, including from MacKay properties, had undercut Scottish Highland producers, like the Sutherlands, driving their farms out of business.

'If ye dinna ask, ye dinna get, lassie', he had encouraged his daughter kindly, jokingly putting on a broad Scots accent.

'I promised you a palace. Now my princess gets the right to name it,' he had chuckled.

Ada had pointed at a nearby prominent hill: 'That's Dulcumbo.'

She grinned at her father:' Let's call our new home Dulcalmah.'

'Aye, that's a bonny name', he smiled in agreement.

He felt a twinge of pain in one of his thighs. Duncan irritably hit the heel of the boot with his crop. His condition had continued to deteriorate. He now walked as if he had two wooden legs. But the doctors in Sydney had been unable to help him. He decided that he'd have to go Home and visit specialists in London.

Chapter 51: The Arabs

Set amid its green parkland and oak trees, the graceful Georgian mansion appeared quintessentially English to its new visitors, as they approached in a pony and trap.

'Welcome to Crabett Park,' a man–servant welcomed the two Australians, before he led them through a large entrance hall, on whose walls numerous paintings of horses hung, and then into a spacious, sunlit drawing room.

They were announced as: 'Mr Duncan Forbes MacKay and his son of Dulcalmah, Hunter Valley, New South Wales.'

Now, rising to greet them in front of a large bay window was an Arab, resplendent in a shimmering gold *thobe* and *keffiyeh* – robe and headdress.

'Sir Wilfrid?' Duncan asked uncertainly.

A tall woman sitting nearby gently admonished the Arab: 'Anne, don't tease your visitors.'

Pulling her headdress to one side, the two men could now see that the Arab had the smooth face and diminutive stature of a woman but features which could be mistaken for those of a man.

The woman smiled: 'No, no Mr MacKay. I am Anne Blunt. Please forgive my rudeness in not making it clear from the start. My husband is up in town, in London, today.' Wilfrid's absence was fortunate Lady Blunt thought. His unusual dislike of British imperialism, and those who profited from it, could sometimes prove awkward.

'I find if I dress like a Sheikh, people dismiss me as an eccentric. If I dress like an Englishman, well, people think..,' Lady Blunt left the unfinished sentence hanging in the air. Noticing that Duncan had stumped along in an ungainly fashion, she quickly ushered her visitors into chairs and ordered tea.

'I trust your journey down from London was easy, Mr MacKay?'

'Thank you Lady Anne. Most of it was by train and very comfortable.'

'Of course, of course. Where would we be without our marvellous railways?' Lady Blunt sniffed disdainfully.

'Quite what my grandfather would have made of it all, I don't dare imagine!' she added.

'Perhaps Lord Byron would have written a brilliant poem extolling the virtues of steam locomotives?' the tall woman said wryly.

Lady Blunt merely arched her eyebrows and glanced at her visitors, inviting them to join in the conversation.

'Give me a good horse, Lady Anne, and I will ride quite happily for months at a time through the Australian bush,' Duncan said.

'I have heard that you too enjoy adventures away from civilisation', he continued.

'Yes, Mr MacKay, for me riding an Arab across the desert is pure bliss.'

Duncan had done his research on Sir Wilfrid and Lady Anne Blunt before writing and asking to visit Crabett Park and its illustrious stud farm, where the Blunts were intent on saving the Arab breed of horses for posterity. He had heard Lady Anne was brilliant at everything: artist, violinist, linguist, athlete, explorer and horsewoman. There appeared to be no end to her accomplishments.

'In fact, if she were a man she would be famous for her talents,' his informant had said. He'd then added dryly: 'Of course she really is more man than woman, if you catch my drift. This explains why her husband, Sir Wilfrid, tries to bed every woman he can!'

'So you are interested in my Arabs, Mr MacKay?' asked Lady Blunt, carefully inspecting the father and son over the top of her tea cup.

'By interesting coincidence I sold one to a Mr Dangar not too long ago. I believe he also hails from your Hunter Valley. Perhaps you know him?'

'We have met on occasion, Lady Ann,' Duncan replied, his face devoid of expression. He did not wish to reveal too much of his insatiable desire to purchase one of the Crabett Park horses, for fear of driving up the purchase price. When he had first seen Dangar's beautiful Arab, he knew he had to own one himself.

'I admired Mr Dangar's horse, which is why I am here. Our family has been breeding horses for many years. One of your Arabs might be very welcome and we would gladly assist your project to save the breed.'

Lady Blunt gaze turned to Duncan's son with the same name as his father, apparently. She saw a tall, handsome young man impeccably turned out in expensive clothes. His suit could only have come from Saville Row. She could tell from the way he looked at her with a soft confident smile that he was used to women finding him attractive. And indeed, if she were that way inclined, she might be drawn to him. For a moment she wondered what Wilfrid's friend, Oscar Wilde, would make of the young Australian. Smiling inwardly, she dismissed the mischievous thought.

'And are you like your father? Do you like riding, young man?'

'Lady Anne, I have ridden horses since I could walk. For me a horse is the most noble of animals.'

'Well said. My sentiments entirely,' Lady Blunt beamed.

Lady Blunt's mind was made up – the MacKays had passed the first hurdle. She stood up spritely: 'Well then, let us walk to my stables. I shall show you my darling Arabs.'

While inspecting the horses the two MacKay men were subjected to a polite but penetrating examination by Lady Blunt on their horse–breeding credentials. Satisfied, the MacKays were leant jackets, jodhpurs and boots and invited to join her ladyship in a gallop across Crabett Park's green fields.

Duncan was helped into his saddle by two grooms. The nimble Lady Blunt needed no assistance. With one foot in a stirrup she pulled herself up with lithe ease. By now used to her eccentricity, the MacKays were only mildly scandalised to see their host sit herself on a man's saddle. Duncan managed gallantly to stop himself from laughing as her robe billowed out behind, like a latter–day Sir Lancelot, as their horses gathered speed. For her part, Lady Blunt could see that both men were expert horsemen and the younger one could ride a horse as quick as a professional jockey.

Duncan was impressed by the two horses, Kara and Habdan, Lady Blunt had selected. Back at the stables he knew he would not get a second chance. A return trip to England would be highly unlikely. He decided to buy them without waiting.

While the necessary documents were being signed in the stable office, Lady Blunt smiled at the younger MacKay: 'I see you enjoy riding. I can't imagine you will give it up during your visit?'

'I will be attending Cirencester Agriculture College, Lady Anne, so I hope to have the opportunity at some stage.'

'Ah, yes. You should find plenty of young men there with similar interests,' Lady Blunt said with a brief, enigmatic smile. The thought flitted across Lady Blunt's mind that the young Australian might grace some of her London parties?

'And you, Mr MacKay, will you be riding elsewhere during your visit to England?' Lady Blunt asked Duncan, as he put the office pen back into its well.

'Unfortunately not, your ladyship. You will have noticed that my legs are very stiff. I hope to find a doctor in London who might find a cure for my ailment.'

'I wish you every success Mr MacKay,' Lady Blunt said sympathetically.

But Duncan was unsuccessful in his attempts to find medical salvation. After three opinions he returned to Australia accompanied by a full–time nurse. Back at Dulcalmah his legs continued to worsen and eventually they became completely paralysed. He could still ride after he was hoisted into a saddle. But by the time Lady Blunt's horses were delivered, the paralysis had crept into his wrists. He could no longer hold reins properly. He would never ride the Arabs.

Chapter 52: The watcher in the tower

Duncan sat high in Dulcalmah's white tower. He loved sitting alone, looking at the distant hills of untamed bush and, close by, the mansion's flowers and green lawns, as the late afternoon sun lengthened the shadows over the estate's thirty thousand acres. The property had never made much money from its cattle and sheep but he had no regrets at making Dulcalmah the family home. He knew that the magnificent building and grounds would be a testament to his life. He was proud that generations to come would recognise he had left his mark – what more could a man want?

His reverie was interrupted by Nora's voice sharply reprimanding one of the maids, her voice reverberating up the central staircase. Dear Jesus, did her ladyship never stop, he thought, shaking his head slowly. God help anybody who did not meet her exacting standards. Love might be long gone from the marriage but he respected his wife for her attention to detail and determination.

He forced his heavy eyelids to remain open and leant over to a small table by his chair. He picked up an atlas of Australia and turned the well–thumbed pages to Queensland. Well, he'd done it; he smiled in satisfaction as he looked towards the top of the page and saw where he had ringed Iffley in pencil. Now MacKay cattle were driven for nine months along the 1,400 miles stock route from the station, stopping at the various MacKay properties along the way until they reached Ravensworth, only 25 miles from here, where they were fattened for market.

Duncan dozed fitfully and the atlas slipped from his hand. The creeping paralysis was in his lungs now. Breathing was a struggle.

He heard the faint sound of a horse from afar. He half–expected to see the Presbyterian minister, Dr White, a regular visitor but no, he quickly realised it was the noise of two horses galloping hard up the drive. Relieved that he would be spared more bible reading, he looked down and managed to force a laugh as he admired his two sons, racing each other on Kara and Habdan up the long drive. Forbes won by a head but Lou's seat was more elegant. The young MacKay men jumped off their snorting, sweating horses. 'Rub them down well,'

Lou ordered, tossing his reins into the hands of two grooms who appeared from the stables.

Duncan rang a small porcelain bell and two man–servants appeared. As they carried him downstairs to the front verandah he caught sight of himself in a mirror. He still had his full head of white, wavy hair but his beard had become straggly. Duncan's eyes, once bright and piercing, were now dull and surrounded by black circles of exhaustion. His blankets failed to conceal that his frame was painfully thin. He whispered silently: 'Not long now.'

The servants carried him out onto the verandah and lowered him gently into an old but very comfortable wheelchair.

Despite the vehicle's snug fit, Duncan grimaced every time he sat in it. He remembered painfully that day on Melbee's verandah when he'd been acting the fool and had hopped into Uncle Forbes' wheel chair and screeched joyfully that it felt made to measure. Well, by malign irony, it was his now.

As he waited for his two sons to join him, Duncan looked across the grounds to the side of one of the hills where there was an abandoned Aboriginal humpy in which Jonathan used to sleep – he'd refused an offer of a room and a bed in the servants' quarters. In his old age Jonathan had discarded his 'whitefella' clothes and had reverted to his traditional tribal way of life. Despite this he had walked down from Bullamon to join Duncan. Strange how they had become close, Duncan thought. He'd never had another good friend after Hugh Bryden had died. Another tradition the Aboriginal had observed was every three years he'd leave his humpy and journey northwards to attend a big corroboree. Duncan was not sure where.

Jonathan had come up to the house about a month ago to say goodbye in the tower. It was the first time he had been allowed into Duncan's home. The Aboriginal had bent his grey head and had shaken the white man's hand, just like the first time they'd met. The two men knew they would never see each other again.

'Jonathan,' Duncan had whispered, as the Aboriginal had turned to leave.

'Yes?'

351

Duncan had clamped on to Jonathan's hand and looked up into the black man's eyes. The white man had felt he had to say something more. After all, they'd known each other for over twenty years. Duncan's family had crossed the oceans to come to this country where they had prospered mightily on land, over which Jonathan's people had formerly roamed freely since time began.

He had searched for the right words: 'I'm sorry,' he breathed eventually, falling back on the wheelchair's deep cushion.

Jonathan had nodded but said nothing. His bare feet had made no noise as he had padded over the thick Persian carpet and down the staircase. Outside he had shifted his possum cloak – the late sun was waning and there was a chill in the air. The Aboriginal had started to lope down Dalcalmah's drive, the thick, hard soles of his feet impervious to stones. Observing from the tower, Duncan saw that after a few minutes Jonathan had changed direction, taking a barely discernible track. The white man had caught the faint sound of the black man singing to himself, as he faded into darkness of the bush.

'Goodbye, my friend,' Duncan had murmured.

Duncan grimaced as his lungs squeezed painfully against his ribcage. A dry smile creased his lips as he heard his sons joshing in Dulcalmah's ducal entrance hall. The large mahogany front door was flung open and youthful boots bounded out onto the wooden verandah.

'There you are Father,' his younger son shouted.

'Did you see us racing up the drive?' Lou demanded eagerly.

His father lifted his hand feebly in acknowledgement. He remembered when he was Lou's age he'd already confronted much danger and hardship in the pursuit of wealth. By contrast his two sons did not have a care in the world. And they fully expected to enjoy their father's money once he was gone. 'And why not?' Duncan thought. Although he had been no saint, he was glad that he would live on through his sons.

Chapter 53: A kingly man

On the 16th June 1887 Duncan Forbes MacKay died at the young age of 53. Not long afterwards his funeral took place at Singleton, about 50 miles inland up the Hunter Valley from Newcastle, not far from Dulcalmah. A light winter drizzle began to fall, appropriately more akin to gentle Scottish Highland mist than the sub–tropical downpours often encountered in New South Wales. The MacKays huddled under dripping umbrellas, held by their servants, to watch Duncan's coffin be lowered by his favourite grooms into the ground.

There were not many mourners. The family had decided to make it a simple, private occasion. The Hookes had come, more out of respect to Nora, than goodwill towards her husband. Duncan had been too successful. Dulcalmah was just too ostentatious. There was whispered, scurrilous gossip too about the unknown disease which had caused Duncan's paralysis and premature death.

Hearing by chance about the funeral, a journalist from the local *Singleton Argus* also came, curious that the death of such a prominent person had attracted so little attention.

The Reverend James White in his booming graveside address said that Duncan Forbes had in the conduct of his affairs 'intuitively apprehended the critical point in that tide which, taken at the flood leads on to fortune.'

The minister described Duncan Forbes MacKay as a kingly man, 'one of whose stuff are made explorers, pioneers of civilisation, colonisers, legislators, heroes and martyrs.

'Take him for all in all, we shall not soon look upon his like again,' urged the Reverend White.

In strict Presbyterian style he then warned the mourners at great length on the evil of sin; the folly of putting off the business of salvation and setting their hearts on earthly things; and the necessity of seeking the kingdom of God.

In truth, the assembly of MacKays and Hookes did indeed thank God when the minister had concluded, although perhaps not for the reason he would have wished.

Duncan's children wept as their father's coffin finally disappeared.

Behind her widow's veil, Nora stood ramrod straight and dry–eyed. She felt fingers seeking comfort, glancing down Nora saw it was Mary Annie, tears trickling down her cheeks. She patted her daughter's hand and bent down: 'Don't cry dear. Father has gone to heaven. Try to remember all the great things that the Reverend White said he accomplished.'

'I know Mother. Father told me so many stories about himself and our family.'

Nora smiled and caressed Mary Annie's face with a silk handkerchief: 'Well, my darling, don't forget them.'

Mary Annie looked up: 'I won't forget Mother. I will always remember.'

Nora turned away from her husband's grave and led her seven children towards the short line of carriages, their hoods glistening through the soft dampness. The congregation followed the family slowly, at a respectful distance.

On the horizon, further up the Hunter Valley, large dark clouds, as black as the sea of undiscovered coal beneath their feet, appeared suddenly, thundering towards the cemetery. Fearful of being drenched, the gathering quickened its pace. Apart from Mary Annie, nobody looked back.

– The End –

Author's notes
Introduction

I first became aware of the fascinating history of my mother's family when I was a young teenager in Perth, Western Australia. I remember coming home from school one day when my father took me to one side and told me Mum's mother had died. Dad told me that she was upset and I shouldn't rush up to her demanding my supper.

I had never met my grandmother but I had gleaned from overheard parents' conversations that my mother had not got on well with her. Nonetheless Mum seemed upset. Her father was never mentioned.

A little while later I asked Mum about my grandmother and she began to outline her family's history.

It seemed the MacKays had left Scotland and gone to live in Prince Edward Island, Canada. They then left Canada in a boat and sailed to Australia and lived in a very big house in the Hunter Valley, New South Wales.

What did they do there? I asked.

They had cattle and horses. It was quite tough to begin with, Mum said.

Why?

Well, it was like the Wild West in America she said.

I was really interested now. You mean with Red Indians?

Well, not exactly. Were there cowboys?

Oh yes, I'm sure there were.

I could see Mum was beginning to get deliberately vague. But I remember her saying that like the Red Indians, the Aborigines tried to steal cattle. And that was very bad because they only wanted to eat part of the animal; they left the rest go to waste. That seemed alright to me. Like most Aussie boys I really liked a good steak.

Did they shoot the Aborigines trying to steal their cattle? I remember my mother looking uneasily at me and saying: 'Yes, my father said they had to.'

I take no pride in recounting this tale which stayed with me, nearly forgotten. But it surfaced again when my mother died and I was in my sixties. Judging 19th century British settlers by 21st century standards is pointless. The same should be said of indigenous Australians.

After my father died in 1992, my mother came to live with my family. While she lived with us I had the chance to talk to her about her own life, snippets of which are on You Tube.

On occasions she even talked about her father and his siblings, the big house in the Hunter Valley which she had visited twice, and the tough time her father had had on the family's cattle station (Iffley) in Northern Queensland.

She also mentioned her grandmother, after whom she had been named, was a Hooke. 'They were butchers who came from Tasmania,' she said. This confused me: a cousin had told me the Hookes were very grand.

I had asked my mother whether the MacKays had been crofters. Her reply was immediate and dismissive: 'Certainly not. They were educated people who were tenant farmers.'

History is often accused of being patriarchal. I hope I have managed to redress this imbalance in this book. Even so, I regret that I may not have done justice to the remarkable women who married into the MacKays: my mother's grandmother, Frances Leonora (Nora) Hooke (and her mother, Mary Ann) Sybella McKenzie, Jane Scobie and Donald's wife Jessie. I'm certain my mother inherited their tough genes.

My mother was born in 1912 and was 101 years old when she died in 2013. Her father was born in 1866 and his father, my mother's grandfather, Duncan Forbes MacKay, was born in 1834 in Prince Edward Island. Genealogically speaking this is a mere blink of an eye. While writing this book I felt as if I could reach out and touch the characters, so close they seemed. On occasions, writing in my garden shed, I even sensed they were standing next to me, peering over my shoulder as I researched and wrote. A frequent, goose pimply–sensation which was strongly reinforced when I looked at their photographs.

I wrote this book for my immediate and extended family and wished to complete it within a reasonable time. In fact the research and writing took four years. I could have easily spent more time writing one twice its length.

The name MacKay

Confusingly the name MacKay is written in the Book of Mackay with either a lower or upper case K. My mother and her grandmother used the upper case but at least one of my relatives uses the lower case. I've used the upper case version. Either way, it matters not.

The Hookes

I know of two theories for the reason John Hooke wished to leave England: did he simply marry beneath himself or was his wife, Mary Ann, Jewish? Which is more plausible? I opted for the latter because an English country squire marrying an attractive village girl was not unheard of and the class differences would not have been insurmountable. But the marriage of a Christian to a Jew could well have been scandalous, particularly in the more provincial parts of Victorian England.

Jessie MacKay

Nowhere could I find the name of Donald's wife mentioned. However, the ship which Donald built was named *Jessie*. Furthermore, Donald's nephew, John, christened one of his children Jessy Johanna. Given the MacKays' habit of handing down names from generation to generation, I think it reasonable to deduce Donald's wife was called Jessie.

Prince Alfred, The Duke of Edinburgh and Nora MacKay

Prince Alfred, the second son of Queen Victoria and Prince Albert, followed his elder brother Bertie's lifestyle. Bertie had, for example, introduced him to the delights of Parisian brothels. And, like Bertie, he had affairs with the wives of the aristocratic milieu in which they moved. Unlike Bertie, though, when he travelled he could cast his net wider and away from scrutiny by his draconian mother.

Apart from Mary Annie's story, I could find no evidence of Alfred visiting Kenneth MacKay's Cangon property (a leading stud farm, still in MacKay hands). But why would Mary Annie lie about Alfred visiting Cangon when she hadn't lied about anything else? Seeking confirmation, I approached the UK's Royal Archivist but did not even elicit a polite acknowledgement of the receipt of my letter. Strange, I thought, given recent claims by his organisation to be far more open to the public. To be fair, my guess is that Alfred kept quiet back home about his Australian escapades and the Royal Archives have little on file. I can, however, imagine the brothers enjoyed a brandy and cigar together, chuckling about Alfred's Australian adventures.

There is a mention in one of the Hunter Valley newspapers about George MacKay being on the welcoming committee for Alfred's visit to the Hunter Valley. Horse races and a ball were indeed planned. As a prominent family, I think it reasonable to assume that this was George MacKay, the eldest son of John and Sybella MacKay and owner of Melbee, near Cangon.

Nora MacKay *did* have a baby, christened Agnes, about nine months after Alfred's visit. Agnes never married.

There was one other possibility for Alfred to have met Nora. In 1868 Alfred also visited Brisbane where he was taken inland by train to Jondaryan, where he was to open the latest extension of the western railway line. His train was late and the welcome dinner did not start until 10pm. The guests included prominent squatters from the area. Jondaryan is a long way from Bullamon so it would have been unlikely that the MacKays were on the invitation list. Mary Annie also makes no mention of her parents visiting a dinner for Alfred in Jondaryan.

My mother took a keen interest in the British royal family. She told me more than once that there were illegitimate descendants of royalty in New South Wales and this was well-known and 'talked about'. She was sincere in her belief. But rumours like these are not unknown in Australia.

All in all, a dalliance between Alfred and Nora MacKay is plausible, if unlikely. But if not her, perhaps someone else among the prominent Hunter Valley families? Highly likely I would have thought. Or maybe at Jondaryan where he also had opportunity that night to indulge in his appetite for what was laughingly described in Australia's pubs as 'horizontal refreshment.' And only God knows how many prostitutes or actresses gave birth to royal progeny after his visit?

I included this chapter because Alfred's visit was the first by a British royal to Australia and therefore a major event, but one which, presumably, the Royal Archivist would prefer to keep out of sight in Windsor Castle.

The word British

I have used the word British for the English, Scots, Welsh and Irish settlers and their descendants in Victorian–era Australia. My understandable focus on the British, particularly the Scots, is not intended to denigrate the contribution of other nationalities in the development of Australia but does, of course, reflect the British birth or descent of most white Australians during the period in which this book is set.

I must add that I find it odd that the term 'European' seems to have replaced 'British' in contemporary Australia during most discussion of its early colonial history. I have yet to meet a German or Frenchman who has thought Australia was formerly part of his or her country's empire.

Aboriginal Cannibalism

Mary Annie in the *MacKays of Dalcalmah* quotes my mother's father (Lou) when he was on the family's Iffley station in northern Queensland: 'He said the heat up there was terrific. Some of the blacks in that part were quite wild...they used to mutilate the cattle...cut their tongues out. Lou said he was a sure shot with a revolver...he used to shoot the poor things out of their misery. The blacks were also fond of Chinese, and once you got a Chinese cook on a station he would never leave you...travel to the next station was too dangerous to him.'

I was perplexed at first. If the Aboriginals were fond of Chinese, why was travel so dangerous? Then I read the paragraph again. And again. (I also wondered later if Robert MacKay Brown had inserted the dots because he did not wish to include some things said by Mary Annie which might have been inconveniently embarrassing).

Searching on the Internet I soon came across several allegations of Aboriginal cannibalism and, worse, here and there a predilection for Chinese flesh because it was less salty. I was initially doubtful about the first allegation and dismissed the second as ridiculous. Through my research I came eventually to believe both.

It is accepted that cannibalism was practised in New Zealand and Papua New Guinea. The distance between the latter and northern Queensland is less than 100 miles with islands in between. I would therefore be surprised if cannibalism was not practised among Australian Aborigines in Queensland.

The first convincing account of cannibalism in northern Queensland I came across was Carl Lumholtz's *Among Cannibals* (1889). Why would a respected Danish botanist invent allegations of this nature, especially when he had no British colonial axe to grind?

The white colonial diet relied heavily on preserved salt beef; the Chinese ate more vegetables. If we are what we eat, to coin a phrase, the British must surely have tasted saltier? In 2008, Olga Ammann, a German anthropologist conducted a study on the last cannibal tribe in the Papuan Pacific Islands. These Papuan cannibals interviewed stated that the flesh of the whites had a smell too strong and too salty. While the Japanese had a much better taste than others. But they come in second place, behind their wives (sic).

The source that finally convinced me on both counts was the account of the Palmer River gold rush, *River of Gold* by Hector Holthouse. This was difficult to obtain and has been dismissed by some Australian academics. One described it, unfortunately perhaps, as a pot boiler. I disagree with this assessment – the book's index of sources is impressively comprehensive. If the reader can obtain a copy (I obtained a second hand one) I leave it up to him or her to make their own judgement.

As historian Geoffrey Partington, hardly an uncritical fan of the British Empire, suggested in 2008: 'Unfortunately in Australia, suppression of inconvenient truths had flourished over the last three decades.'

I pondered for some time whether I should include a chapter in this book on Aboriginal cannibalism. But, because it must surely have influenced the colonial opinion of Aboriginals, to omit it would have been an act of politically correct self–censorship.

The problem however is that all the allegations of Aboriginal cannibalism I could find, although numerous, were anecdotal. Until such time as Australian anthropologists really start digging, proof will not be completely conclusive. The Palmer River would be a good place to start.

The British Invasion and the Aboriginal Wars

I know some disagree with the use of the word 'invasion' to describe the British conquest of Australia; they say it was more a gradual expansion from the original colony in Sydney. True, it was not an invasion like the WWII Normandy or Pacific island landings, but from the indigenous Australians' perspective it was most definitely an invasion of their lands with deadly consequences for their traditional life and culture.

As a schoolboy in Perth, Western Australia I do not recall learning much about Aboriginals resisting the British invasion. Yes, there were spears thrown and a few explorers killed but widespread fighting? It was the research for this book which opened my eyes to the fact the indigenous Australians did, in fact, resist fiercely the invasion of their lands.

I read about the First Black War in Tasmania. And that celebration of conquest, *Triumph in the Tropics*, revealed that in Queensland 'The Black War' flared after the great bunya (bonyi bonyi) festivals of 1841 and 1844. 'This piecemeal slaughter grew into actual war again in Cape York Peninsula and in the Cloncurry district in the final wrecking of the fragmentary Aboriginal frontiers in the seventies and eighties.....the Kalkadoons (Kalkadunje) merit more than passing mention – they were the elite of the Aboriginal warriors of Queensland. With courage and resolution they fought to the end – but it was, indeed, the end.'

I found it puzzling why I was unable to find any comprehensive history of the wars between the British and indigenous Australians – along the lines of *The Fatal Shore* by Robert Hughes – which, according to the Australian War Memorial, continued until the 1930s in Western Australia, less than one hundred years before this book's publication.

The Australian War Memorial estimates 2,500 British settlers were killed in these black wars. In return, about 25,000 indigenous Australians were, there's no other word for it, slaughtered. Others consider the latter figure to be an underestimate. Many white Australians feel guilty about the mass killings committed by the British colonists and their descendants and the issue continues to cloud discussion about Australia's recent history and influences government policy today.

Several countries in the world have a violent past of recent or historic atrocities, which can still cause bitterness today. Race and religion are the cause of many of these troubles. But eventually most people, be they victims, bystanders, aggressors and their descendants move on and learn to rub along together. Continually and vehemently revisiting past grievances becomes a self–defeating minority activity at the margins of society, risking the creation of a majority which becomes dismissive or, even worse, bored.

I agree with journalist, Juliet Samuel, who wrote in the UK's *Daily Telegraph* in early 2017 about continuing German guilt for the Holocaust when she said: 'But guilt is no sound basis for a society and atonement cannot be an unlimited policy objective. Learning from the past is one thing. Being blinded by it is quite another.'

Bibliography

The MacKay family

The MacKays of Dulcalmah: the tales of Mary Annie Mackay, recorded, expanded and annotated by Robert MacKay Brown, circa 1940s?

Correspondence between Duncan Forbes MacKay IV of Sydney, NSW and various MacKays living in Prince Edward Island, Canada, 1970s

Recollections of Robert MacKay Brown, Brian France, 1997

The Hooke family

Handwritten observations by Robert MacKay Brown on the Hooke family history

Extract from *Hooke of Crookes Park*, Nancy and John Hunter

Strathnaver – the MacKay country in the Scottish Highlands

The Book of Mackay, Angus Mackay, 1906

The Reay Fencibles, John Mackay, 1890

The History of the Highland Clearances – Trial of Patrick Sellar, ElectricScotland.com

Prince Edward Island, Nova Scotia and New Brunswick

Pioneer Life of PEI, Jessie Rosina (Norton) Beck

Letters to Duncan Forbes Mackay (IV) from William E Johnstone, 1970

Bristol Notes, The Guardian (PEI), Walter O'Brien, 27/1/1973

Ann Calder's Children, John Carleton McKay, 1983

Plagues of Mice, Ian MacQuarrie, Island Magazine, 1987

A History of the County of Pictou, Rev George Patterson, 1877

Smuggling in Maine during the Embargo and the War of 1812, Harvey Strum Colby, Quarterly, 1983

Roadblock 1810, Chester B Stewart, The Island, 1983

The Rogues of 'Quoddy': Smuggling in the Maine – New Brunswick Borderland 1783–1820, Joshua M Smith, abstract from thesis, May 2003

History of Presbyterianism on Prince Edward Island, Rev John Macleod, 1904

Shipwrecks & Seafaring Tales of Prince Edward Island, Julie V Watson, 1994

The Island Register

Bold Privateers: Terror, Plunder and Profit on Canada's Atlantic Coast. Roger Marsters

Unfortunate Events, What was the War of 1812 even about? Caleb Crain, The New Yorker. October 22, 2012

1816, The Year without a Summer, Gillen D'Arcy Wood, branchcollective.org

The Descendants of William MacKay, abt 1746 – 1826 and Jane Scobie, 1756 – 1834, George Edward Hart, Island Register, 2011

Rural Protest on Prince Edward Island: From British Colonization to the Escheat Movement, Rusty Bitterman, Sep 2006 and book review by Sean T Cadigan, *Acadiensis, 2007*

Lord Selkirk: A Life, JM Bumsted

Wikipedia

Australia: New South Wales and Queensland

Dungog Shire Council Thematic History, 1988 and addendum to *A History in Three Rivers*, *Dungog Shire Heritage Study Thematic History*, August 2014 Michael Williams

Early Days of the Law in Country Districts, The Australian Law Journal, Vol, 46, November, 1972

This anomalous community, Dungog Magistrates' Letterbook, 1834–1839, Macquarie Law School

Among Cannibals, Carl Lumholtz 1889

The Rockhampton Delusion, Laura McDonald, Queensland Heritage

Military Settlers, the men of the Royal Veteran Companies Royal Staff Corps (1825), Christine Wright, Journal of the Royal Australian Historical Society, 1st November 2009

On the Overseas Chinese Secret Societies of Australia, Carl Shaoqing, Nanjin University, New Zealand Journal of Asian Studies, 2002

Singleton of Other Days, Sir Solomon, Singleton Argus, 29th April 1935

Triumph in the Tropics, Sir Raphael Cilento & Clem Lack, 1959

Some notes on cannibalism among Queensland Aborigines 1824–1900, EG Heap, Queensland Heritage

Pioneering Days: Thrilling Incidents, George Sutherland, 1913

Remembering the droving days, Megan Stafford, North Queensland Register, 20th March 2012

The Brutal Truth, The Monthly, Tony Roberts,

Early Days in North Queensland, Edward Palmer, 1903

The Fatal Shore, Robert Hughes, 1986

Boiling down in the 1840s: A Grimy Means to a Solvent End, Labour History No. 25 (Nov. 1973), pp. 1–18, Australian Society for the Study of Labour History, Inc. K. L. Fry

1843: The Year it All Began, Australasian Study of Parliament Group, David Clune, Autumn 2011

Early Days of the Law in Country Districts, The Australian Law Journal, Vol, 46, November, 1972

Problems of Police Administration in the New South Wales 1825 – 1851, Hazel King, Royal Australian Historical Society Journal and Proceedings Vol. 44 1958 Part 2

Visual Ephemera: Theatrical Art in Nineteenth Century Australia, Anita Callaway, 2000

Selling Sex: A Hidden History of Prostitution, Rachel Frances, 2007

Queen Victoria's Children, BBC TV, 2016

Before the Line, Melanie O'Flynn

The Native Police at Callandoon – a blueprint for forced assimilation? Mark Copland, Griffith University, 1999

Our killing fields, , Eurekastreet.com.au, Bob Reece, 24 June 2006

The Queensland Native Mounted Police, Sergeant A Whittingdon, The Royal Historical Society of Queensland, 1964

The Conspiracy of Silence: Queensland's Frontier Killing–Times, Timothy Bottoms, 2013

Queensland's Frontier Killing Times –Facing up to Genocide, QUT Law Review Vol 15 Hannah Baldry, Alisa McKeon, Scott McDougall 2015

Tribal Alliances with broader agendas? Aboriginal resistance in Southern Queensland's Black War, Ray Kerkhove, Cosmopolitan Civil Societies 2014

Cannibalism: A White Colonist Fiction? Geoffrey Partington, Quadrant, May 2008

Bushranger Thunderbolt and Mary Ann Bagg, Carol Baxter, 2011

The Hung Society and Freemasonry the Chinese Way, Australian and New Zealand Masonic Research Council, RW Bro and Graham Stead, 2002

The Australian War Memorial www.awm.gov.au

A Private Empire, Stephen Foster, 2010

Glossary

Blacks: The term still commonly used in Australia to denote indigenous Australians or Aborigines. 'Wild blacks' was the pejorative term used in colonial times to describe indigenous Australians who had not been 'civilised' and were hostile to the invasion of their lands by the British and their descendants. 'Tame blacks' was the pejorative term to describe indigenous Australian who had been 'civilised'. Lubra was the pejorative term used in colonial times to describe an indigenous Australian woman.

The Clearances: the eviction by Scottish clan chiefs, mostly during the 18th and 19th centuries, of the clans from their Highland farms and their replacement by more profitable sheep.

Brig: A two-masted square-rigged ship, typically having additional front and back sails.

Bushranger: Australian term for a robber (usually mounted) who lived and plied his or her trade in the country areas (the bush). Roughly equivalent to an English highwayman.

Escheat: The reverting of property to the state. In colonial Prince Edward Island, the disgruntled sub-tenants formed the Escheat Movement which wanted the British state to exercise a compulsory purchase of the government-owned land from its leaseholders (proprietors) - often absentee landlords - and subsequent sale to those who had settled on the land i.e. the sub-tenants.

Fencibles: British Army temporary regiments usually confined to garrison and patrol duties, thereby freeing up regular regiments for action.

Humpy: a small hut or shelter made by indigenous Australians. Often temporary accommodation for nomadic tribe members.

Kirk Elder: A person elected by the congregation of a Scottish church (Kirk) to be a governor of its church.

Manu forti: The Latin motto (English translation - with a strong hand) of the MacKay clan. The clan's crest is an upstretched arm with the hand firmly holding a dagger.

Pastoralist: Somebody whose business is the raising of livestock. Commonly used in Australia and is the loosely equivalent term for an American rancher.

Privateer: A private person or private warship authorized by a country's government to attack foreign shipping.

Quitrent: The rent imposed by a government on people who lease government-owned land.

Sassenach: The Scottish Highland Gaelic word for a Lowland Scot or English man or woman.

Schooner: A sailing ship with sails on its two or more masts. A schooner could sail at a greater angle into the wind than a square rigged brig and was consequently more manoeuvrable and often faster when sailing into the wind.

Steerage: The cargo deck of ships which was also used to carry passengers. Its primitive shared facilities meant the cost was cheaper than 'cabin class'.

Squatter: In colonial Australia, a person who occupied a large tract of land (owned by the State) outside the legal limits of the British colony in order to graze livestock. Initially often having no legal rights to the land, they gained its usage by being the first white settlers in the area.

Tacksman: A person who was a tenant of an often large area of the Scottish clan land owned by the clan chief, which he or she sub-let in smaller parcels to other clan members. A tacksman could act as an agent of the clan chief, managing the clan chief's land, collecting rents and buying and selling livestock and arable produce.

About the author

The son of a British Army officer, Jonathan Rush was brought up in England, Germany, Cyprus, and Australia. He has also lived and worked in Switzerland, the Netherlands and the Middle East. His experience living through the 1979 Islamic Revolution in Iran provided much of the material for his novel, *My Persian Girl*, first published in 2012.

He lives near London, England with his teacher wife. They have three grown-up, married children.

CPSIA information can be obtained
at www.ICGtesting.com
Printed in the USA
FFOW02n1723101217
43992718-43179FF